NEVER TOO OLD FOR A PIERHEAD JUMP

NEVER TOO OLD FOR A PIERHEAD JUMP

The Sixth Harry Gilmour Novel

DAVID BLACK

LUME BOOKS

LUME BOOKS

First published in 2020 by Lume Books
30 Great Guildford Street,
London, SE1 0HS

ISBN 978-1-912982-03-5

Typeset using Atomik ePublisher from Easypress Technologies

www.lumebooks.co.uk

To Jack, who else?

Pierhead Jump:

A draft or appointment that has to be taken up at very short notice; derived from the need to take a running jump from the end of the pier, because your new ship has actually slipped and is already proceeding to sea.

(Ref: "Jackspeak: A guide to British naval slang & usage", compiled by Surgeon-Captain Rick Jolly RN, OBE)

Author's Note

This is the sixth, and final (probably) Harry Gilmour story. In telling his tale, I deliberately set him on a course in the autumn of 1939 that would steer him through the heart of the tumultuous events about to engulf the world.

I thought that by using the war as a frame upon which to hang my tale, it would free my febrile imagination to embellish and create a set of epic adventures that would amaze, thrill and entertain.

To that end I immersed myself in the lore of the Trade, only to discover that the reality of what those young men actually went through; their daring, fortitude, and sheer belligerent and bloody-minded inventiveness in the face of adversity was far more epic than anything I could ever have conjured forth.

So the truth is, these Harry Gilmour books are not so much mine, as theirs. Because every action, every deed of derring-do and reckless courage you will read in this book, and all the previous five, actually happened, on a Royal Navy submarine, somewhere, at some time during the Second World War.

One

The smell. It was like he'd never been away. Diesel and feet. It wasn't the worst submarine stink he'd ever inhaled, but then she was still a relatively new boat, and at least summer was still a long way off, so the stifling heat hadn't had its way with her yet, enough to make her truly whiffy. Where he was standing helped too; his backside being jammed between the two hydroplane wheels meant he was in the breeze coming down the open conning tower hatch.

The other thing he noticed was that it was unnaturally quiet in the submarine's control room, despite it being crammed with what remained of the boat's crew. Thirty-four officers and men. The majority pressed into the space, with the rest pushed out into the main passageway. The only sound was the muffled clanking of a busy port.

Alexandria.

Most of the light in the control room was from a solid shaft of Egyptian sun, slanting down from the same hatch as the breeze. It put all the faces serried before him into shadow, the front rank barely two feet from his chest, staring back at him. Looking all the more surly.

'My name is Lieutenant H J Gilmour, RNVR,' he said. 'I am HMS *Saraband*'s new commanding officer, henceforth to be known as the captain.'

Harry had already read himself in as the new CO, completed all the paperwork. This was his first address to the crew. Harry didn't like giving speeches to crews; in his short career as a Royal Navy Volunteer Reserve officer he'd become a follower of the 'by their deeds shall ye know them' school of thought.

11

'I don't like giving pep talks to grown men,' he said. 'However, it has been impressed upon me that I should say something to you, in light of certain recent events.'

Nobody said a word; nor should they have. But there are silences, and there are silences.

'As far as I'm concerned, recent means past,' he said, 'and I'm not interested in the past. I don't know exactly what has happened here on *Saraband*, but more importantly – and I want you all to listen to me very carefully here – I don't care. I am the Captain now, and as far as I am concerned, this is a new command. A clean sheet. A new start. There are no past problems, previous difficulties. Nobody brings old baggage onto my boat.'

Harry paused there to let it sink in. Another of his pet hates was asking stupid questions, like: *Is that understood?* Especially when directed at a mob. How was anyone expected to answer?

There wasn't even a shuffle.

'I shall be announcing the appointment of a new first lieutenant and a new cox'n directly,' he said, 'and then new standing orders and procedures will be posted, and we will get our boat ready for sea and continue on to our deployment. That is all. Carry on.'

Then there was a shuffle. He watched them all peel off to their respective duties; whatever those might be, he knew not. He urgently needed to speak to someone who did. He turned to the boat's second cox'n, who was standing next to him, all pensive and lip chewing.

'Pass the word for Sub-Lt. Laurie,' he said. 'I'll be in the depot ship wardroom.'

He climbed up the conning tower ladder back out into the light, and looked around him, checking the real world was still there. Because he wasn't sure what kind of world he'd left down that ladder. He'd find out soon enough, he supposed. Wasn't *that* something to look forward to?

The sprawling port was crammed. Not a lot of naval stuff now; it was 1944 and the war was long gone from this end of the Mediterranean. A lot of merchant shipping, though; the entrance to the Suez canal being just down the coast, and in a permanent state of traffic jam, or so he'd heard, now that the sea lanes between here and Gibraltar were all but free from Axis threat.

Alexandria. Busy and noisy, with an ugly skyline. Nothing like Beirut. He was only two days away from that city on its beautiful bay, and was already missing it. He looked up at the bashed, dented, and distinctly un-naval-looking sides of the depot ship. She was the old HMS *Ellan Vannin*, the converted Isle of Man Steam Packet company tub he remembered so well, now dumped here to be mother hen to subs transiting to the Far Eastern Fleet. Subs like *Saraband*, touching for maybe twelve hours or less; just long enough to top off tanks and load up on new bread and fresh fruit and veg before heading down the canal to the Red Sea, bound for Aden and Ceylon.

Except *Saraband* had been here almost a week.

There had been trouble on board. Harry really didn't know the full story. Everybody had gone quiet, which was almost unheard of in the Trade – as anyone who joined it quickly learned. The Trade was the submarine service's name for itself. However, for an outfit that also liked to be known as the Silent Service, it was awful fond of tittle-tattle.

The story he'd heard was that *Saraband* had sailed in on schedule, nothing amiss, on her way to join Fourth Flotilla at Trincomalee, the Far Eastern Fleet's huge anchorage and base on the north-eastern coast of Ceylon. And then, within an hour of her coming alongside, her captain, first lieutenant and coxswain had all been relieved and several other hands removed from the boat. No formal charges, yet, but the word was of 'conduct prejudicial to naval discipline'.

Now *there* was a catch-all phrase capable of covering a multitude of sins.

But the reasons behind these events had been less important than the fact there was now a boat en route to Ceylon that was suddenly short of a captain and several other key members of her crew. And with the war moving on, there hadn't exactly been a surfeit of spare and available skippers hanging around at this end of the Med.

So that was why Lieutenant Harry Gilmour had been summarily plucked from his idyll in Beirut, the Paris of the east, and appointed to *Saraband*, in command. Well, that was the navy for you. They gave you a nice long lie on the beach, and then a pierhead jump.

Sub-Lieutenant Bill Laurie RNZNVR was not in the control room to hear his new captain's pep talk. He was *Saraband's* most senior surviving officer, and right then he'd been on the depot ship trying to convince her pusser that his signature was enough to release *Saraband's* spirits ration, as there would not be enough rum left on board for all her remaining ratings when the time came to pipe 'Up spirits!' in exactly 45 minutes. Miss that and there might yet be a bloody mutiny! Or words to that effect.

The pusser was having none of it – then *Saraband's* control room messenger found Bill and delivered the summons to meet his new CO.

Harry was sitting in *Ellan Vannin's* empty wardroom, with *Saraband's* confidential books spread before him. They'd just been updated by the depot ship's office, which had added Lieutenant H.J. Gilmour as CO and deleted all those who'd been relieved. He was staring blankly at the meaningless list of names that constituted his new crew when a big, bluff figure slid silently up to him, blocking the light. The figure snapped to attention.

'Sub-Lt. Laurie, sir, reporting.' It was a deep voice, with an easy Kiwi accent, warm as caramel. One that, if you'd heard it on the BBC, you'd trust implicitly. For here he was; *Saraband's* navigator and the man who'd been notionally left in charge of her until *Ellan Vannin's* submarine staff officer scratched Harry's name onto her books. Bill Laurie. Over six feet of rude colonial health, black hair in tight curls neatly cropped, square of jaw and broad of shoulder, cap on and in a uniform so neat and squared away you knew he was fresh out from Blighty.

The wardroom was empty, just lots of little islands of frayed armchairs and the odd knot of tables and chairs round the edges. Harry was at one such knot. The sun was slanting in through the open scuttles, making the whole space bright and airy, and a pleasant breeze wafted in, making all the dust motes dance. Harry knew it would be empty at this time of day; breakfast over, lunch a long morning away and no watch changes due. That was why he had chosen it to meet this Laurie fellow.

Harry wasn't wearing a cap, so no salutes. You didn't salute in the Andrew, if you weren't wearing a cap.

'Ah, Mr Laurie, a pleasure to meet you,' said Harry, standing up and offering his hand. 'Stand easy. Sit, please, and tell me about the boat.'

The bare facts, Harry already knew. Some were in the confidential books, others in her specs. HMS *Saraband* was a 'third batch' S class submarine, over 840 tons surfaced, more than 900 tons dived; 217 feet long and 24 feet in the beam, which made her bigger than earlier boats of her class; she was powered by two eight-cylinder Paxman diesels delivering 960 brake horse power, which made her capable of almost 15 knots surfaced. The Admiralty-designed electric motors, however, were only capable of 8 knots submerged. Her armament comprised the usual six torpedo tubes forward, and a single, external tube aft – external meaning it could not be reloaded. The six for'ard tubes all had re-loads, so thirteen torpedoes altogether. She was also fitted with a 20 mm Oerlikon cannon mounted on a band-box abaft the bridge, as well a clutch of bridge-mounted .303 Browning machine guns.

Much of *Saraband's* extra size was given over to bigger fuel tanks, the entire ethos behind the design changes being to extend her range for operations in the Indian Ocean and the Pacific. It also meant she had to carry a larger crew; her full complement was supposed to be forty-nine officers and men. Launched fewer than five months previously by Cammell Laird in Birkenhead, she had completed her builders' trials and her first operational work-up patrol off Norway without ever hitting her regulation manning level. So, she had been short-crewed to start with and was even shorter crewed now.

'So, what's her vices?' asked Harry. All new boats had teething problems; some got sorted right off, others lingered, sometimes infuriatingly or to the point of making the bloody boat dangerous to go to sea in.

Bill Laurie had the list; all the usual glitches to do with propeller gland packing leaks, ditto the periscopes; electrical power problems on the main ring; mostly sorted now. Her main vice however, at least according to Bill Laurie, was that she persisted in being 'sneaky.'

Harry knew exactly what he meant. Everything going smoothly, then *bang!* She'd throw a new fault at you. Something you weren't expecting, exactly when you weren't expecting it. There'd been quite a lot of that apparently, all down the bay, and up the Med; stuff going wrong.

But what Harry really took from Laurie's report was not the list of breakdowns and malfunctions, but rather his command of the detail. *Saraband's* navigator knew a lot about his boat. And what he didn't know, he'd admitted. No flannel.

'Although you'd need to speak to the warrant engineer, Mr Kershaw for a full breakdown on the fault lists, sir,' said Sub-Lt.Laurie, winding up. He did it with a furrowed brow, 'eh, except I'm not sure if … '

'… if he's still with us?' said Harry. 'Yes, well, I understand he is. Nobody's told me otherwise.'

Warrant Engineer Gilbert Kershaw was *Saraband's* most senior engineer, and the instigator, apparently, of all *Saraband's* current troubles; or perhaps to be more accurate, he was the revealer. That was according to the precious little Harry had heard from the depot ship's commander.

'*Saraband* came in, her gangplank was hardly aboard, and our Mr Kershaw was right up it,' the commander had recounted in hushed, still astonished tones. 'Into my office, demanding an immediate table with the RAA!'

He was referring to the Rear-Admiral, Alexandria, boss of the entire Alexandria naval base.

'Announcing – very cool, calm and collected – that he was never going to, set foot on "that fucking boat" again, and we could do with him what we liked. And *that* was when, as they say, events began to unfold. Remarkable.'

Those events, however, were the least of Harry's immediate concerns. 'Take me through the crew, Mr Laurie,' said Harry, pulling the list towards him.

Laurie drew a deep breath, and began. 'Well, after me, there's our guns 'n' torps, Sub-Lieutenant Adrian Gowers. He's RN. Then there's Sub-Lt. Ian Caudrey, another RNVR, he's our fruit machine man as well as doubling as our pusser …'

Harry interrupted, 'Just one thing, Mr Laurie. As you go, I'd much appreciate an idea of each man. Your personal assessment. Nothing too detailed, unless you think they merit it. Essentially, I suppose, I'm asking what I can expect from them.'

Sub-Lt. Laurie nodded and began again. 'Well, sir, guns 'n' torps like me sir, has war patrol experience, all of it on home flotilla boats. Knows his job, gets on with it. Reliable, but no dazzler, if you'll pardon the non-military language, sir.'

Harry smiled, and gestured for Laurie to continue. So he did; on down the list, every petty officer, engine room artificer, seaman and stoker. He read out each name on the list and seemed to know each immediately; some he had a few words to say about, a very few others, mostly back-afties, he confessed to having not enough personal knowledge to say. That wasn't particularly surprising; life in the engine room spaces took place on another world in most boats, the gap between the stokers and the seaman was wide; oil and water not mixing, as they used to say.

Harry let him press on to the end without further interruption, which Laurie did with methodical precision. Poor, innocent Sub-Lt. Laurie didn't know it at the time, but he was being put through a test. One that was about to transform his entire naval career. And he didn't have an inkling.

Harry, parachuted in with no clue of what was awaiting him, no idea of the nature of the beast he was now expected to control, and possibly even tame first, urgently needed someone who already knew his way around.

Harry thanked Laurie for his comprehensive brief; he was sure he would get to know all the crew in time, but that overview was invaluable for now. Then, they had a jokey chat about the vagaries of life as a volunteer reservist. All the while, Harry was silently weighing all he had just heard and coming to a decision he hoped he wouldn't regret.

'Now, Mr Laurie,' he said, becoming formal again. 'I have one more thing I need from you. *Saraband* no longer has a first lieutenant. I want you to be that man. What do you say?'

'Umm … before I answer, sir, there is one really pressing matter … I need your signature to release our grog from the depot ship's bond. It's less than five minutes to "Up spirits!" sir, and we don't have enough on board to go round.'

Two

The sun was exquisitely warm on his face. He could even feel its heat working its way into his old bones; because these days, being 24 felt as though it qualified as old.

There was a warm breeze on his left cheek, ruffling his hair as it came wafting out from the depths of the Sinai Desert, and beneath his feet was the diesel thrum coming through the bridge deck plates. He felt something that frankly, he had never expected to feel again; being aboard an operational submarine, under his command and underway.

The desert ended abruptly at the water's edge, a bare five yards off the port beam. *Saraband,* snugly tucked into a daisy-chain convoy of ships, mostly merchantmen, puttered on, heading down the Suez Canal at a stately seven knots while keeping her allotted distance from the ship in front. There was an extra lookout on the bridge, eyes permanently aft on the ship behind, making sure there was no tendency for it to gain on them, lest the next thing you knew, it had rammed you up the arse.

If you looked to your right, the land was quite lush, with a few fishing settlements dotted along the bank. However, on the eastern side of this thin blue ribbon of water they navigated lay vast expanses of sand; unbroken, featureless. No landmarks except for the odd canal-side shack; and no people, unless you counted the half-dozen or so local men they'd been hailed by earlier, all squatting in a row by the water, jellabas hitched up for a spot of sociable morning bowel-voiding. They were all grinning white teeth and burnt brown faces, waving cheerfully while *Saraband* and the other ships passed less than a falafel-throw away, pleased to see their fellow man going about his business as they went about theirs. The wonders of the orient.

It should have been a laugh but was not. As they passed these well-meaning Arabs, *Saraband's* crew on deck did not wave back. The dozen or so of her sailors up there on the casing had been granted permission because the canal was safe; no enemy ships or aircraft could reach them and no foul weather would swamp any open hatches. So Harry had ordered a roster for those off watch to come up for a smoko and instructed the engine room hatch and the torpedo loading hatch should be left open to let fresh air circulate in the boat for those still below.

As a mark of respect, any other crew would have bared their backsides to the waving natives. The *Saraband's* just stared. Apart from one, who yelled, 'Oi! Abdul! When yer done crimpin' that one off, you should enter its name for Dartmouth!'

Dartmouth was Britannia Royal Naval College, where the Andrew bred its officers. On any other day Harry would have found the comment rather witty. Today, however, it had confirmed something he didn't like to know. *Saraband*, after three days under his command, might be back to Royal Naval business as usual, but she was not a happy boat. There was a current of sullen disengagement running through her, he could feel it every time he dropped down through that coning tower hatch.

Which is just what I need at my time of life, he thought to himself. The previous autumn, Lt. Harry Gilmour RNVR, DSO, DSC and Bar, had been blown up and buried under half a house by a bomb from a Stuka while running through the back streets of some obscure Greek island town, trying to get back to his boat; that he knew he should never have left. He should have died, but instead he'd spent most of the past few months in a very nice rear area hospital overlooking the port of Beirut, being tended to by a lot of very, very nice New Zealand Army nurses.

Talk about dying and going to heaven.

All those months ago, he should have been sailing for home aboard his then command, HMS *Scourge*, after she'd been recalled to Blighty for refit. But the Stuka bomb had put paid to that, and *Scourge* sailed without him.

Which meant, when they took the bandages off and told him he could finish his recovery at the beach, he found himself spare in every sense of the word.

A non-taxing billet was created for him on the shore staff of First Flotilla, and he cycled to work every day from where he bunked (in some style) in an old pension just back from the Corniche El Manara that had been requisitioned as officers' quarters. Work done, he usually ended each day with a swim off the Corniche's lido. Then there were the nights, when he devoted himself assiduously to the pursuits of the city's burgeoning café society. It was a lifestyle, that after almost five years of war, he sort of felt he had earned. There was plenty of time to wonder what the future held, if he could be bothered.

On current wisdom, he should have expected another five years at least as a submarine CO. After that, he would be on the beach, or, if the war was still on, revert to general service because the Trade didn't like the idea of COs over the age of thirty. It was thought their necessary edge of aggression and mental agility would have been blunted by then.

But as his wounds had laid him up for quite some time, there must have been questions asked somewhere as to whether he would ever get enough of his stamina back to survive the strains and stresses of three-week war patrols anymore.

Then there was the war; it didn't look likely to last another five years anyway. And given the sheer number of new officers coming through now, the chances were he had already been nudged off the command ladder to make way for the new blood. All of which pointed to the remainder of his life in a blue suit being spent tucked away in some 'Staff Officer, Submarines' billet, aboard some nice, big, comfy depot ship, counting toilet rolls and keeping regular meal hours. It hadn't sounded half bad, if he was honest with himself. Oh, for such a lot of reasons, not least being the prospect of actually surviving this war after all.

Except now here he was, on the bridge of HMS *Saraband*, a new boat, with a new crew, heading off again to engage the enemy more closely, and he was grinning to himself. But then, that was probably what you did, he supposed, when you had a trade you were good at, and you were back to doing it. Even if you knew it might yet kill you. If only his new crew had felt as chuffed. *God help them all*, he thought.

*

He never left the bridge for the twelve-hour transit of the canal. Once they departed Port Tewfik, at the southern end, and were heading out into the Red Sea proper, he dropped down to the chart table at the corner of the control room for a quick chat with the new Vasco. With Bill Laurie now *Saraband's* first lieutenant, she'd needed a new navigator and Sub-Lt. Adrian Gowers RN had got his step up. Gowers, on initial impressions, was a serious looking young man, who as Laurie had said, appeared to have little of the 'dazzle' about him. However, the first thing that struck Harry was his prominent front teeth – not that Harry hadn't been warned. 'Which one is Gowers?' he'd asked, when he first set off to look for him in the wardroom. And the depot ship's staff officer had replied, 'Just look for teeth. If you see a set that'd make a queer mess of an apple, that's him.' As a result, every time he met the unfortunate young man, Harry had to stifle a smirk.

So far, Harry had no evidence of Gowers' ability as a navigator; playing follow-my-leader down the canal didn't count. So he was looking over his course planning for the run down to Aden. *Saraband* already had her slot window alongside the bunkering tanker to top off her fuel, and Harry could see it left plenty of time, so he had no intention of flogging the boat. For he had plans for the crew on this leg, and they weren't for leisure.

There was a way of doing things in the Trade and on submarines in general, that when you joined, you had to sign up to. There was a particular understanding about how a boat worked, had to work. Just thinking about it took him back to that night, when the war was young, sitting in the motor room of the old *Pelorus*, his first submarine, with Jim Gault, one of her chiefs, and that old rogue Ted Padgett, her engineer. He could practically recount the conversation word for word …

… *it will not have escaped your notice, sir, that in the Trade, we're a very traditional bunch*. He could practically hear the sonorous tones of Gault still, expounding the popular myth that it was all lax discipline aboard submarines, and an easy berth, and him having none of it. *It don't work in the Trade if you just look at life as a sort of search for opportunities to swing*

21

the lead, take it easy, bunk off. I'n't that right, Ted? And Padgett, summoning up all his sagacity, *Aye, Jim, the thing about the Trade is, Mr Gilmour, unlike with that lot of skimmers upstairs, with us, every man has to know his job and do his duty exactly right, and if he does, then there's a good chance we all live. If he don't, then we don't. It's simple as that. You can't arse about on a submarine, Mr Gilmour. Some berk tripping over his own feet … something you havin' been to officers' school, sir, you'll know all about …* and Ted Padgett and Jim Gault grinning at each other … *and the next thing, the halfwit has grabbed a vent valve or dropped his wrench into the battery space, and before you can say 'any more for Winnie More, before she pulls her drawers up', we're all sharing our tot with Davy Jones.*

Their message had been clear; you might get to slob about in shapeless white pullovers and not wash every day and give cheek to your officers, but that didn't mean there was no discipline. Because the way it worked in the Trade, you brought your own discipline aboard with you. Purely and simply because the entire boat was relying on you, and you on it. That was how it worked.

And their sage sign off. How could he ever forget that? Before that tramp steamer had rammed them, beam on; been allowed to come up on them on the surface in the middle of a dark, dark night, and send them to the bottom, because there had been one person aboard the old *Pelorus* whom none of them could really rely on.

Gault saying, *We don't like gormless people in a boat*, and Ted Padgett agreeing. *Right, Jim. On a boat yer first job is to keep yer 'gorm' about yer at all times.* Except their skipper had lost his 'gorm' long ago, into a bottle of gin. Just like this bloody boat of his now, just going through the motions. Something about her, not sound; her people on board, completing their allotted tasks, and not a jot more. The *esprit* gone.

A boat that couldn't rely on herself was highly likely to get everyone in her killed, and that included him. Once they were into the Red Sea proper, he was going to put them through their paces; see what they were capable of. Diving times, how long it was taking them to get *Saraband* under; gun exercises to see how her gun-layer and loader performed; and torpedo handling and firing drills. He'd get the TGM, the torpedo gunner's mate, to strip down and check their torpedoes too, not so much to see if he knew what they were doing – if they didn't by this stage of their training, it was too late – but to make sure they were paying attention. Plus, all the heaving and shoving involved in removing the one-and-a-half ton buggers from their tubes, then reloading them again would keep the for'ard end crew's minds off moping.

One bright star on the horizon was *Saraband's* new cox'n, Chief Petty Officer Garbutt, a twenty year man, Andrew through and through, who had been handed what most certainly wasn't his first pierhead jump and had taken it in his stride, as he had every disruption and unforeseen event handed to him in a long career. One minute he'd been grand enough in the admin pecking order aboard *Ellan Vannin* to have his own office and cabin, and the next he was heading to the other side of the world to fight the Japs aboard a fresh-out-the-wrapper submarine that had somehow already managed to acquire a 'past'.

Even if CPO Garbutt had broken down and cried when Harry had told him his orders, you wouldn't have noticed any change in expression, because there was a beard and moustache that must be the definition of a full-set. The instant Harry clapped eyes on him, he knew he was going to be a great help. And what Garbutt said to him later, cemented it.

'I was chatting to my old mate Jim Gault a while back. He knew you. Mentioned your name.'

Harry and Jim Gault, he of the sage counsel, had been among the few to have escaped from the stricken *Pelorus* all those years ago.

'He said you were out here now, sir.'

For an RNVR officer, Harry had acquired a bit of a reputation in the Trade, not least with his saving of Trade legend Ted Padgett from the sunken *Pelorus*.

'What about old Ted then, these days, eh?'

Garbutt continued, 'Going to work on a bus, and a grandpa, too. You've got a lot to answer for, sir,' and then a grin, or at least Harry was sure he saw *something* glint behind all the facial foliage.

Ted Padgett. *Twenty years of undetected crime*, they used to say about him. Ted, who had been more dead than alive when Harry had dragged him from *Pelorus'* shattered, sunken hull. Now, wounds healed, Padgett was an instructor at the Royal Navy's engineering school in Plymouth. And the fact that he'd survived at all had made a bit of a legend of that newly minted Sub-Lt. Gilmour.

Garbutt wasn't the first of old Padgett's legendary cohort of friends in the service that Harry had encountered since, so he knew what his words meant. Garbutt was going to look after him; the way he'd looked after his friend.

But oh, what a different story it was when he met his new warrant engineer, Bert Kershaw, another Trade legend. He knew immediately Kershaw was a problem that would take all his subtlety to turn around. From the moment he clapped eyes on the warrant engineer, Harry realised the man had already decided to take against him. There was nothing in the rules that demanded men in their roles should start exchanging Christmas cards, henceforth and forever more. But if *Saraband* was going to be an efficient fighting boat, then the chief engineer and the captain had to have a working relationship. Alas, it very quickly became apparent that Harry was going to face a stubborn wall of intransigence and a sheer bloody-minded lack of co-operation, from the instant Kershaw, on being required to present himself, pointedly looked at Harry's shirt epaulettes and their two wavy-navy RNVR rings and paused, just for a moment, before saying 'sir.'

A younger Lt. Harry Gilmour might have felt dismay. But the war was too old now for dyed-in-the-wool Royal Navy regulars to be afforded the luxury of looking down their noses at volunteer reserve officers. All Harry felt in that brief, but oh-so-significant pause was a full flash of anger. *So it's going to be like that, then*, he thought to himself. *So be it.*

Three

Scobie, their pinched, fastidious little steward, put another coffee pot on the wardroom table and tested the can of condensed milk to see how full it was before withdrawing across the passage and back to the galley. Harry sat with his first lieutenant and Caudrey round the L of the table, perched on the banquettes forming the three sides of the alcove that made up *Saraband's* officer country. It was a tight, cosy little space, wood panelled walls with a series of small wall lights casting a weak yellow splash over the crew lists and watch bills covering the tabletop. Looking down on them was a small portrait of the King, and a set of three neatly framed prints of Jane, the leggy cartoon character from the *Daily Mirror* whose hapless adventures invariably ended up with her in various states of undress.

Harry was reviewing the series of exercises he had put the boat through that day, testing their gunnery and their torpedo room procedures; he had even carried out a simulated attack on an unsuspecting small northbound Allied convoy, to see how the control room crew performed. Their performance was not entirely dismal. Everywhere he had looked, however, there had been slackness, and a total lack of urgency and application from nearly every individual concerned.

Since entering the Red Sea the previous day, he had *Saraband* hard at it. All the way down the canal, Scobie had been bagging and storing the boats gash as per the local by-laws – no dumping in the canal. Now, he had him buoy each bag before lobbing it over the side. He then dived the boat to periscope depth, on the stopwatch. The dive times were so bad they were barely believable. Then it was hit the tit for the klaxon and, 'Surface! Gun crew close up!' Stopwatch out again to see how long the gun crew took to get up and start firing.

'They do know the idea is they're supposed to hit the bag,' he observed to the new guns 'n' torps, Caudrey, after several minutes of his gun team's wild blasting away. Poor Caudrey, his gun crew's times on deck and times to first round away had been lamentable too, and the first bags they fired on had actually drifted away unpunctured.

Harry was now addressing *Saraband's* performance. 'That's twice now we've almost gone through thirty seconds to get down, Number One,' he said to a stone-faced Bill Laurie. 'And our best has been just under twenty two seconds. You know that will get us killed.'

Harry's last boat, HMS *Scourge*, could routinely get down in 14 seconds. But he didn't say that; he didn't think the 'my-last-boat-was-better-than-your-boat' approach was a grown-up way to deal with the problem.

Harry topped everyone's coffee up. 'Right,' he said. 'Moving on. Our gun-layer is useless. Admittedly, his team being so slack wasn't helping. But he genuinely isn't fast enough getting his eye in on a target. Not his fault, but he's off the team. The loader. however, is just a slack bastard who's not trying. Mr Caudrey, I want you to inform him that he too is off the gun team, and that from now on the captain has ordered he be permanently assigned to gash duty. He is now the boat's official bin man.'

'Yes, sir,' said Caudrey, making a note to save himself looking into his captain's implacable eyes.

And on Harry went, down through his list of things to fix and replacements to be appointed. During the mock attack on the convoy, he had been impressed by how most of the control room team had pulled together. Caudrey had kept his cool on the fruit machine – that trusty, clanky old mechanical angle solver that told a captain where his target was going to be when his torpedo arrived. And Gowers had been steady in drawing the plot. Both had done solid, workman-like jobs.

Garbutt and Petty Officer Newbold, his second cox'n on the planes, had been all he could have wished, and the helmsman too, had been sound. The wrecker, however, had lived up to his name in an all too literal sense.

The wrecker was the Trade's name for the outside engine room artificer – the ERA – responsible for all the machinery outside the engine room from periscopes to trim tank pumps. He also ran the boat's dive board under the direct orders of the first lieutenant.

This one had conducted himself in a spectacularly surly and slow fashion, bordering on the insubordinate. Harbottle was his name, and on more than one occasion he had been perilously close to losing the boat's trim despite timely orders from Bill Laurie, who had become more and more quietly furious with him as the mock attack progressed. It was almost as if the wrecker had determined to take a lead from his department boss, Warrant Engineer Kershaw, by playing the silly bugger at every opportunity. This was not a good thing. And Harbottle should not have needed telling. Everyone knew submarines were not safe places to be. If you stopped being one step ahead of a sub at sea while you clowned around, it would bite.

'You reckon this leading stoker, Priestly, is up to it, Number One?' Harry asked, taking another swift gulp of coffee. Priestly was the lead rating among those who stood in for Harbottle when he was off watch.

'Yes sir,' said Bill. 'Steady hand, definitely not a silly bugger. He should be in line for a bump up to senior rate anyway, on his record.'

'Well, Number One. Priestly to replace Harbottle as wrecker. Make it so. I'm sure there'll be more than one back-aftie to fill Priestly's space as stand-in, if only for a spot of peace and quiet away from the diesels. And tell Harbottle, he's relegated with immediate effect to repair and maintenance duties only. Now that he's off the dive board he's another one the boat can wrench from Mr Kershaw's over-stretched department for the bridge watchkeeping bill.'

'A senior rate, sir,' said Bill. 'He won't like that.' Petty officers or the equivalent weren't expected to stand watch in all weathers on the bridge. That was supposed to be a young man's game.

'If he quibbles, tell him quietly that the captain is looking for candidates for off-loading at Aden, if he's interested in getting on the list.'

This took them into the even more delicate subject of the warrant engineer. As part of his heel-dragging, he'd been objecting to any of his engine room crew being taken away for other watch duties on the boat, such as the bridge watch or control room messenger, or even for the shell line, passing rounds from the magazine to the gun crew when in action. Or even as stand-in gunners on the .303 machine guns or the Oerlikon.

Harry hadn't lost any time in asking for an explanation the first time Kershaw had refused to release any stokers. 'My engine room crew is critically undermanned ... sir. I can't afford to have them being dragged off for non-essential duties ... sir.'

Always the pause before the word 'sir' now.

It was a response Harry had been expecting, seeing as it was the same one Kershaw had given the cox'n, his old Trade pal CPO Eddie Garbutt, when he presented the warrant engineer with the first lieutenant's first watch bill since leaving Alexandria.

Of course, as captain all Harry had to do was order his warrant engineer to do exactly what he was bloody well told. But something was eating at Warrant Engineer Kershaw, and Harry was all but certain it wasn't just the fact that a wavy-navy officer had been put in charge of his boat. And everything to do with why, the minute *Saraband* had touched at Alex, he'd stormed off the boat refusing to serve a minute longer aboard. It should have ended Kershaw's career and flushed his reputation down the heads. But the runaway train that was the war had meant there was no time or leeway to throw him off. *Saraband* was bound for Trinco and she needed an engineer to get her there; so, Kershaw remained.

But from where Harry was sitting, it was obvious the reprieve hadn't ended the matter for Mr Kershaw. It hadn't brought him back to his duty, and instead he was picking away at whatever this 'big something' had been. And that wasn't good. For anybody. Because for this to be a successful commission, for them all even to survive it, it was part of the deal that everybody, especially the boat's heads of department, saw eye to eye, bonded, pulled together; all those morale clichés, which had become clichés only because they were true.

Harry's father's old bon mot that *a man convinced against his will, is of the same opinion still*, most certainly applied here, which was why Harry didn't want merely to bang Kershaw round the ears with the Kings Regulations & Admiralty Instructions, and leave him still seething and resentful. He wanted whatever this 'big something' was, out of his system, and since

Saraband wasn't on front line duty quite yet, Harry thought there was still time to get the old bastard back to concentrating on his bloody job.

Harry and Kershaw's chat on the matter had gone something like this:

Harry: 'Mr Kershaw. I will not seek to interfere in your running of the engine spaces while we are at sea. That would undermine your authority and I will not do that, Mr Kershaw. However, I will log each incident, and I do demand that you enter in writing your reasons for dissenting from my orders.'

In the course of Kershaw's long and distinguished career in the Royal Navy, seldom had a blemish tarnished his record – until, of course, his meltdown back at Alex. He had certainly never been logged for anything. The prospect of it happening now, every time he played his obstruction card, had not sat well with him. Especially since his excuse for not releasing stokers for other duties was palpably a parcel of bollocks, and both he and Harry knew it. For, after *Saraband's* previous captain had been removed, in the brief cull of other crew, none of the engine room crew had been sent up the gangway. Kershaw still had the complement he originally sailed with.

Kershaw: 'Sir … for the very reasons I can't afford to lose crew willy-nilly, I don't have the time to be continually buried under unnecessary paperwork … sir.'

Harry: 'Mr Kershaw, as I'm sure you understand, it is customary in the navy that the captain decides what is necessary or unnecessary on his boat. However, if you decide your requirements are more important, then I'd say that it is equally important that you set out why. And just to clarify, lest there is any doubt, Mr Kershaw, that *is* an order.'

Cruising down the canal, the absence of stokers from that watch bill hadn't caused any problems; the extra bodies weren't needed. But Bill Laurie had his latest watch bill laid out ready for Harry's initialling, and it *did* require crew from back aft. It was, he said, much the same as the one *Saraband* had operated since sailing from the Holy Loch on her first shake-down war patrol to the north of Norway. Kershaw hadn't objected then; in fact, most of the stokers welcomed a break on the bridge even if just to remind themselves the sky was still up there; as a duty it was regarded as a bit of a morale booster. The same with a spot on the shell line, especially if you ended up on the gun end and got to be part of all the flash-bang-wallop. It was a truth held to be self-evident throughout the entire 300 years of unbroken naval tradition, that nothing perked Jack up more than getting himself on the firing end of explosive ordnance.

Harry, with a flourish of his pen, handed the bill back to the first lieutenant. 'Make it so, Number One,' he said, confident that Kershaw wouldn't be sticking his neck out this time.

*

Saraband was at watch diving, about 40 miles north west of the island of Socotra at the mouth of the Gulf of Aden.

Caudrey was in the control room and the boat was at periscope depth moving slowly eastward with their leading Asdic hand, Leading Seaman Meek, on the set, ears pinned back for any rumbles echoing from the depths. He was listening for hydrophone effect, generally called HE; the noise a ship's propeller makes as it slices through the water and the first tell-tale sign for submariners that a target might be coming their way.

Regular signal traffic had alerted Harry to the impending passage of a small Allied convoy, Red Sea-bound and lightly escorted by a single Indian Navy sloop. And, given that sound travels four times faster under water– and in these warm seas, ridiculous distances – Harry thought the Asdic set should give him plenty of warning of its arrival. Which was why he'd ordered the boat to be ready to go to diving stations for another mock attack. He was taking every opportunity that came along now, to get this slack-arsed crew tightened up.

Caudrey paced the control room; three steps one way, three steps back, peering at the helmsman's course on his compass repeater against the for'ard bulkhead, then at the boat's depth on the diving board against the starboard hull, and the bubble there, steady like a spirit level, showing the new wrecker still had the trim just right. Against the port hull, he checked again the diving plane angles over the planesmen's shoulders to make sure they were doing their bit too, to keep the trim. Then to the chart table, checking the instruments there, that they still had motor revs for 3 knots, filling the time to when he next had to mark up their progress on the chart and then stick the periscope up again for another all-round look. It was about three-quarters of an hour into the forenoon watch, and it was watch diving in all its tedious monotony.

And no chit-chat to relieve it. Surly *Saraband* wasn't a chatty boat these days. Everybody knew why of course. Except the new skipper. And he didn't want to know. It was all bash-on with him. Drill, drill, drill. No time to mope. Everything against the cox'n's bloody stopwatch, and never good enough. Every time it had been, 'Do it again!' And then, 'Again!'

The entire length of the Red Sea, the bloody boat had been up and down like a whore's drawers.

That bloody new cox'n, Garbutt, and his bloody whistle, blowin' it every time you were supposed to start some new drill, and blowin' it every time you were supposed to finish it, and then the bollocking for being too slow. Again.

McTeer, one of the radar ratings, the one from Glasgow with the accent that sounded like some poor bastard in the terminal throes of TB, had summed it up in one of his mutterings. 'If that bestirt blaws yon thing wan mair time, ahm gonnae ram it so farr doon his throat, every time he farts, his granny's gonnae think the kettle's boilin'.'

The crew had breakfasted, and all the paraphernalia of dining had been cleared away. Those not on watch were deep in Egyptian PT – Jack's euphemism for sleep. All except the captain, it seemed. The boat was so quiet, everyone in the control room could hear the clack-clacking of that new toy of his coming from the wardroom. However, it wasn't the captain tapping on the typewriter. It was their yeoman of signals, Petty Officer Lionel Cantor, the captain's new favourite, typing up the captain's scribbling.

The two were hard at work.

Harry had acquired his new toy, as well as a box containing a ream of foolscap paper and another with three quires of Roneo stencils, from the port office at Djibouti. *Saraband* had been diverted to the French colonial port for refuelling because there was an outbreak of cholera at Aden. From what Harry had heard of that fly-blown hellhole, he was convinced they'd got the better deal.

Especially when he spotted the typewriter.

An idea had been floating around in Harry's head for some time now. It had first surfaced after he assumed command of his last boat, *Scourge*. Her former CO, Bertie Bayliss, had got the boat into the habit of holding a Sunday service, which was one part God-bothering, three parts general chat about where the boat was headed, what they could expect when they got there, and what was happening elsewhere in the war. Harry liked that idea, of the captain talking to the crew; he had never much liked the God-bothering and hymn singing aspects, however.

What to do?

The first germ of an idea for avoiding the psalm singing had come from the *Daily Mirror*'s dedicated newspaper for the submarine service, *Good Morning*. Since early 1942, the *Mirror* journalists back in London had been printing off weeks' worth of numbered editions of *Good Morning*, filled with timeless features and cartoon strips – most notably, *The Misadventures of Jane* – and loading them aboard submarines heading out on patrol. They were to be opened in the correct order and distributed amongst the crews when at sea. What if Harry were to publish his own newspaper, all about events on board his boat, and distribute it alongside the professional paper? But how to do that?

And then he'd spotted the typewriter lying in a corner; on top of a rusting 1938 Roneo machine. The typewriter had an English keyboard, so no French accent keys, which meant he got it for nothing. The Roneo machine was *défectueux*, so that was *gratis* too, but the paper and the stencils had cost him a bottle of scotch from the wardroom stock.

Now, he was sitting with Cantor, who could type with more than two fingers and without lots of xxx-ing out, and they were putting together *Saraband's* first newspaper. Harry hadn't a title for it, but he was going to get round that by launching a competition in the first edition. He was also writing his editorial, in which he was announcing his intention to throw open the pages of this new journal to the boat's crew. He'd write up all the 'big picture' stuff and the need-to-know, operational guff; but all the entertainment and gossip would be theirs. *Submit, and ye shall be read!* he scribbled, and thought his headline very press-savvy.

Discovering Cantor was *Saraband's* yeoman had been one of the few bright spots of the handover. Harry and Cantor went back a long way. To the early years of the war, and the Free French submarine *Radegonde*, where Harry had been seconded as the BNLO – British Naval Liaison Officer – and Cantor was one of two Royal Navy wireless telegraphists already on board. Harry had hardly been able to believe his eyes when he'd squinted twice at the face in the gloom of *Saraband's* radio cubby. Cantor was no longer a boy; his face fleshed out now and harder. Promotion obviously suited him, thought Harry, when Cantor grinned back his, 'welcome aboard, sir.' They'd been through a lot on that Free French boat together, not least the time they were nearly sunk by a hurricane in the Caribbean, and then a rogue French super-sub tried to blow them out the water with its preposterous, bloody great 12 inch gun; until the hurricane got it instead. Cantor was going to be a great help on this newspaper lark. His presence also meant Harry knew he would never have to worry about *Saraband's* signals department, for the entire commission.

Harry was finishing his tracing of a map of the Arabian Sea, from the wardroom's schoolboy atlas, to show in the new paper *Saraband's* course from the Gulf of Aden down round India's Cape Comorin to Ceylon. Suddenly, he was aware of Caudrey looming over him.

'Sir,' said Caudrey. 'Asdic says he has multiple HE on zero eight five degrees. Very faint still, sir.'

Harry scowled up at him, as he shuffled his way from behind the banquette. Caudrey should have yelled that fact the instant he knew it. Harry stepped towards the Asdic cubby, but when he looked in, their leading Asdic operator was not on the set. Not Leading Seaman Meek, who'd shown distinct signs of improvement at his job with every exercise Harry had put him through. Instead, the operator sitting with the headphones clamped to his skull looked like a schoolboy.

'Pass the word for Meek!' called Harry. Caudrey should have done that already.

'Umm, sir.' It was Caudrey, at his elbow. 'When Asdic alerted me …' Caudrey obviously didn't know the name of the rating on duty. 'I stuck the 'scope up, sir, to see …'

A now cold, angry Harry was thinking, *You did what? Before alerting me?*

'… there was nothing on the bearing, sir. But when I did a quick all-round, sir, I picked up an intermittent mast on the horizon line, sir. On one one zero, sir. But there's no HE on the bearing, sir …'

Harry would have to take this young man aside. But later. Now was not the time. Not in front of the whole control room. Before Caudrey had finished explaining, Harry reached over and hit the general alarm. Behind him, Meek was already slipping into his seat on the Asdic, sliding the headphones on, tuning in. Suddenly there were running feet everywhere.

Here, on the extreme western rim of the Arabian Sea, there were no enemy aircraft or surface raiders any more. The only threat could come from an enemy submarine. The Germans had been known to send the odd U-boat this far from home, hunting the careless; and according to all the intelligence reports Harry had digested before sailing, Jerry even had a flotilla of them operating out of Penang Island. But that was a long way away on the other side of the Indian Ocean.

The real threat was Jap submarines, but they had rarely been seen this far west, having shown little interest in getting in amongst the Allies' merchant shipping lanes. And they hadn't sent a carrier strike force into the Indian Ocean since April 1942, being more occupied with the Yanks in the Pacific these days.

Harry ordered the periscope up, and he ordered Cantor, who'd slipped into the control room behind him, to put him on one one zero. Up came the 'scope, and reading off the bezel, Cantor guided Harry – whose eyes were stuck to the 'scope's lenses – round onto the bearing. And there it was. Looking like a hair on the lens, except that it was far too straight; a long, thin pole, a long way away, just nicking the horizon line. One tiny blemish, in the middle of a pristine sea.

Harry did a slow all-round, just in case. As he did, he said, 'Meek. Any HE on one one zero?'

There was a moment.

'Yes sir,' said Meek. '… but it's just there and no more. I think it's a diesel, sir, but whatever it is, it's definitely not flogging itself, sir. Dead slow. Could be a dhow, sir.'

Just there and no more. No wonder the schoolboy hadn't heard it.

34

Harry swung the periscope back to look for the pole. Even before it moved back into his view, he knew in a flash of inspiration exactly what it was, barely moving on the long, slow swell.

It was another submarine, on the surface, probably with barely manoeuvring way on her, and her periscope fully extended; looking for the approaching convoy coming over the horizon, while keeping her own profile below it. And what a nice, sunny day they had for it too.

'Down periscope,' said Harry, as he stood back and thrust his hands into the pockets of his shorts. The shorts were part of the new tropic dress code he'd been writing about in his new newspaper but had yet to share with the *Sarabands*. That was why the control room crew were looking at him out of the corners of their eyes. Harry looked at the gyro repeater above the chart table. *Saraband* was steering zero nine zero. The telegraph was showing turns for three knots, just. He reached for the sound-powered telephone, tacked to the hull stringer above his head.

'Forward torpedo room, Captain here,' he said. 'Bring all tubes to readiness. Set all torpedoes for 5 feet.'

He leaned back to speak down the passage, to the Asdic cubby. 'Meek. What's the convoy doing now?'

Meek called back the bearing.

'And our target on one one zero?'

'Still on bearing, maybe drawing slightly left, sir. Still very faint,' said Meek.

'Mr Gowers, start the plot,' said Harry. 'Mr Cantor, crank up the fruit machine and dial in bearing one one zero, range … six thousand yards. Speed …' Harry paused to ponder. Certainly no more than *Saraband* was making. He should make a guess now, firm it up later. 'Three knots.'

Caudrey was staring at him, appalled. The fruit machine was his station. Harry gave him a wink. It didn't help matters.

Harry turned to face the control room. 'Gentleman, it is my opinion we have a submarine just over the horizon, on the surface ahead of us, on our course and apparently waiting for our little convoy. Since no Allied submarines are reported in our area, we must assume she is an enemy, and not planning a practise attack as we were about to.'

Quizzical glances all round; the captain was talking to them – about what was happening. Folk had barely time to take it in before the bugger was talking again.

'Mr Laurie.' Harry was speaking to their new jimmy, at his new station on the dive board. 'I want you to bring the submarine toward the surface with zero bubble until the casing has broached. Once broached, I want the dive team to control her with the planes.'

Now that was going to be a very unorthodox manoeuvre. The older hands knew it was viable, but what did that big galoot of a Kiwi know? He who was used to playing with dividers and compasses only at the chart table. And now here was their captain, expecting him to make 900 tons of submerged submarine perform nimbly, like some steel Nijinsky. 'Try to make not even a ripple, and even less noise. And keep us steady when we get up. Take your time, now, Number One.'

This new skipper didn't believe in asking much of his men.

Saraband rose without a tilt on her deck, dead on the bubble, her trim under perfect control. The only way Harry could tell they were going up was by the bar on the depth gauge.

Bill Laurie might have been many things, including a Kiwi, but he wasn't a *big galoot,* of any stripe whatsoever. He was a steady, keen-eyed farmer's son from Hawke's Bay, with just the right unflappable feel for handling a boat, as his trophy cabinet full of cups for dinghy racing would have testified, and as Harry was coming to realise.

Leading Stoker Priestly's un-alloyed joy in machinery, and the fact that he quite liked big Bill Laurie as an officer, also helped. Priestly hadn't been able to believe his luck when this new skipper – or should he say captain – stuck him in the wrecker's billet. Fucking up was out of the question.

Even though he didn't know it yet, all in all, Harry had put together a pretty damned good dive team.

He didn't even have to tell Number One to put the brakes on. They were on the surface. Just.

'Mr Caudrey, up you go with the lookouts!' said Harry. Caudrey's crestfallen frown turned to a big smile. 'Aye, aye, sir!' And he was gone with the rest of them, all scrambling up the conning tower ladder. Harry lifted the sound-powered phone. 'Engine room, captain. We will be remaining on motors.'

He didn't want to alert any enemy, with his ears stuck to his hydrophones, by letting engineer Kershaw blast *Saraband's* diesels to life in all their thumping glory. Then he spoke to the helmsman, at his station at the far end of the control room. 'Helm. Maintain heading.' Then to the wrecker, over his shoulder, 'Up periscope. All the way.'

He was going to emulate his target – hoping now to see it, over the curve of the horizon – without it seeing him.

Harry wasn't sure what he expected to see. His best guess was that it was a Type IX U-boat. If Jerry had one or more of them at this base of theirs on Penang, then it had the range. The Type IX had an operational radius of over 11,000 miles. And they were big buggers too; 1,200 tons, over 250 feet long, armed with twenty-two torpedoes and a veritable forest of 37 mm and 20 mm anti-aircraft guns. A bigger bite than he had. Careful, Harry.

With the 'scope up, Harry peered at the bearing bezel that ran around the top of the eye-piece, turned it onto one one zero, and leaned in to look. What he saw was indeed a big bugger. Much bigger than a Type IX.

She was a Jap.

Four

Harry was looking at the target's port quarter, her bows pointed almost directly north east. From the lack of propeller churn at her stern, Harry guessed she must have practically no way on her at all. A huge, long, sleek, black hull, elegantly riding on the long, slow swell. He didn't have to see the small painted flag, curving along the base of her conning tower, the white rectangle with the bright red 'meat ball' in the middle, to know she was a Jap. He recognised the shape of her immediately from his teenage hobby magazines; 1935 and Japan exiting the London Naval Treaty for the Limitation and Reduction of Naval Armament – and two years later they produced this. The Type I-16, a monster of a boat. Over 3,500 tons displacement dived, almost 360 feet long and 30 feet in the beam, with two marine diesels capable of delivering almost 12,500 horsepower. They gave her a surface speed of almost 25 knots. Each boat in the class carried a crew of 100 and was armed with 20 torpedoes and a 5.5 inch deck gun. But most importantly, the I-16 class had a range of over 14,000 nautical miles. So out here was an easy reach for her; the wide Indian Ocean no barrier.

And indeed, there was every reason why a major, long-range Japanese boat should be patrolling astride one of the main Allied shipping lanes into the Suez Canal. What better choke point for a submarine lurk? So why was Harry surprised? No; he was more than surprised. Beyond surprised. He was suspicious. What was this bugger doing here?

Even before the war, it had been all over the popular naval press, how the Imperial Japanese Navy trained to use its burgeoning submarine force. Not as commerce raiders, but in whole flotillas as part of its main battle fleet. So, what was Tojo doing here, casually casting aside a decade or more of Japanese orthodox naval doctrine for a pop at a few rusting merchantmen? When he should have been further south, off the main naval base at Mombasa. Saving his torpedoes for fat men of war; a battleship or an aircraft carrier – even a cruiser should have been a better target.

But there was Johnny Jap anyway, in an almost perfect attacking position. And there was the Allied convoy coming on, with no expectation of encountering an enemy. And just one escort.

'Meek. What's our convoy doing?' said Harry. 'Are they zig-zagging?'

'I have eight, possibly nine distinct contacts, sir,' called Meek. 'I have detected no zig-zag since I picked them up, sir. They are maintaining course, sir.'

Harry stepped to Gowers' plot. He had extended the convoy's track in thin pencil, right down the Gulf to where it must alter course north west to hit the Bab-el-Mandeb Strait and enter the Red Sea. From where she sat now, the Jap need only come 10 to 15 degrees to port and run a couple of miles on the new course to put herself well under 1,000 yards and on a 90 degree track angle to her targets. You couldn't ask for a better set up. But the Jap had to get there first.

'Helm. Port fifteen, steer zero three zero,' said Harry, opening the angles in his head; seeing *Saraband* run out not quite parallel to what must be the Jap's new course, all the while closing the range, then turning in on his own 90 degree track angle and hosing her with a full salvo. What a coup that would be. If *that* couldn't put a smile of the faces of this set of miserable sods he had for a crew, then what would?

He was about to order, down periscope, when a great tumble of white water burst from beneath the stern of the Jap, and instead of coming up to port, her bow fell sharply away, and almost like a greyhound out the trap, the enemy boat was showing him her backside and speeding away on a course he estimated to be zero nine zero.

'Midships, steer zero seven zero,' he said, steel in his voice, cancelling *Saraband*'s course change. What the hell was going on? The Jap had just thrown his tactical advantage overboard, completely. Instead of closing her target, she was veering away to run parallel to it, except going in the opposite direction, and too fast, by the looks of her wake. It would take her away from what would have been an advancing attack, where her targets would be running into her oncoming torpedoes, to a withdrawing attack, where the merchant ships would be pulling away from her and her torpedoes would have to chase their targets.

It didn't make sense.

He said into the phone, 'Engine room, Captain, start both diesels – clutch in.' Then, 'Helmsman, full ahead together starboard thirty, steer one two zero.'

It didn't matter what noise he made now; no Jap hydrophone operator was going to hear *Saraband* behind all the racket coming from his own baffles. He also ordered the periscope down, lest *Saraband's* own acceleration whiplash the fully extended periscope mast out of shape.

He couldn't work out what was going on in the Jap's head. So the only thing for him to do was to get between the Jap and the convoy, and then maybe alert its escort to the presence of an enemy submarine. Although he didn't give much credence to the abilities of the escort's captain; what was he thinking about, not zig-zagging his charges? U-boats really did turn up in the most unexpected locations. Still.

Anyway, wherever the Jap was going, it was obvious he was going to get there before *Saraband*, given he was capable of almost 25 knots, and *Saraband* was lucky if she could make 14 knots.

Harry stepped over and leant against the chart table, looking at his new crew, tight around him. Not one of them had the remotest idea of what was going on upstairs. But then, that was how the Trade worked; you had to hope your captain knew, *and* knew what to do about it.

Except right now, he didn't know what to do. He looked around the control room again at all the hunched figures, wondering what their thoughts were. He could always find out by asking them.

'The Jap has just cut and run … blown his best chance of a crack at the convoy,' said Harry.

'High speed HE on the target's bearing, sir,' called Meek in the pause that followed, as if to confirm. 'Target getting fainter on zero nine zero, sir.'

'I'd like to think we've frightened him off,' said Harry with a little irony and a bit of a laugh in his voice. 'But I don't think he even knows we're here.'

No smiles. No guffaws. Silence in the control room apart from the loud diesel thump, now.

'Sir.' It was Cantor, at the fruit machine.

'Mr Cantor?' said Harry.

'If he's not after the convoy, it could be the *Howe* he's after, sir,' said Cantor.

The silence froze the humid air. Even senior rates seldom had the nerve to offer advice to captains in their own control rooms. Usually. Maybe favourites could get away with it? Everyone wondered what was going to happen next.

Harry didn't let him finish, because he'd just remembered. 'Yes. The signal you showed me regarding warship movements, Mr Cantor.'

'Yes, sir, HMS *Howe*,' continued Cantor. 'She's fourteen hours behind us. In transit. She's been in the routine traffic reports since we cleared Port Tewfik, sir.'

HMS *Howe*. The Royal Navy's newest King George V class battleship, and likely fresh from her builders' trials on the Clyde. All the new stuff was heading out to the Pacific these days, so Cantor's guess was almost certainly right.

'Maybe the Jap's after her, sir,' said Cantor. 'It wouldn't be a surprise if he knows she's coming through. Kind of hard to keep it a secret, a forty thousand ton battleship coming straight down the middle of the canal, sir.'

'Maybe you're right, Mr Cantor,' said Harry, who'd forgotten there was a battleship following him out to Ceylon; thinking more about the war ahead of him than what was happening behind. 'It's a better explanation than any I've been able to come up with.' He spoke knowing that of course Cantor was right, and where better to attack an enemy prize from, if not the middle of one of his own convoys? The only problem now was, what was Harry going to do about it?

*

Night had fallen just over 40 minutes previously, and *Saraband* was powering in on the convoy's southern flank as fast as her diesels would drive her.

Since the Jap shot off, running fast to the east, Harry had hung about for the convoy to come up on him – all the while waiting just over the horizon with the periscope up, for the merchant ships to heave into sight. When they did, he slinked round onto their course, lowering his periscope and trimming down *Saraband* to her lowest profile to shadow them at their mean speed of eight knots. It put him out quite a few miles from the convoy, but the noisy merchantmen were still trackable on Asdic.

The Jap, he had reasoned, would've done a much larger swing around before coming up astern of the convoy; keeping his distance, just peaking above the horizon every so often, while matching their speed and hoping no reconnaissance aircraft from Aden came prowling close. That way he'd be reasonably sure of the convoy's course. The Gulf of Aden was one big funnel at this point, and there was only one direction for ships to go. Once night came on, however, all the Jap had to do was speed up, get in amongst the merchantmen, and wait. Given the closing speeds between *Howe* and the convoy, it probably wouldn't be for that long.

Harry was on the bridge, next to certain the Jap would still be running on the surface, too. That was what he would have done. His guns 'n' torps, Sub-Lt. Caudrey, was up there too, fussing over the target bearing transmitter, or TBT, which Harry had ordered him to lug up.

'I'm minded for a surface torpedo attack, Mr Caudrey, so I hope you know how to use that thing,' Harry told him. Caudrey had said, 'Yes, sir,' but he hadn't looked that sure.

The TBT was a great lump of kit, centred round a set of binoculars that, when attached to its fitting on the bridge front, transmitted information about a target down to the fruit machine in the control room. When the time came, this would allow PO Cantor, who was currently sitting at the fruit machine down in the control room, to calculate the accurate firing of the torpedoes.

It was Meek, however, from whom Harry was waiting to hear. He was impatient to know the minute his Asdic set picked up any HE coming up behind. Harry would have preferred to have *Saraband*'s radar lit up instead, but after a chat with McTeer on the capabilities of the set, he'd decided against it.

McTeer had been picking up radar sweeps from the convoy's escort for most of the afternoon. It seemed the escort's captain would order one at random, presumably every time he got nervous. Why his set hadn't picked up *Saraband* was anyone's guess; maybe it was because they were too small for the operator to recognise as a threat, or maybe the escort's set and its operator were just crap at their jobs.

But McTeer had told Harry that, if he were to order *Saraband's* radar fired up, there was a good chance the escort would pick up their signal and come investigating. That would blow his cover – and Harry didn't want that. Then there was the Jap.

From the stack of intelligence bumf on the Imperial Japanese Navy that he had read before *Saraband* sailed from Alex, only one thing had been clear; nobody had any firm idea of what kit the Japs had or didn't have, especially when it came to the electrical-based stuff like radio direction finders – or radar, as folk were now calling it – and Asdic, or as the Yanks were calling it, sonar. The only advice the reports had was that the Japanese, 'were working hard and making strides in this area'. So, even supposing the Jap didn't have any effective radar, he might have some sort of detecting gear, and then he'd pick them up too; and promptly hare off into the night. Lost, but still lurking there, and looking for *Howe*, with *Saraband* no longer in contact and able to stop him.

So that was why, whatever he was planning here depended on staying hidden.

He stood there on the bridge, in the tropical warmth of the night, with everything he remembered about submarines and command and war tumbling back to him, everything he had to think about, all of the events he had to foresee and plan for. For here he was, back again. In the infuriating, exhilarating and depressing knowledge that he was doing something he was really good at, but at the same time he wished it would all just go away and leave him alone. The same question coming back again and again, just as he remembered it. Just as it always had.

Who the hell was he going to be when all this stopped?

Always assuming of course, 'all this' hadn't stopped him first.

It was just the fucking war. And certainly no time to be fretting over all that nonsense now. Put it in the box and get on with it.

'Ship!' called the portside lookout. 'Bearing red four five, sir! Can only make out shadow, sir, but it looks like a big freighter.'

Harry didn't bother raising his night glasses; with the state of his night vision, even after all this time up here in the dark, it would have been a waste of time. 'Well done, keep your eyes peeled for others,' he said.

Then in quick succession: 'Two more contacts, sir!' said the lookout. 'Ahead of the first target, sir. I can make out their wakes, sir.'

They were all on the bearing Meek said the convoy was on; just a small box of merchantmen bumbling along in the dark. Good. Harry wanted to tuck himself in astern of them, a little off to port, and then wait for Tojo to come barrelling up. And now … that was exactly where he was. Meek's voice came again, a disconnected, tinny rasp in the darkness, echoing out the bridge voice pipe.

'Bridge, Asdic! I have high speed HE on green five five, sir. Getting louder.'

It was the Jap. Harry looked to starboard, and saw nothing but a wall of night, broken only by the speckle of stars. The starboard lookout, however, was concentrating his night glasses along the bearing. Harry wasn't sure what would happen next. He'd been trying to work out all the possible scenarios the Japanese captain might follow, to put himself in the best attacking position when *Howe* came past. But if command at sea in wartime had taught him anything, it was the folly of trying to guess what the enemy might do. *Attack what is in front of you*, Teacher had always said. So that was what Harry intended to do.

He stepped to the conning tower hatch. 'You have the bridge, Mr Caudrey,' he said, and instantly dropped down it. He needed to see Gowers' plot.

The boy was sharp. The Jap's progress was already recorded, his track pencilled in, heading right up the ends of the convoy, and any minute now the Jap would be crossing green four five off *Saraband*'s bow. With the convoy withdrawing to port, all Harry had to do was give *Saraband* a quick burst of speed and he'd be sitting on a 90 degree track angle to the Jap, at well inside 1,000 yards.

While he was thinking all that, Gowers, the slide rule still in his hand, spoke. 'If we maintain our present course and speed, we'll be seven hundred and fifty yards off his track … on a ninety three degree angle … right here, sir.' And he jabbed the plot. Harry turned; in the tight confines of the chart table, he was looking right into Gowers' face, every gawky, toothy contour thrown up in gargoyle relief by the control room's red light. And he saw nothing but blandness. Yet this child had just read his mind. In fact, he had read what Harry had been thinking better, and faster than Harry had thought it. *There might be hope yet*, Harry thought. Especially since, if he'd ordered the spurt of speed as he'd been about to, he might have ended up too close to the Jap's track to fire – a torpedo needed a good 500 yards to settle on its depth and arm. And another thing; by cranking up the revs on *Saraband*'s propellers, he would likely have generated enough wake glowing in the dark to alert even the most myopic Jap lookout.

But all he said to Gowers was, 'I concur, navigator. Well done.' All delivered with a commanding knitting of the brow. He lifted the sound-powered telephone. 'Torpedo room, captain. Open all bow caps. Prepare to fire a six-shot salvo. To be fired on the stopwatch at -two second intervals. Running depth, ten feet.' He listened while his orders were repeated back, then hung up.

As he did so, Meek called another bearing on the Jap. It was closing fast. Harry looked at his watch. Time was of the essence now. Then he turned to the voice pipe. 'Bridge, captain. Do you have the TBT on the new bearing Mr Caudrey, and do you have the enemy in sight yet?' Cantor would be needing a range and accurate speed, right now, to calculate a director angle in time for *Saraband* to start firing.

'Captain, bridge, TBT on the bearing. But can't see a thing, sir. There's not enough starlight. It's just … too dark, sir.'

Harry took the few steps aft out the control that brought him to the radar cubby. 'McTeer, switch your set on. And get me a range to the target coming up on our starboard bow.' He didn't wait for McTeer's, 'Aye, aye, sir.' Just patted Cantor's shoulder on the way past to the control room ladder. 'We'll have you in business in a jiffy, Yeoman,' he said, as he scrambled up it and back onto the bridge.

It didn't matter who picked up his radar emissions now; only time was of the essence, the convoy escort skipper could think what he bloody well liked. And even if Tojo did have some gimcrack radar detector, he'd probably think it was just the convoy escort getting jittery again.

45

He was at the voice pipes again, and about to start yelling at McTeer for results. Until he remembered that these bloody contraptions took ages for their valves to heat up. He was about to start cursing himself for not ordering that sooner when McTeer's guttural barks came up the pipe, … bearing … range. Bloody marvellous! Cantor was dialling them in, Caudrey correcting the TBT. For a moment, Harry couldn't work out how it had all happened so fast; and then he did. The boat was going into action. McTeer hadn't needed to be told to get his machine switched on. It already was. Just not transmitting. *Good man!* thought Harry.

In fact, they were all performing like good men; still a bit clunky at the edges, a bit too ponderous, but then they were new to this game. The chivvying and whistle-blowing all the way down the Red Sea must have done some good.

'I can see a bow wave, sir!' called Caudrey, except that he was so excited it came out more like a squeak. Then he remembered to call the bearing, without having to be reminded. Which was good.

Harry repeated the bearing down the pipe to Gowers. 'I'm going for a one-and-a-half ship length spread, Mr Gowers.'

'Aye, aye, sir. One-and-a-half spread, sir,' Gowers replied. It meant the first torpedo should be aimed just ahead of the oncoming target, lest their speed calculations were a little bit out, and given the salvo rate of 6 seconds between shots, the last would be aimed just astern. So, if the target was either faster or slower than they'd calculated, at least one of the torpedoes should hit.

All information Cantor would be dialling in.

'Ninety-two degree track angle, sir,' Gowers called back, after he'd done his slide rule work on the plot. 'Range to track, seven hundred and forty yards, sir.'

Cantor would be dialling all that in too, thought Harry, and even while he was thinking it, up came another voice from the pipe. It was Cantor's; 'DA is green two nine, sir!'

The director angle; the angle off your track, that when the target crosses its line, you fire your torpedo, hoping you've got your sums right, so that when your torpedo crosses the target's course, he's already there, at x-marks-the-spot, and takes it right in his belly.

Harry had a thought; then he made a decision. One of those make-a-virtue-out-of-necessity decisions he hoped would be right. He picked up the bridge microphone this time. 'Torpedo room, this is the captain. Stand by … intervals on the stopwatch.'

His orders crackled back to him out of the speaker.

'Mr Caudrey,' he said, quietly into the young Sub's ear. Hoping his decision would pan out.

Caudrey stood up from leaning into the TBT. 'Sir?'

'Your DA is green two nine, Mr Caudrey. When that bow wave crosses the graticule, yell out.'

Caudrey's jaw dropped. Harry nodded, with an arched brow, at the TBT, and Caudrey immediately dropped back into position. Harry watched his rigid back, as he precisely adjusted the angle to put himself on green two nine. Harry could see the lad's whole body was as rigid as girder. Good. He was obviously completely aware that responsibility for firing *Saraband's* salvo was now entirely down to him.

Harry knew the time it would take to get his eye in on the view through the binocular lenses; not to mention his below-par night vision; so why waste the time when Caudrey was there to do it for him? Because Caudrey was going to have to learn at some time. And this was war, not a fucking play school. So he'd better just bloody well get on with it. It was what he was fucking here for.

Of course, none of this did Harry say to him. He just leaned against the bridge wing, the microphone to the forward torpedo room clutched, digging into his chin until it was hurting, and waited, aware of the knot in his own stomach.

He was wondering if he should risk another breath, lest the racket of it should distract Caudrey, when a mighty shout exploded in his ear. No squeak, this!

'Target on green two nine!'

'Fire One!' called Harry into the mic.

Saraband shimmied beneath his feet. And before he knew it, the next torpedo was on its way. He looked around the bridge. Caudrey was still fixed to the TBT, obviously willing his shots home. And so were the two

47

lookouts, their binoculars fixed out on the target's last bearing, and not on the section of sea they were supposed to be covering.

'You two!' yelled Harry. Yelling was something he seldom did. The lookouts spun around as one, binoculars down, revealing faces suffused with guilty shock. 'Where do you think you are? The finish line at Cheltenham? Eyes on your duty!'

A voice came up the pipe. It was Gowers'. 'First torpedo, ten seconds to run …' He began counting it down, until it ran out; and then he started on torpedo two, 'four, three, two, one …' Again, nothing. And again, he began counting.

'Target has definitely turned towards, sir.' It was Caudrey's voice, sounding crushed. 'Bearing is now gre …'

It was obvious to Harry what he meant; the Jap sub had spotted their torpedo wakes and was turning to comb them.

Except, while Caudrey was telling him this, there was a flash. Not bright, suffused rather. Caudrey obviously saw it more clearly through the TBT, but before he could speak further …

Buh-DUUUMMM!

And Harry was smacked in the face by a shock wave.

'Yeoman!' Harry shouted into the voice pipe. 'Send, *en clair*, our call sign and say, "have torpedoed and sunk Japanese submarine, position …" and give our co-ordinates. Make it to C-in-C Eastern Fleet, on-pass Flag Officer, Submarines. Do it now and tell me when it's sent.'

Down in the control room Cantor was running down the passage and into his seat in front of *Saraband's* main transmitter, sending before he'd taken a third breath.

Above him, Harry said, 'Un-ship the TBT, Mr Caudrey, and get it below fast as you like,' while he peered into the night, hoping to see something; hoping he hadn't been a bit too previous about the 'and sunk' part of the signal. Behind him he heard the distinctive *whoop! whoop!* of the Indian Navy sloop's hooter from way over the water, and suddenly, out the corner of his eye, he became aware of two searchlights probing the night. He shielded his eyes to protect what night vision he had – and that was when the star shell burst way above him and about quarter of a mile directly off *Saraband's* bow.

In its chemical glare he could suddenly, clearly, see now a huge, spine-like shape, resembling some modern sculpture – jabbing maybe as much as 100 feet into the air – pointing like some Nazi salute, straight out of the light-shimmered sea, up, at an angle of at least 50 degrees.

It took him a moment to realise that it was the huge bow of the Jap sub. And then it seemed to lurch a few degrees more towards the vertical, and *whumph!* – there was gout of bubbling foam and smoke, and it went straight down into the churning sea and was gone. *One hundred men*, thought Harry. His next thought was, *what happened to the other three torpedoes?* But what he was looking at told him all he needed to know; the Jap must indeed have spotted the tell-tale fingers of bubbles and froth coming right at him and flung his helm over towards them. The timeliness and tightness of his turn had neatly swung his bow out of the path of the first two torpedoes, and stern from the paths of four, five and six; but at almost 360 feet long, just enough of him had remained left in the way of torpedo three. And it had done the job it was intended to do, and blown his arse off.

Harry knew immediately how lucky they'd been. That Jap sub skipper must've acted with split-second judgement, when his lookout called the threat. If his had been a smaller boat; even a Type IX Jerry job, which Christ knew was a big bugger by anyone's standards, he would have got away with it. But no; he'd been an I-16. As big as a bloody destroyer.

'Signal sent, sir!' came from the pipe, and Harry snapped back into the world; with that sloop ranging wild all over the place up here now, this was no place for any submarine to be lingering, even a friendly one. He immediately hit the tit twice. The klaxon roared and he shouted, 'Clear the bridge!' The two lookouts were already on their way down the hatch. Harry followed, slamming shut the lid and calling down the tower, 'One clip on, two clips on!' as he secured it. His feet hit the control room deck, and he looked around at all the red-shadowed faces, gawping at him, some grinning ear-to-ear. It was obvious that nobody could believe what they'd just done.

Caudrey stood holding on to the chart table, breathing as though he'd just run a four-minute mile.

Harry beamed at him, 'Bloody hell, Mr Caudrey! You certainly know how to make it look easy!'

Caudrey looked as though he didn't quite understand.

Harry addressed the entire control room, 'Young Caudrey here has just sunk his first Jap, and a bloody great bugger he was too. You might look a bit more pleased about it, Sub.'

Gowers belted Caudrey on the arm, and gave him a big grin, and there were voices too, 'ya beauty! ... yes!... bloody good show! ... nice one, sir!'

Harry turned to Bill Laurie and said, 'Keep one hundred feet, Number One. Helm, starboard thirty, steer two zero zero, slow ahead together and let's clear the datum. We don't want to be hanging about while our convoy escort chum upstairs tries to work out what's just happened. Right, where's Scobie? I need a cup of coffee.'

Caudrey had indeed done well up there on the bridge. Kept his head and got on with it. However, Harry hadn't forgotten all his faffing earlier, not yelling out right away when a ship, a target, even just the stick of a masthead, broke the horizon; deciding to, 'just make sure' before calling 'Captain to the control room'. Not paying attention to the fact that it is the captain who decides what needs to be worried about. A good pointing out of the error of his earlier ways was still called for, just to make sure young Caudrey didn't get *too* cocky.

So, as he stepped past the young Sub, on his way to find the galleyman, Harry spoke quietly into his ear. 'Oh, and once we've secured from diving stations, Mr Caudrey, report to me in the wardroom for a bollocking.'

Five

It was a good place to watch the world go by. A street café-cum-bistro in the classic Parisian style, on a corner where five streets and alleys converged, just in from the Boulevard des Almohades and so close to the docks that, if you leaned out far enough, you could see the forest of masts at the end of one of the streets. All narrow, classic, four or five storey French facades, with striped awnings and gaudy shop fronts, and a steady flow of human traffic – mostly European, or at least dressed that way – threading and weaving their way through the warm, late morning shadows. Captain Bonalleck sat at his pavement table with a glass of *vin rouge* and watched it all go by. Here, in this smart enclave of Casablanca, you might never have known there was still a war going on.

Charlie, 'the Bonny Boy' Bonalleck looked like he'd seen better days. His tropical whites were more grey than dazzling and the tanned face was gaunt and crêpey ; which was a shame, because he thought he looked a million dollars.

He was waiting for somebody. And if that somebody turned out to be all he said he was, then the old Bonny Boy was going to be looking a whole lot better, very soon.

It was about time he had a change of luck. The laws of chance dictated the world could only gang up on you for so long before fate got bored and moved on to annoy some other poor sod.

Yes, he'd got the heads-up in time to stay one step ahead of all the bastards out to do him down. But had that been luck? He preferred to think of it as good planning; keeping his feelers out there, sensitive fingers on all the trip wires so that when the bastards moved, he knew about it. You had to be up early to catch the Bonny Boy. It had always been like that; them always coming after him because he was always brighter and better than they were. The biggest mistake a chap could ever make was to be right, eh? But that was what it was like when you lived in a world full of wretched little things, always scratching and clawing at you, trying to drag you down into their morass. And if you should ever be fool enough to turn and fight, they swarmed all over you like bacteria spilling out from a petri dish.

Stop. Keep your mind on what you could be getting out of this. Think of the money. And the new life. Although he wasn't sure he liked the idea of having to go all the way to Brazil for it. But Portugal could be nice. She was a neutral country. They couldn't touch him there. Maybe he could just fulfil all the terms of the contract through detailed, written reports. He'd be doing that anyway, sitting and writing them in some fly-blown office with a squeaky ceiling fan in Recife or Bahia or whatever dump they chose to lodge him. It would never be Rio, oh no. Nowhere nice. What was the point of having to be there in person? Surely even your average, educated dago could read a set of instructions?

The getting away from Algiers to Casablanca had been the easy part. Rear areas in big military operations are always a crucible of chaos, and those Yanks could always be relied upon to be as gullible or careless as you needed them to be. God bless 'em. A couple of forged travel passes with all the right stamps on, when they were too busy invading Italy to notice, and then a palmed book of requisition chits, all stamped; he had flashed a few of them around the black market when he'd got here, and right away generated all the readies he needed. Bob had, indeed, been his uncle.

And life was alright. He'd found some back-street tailor to alter his Royal Navy captain's uniforms to those of a merchant navy captain, and managed to pick up a company cap with an Elder Dempster Line house badge; and he had a cover story about being a landed survivor from some sinking that he didn't ever want to talk about. He also changed his surname. No point in making it easy for anyone on his tail. He was now Captain Chaplin. Captain Charles Chaplin: he liked that, just the right degree of cheekiness. He'd also acquired, through a chance acquaintance, a small but comfortable rented room in a small pension run by exiled Libyans who, even though their country had now been liberated, didn't want to go home. So everybody was doing very well here, thank you.

But he knew it couldn't last. He was still in an Allied-controlled area, and sooner or later someone would find him. And it wouldn't be to give him a medal.

How had they known? How had they discovered his plan? To go after that jumped-up little shit of a civvy in a blue suit, Gilmour. To crush him, kill him, annihilate him and grind his bones and memory into the cesspit of history.

God knew Gilmour deserved everything he'd tried to throw at him. Sub-Lt. Harris John Gilmour, the new rising star; we'll send him on to your boat just to show you what you could have been, if you'd kissed our arses like you were supposed to. Oh, and he's an RNVR officer, just to rub it in. And then … they'd given him medals and glory. But they look after their own, don't they? Always have. All the captains of all those battleships he'd 'torpedoed' during that fleet exercise all those years ago, before this bloody war; how he'd shown them. But it wasn't them that got hounded out of the navy, was it? It had been him, their very own submarine ace from the Great War, who knew how you sank the bloody enemy; who wrote the bloody book on it; knew how it should be done — and did it. It was *that* man they went after. Too cocky, they said. Too flash, too young. To bloody right, more like it. Until the next war came along, and then they needed the chap who knew how to sink bloody Jerries again. And he had come back and shown them, again. He'd only gone and sunk the *Von Zeithen* for them, hadn't he? Like they asked him to. But oh no. They preferred to listen to that little shit Gilmour, spreading his poison about how his captain had been drunk; had been lying rotting in his flea pit, all while perky little Harry, barely out of his short trousers, had really done it all by himself. The Bonny Boy wondered where Gilmour was right now. He hadn't heard for months; but then you didn't, did you? If you were out of the loop, and on the lam, as the American cousins were wont to say.

Then, the inner voice in his head stopped abruptly as the man he was waiting for materialised from the crowded street. He half rose to greet him,

53

and then stopped. The man had a companion with him the Bonny Boy didn't recognise, a tall man in a light brown double-breasted suit, panama hat and two-tone brogues. The Bonny Boy was at a stage of life when he didn't appreciate surprises. He sat down again and stared hard at the two men; if he kept his hands under the table, he could have it up and in their faces, if …

'Charles! Charles!' The man he had come to meet, his chance acquaintance, greeted him with the usual expansive gestures that the Bonny Boy always thought made him look like a clown out of dress. The sweat stood out on the man's forehead and glistened on his pencil-moustachioed lip. He looked too hot, as he always did, in his entirely unsuited-to-the-climate, grey gabardine suit.

Jerome, the ubiquitous French *boulevardier* and local fixer. He'd been poncing drinks off the Bonny Boy since that day on the Corniche when fate dropped them at same café and placed them at adjacent tables.

The Bonny Boy – two days in town – remembered Jerome sitting and looking at him, and how he'd contemplated offering violence to the impudent spiv. Until Jerome said he hoped he didn't mind, but that he couldn't help but recognise a fellow citizen of the world; what he'd meant was, *so you're the ingénue with all the Ami supply chits I've been hearing about.* And over a couple of amicable absinthes, he'd offered to ease *M'sieur* Chaplin's path into Casablanca life with a few contacts. The tailor who'd gone to work on his uniform, and the Libyan pension owners for a place to stay, to name just two.

'Meet *Senhor* Miller,' said Jerome. 'The man I said you should meet. You must meet. That fate has decreed you meet!'

They all sat down. Fingers were snapped, coffee arrived.

Senhor Miller spoke with an accent that wasn't quite place-able. He was Brazilian, he said, 'but please, call me Ademar, Charles.' Except his tone hadn't sounded as chummy as his words. Maybe it was just the accent.

He wanted to discuss the idea, Jerome's idea, your idea. It didn't matter. It was a good idea, and he'd like to explore the possibility of taking it on a step, to maybe a plan. What did *M'sieur* Charles think?

'I know I said we two together, alone, would discuss first how best to begin the talking on this matter, Charles,' said Jerome at his unctuous best. 'But *Senhor* Miller, when I intimated a … possibility … he said, "*Não!* No time for beating about your English bushes! Let us meet now and see if minds are meeting! So here we are, Charles. Men of action. Men of the now.'

From the look on Miller's face, the Bonny Boy knew the Brazilian would never dream of uttering any such words; but he guessed the meaning of what he must have said.

Miller took his turn to expound. 'As you know, Charles, Brazil is in this war too,' he said. 'Since August nineteen forty two, our President Vargas has said we must fight the Nazi dictator.'

Which the Bonny Boy thought a bit rich, since President Vargas was a dictator, too.

'We said we'll help the Americans, we'll help the Allies. We'll help them stop the U-boats sinking our ships, then we'll send soldiers to fight alongside you. To Italy. So we did. But we have a problem. With the Americans. Not a big problem, but an irritation.'

'They're treating you like children,' broke in the Bonny Boy.

'You're British, so you know,' nodded Miller. He paused to sip his coffee and light a cigarette. 'We think you, as Jerome has assured us, being a former British convoy commodore, you might be able to help us set up our own … ways of doing things … at sea with our convoys, our trade routes. Without always having to go with … our hands out, to the Americans. Nice and helpful people though they are.'

'Oh, I think I can probably do that, and then some,' said the Bonny Boy. 'Depending, of course, on … oooh, the outcome, for me, Ademar.'

'Of course, Charles,' said Miller, with his thin smile. 'Always dependent on the outcomes for everyone.'

*

Two hours later, across town, in a back room of the British Legation, a conversation took place between two middle-aged, avuncular and extremely clubbable gentleman diplomats.

'That shit Stroessner is on the loose again,' said Alex, coming through the door, and flipping his soft hat onto the stand. He was the one who always liked to sport a flower in the lapel of his linen jacket.

'Really?' said Compton, the other one, who insisted on wearing a monocle even though it made him look not quite as serious as he'd have liked. 'I thought he was staying indoors these days in case the French lifted him.'

'I've just seen him talking to some washed-up old merchant navy skipper outside Celine's ... the old sea-dog was one of ours, would you believe? It looked decidedly rum. And they had some local spiv in tow. I'm thinking we should find out what's afoot. What are you thinking?'

Stroessner was a local, a former Vichy apparatchik, but these days more often spotted sporting a Cross of Lorraine lapel pin, and clapping politely every time anyone shouted, 'Vive de Gaulle!' The word out on him, however, was that back in the bad old days he'd collaborated not out of convenience, like most folk, but because he believed the right side had won in France in 1940, and that it was only proper that Europe should have strong leader. And that the current man in Berlin was just the man for the job.

Six

Harry was on the bridge, thinking about girls.

The whole vast panorama of the Indian Ocean was spread before him in all its seductive, turquoise majesty, with just the single jagged slash of *Saraband's* white, frothing wake, zig-zagging away astern until it too was swallowed into all the shades of sea and sky.

Except he wasn't looking at the view, his mind was back in Beirut, and the New Zealand base hospital and all its lovely Kiwi nurses.

It had been like dating sunshine, going out with those strapping and utterly enchanting girls, all exploding with rude health, silken skin, luxurious sun-bleached tresses; all those leggy, laughing, careless, wonderful Kiwi girls.

First, they'd saved his life when he was carried ashore off his last boat, HMS *Scourge*, with all manner of holes in him. His wounds from that fiasco in the Dodecanese had been serious, but the body heals. However, he'd gone into that Greek operation tired already, which hadn't boded well for his mental recovery. There, the girls, most assuredly, had saved his head.

Convalescing, even in the relative paradise of Beirut, offered all sorts of potential to wallow in the dark places of the mind – and coming from north Britain, he was certainly culturally disposed towards it. But those girls had no sympathy for that. They brought their south Pacific sun with them, everything light and fun. There had been lots of dates, and kisses and cuddles and hand holding; strolls along Mediterranean beaches, all a long way from any fighting. They had saved him from war-weary despair.

And, even though he didn't know it, he had done the morale of a fair few of them a power of good too. A lot of homesick girls, dealing with the real aftermath of war, day in, day out; and along had come Harry Gilmour, the quietly spoken, slightly self-deprecating west Highland gentleman. He had arrived all bashed up, but still managed to be handsome in a lop-sided sort of way and was brave and daft and funny and you knew you were utterly safe with him; you just knew nothing bad was ever going to happen to you when you were with him.

Harry tried to imagine his younger self, sitting at his desk in the grammar school with the rain slanting down outside, doing India for history and geography, looking at the teacher's be-gowned back, scraping chalk across the blackboard, a voice droning in monotone. What would that Harry have said, if he'd known all of this awaited him? All those Kiwi nurses. The beaches of the Beirut Corniche. Or that one day he'd be bestriding the deck of his own command, with the Nine Degree Channel through the Laccadives over the horizon astern, and Trivandrum, and Cape Comorin and the entire sub-continent just over the horizon to port. What would the young Harry have said? About this life less ordinary; unimaginable then, yet awaiting him all the same.

And what did the Harry now, think about all the paths he might have taken? All of them obliterated by war. And the path that had brought him here? He felt such a terrible loss of innocence right then that he was actually relieved when Number One appeared through the conning tower hatch and wrecked his reverie.

The first lieutenant asked Gowers, who had the watch, for permission to come on the bridge, then he joined Harry on the Oerlikon bandbox, leaning on the rail, watching the wake. He produced a packet of cigarettes, offered one to Harry and they stood in companionable silence for a few moments, puffing away.

They were heading for Colombo first, where Walker's yard were to fit another upgraded gizmo to their new radar set, and a newer, improved version of the TBT that didn't require connecting to the fruit machine, and then they'd go into drydock briefly, so the whole boat could receive her new, tropic service coat of dark green paint. So there was ship's business to discuss.

'Sorry, I really didn't want to disturb you, sir,' said Bill Laurie, taking a final drag before flicking the end into the sea. 'But there's a small matter I wanted to talk you about, out of the range of flapping ears, if you get my drift.'

Submarines were notorious for their total lack of privacy. Even alone, locked in the heads, people could hear if you even so much as scratched your beard. Ship's business didn't merit privacy, so Harry assumed it would be about the remarkable change in the atmosphere aboard since they'd sunk that Jap sub. He was wrong.

'It's McTeer's suggestion for the title of your new newspaper, sir,' said Bill, obviously struggling with how best to broach this subject. Which was unusual for Number One. Highly unusual, since even on their short acquaintance, Harry had never known him to be anything other than completely direct. It should have alerted Harry to what was to come.

'The only suggestion, Number One, if I might remind you,' said Harry, with a smile that said he was totally unsuspecting. Harry had brought out his new baby with a single typed line for a masthead, that just said, 'Today on *Saraband*', and with a note attached that opened the choice of a permanent title to the crew; place all suggestions in the envelope stuck to the galley door.

'Yes sir,' said Bill. 'This name. *The Bugle Blower*. It's not a good idea, sir. I strongly suggest you don't adopt it.'

Harry turned sharply to look at him, to see if the first lieutenant was somehow trying to take a rise out of him. 'What are you talking about, "strongly suggest"? I grant you its pretty lame. But at least McTeer bothered his backside and entered. It is a start.'

'Oh, it's a start alright, sir. In fact, I fully intend to have words with McTeer later. He is deliberately setting out to embarrass you, sir. And everybody on board will know it.'

'You're going to have to explain, Number One.'

Harry would swear later that Bill Laurie had actually squirmed, before he visibly forced himself to plunge ahead and answer.

'It is all to do with the trouble on board, before you were appointed, sir,' he said. A long pause followed, and then he added, 'You said at the time you weren't interested in any of the details. We were to have a new

59

start. Well McTeer, obviously disagrees, and with this "lame" title of his, he's out to dig up what happened, and he's trying to take the piss out of you in the process.'

'You really are going to have to explain, Mr Laurie.'

A deep sigh from Bill Laurie, a look around the horizon as if he was searching for someone to come and save him, then: 'The last skipper got binned because there were incidents of certain members of the crew … not jumping high enough at the leapfrog. And the reason some of the others went too, especially the senior rates, was that they didn't do anything about it. So, it only takes a moment's pause to see what McTeer's wheeze is about. *The Bugle Blower*? It's hardly subtle, sir. And very insubordinate.'

Harry was aware that his jaw was open, and he covered this by letting out a laugh; he saw the humour right enough. But equally, he knew it wasn't on. The two men stood for a moment, silently regarding the sea. Then Harry asked, 'Which accounts for the fact the warrant engineer is angry all the time?'

'Yes, sir,' said Bill. 'He blames … everybody. Not so much you … you not having been directly involved. He is at least prepared to still have conversations of a sort with you. With everyone else … especially us officers … for not doing more to stop it … he's furious. When was the last time you heard him do any more than grunt at me?'

'And none of his stokers were …?'

'No, sir. His anger is pure.'

Harry tried to imagine everything that must have gone on aboard the boat … and then decided he really didn't want to know. The navy was usually draconian in punishing such disciplinary breaches. Since the origins of the service, sodomy had been prohibited under, first, the Articles of War, and then the KR&AI. In the previous century you could be hung for it. Of course, you didn't need to spend long in the Andrew to know it went on. And Harry could easily understand the Navy's abhorrence; how it really was conduct liable to be most corrosive and undermining of a ship's discipline at sea. He never expected however, to be confronted by it. And he could only surmise someone on the FOS' staff had thought the quickest way to get this particular incident sorted was to shut it down and pretend it never happened. And Harry was alright with that. After all, ashore, it should be nobody's bloody business. Except it was a crime there too, even in civvy street.

Not for the first time, he wondered at what a truly impertinent intrusion into a person's private life that law was. But he had other things on his mind these days; and he returned to his initial verdict on what had gone on aboard *Saraband* before his arrival; that he hadn't wanted to know about. And he was now more convinced than ever that he'd been right on that call.

Another pause ensued, while each lit up another cigarette. Harry had never been much of a smoker, but he was finding the damn things particularly helpful right now.

'*The Bugle Blower*,' he said. 'Cheeky bastard. Cheeky, dirty bastard. He wasn't ...?

'No, no, sir. Definitely not. Everybody ... involved ... is long gone now, sir.'

'An exceptional radar man though, wouldn't you say Mr Laurie?' Another pause, then he said the culprit's name out loud, as if to test the sound of it. 'McTeer ... It's funny how all that pure physics and grasp of elegant technical function can live quite happily in the same brain alongside all that talent for lurid filth, don't you think, Mr Laurie?'

He said it, chuckling to himself, paused again, then added, 'It's quite funny, though, isn't it? His title?'

'Yes, sir. But I'm not sure I'd tell him that,' said Bill, grinning too. Almost relieved to find his new captain wasn't a complete up-his-own-arse pom. 'Because I'm still going to have a bloody good talk with ...'

'Don't,' interrupted Harry. 'Let me talk to him. I'm in the mood to have some fun too, Number One.'

'Sir?' said Bill, his curiosity piqued.

'I haven't shown you, but as well as coming up with his bright idea for a title, McTeer drew a series of caricatures ... of me, you, the cox'n, Bert Kershaw ... Mr Gowers,' and Harry gestured to himself making a goofy mouth. 'I haven't decided yet whether they're this side of insubordinate, but I did laugh. The only thing was, it would've been too bloody finicky to get them into the first edition, but I'm thinking now, maybe if Leading

Seaman Gordon McTeer is so interested in our new newspaper, he should be encouraged to play a far bigger role. What do you think, Number One?'

'Oh, I'm a great believer in not letting any crew member hide their talents under a bushel, sir. As I'm sure you know, sir.'

'I'm sure I do indeed, Number One.'

And they both had another little chuckle to themselves.

*

It was 20 minutes into the last dog watch and Harry was sitting at the wardroom table, paperwork strewn across it, decoding a for-captain-only signal from Northways, the north London headquarters of Flag Officer, Submarines. It was some housekeeping nonsense that had little to warrant all the security. Bureaucracy. He was suddenly aware of a figure standing over him.

'Leading Seaman McTeer, reporting as ordered, surr!'

Harry was happy to see that his visitor was compliant with all the dress instructions he'd written into the new paper, about how to combat the debilitating effects of heat in the tropics; PT shorts, a drill shirt, and since he'd been summoned to the captain's table, cap on.

'Ah, McTeer,' said Harry, rummaging for another piece of paper in the pile. 'Cap off. Stand easy. Um, have a seat, McTeer, while I find …'

McTeer obeyed with all the woodenness required for a show of military discipline. Harry found the paper, a watch bill. 'Now, are you familiar with this new bolt-on we're expecting for your radar set?

Harry could see that McTeer had expected his summons to be for something else entirely, such as taking the piss out the captain with his *Bugle Blower*.

A technical discussion ensued, which then moved onto manning requirements for Harry's new watch bill, which was to continue to require a radar watch to be maintained throughout the boat's surfaced hours. It was something *Saraband* had operated since she'd sunk the Jap; Harry's idea, lest it should have a pal in the area, and just to keep the boat on its toes and generally tighten up her performance. The standing order was, the instant any target came within a set range, the officer of the watch was to hit the tit and dive the boat, regardless of whether the target was a 'friendly' – which was the most likely in these waters – or not. 'The more we keep doing it, the faster we're going to get,' Harry kept parroting, just so everybody got the idea.

He'd even written an article on it, 'Diving, in time!' in the first edition of the new newspaper; pointing out that 'friendlies' had a bit of a track record for attacking *any* submarine they spotted. So diving *every* time you spotted a dot on the horizon was always a good idea.

Then he came to the new watch bill, which was going to involve McTeer and his oppo on 4 hours on–4 hours off; a knackering bill to maintain, and that wasn't even allowing for any routine maintenance work. However, he added, 'we'll be getting an additional hand at Trinco to help make it work. Can you keep things ticking over until then, at your end?' Harry wasn't asking permission.

'Aye, sur. Nae problem, sur,' said McTeer, now quite relaxed that he knew he wasn't in any 'soapy-bubble', as he might have termed it.

'Now, there is something else I want to chat about, McTeer,' said Harry, who then leaned into the passage and called to the galley, 'Scobie! Be a good chap and bring us a pot of coffee, fast as you like please.'

McTeer felt a spasm of alarm. Captains didn't invite ratings to have coffee in the wardroom.

'First, McTeer, thanks for your contributions to the newspaper. I especially liked your suggestion for a title. *The Bugle Blower*. Very catchy.'

Oh-oh! thought McTeer. *Here we go!*

'But not quite there yet, I think. I was at a loss as to what it needed to round it off, until I saw your draughtsmanship ... your caricatures. Then it hit me,' and Harry paused to beam a guileless grin. 'Let's have an icon, I thought, like the *Daily Express* does ... you know ... the crusader. Except for us, I see a face with a big set of lips, all puffed out, about to ... fix on said bugle. Blow out your lips, McTeer, so as I can see how it might look.'

'Sur?' said McTeer, not knowing where to look. 'Ah doan't unnerstan', sur.'

'Of course you do, McTeer,' said Harry, smiling benignly. 'Pucker up, Leading Seaman, and let's get a look at it ... imagine your gob is about to clap on to a bugle. You won't know what to draw until you try it ... there! That's it!'

McTeer could feel the red suffuse his face, as he puckered out his lips obediently. He cringed from the vision of what he must look like.

'Excellent, McTeer. Now I want you to imagine … the figure of a bugle blower … right there by the title, as drawn by you, and close your eyes and then imagine the figure as your own profile finely drawn in caricature, ready to close up for action, depicted in exquisite detail, and then imagine that image sitting there every week, right on the title – the masthead I believe it's called in printing circles – alongside your excellent idea for that title … *The Bugle Blower* … and how it will all look to our admiring readers. I think that is the ideal solution, don't you?'

McTeer knew exactly what his captain was up to now. What a bastard. Except he had to admire him for it; for playing him back at his own game. What a sneaky, cunning bastard.

Scobie broke the silence by banging down the coffee pot, two tin mugs and a pierced tin of condensed milk. He just said, 'sir!' and was gone. Neither Harry nor McTeer had looked up in time to see the withering horror on the wardroom steward's face. They hadn't realised he'd been listening.

Harry poured. 'You know I really do enjoy your caricatures … even though you sail a bit close to the wind. Mr Gowers especially might have some cause for grievance.' And at that, Harry treated the uncomfortable rating to raised eyebrows. 'Did you do that line of work in civvy street, McTeer? Cartoonist? On a magazine, maybe … a local paper?'

'Naw, sur. Printer, sur. That's whit a wus, sur.'

'A printer, eh? You know, given your obvious enthusiasm for my idea, I think you could be a very real help to me, McTeer. I'm very keen to illustrate *The Bugle Blower* … in addition to that little icon of you, I see informative maps, cartoon strips of our own, that sort of thing, so you've no idea how much I appreciate the fact that you've just volunteered to take on that responsibility. Just me and Petty Officer Cantor doing all the work makes it all look a bit too pedestrian at the moment.'

'Volunteer sur? Ah doan' remembur …'

'… its implicit in your enthusiasm, McTeer. And it will be noted. Now, drink your coffee McTeer, while I tell you some of my ideas.'

Ah've been fucked, thought McTeer.

The leading seaman sat through Harry's discourse looking utterly crushed, obviously imagining a future as an object of scorn and ridicule, certainly throughout the boat, and more than likely far beyond, once his crewmates had explained to the rest of their new flotilla what it all meant. He hadn't really heard half of what Harry had said, and so was brought up short when his captain suddenly announced, 'Oh, and one more thing before you're dismissed … having just gone over all this out loud, it strikes me it is going to be rather a lot of additional effort for you. So how is this for an idea McTeer, to lessen the workload? Why don't we shrink the title to just *The Bugle*, eh? And maybe dump the idea of that little icon of you blowing it altogether? How would that suit you? You wouldn't be too disappointed, would you?'

McTeer's eyeballs involuntarily rolled backwards, and he exhaled, audibly. 'Naw sur. That sounds like a great idea, sur,' he breathed, seeing his life come back to him.

Seven

'Sir! Sir! There's a line of lights on the port bow, coming out from shore!'

Harry woke from his doze. The voice was Gowers. Harry was aware of the air, cloying at him like a warm bath in the darkness. He could not for the life of him think of where he was. Then, of course, he was on the bridge. And Gowers was the officer of the watch. Harry felt his back creak as he rose from his little cat's' cradle hammock. Even he could see the little daisy chain of guttering yellow blobs creeping seaward to cross *Saraband's* bows. He rubbed his eyes, trying to work out what they were.

Saraband was at the entrance to the Penang Strait, north channel, about 3 miles west of the mouth of the Muda River. They were deep within the Japanese-controlled waters off the Malay peninsula. Harry checked the time on his wrist. The glow from his watch face showed it was coming up to 2100 hours.

'Can you make out how close they are?' he asked.

'Hard to tell, sir,' said Gowers, peering through his night glasses.

It wasn't just dark around them; it was deep, tropic night; impenetrable, obsidian. There was no horizon, no sense of the coast, or of the jungled hills that Harry knew rose up behind the flat coastal strip. He knew they were there only because he could smell their fetid presence on the thick air. Bloody hell, how was he expected to sink enemy shipping if he couldn't even see the buggers?

'But probably local fishing boats, sir,' Gowers added. 'I think.'

'You *think*,' said Harry, unable to master his irritation. Then, more charitably, he thought, *it could be Flash Gordon newly crash-landed back from space … with Ming the Merciless hot on his tail … for all any of us can see.*

Everything seemed to be entombed by darkness, except these disconnected blobs of insipid light, bobbing away out there to the accompaniment of *Saraband's* diesels, which were burbling away, nudging her forward at barely three knots with the rest of their racket going towards topping up her batteries. Even up this close in the confines of the bridge, all he could see of Gowers and the four lookouts were their pale faces, like suspended smudges, because their blue drill work shirts had lost all definition against the night.

And it was hot. Humid and hot. So that you could feel the trickles of sweat … down the line of your jaw … from your armpits … pooling in the small of your back.

He already knew how bloody awful it would be right now, down below in the confines of the control room, but he couldn't imagine what it must be like back in the engine spaces, with the diesels going flat out. At last watch change, the engine room temperature had been 98 degrees Fahrenheit, with 92 percent humidity. Nobody was laughing now, about his ranting in *The Bugle* about kit to be worn; no more jokes about, 'yes, but what does our fashion editor say?' Or, 'Oh! Where *are* hems this season?'

'Don't wear belts!' he'd bellowed from the health section. 'Or any tight clothes! They prevent air wafting round your bits and evaporating your sweat. And pooling sweat is a come-hither for prickly heat. You won't like that! Also, wear your shirts outside your shorts – it doesn't look so squared-away, but it helps the air waft about you, too. And as we get further into the summer months – and it gets hotter and more humid – you should start thinking about sarongs – which will be buyable cheap at any local market – or even towels wrapped round your waists. Anyone caught wearing underpants will be on a charge.'

The Bugle was equally strident on cleanliness. 'Keep yourself clean! If you've been sweating a lot, wash it off, or at least wipe it off with a towel or flannel. If you leave sweat to dry off, the salt residue will bung up your pores and you'll end up covered in irritating rashes. And don't keep wearing dirty clothes. They'll infect any skin problems. Dhoby your dirty overalls!'

It was amazing what you could learn by just flicking through standard operational procedure notes in a depot ship sick bay. He had a whole wedge of handy health hints left, still to slip in to *The Bugle*'s pages.

He was still lost in reverie when a shout from Gowers rang out like a gunshot. 'Starboard thirty!'

Harry felt *Saraband* gently commence her hard right turn. He followed Gowers' line of sight and saw the reason for his alarm; just under the bridge wing there was a face staring up at him from the thwart of rough-hewn, canoe-like craft already starting to bounce on the submarine's wake. It was a brown face, no, it was two, no, three faces, amidst a mess of tackle and grass cordage in the bilge of their craft, all summoned forth out of the darkness by the wan glow of two lanterns propped up on sticks.

The shape of the tiny craft and its crew had simply materialised out of the dark, as if from nowhere. For the night was so immaculate, there was no sense of distance for the lookouts to measure. Just the lights, bobbing away, those closest, the forerunners of the chain, were merely disconnected points in blackness, until suddenly *Saraband* had come close enough, without warning, to catch a weak reflection that showed the lights joined to something more substantial; a local fishing prau about to go right under *Saraband's* saddle tanks.

'Jesus Christ,' Harry muttered. 'Heave her to, Mr Gowers!'

He heard Gowers ring the engine room telegraphs, and call down to the control room, 'Stop together!'

Harry leaned over the bridge and called down to the prau, 'Terribly sorry lads, we didn't see you!'

Then he turned to Gowers, 'Well that's our surprise gone. We'll be the talk of the fish market tomorrow. It won't take long for word to get round that a bloody great submarine's lurking about in the offing.' Harry had hoped to delay announcing their presence in the area until he'd launched a few torpedoes into some nice Jap target.

'Ingrish? Ingrish?' The voice was coming from the prau. When Harry looked back over the bridge wing he could see the daisy chain of lights had started to concertina, and two of the men in the prau were hauling in slack from what looked like a seine net. It was what he'd feared, as soon as he saw they were fishing boats; why he'd ordered stop, together. He didn't want to think about the mess they would have been in if that net had got tangled round *Saraband's* propellers.

'Yes! Yes! English!' Harry called back. He was greeted with big grins from the prau.

'Japan man there!' The fisherman doing all the talking had stood up and was gesturing south into the night. Harry had an idea. 'Mr Gowers. Pass the word for the cox'n and Scobie.'

*

Saraband was at periscope depth, a good 2,000 yards north of Tikus Island, still at the head of the Penang Strait but further to the west, and just on the shelving line where the sea bed fell away to almost 300 feet. The sun had been up for at least an hour, and the ship Harry was looking at through the small periscope still hadn't moved.

The waters along the full length of the Malay archipelago were notoriously shallow, never more than 350 feet anywhere, and shoaling to the point of useless for submarine ops the further you went down towards the Malacca Straits.

The ship he was watching was sitting on the shelving line, too.

She was an elderly coastal trader with a tall, spindly, natural draught funnel amidships, behind a wooden wheelhouse, with two deep well-decks between her central superstructure and her fo'c'sle and poop. She looked as if she weighed in at a bit over 600 tons, and her distinct lack of freeboard said she was fully laden, so arguably deserving of a torpedo – just. Which made Harry wonder what she'd been doing hanging about here in the early dawn, instead of running for Georgetown.

Then there were her proportions; the more Harry looked at them, the more they seemed not quite right; too much fo'c'sle and poop, and not enough well-deck. In other words; a lot of ship, for not much hold space.

The poop had an ancient pea-shooter deck gun perched on it, and although she was fewer than 600 yards away, Harry could see nobody on deck.

She looked like she was waiting for somebody.

Harry sent the periscope down yet again and leaned against the chart table, lost in thought. The control room crew covertly watched him pulling that bottom lip of his again, looking for clues as to what was going on.

Harry was thinking about what the Malay fisherman had told him the previous night.

Having almost run down the poor man's prau, Harry had the cox'n haul him aboard so that he could say 'sorry' in person. And what had Harry learned from the encounter? That the man had been pleased to see they were 'Ingrish' and not Jap; that his limited grasp of the English language came from having been a British District Officer's driver before the war; and that he and his fellow villagers had been out stringing a home-made seine net when they first heard *Saraband*'s diesels, without realising she was so close. Harry also gained what he'd hoped for; intelligence.

Mostly just little snippets: that the Japs had strung anti-torpedo nets between many of the fishing gillnet stakes that you could see lining the main shipping channel either side of the Strait. And there were many of them; as Harry had already noticed, even on his short acquaintance with this coast. As a result, smaller coasting vessels were passing inside the gillnet stakes with a certain degree of confidence that any marauding Allied sub taking a pop would see their torpedoes 'premature' in the nets – that is, detonate short of their target – thus allowing them to escape.

But there had been other, more pertinent stuff.

For example, there was frequent traffic in and out of Penang at the moment, and one big ship in particular, with a big, puffing funnel was always going up and down, and whenever she was about, other cargo ships invariably showed up too. There had been many theatrics performed to get the point across on that one; enough to suggest the ship upstairs right now was the one the Malay had told him about. Certainly, this ship was exactly where the Malay said he'd last seen his 'big puffer'. And Harry supposed 600 tons was big, to a man whose own marine conveyance could be easily lifted by himself and a friend.

The fisherman had also been eager to pass on information about George Town harbour, and what sounded to Harry like the infamous Jerry U-boat base away from home. From his descriptions it sounded as though Jerry did have Type IX U-boats in there: up to four of them.

In return, Harry told Scobie to offer the Malay treats from the pantry to take back home. In the end, the fisherman settled for a big tin of barley sugar sweets and two tins of gammon. He was more interested in the bandages and antiseptic cream on offer, as well as a small tin of surgical needles and a bobbin of suture. They'd parted as friends.

All of which raised the question; why had he still not attacked the ship upstairs?

His answer was easy; something didn't feel right. This was his second sweep round to take a closer look. The strange ship might be quite happy sitting there, her engines at 'all stop', but it was a bugger for a dived submarine to hang about with no way on her, trying to keep her trim while watching discreetly. But why watch? Why not just stick a torpedo in her?

Well …

If the target was going nowhere, and only had a pop gun, which was ostentatiously tacked to her arse-end, wouldn't it be the smart idea to surface and sink the damn thing by gunfire, saving the torpedo for something better that might come along? On the other hand, the Malay had said that other cargo ships invariably turned up when this one was around. So why announce your presence and send all other potential targets scurrying to port, when you could wait and sink them all?

Harry gave his bottom lip another pull. Yep. There was indeed something he didn't like about the ship upstairs. And he knew what it was. Or rather, suspected.

She was a Q-ship.

He hadn't read any intelligence that the Japs were using them; but then that didn't mean anything. A Q-ship was the classic submarine trap. You took an ordinary rusty old tramp steamer; the older and clankier the better; and you put a naval crew aboard and a battery of modern naval ordnance – a brace or more down either side of 4-inch quick-firing guns; depth charge racks, modern hydrophone listening equipment; and you modified the rusty old hull internally so that she could take punishment and was capable of accommodating a modern, high-speed turbine in addition to her old boilers. Then, you sent her out to trail her coat.

The unsuspecting submariner would see only an easy kill, and when he surfaced to dispatch it – it would be too late.

Harry knew that he wasn't going to surface, but he couldn't make his mind up whether to fire a torpedo and blow his cover on this coast for just an old, 600 ton bucket. However, one thing he definitely couldn't do was hang around treading water.

'Keep sixty feet. Slow ahead together,' he said, eventually. 'Port twenty.'

And they were off again, on another slow turn around their target, in the hope that when they circled back, something would have changed.

It did.

'High speed HE on three one zero,' said Meek, whose quiet tones from the Asdic cubby could still be heard even in the silence that enveloped the control room. 'It's a good distance away, sir, but getting louder … yes … moving away from our turn … south … on three one five now, sir … coming a-beam of us, sir … wait one … further, multiple HE, sir … beyond the target … slower … their bearing is drawing right too, sir.'

Harry stepped to the plot, where Gowers already had their target ship marked. He was pencilling in projected courses for Meek's new targets, way over towards the coast.

Harry said, 'Do an all-round sweep, Meek.'

A pause, then: 'More HE, sir. Multiple … on two zero zero. Faint, so some distance away … closing from the south, sir … wait one!' Meek paused to turn his wheel again, listening, then he called, his voice getting a wee bit excited now, 'HE from our target ship now, sir! She's started up. Reciprocating engine noises, sir … she's under helm … moving … What a racket! Moving away … out into the channel.'

'Starboard thirty.' said Harry, excessively *not* excited. 'Group up, full ahead together.'

Harry had halted *Saraband*'s veer away and was turning her back. He watched as her head came round on the gyro repeater, then stepped back again to study Gowers' plot. Except Gowers was slow; slower than Harding had ever been at laying out the picture of what was happening upstairs. Harding, *Scourge*'s navigating officer, whom Harry, right now, sorely missed.

However, he knew he shouldn't, couldn't think like that. It wasn't helpful. So he stopped, held his breath and let Gowers finish filling in all the targets that Meek was calling. Shouting at Gowers wouldn't make it happen any faster, in fact it would probably make him even worse. He knew that. *But for fuck's sake, hurry up, man!* he incanted to himself, over and over.

A picture was, none the less, emerging.

Meek continued to call what he was hearing; the multiple HE beyond his high speed target indicated as many as six; slow ships, that sounded like they were labouring – almost certainly small merchantmen of some description, and old. The high-speed target, however, it turned out wasn't that high speed after all, doing no more than 18 knots. A product of Meek getting a bit too excited. A Jap E-boat, by the sounds of things, he said – now that he'd calmed down – ambling along. And the multiple HE coming up from the south turned out to be just two targets. Marine diesels, Meek was sure, but nothing heavy. *Escorts*, thought Harry. More than likely some type of sub-chaser; their numbers initially multiplied by Meek's inexperience, he decided.

Harry ordered, 'Group down, slow ahead together,' then, 'periscope depth.' And he felt *Saraband* rise beneath his feet.

He already had the periscope on the bearing of the multiple merchantmen when it broke surface, and was instantly aware of mastheads, and at least two bridges and funnel tops just visible over the curve of the waves and against the verdant mush of the land in the background. But there was something else between him and the ships; small, regular, like fence posts. On instinct, he cranked back the periscope head to do a sky sweep. He'd barely gone a few degrees around – fewer than five seconds had passed – when he ordered the periscope back down again, and *Saraband* back to 60 feet.

Two shagbats. The first less than a mile away, and the other, echeloned behind it, coming up on the little convoy on the other side of the straits. They were flying at about 1,500 feet, both single-engine floatplanes like the Jerry Arados that he so disliked; so both probably a 'Jake', which was the Allies' code-name for the Aichi E13. Nasty buggers: carried a 500 pound bomb load, or depth charges, if they were after subs.

Also, it had dawned on him what the 'fence posts' were. Fishing stakes, for gillnets. The convoy was creeping south down the coast behind rows of gillnet stakes. Their Malay fisherman friend had told him all about them, how the Japs had now festooned them with anti-torpedo netting.

He looked at the plot again. Gowers was up to date. The plot was good, but tactical situation looked buggered.

At a glance he could see that all his possible targets were moving beyond easy range for an attack, funnelling themselves into waters that were too narrow and too shallow. If he were to try and get *Saraband* into a firing position he'd need to run fast, motors going flat out and eating amps from his battery. Amps he would need later, given how many hours of daylight were left in which he'd need to remain submerged.

Then there were Jap escorts coming up to meet them, and the very dubious tub he'd been watching since sun-up, which was now buggering off in the opposite direction. It was withdrawing at an angle that, by the second, was making it more and more difficult to get into a firing position.

And what if he did catch up with all these departing ships in their little convoy? There were the fishing stakes and what was strung between them. Even if he could manoeuvre in time to get behind the stakes, to where the enemy was, there wasn't enough water 'twixt stake and shore for him to turn onto an attacking angle. And if even if he did, would there be any room to turn and get out again?

He issued a series of orders. He'd decided it was time to turn around and bugger off. Right now, his boat wasn't in any danger. From what he could see of was happening on the plot, and what he'd seen in his brief look through the periscope, he guessed the Japs probably didn't even know he was there. But if he pressed on, that would change. Fast. And frankly, from what he'd seen of the potential haul, it wasn't worth the candle.

Harry ordered *Saraband* to 80 feet and told Gowers to lay in a course to take them back up the coast to just north of the Muda River estuary. 'No hurry,' he said, and ordered the telegraphs rung for 'sedate motoring' – Bill Laurie knew what he meant and rang slow ahead together. His plan was to hang around up there, about 5 or 6 miles out and wait and see whether any other targets popped up. Then, he ordered the boat to watch diving, handed over the con to Bill Laurie and stepped forward into the wardroom in search of Scobie and a cup of coffee. Even though sweat was dripping off the end of his nose, and the heat couldn't be less conducive to a hot drink, he felt he needed the kick.

It was only when his mug sat before him on the wardroom table, that it had dawned on him he hadn't given his usual running commentary on what had just happened upstairs, and where they were going now, and why.

When he thought about, he realised he hadn't given a commentary since he'd assumed command. He wondered why. Throughout all his previous commands, his commentaries had become legendary, and the crews had always appreciated them. They had liked to know what was happening. It helped reassure them their captain knew what he was doing.

But things were different on this boat.

Not a happy ship.

Not surprising really, bearing in mind what had gone before. The boat was unsettled – and he didn't have a handle on her.

He had thought at first, after sinking the Jap submarine, and the subsequent signal from HMS *Howe's* captain, that that had got them over the hump; bonded them again, made them more like a normal submarine heading out on patrol. *Thank you* Saraband *for sweeping the seas for us,* the signal had said. *Can we have the next baroque dance with you?*

A reference to their *baroque* name.

But then *Saraband* had made Columbo, and all the puffed-up swagger he'd expected from a crew that had sailed in with bunting representing a 3,000 ton Imperial Japanese Navy submarine sewn onto their jolly roger, simply failed to materialise.

And that was even before he'd carried out his purge. Which had put a real dampener on matters. Harbottle, the disgraced outside wrecker, had been sent ashore, as had the lacklustre original gun-layer, since relegated to full-time gash disposer; both replaced with likely bodies from the local spare crew pool. A couple of other weak links were disposed of and replaced in similar fashion, notably from the torpedo room. Normally Jack didn't like slack arses who failed to pull their weight. But maybe those weak links had been liked more than he'd allowed for.

On the plus side, he'd got Leading Seaman Priestly bumped up to Acting Petty Officer and had confirmed him as *Saraband's* new wrecker. He had hoped that would please the crew – to have, at last, someone who knew what he was doing on the dive board. But if it had, nobody was showing it.

Back in Columbo, even when leave had been handed out, the watch going ashore tramped off the boat without a whoop or a holler. And when they reported back, all on time, they were biddable alright, but what a surly shower. Obviously, they had no steam to let off.

Only four idiots were brought to the first lieutenant's table; one for assaulting a local trader, whom he accused of trying to diddle him over the price of a teak elephant barely the size of a grapefruit, and another two for brawling ashore with pongos from Fortress Command. In a perverse way, it was a disgrace for a fighting boat's crew to generate so little mayhem on a run ashore. Where was their fighting spirit? This was supposed to the Royal Navy. Only the fourth defaulter had given him hope. A young AB called Duncan, who had shown much promise as a replacement on the gun team. He was just a slip of a lad, but very drunk when some huge three-badge stoker started claiming he'd heard *Saraband* was a boat full of bum boys. Duncan had gone straight at him with a bar stool. Needless to say the stoker won that one, but the other *Sarabands* had been so proud of the young lad sticking up for his boat, they'd re-christened him 'Duncan Disorderly', and told him to always answer to that title with pride.

Bill Laurie said the boy had come before his defaulters' table, his face seven shades of black and blue, but with a big grin still on it, and his chest puffed out. So Bill had only awarded him a month's stoppage of grog, omitting to mention that Duncan, not yet being 21 years old, wasn't entitled to it in the first place.

The only other light spot during that run ashore had been Caudrey piping up, 'Why do we call them pongos, Number One?' And Bill Laurie explaining, 'Personal hygiene in the British Army, especially when on operations, has always been a bone of contention between our two services, young Caudrey. Hence we navy types are wont to say, wherever the army goes, the pong goes.'

And now look at them, thought Harry, sitting over his coffee at the wardroom table, peering down the gangway to the hunched backs in the control room, going through their watch routines. It set him ruminating. *Their captain's just shied away from a fight, and they're not even bothered. In fact, I get the feeling that they're actually more relieved than anything else. What a shower. All the fighting spirit of a pet dormouse with acute anxiety.*

Harry wasn't happy.

Eight

'Captain to the control room!'

It was Bill Laurie's voice. It hadn't long gone 1600 – the start of the first dog watch, so it was Bill who had the watch.

It only took Harry three steps from the wardroom table, where he'd been looking at the charts for this patrol billet, wondering where to lay a course for next in the hope of better targets. *Saraband* had been assigned this box under the system that was common to all Royal Navy sub operations; you were given a designated area, and your boat alone could patrol in it. No other Allied boats were permitted. The rationale was simple; it meant if you saw another sub, it had to be a U-boat, so you could sink it. 'U-boat' was the designation applied to all enemy submarines, not just German ones; Eyeties, when they were in the war, and Japs too.

Saraband's box was large for this patrol. Latitude 5 degrees north to 7 degrees north, and longitude 95 degrees east to the Malay coast.

The Asdic watch had picked up faint HE coming from the south. Harry ordered the periscope up and he did a quick all-round look – sky and horizon – before getting the wardroom messenger to lay him on the bearing. And there it was – what looked like the mast and bridge structure of one of those Jap escorts, coming up over the horizon. Harry sent the 'scope back down and pulled out *Jane's Fighting Ships*. Even he wasn't familiar with all the minor puddle-jumpers in the Jap navy's order of battle. He wanted to broaden his repertoire.

When he sent the 'scope up again, what he was looking at didn't tally with anything in *Jane's*. It looked more like a glorified tug, with a deck gun and shield – that were too big for her and completely out of proportion – perched on her short bow and two depth charge racks running the length of her commodious stern. The auxiliary sub-chaser, for that was what she obviously was, looked as though she was beginning a sweep. Harry sent the 'scope down again and said to Laurie, 'Don't bother waking Gowers, she's hardly worth the bother of starting a plot.'

'Target's stopped, sir,' said the stand-in Asdic watchkeeper, the one Harry had thought a schoolboy. 'Yes … he's finished with engines, sir.'

Which probably meant the Jap's anti-submarine detection kit was just some primitive hydrophone, that couldn't hear anything if the sub-chaser's own diesel was running. Not worth a torpedo, and not worth betraying their presence for, although Harry was tempted to surface and risk an engagement just to see that bloody great Jap gun firing. It looked like a 5-incher, and he'd put money on the thing doing more damage to its own deck fittings than any target.

Harry went back to his charts. Some time later, Laurie joined him for coffee, claiming he too needed the hit just to keep him awake. The two of them, in crumpled white uniform shirts open to their chests, sat there blinking in their own sweat. Eventually, Laurie said, 'Our chum upstairs every now and then gets the urge, and chuffs his way over to another patch of muddy water, and just sits there. Just as he did over the last muddy patch. It's like watching paint dry.' Then he yawned and mopped round his neck. The temperature in the boat was in the high eighties now and there wasn't even the murmur of idle chatter to be heard. 'You know the bastard passed within five hundred yards of us, sir,' Laurie added, 'executing one of his arse-shifting manoeuvres. Not even an inkling we were here. I know I should have called you, but … you know … you could tell he didn't have a clue. If they're all this sloppy, we could be in for a very boring deployment.'

And then, right on cue, a voice.

'Captain to the control room!'

There was HE coming south. A reciprocating engine. When Harry stuck the 'scope up, there was an old three-island tramp puffing down the coast. She was a good 1,500 tons, he reckoned, and well worth a torpedo. What he also saw was a Jake floatplane circling in lazy eights over her, and then their sub-chaser chum fired up her diesel and clunked her way over to slip in and run alongside her. Except the tramp was inside the fishing stakes. He tried ordering a quick group-up dash to the south, trying to get to a gap between the end of one line of stakes and the start of the next. But when he did, the sub-chaser just happened to get there before him. Pure, dumb, rotten, fucked-up luck.

And now he was on the wrong side of the ten fathom line.

Another dash to the next gap was out of the question. Even though he was in very shallow water, the number of rivers emptying all the gunge of the jungle into the waters here meant the sea was anything but clear, so little chance of the 'Jake's' spotter identifying the tell-tale, long dark shadow of a submarine in the pellucid depths. But he wouldn't miss the churn one would make, speeding up to 9 knots with barely a few feet between its conning tower and the surface. Harry broke off the chase.

This day was getting to be a pain. Just like the whole patrol. *Saraband* went back to watch diving.

Nobody seemed to mind. Harry could tell. It wasn't a matter of somebody saying something, or not saying anything. This was the bloody Royal Navy after all, not a debating society. It was the feeling abroad. You could sense it, breath it in, like the smell of feet and diesel. And what he was 'smelling' was that nobody gave a stuff that they were breaking off another attack. They were quite happy to be going back to boredom. A *total* absence of fighting spirit.

Maybe it was the heat and humidity in the boat, sapping it. Or maybe it was just the war; it had been going on so long now, the crews coming through were really nothing more than thorough-going civvies in blue suits. The leavening of old Trade hands that could be relied on to show everyone how it should be done, and to inject the requisite doses of good old-fashioned naval gumption, they were few and far between these days. Nearly everybody was new; Hostilities Only matelots whose primary aim was to get back to civvy street, warm beer and a cuddle with the wife in a proper bed. Maybe that was why he wasn't giving his trademark running commentaries anymore? Because he sensed that nobody aboard this boat seemed interested. And when he thought that, he started to feel frightened.

If it was true; if that *was* the settled attitude of this crew, it was going to get them all killed.

To have come this far – and to die just because this rabble of sweepings couldn't be arsed.

'Captain to the control room!' The officer of the watch's voice. Harry obeyed with an alacrity he didn't feel.

'The search periscope seems to be flooding, sir,' said Gowers, looking crestfallen, as if it was his fault. 'I was just doing a regular all-round look and … the lenses weren't clearing of water, sir.'

Saraband, like all submarines, had two periscopes: large, bronze tubes in housings that rested practically on the keel. Bronze, because they had to slide through the hull glands and so couldn't be painted, so they had to be made of something that wouldn't corrode. The smaller of the two was the attack periscope; with one eye piece that ended in a tiny head, so small as to be all but invisible in the chop of open water, when the boat's captain stuck it up to carry out the end manoeuvres of any attack. It was good only for those final observations. The search periscope, however, was much bigger, with binocular vision and all manner of fine instrumentation attached – devices to tell off bearings and ranges and a swivel that let the viewer raise or lower the periscope head to search sea or sky, and an adjustable magnification that let you see to the horizon or bring the pimple on the end of an enemy watch-keeper's nose right into the control room beside you, at a range of five miles. A boat without a search periscope was blind.

Harry ordered the search 'scope up. There was the whirr of the actuator motor as it spooled the riser wires on their sheaves to lift the giant tube from its housing. As the periscope's training handles cleared the deck plate, Harry stepped in to lower them and look through the bifocal eye pieces. First, he could see the familiar streaming water, draining from the top lenses' facings, and expected his view to come clear. Except it didn't. A continuous film of water obscured his view, light dancing and reflecting in the rivulets so that he could see nothing, not even shadow.

'Down periscope,' he said, stepping away. Bill Laurie, standing right next to Harry, saw only a sanguine face, until he looked down and saw his captain's hands flexing and fisting in fury, before Harry rammed both into his pockets.

*

There had been only another hour and a half of daylight left when Acting ERA Priestly went up onto the periscope shears to try and fix the search periscope.

Harry had taken *Saraband* well out into the offing off Langkawi island, away from prying eyes and out beyond all the normal shipping lanes before coming to the surface, trimmed right down, so the wrecker could shimmy his way up to check whether it was the obvious that had gone wrong. He was there to look at the staunching window, an inspection panel on the 'scope's head that wreckers used to polish the lens prisms from the inside with jewellers' rouge. It was the likeliest place for a leak, but in this case there were none. The fault must be far more far more serious, said Priestly. Number One had to ask the warrant engineer to help the new wrecker – nothing was volunteered. Once requested, however, another ERA came forward with all the necessary spanners to begin a more comprehensive search for the leak.

Right then, sitting on the surface, engines at stop together, *Saraband* was supremely vulnerable, especially to enemies from the air. Harry had four lookouts on the bridge and downstairs, McTeer on their radar set carrying out a continuous air and sea search. Upstairs, the men worked under a relentless sun, using a makeshift pump to drain the 'scope's tube then, just before night fall, they dived to test it. The fix worked for a few minutes, then failed again. Except it wasn't nearly as bad as before. So, it was back up again, and the two engineers went back to work, this time having to use shaded torches to see, because by then the tropical night had fallen, as it did, in matter of minutes.

Without a functioning search periscope, *Saraband* might as well abandon the patrol. She would have hauled all those torpedoes well over 1,000 miles for nothing. Towards the end of the first watch Harry called a meeting on the bridge; Number One, Priestly and Bert Kershaw, the warrant engineer.

'I think it might be an engine vibration that's causing it,' said Priestly, daubs of fine machine oil glistening on his bare arms and chest and in his hair. Harry couldn't believe how much light came from the cloudless, star-crammed sky that had opened up a few minutes previously. No tropic darkness now.

'There's no vibrations coming from my engines,' said Kershaw.

'It wouldn't have to be big, or even continuous,' said Priestly. 'Just an occasional resonance, building up, might do it, loosen something.'

'It was what I was saying about her being a biter,' said Laurie. 'When you first joined, sir, and asked me. She has habit of hiding her vices until she springs them on you.'

'There's no vibrations coming from my engines,' said Kershaw, again.

Saraband rolled gently on the deep ocean swell as if she were innocence personified, engines shut down, not even cramming on amps. He could feel the surliness coming off Kershaw. And it was suddenly plain to Harry that it was all directed at him. A statement of resentment endlessly repeating. *Why do I have to put up with this whipper-snapper civilian in his blue suit? A youth who couldn't command a duck in a bath!*

It suddenly dawned on Harry that all this wasn't anything to do with what had transpired before on *Saraband*. That wasn't the gripe that was riling Warrant Engineer Kershaw. Oh, it might have contributed, been part of the build-up, a symptom. That, and the fact that the lieutenant who had commanded *Saraband* before had failed to stomp on it. No. This really was all about Harry now, and his wavy-navy stripes. This grumpy old bastard didn't like what was happening to *his* navy in *this* war; all these new bodies filling up the berths and none of them with a clue about the real Royal Navy, telling him what to do. *Well, I'm not playing any more.* That was what he was really saying. That was what was wrong with Kershaw. This whole fucking set up was a personal affront to him! He was too good for this lot, and this skipper. Harry didn't know whether to burst out laughing or punch the old git. Here they were, sitting on the surface, in Johnny Jap's back yard and effectively blind – and the whole boat was having to put up with this kind of prima donna mincing about.

'… if we could stop the vibration then a few bags of silica gel in the tube might soak any residual vapour,' said Priestly.

'Gel sacks are needed for the motors,' Kershaw started to say. 'The torpedo men working with electrics …'

Harry had had enough. 'Number One, take Priestly down to the engine room stores and get as many gel bags as are needed.'

Kershaw opened and then closed his mouth, like a landed mullet … after he'd taken a look at Harry's face.

*

The pumping of the periscope tube and the placing of silica gel bags to soak up remaining moisture didn't work, either.

After closing the tube, *Saraband* had run on the surface – topping up battery amps and letting the silica start to its work – until dawn, then she had dived and closed Langkawi submerged, before coming back up to periscope depth to view the coast. The periscope lenses remained stubbornly fogged now. Neither Priestly nor the ERA who'd been helping him knew whether this was a result of the original flooding, or just because the damned humidity had got in and was refusing to succumb to the silica. Kershaw had muttered some gnomic technical gibberish that was utterly unhelpful. But Harry knew a refusal when he heard one. This was the safety of Kershaw's own bloody boat at stake. And the bloody-minded, cross-grained, mean-spirited, ill-natured bastard wasn't prepared to help. For what? Because his sensibilities had been ruffled? Aw, bless!

For the first time, Harry began to consider having him removed as *Saraband's* chief engineer. Even though he knew that, for an old Trade senior rate like Kershaw, it would have been the Andrew's equivalent of sending him into an empty room with a bottle of whisky, a revolver, and a single round.

Harry ordered *Saraband* turned about and back out into the offing. Priestly wanted to try again and find the fault. He'd already been working on the damned thing for 27 hours without a break, but Harry listened to him, then ordered the boat back to that unremarkable spot on the empty sea and told Priestly he could have another couple of hours on the surface. Later, Harry wrote him up in the log, remarking on his ingenuity and determination when everyone else aboard was prepared to give up, and of his pride as captain in having him as a member of his crew.

Saraband surfaced into another cloying hot day with the sun directly over-head, burning directly down through air that looked like it was congealing so that visibility came and went in mirages and the lookouts' jobs were rendered almost impossible. Only the rhythmically-turning radar head was there to shield them from the sudden appearance of any Jap air patrol or sub-chaser. Priestly worked on, up on the periscope shears and down in the control room; him and his new mate, the ERA, whom Harry had belatedly realised was technically senior to Priestly but obviously had had the sense to realise he was working with a bloke more skilled when it came to optics. Harry noted his name. Young. He'd remember that.

The boat wallowed well into the afternoon on the long, slow swell. Engines at stop together so as not to develop the vibrations that Kershaw said weren't there. The clock ticked towards nightfall.

Then, it was time to call time.

Harry had decided. They'd be going home with a full load of torpedoes, but he had a plan that, hopefully, would at least add some needlework to their jolly roger.

The periscope tube was cleaned up and sent down. A silent Priestly and his mate went below, and Harry ordered the telegraphs rung for full ahead together. He intended to head west through the night – surfaced, to get there fast – and to get as much charge into his batteries as possible against the time to be spent dived on the following day. The aim was to get in amongst the inter-island junk traffic running up from Banda Aceh to the Nicobars. A few brisk gun actions should make the difference between going out for a duck and salvaging at least some pride before they joined their new flotilla at Trincomalee. Sad to say, Harry wasn't actually sure whether most of the crew minded one way or another. But *he* bloody well did.

He was already composing in his head the signal he'd get Cantor to flash to Captain S, Fourth Flotilla, alerting him to their intention to return from patrol early, when he heard the telegraphs ring behind him, and then there was a discordant grinding sound and a cough beneath the expected bang of the diesels starting. Suddenly, *Saraband* was slewing off her heading.

'Stop together!' Harry heard the watch officer order the rating on the telegraphs, then he ordered into the voice pipe, 'Helm midships.'

Harry stepped to the voice pipe after him and said, 'Captain here. Somebody get somebody to tell me what the hell is going on.'

*

Having digested the news, Harry decided not to go aft to the engine room to see for himself. He'd let Kershaw get on with fixing it, and he'd let him stew while he was about it. Harry could see all too clearly what must have happened, or rather how it had happened.

Standing in the control room, trying not to let the way his shirt was sticking to his back in the heat distract him, Harry listened patiently to the ERA who had been dispatched to enlighten him. It turned out that he only had one remaining main engine now, to drive the boat and charge the batteries. Sweat was cruising in rivulets down the man's oil smeared chest as he explained.

'Mr Kershaw is a stickler for clutchin' in the main engines right away, sir,' he said, getting his excuses in early. 'The minute the telegraph rings, you pull the starting levers, and your oppo opens the starting valve. No ditherin' allowed, sir, or you get a roastin'. And that was what happened. Mr Kershaw was on the levers himself, sir, and when he yanked 'em, I opened the valve, sir. 'Ceptin', sir, Mr Kershaw, he hadn't checked the turning gear first, sir. We'd been doin' some routine maintenance on the starboard main engine while it was shut down, and we hadn't finished, when the bridge rang down for full ahead. The turning gear was still engaged, sir. It's a bloody mess, sir, all jammed up, sir. Starboard engine's solid, and Mr Kershaw's workin' on it now sir, to free it up.'

Harry's limited knowledge of diesel mechanics had been enough to fill the gaps in the ERA's woeful tale. The turning gear was the device engineers used to precisely position the crankshaft, the biggest and heaviest moving part of a diesel engine, when they wanted to get access to its every nook and cranny. The shaft weighed in at God alone knew how many hundred pounds, so it needed the gear to turn it.

When anyone wanted to start the bloody thing, they had to blast it with HP – high-pressure air – just to get it going round fast enough to catch.

But if the teeth of the turning gear were still in it, well, the shaft couldn't turn, and then, what a bloody mess indeed.

Harry should have rung down, 'stand-by' on the telegraph, before ringing for 'full ahead'; to warn the black gang orders were coming. He realised that now. *His* mistake. But, for God's sake! For a boat's warrant engineer not to know what work was being undertaken at any given time, in his own engine room, was unheard of. And knowing, Kershaw should have realised the turning gear might still be in, and checked. Harry didn't have to close his eyes to know what must have happened next.

The telegraph ringing down. Kershaw, in high dudgeon. Steam coming out of his ears. Already fulminating to himself over that whippersnapper on the bridge over-ruling him on the allocation of his own stores, issuing orders like he knew what he was doing, when he didn't. And now he wanted 'full ahead together'? Well, he was going to get it, and smartly! Bert Kershaw would show him, Royal Navy fashion!

And, clang!

Captain Gilmour couldn't resist a little snort of amusement to himself, even though it was no laughing matter. Stupid old bastard, he could hardly imagine what must be eating at him now.

*

And here they come, Harry said to himself, his good eye stuck to the attack periscope, as he counted the scatter of motor junks puttering over the rim of the sea.

'Gun crew, close up in the gun tower,' he said. 'Oerlikon gunner and loader below the conning tower hatch.'

This was going to be their baptism of fire, Laurie had assured him. Neither their new gun-layer on the 3-inch deck gun, Leading Seaman Purdie, nor his mate, Able Seaman Tupper, nor the two lads detailed to man the 20 mm Oerlikon on the bandbox abaft the bridge, had ever fired their weapons in anger since leaving HMS *Excellent*, the navy's gunnery school. So, this was their first chance to prove they had earned their newly woven 'crossed-guns' flashes.

Harry, eye still to the attack 'scope, heard all the shuffling as they got into position. They'd drilled what was about to happen often enough coming down the Red Sea, now it was for real.

Harry reeled off his orders. 'Five enemy junks, closing from south east, three points off the starboard bow. We will surface within five hundred yards of targets. Trailing junk is not to be fired upon, repeat not to be fired upon. Stand by.'

Harry had explained to the crews earlier that in the attacks he intended for the following day, one junk must always be left afloat and undamaged, to carry off the crews of those they'd sunk. It was only fair; the poor bloody locals were in this war not of their own choice and it was bad enough the Royal Navy was sinking their livelihoods for them. Also, every chance must be given to allow the crews to abandon their vessels before the shooting started.

The order was given to surface, and Harry took his place under the conning tower hatch; he was going up first, this time. He perched there, hands on the steel clips, ready, in his white officer's shirt and cap – just to make sure the junk crews knew who they were dealing with. He had insisted the gun crews wore their caps, too. Shirts were optional.

'Surfaced!' called Laurie from the dive board. Harry remembered just in time to stuff his cap into his shirt front before he flung wide the clips and released the upper hatch. He called down, 'All gun crews close up for action!' as a *whumph* of air rushed up past him, billowing his shorts and shirt, reaching the parts other breezes didn't normally reach; it was the residual pressure still in the boat from all the tiny airline leaks and seepages you always got, and would have been enough to have sent his cap over the side if he'd had it on his head. And then he was on the bridge, and into the relatively mild post-dawn light.

And what a lovely, Conrad-esque vista it was; the vast expanse of riffled, turquoise ocean, stretching away to a line of verdant ridges some few miles to the south, a cloudless sky, and close in, the junks, all low and heavily laden, one about 45 tons, the rest about 70-odd to 80; broad-beamed craft with sweeping oriental lines ending in carved verandah stern-castles, oddly raked masts with one or two of them sporting slatted sails the colour of cinnamon, coming on at no more than a sedate five or six knots, pushed along by their chorus of wheezing and cackling petrol engines, bluey fumes smudging out over the laboured wakes each was dragging behind her. Their decks were empty; not a figure to be seen on any of them.

According to the intelligence reports Harry had read before sailing from Columbo, such was the demand on Jap merchant shipping these days, that when it came to re-supplying outposts such as the ones on the occupied Nicobar and Andaman Islands, they were routinely commandeering local native craft and sailing them in convoy instead of using even their decrepit fleet of ubiquitous inter-island tramps. And here they were; a local junk fleet. But where were their crews?

While he was wondering, there was a big bang from the for'ard deck; Purdie and his mate had the first round on the way. Behind him, he heard the Oerlikon gunners slamming their ammo pans into place, and then Caudrey was up beside him to adjust the fall of the 3-inch gun's next shot.

The first round detonated about 20 yards off the bow of the first junk; a sharp crack and a tall plume of water. The warning shot, to allow the crews to surrender, or jump. Two figures rushed out of the junk's wheelhouse to see what was happening, saw *Saraband*, and ran away again, disappearing below. When Harry took his eyes away from their antics, he could see the other junks were moving under helm, starting to peel away from each other as if they were scattering, intending to run.

Harry leaned back and called to the Oerlikon gunner, sitting in the weapon's seat, his eye to the open sight, 'Tully! The ones turning away! Bracket them in! Short bursts to head them off!'

Bump! Bump! Bump! Bump!

The first rounds pumped out, then the gun traversed, and another burst followed. Lines of water jets skittered across the paths of the diverging junks like magically appearing picket fences … and all the way came off the veering vessels, until all five were wallowing in the long, almost imperceptible ocean swell. That was when their people began tumbling up and out onto their decks. Nut brown bodies, all skin and sinew in only sarongs. There was shouting now, and waving, and that was when the women appeared, on two of the junks, a couple of them obviously cradling babies.

'Check fire!' shouted Harry.

Some of the men began manhandling what must have been some type of coracle, like woven lifeboats, that had been resting on the deck cargoes of every one of them.

At least they're getting the idea, thought Harry, *and getting off the damn things before we sink them.*

First one junk, then all, were dropping these floating baskets into the sea. That was when Harry suddenly swung to see what all the screaming was, coming from the junk on the extreme left of the gaggle. A little bandy-legged figure in a faded sand-coloured uniform had started to leap around, brandishing what looked like a Malay pedang sword. He looked quite comical, screaming and gesturing, until he started laying into some of the figures crowding to get into one of the coracles. Two figures went down under blows and all the rest began jumping into the sea. There were blood-curdling screams.

Harry froze, watching the horror of it. So did everyone else, all eyes now on the far-away junk.

Then, Harry was at the conning tower hatch. 'Number One! Get a small arms party up here right now! Get the Browning teams up here too. Hurry up man!'

Harry looked back to the junk. The uniformed figure – Harry realised he was probably some kind of Jap guard – was now running up and down the length of the junk's gunwale, screaming at the locals in the water.

'Tully!' yelled Harry. 'That junk with the Jap on deck. Rake her!'

Tully opened fire.

Nobody on the bridge, or even on the forward deck gun, had actually realised just what a fearsome weapon their Oerlikon was until they watched it, right there and then, go to work on the junk.

Even for an automatic cannon, it had an extremely high rate of fire – at least 450 20 mm rounds per minute at a muzzle velocity of over 2,700 feet per second, so it was possible to empty a 60-round ammo pan in just eight seconds. And that pan could be loaded with all manner of rounds, from ball shot and tracer, to high explosive, armoured piercing and incendiary.

The screaming Jap was there one second, and a wisp of pink mist the next. Gouts of splinters went careening off in all directions; one of the masts seemed to skid at its base and tumble slowly over the side, plucking rigging out of the deadeyes as it went. The sun was so bright, they didn't notice the flames at first. It was Caudrey's shout that alerted Harry to the fact that two other figures in sandy uniforms had appeared on the decks of two of the remaining junks. One of them was lugging some kind of general purpose machine gun with him, the tripod-mounted weapon trailing a bandolier of bullets.

However, *Saraband's* Browning .303 machine gunners were already mounting their weapons, and Harry ordered the first one secured to open up on the Jap. One of the figures on the junk didn't wait to pull the trigger on his gun, but threw himself over the side before the tattoo of *Saraband's* bullets reached him. His pal wasn't so lucky.

By now, the sea around the junks teemed with bobbing coracles, and some heads too, ducking up and down in the water. Harry ordered *Saraband* to proceed dead slow towards the small junk at the back of the gaggle; they gently passed through the edge of the survivors and as they did so, Harry kept gesturing at folk to follow.

Down on the forward casing, as arranged, the first lieutenant was assembling his boarding party. The two tommy-gun toting ratings whom Laurie had sent to the bridge when Harry called for small arms, dropped down to join them.

The night before, Harry had explained to Bill Laurie that he would be sending him aboard the junk he intended to spare, to dump as much of its cargo over the side as possible before he allowed all survivors onboard and let it go.

'I want you to go, Bill, because I want someone sensible there first time,' he told Laurie while they sat at the wardroom table alone. 'Once our crew get the idea … men, *and* officers … then we can delegate for subsequent actions.'

'Aye, aye, sir,' Laurie had replied with a knowing smile.

Saraband, her for'ard diving planes deployed, nudged up to the abandoned junk. She looked all toy-like and prissy-prim from water line to deck, but when you looked above, she was just a huddle of bales and lashings. Harry was looking down, right into the empty wheelhouse with its little shaded patio beyond, now littered with upturned stools and the wreckage of a breakfast.

Laurie was first to step down onto the port plane and nimbly onto the junk. From even this little distance, he managed to look quite cool in his officer's whites and cap. His holstered Webley Navy .45 looked rather martial on his hip. Two ratings with Thompson sub-machine guns followed him, then a handful more with marlinspikes and other tools for ransacking a cargo.

The party had barely stepped a few paces down the deck when two Japs appeared out of what passed for a fo'c'sle on the junk. They separated and stood crouched, staring wildly all around them; at Laurie's party, at *Saraband's* hull that must've appeared huge merely by proximity; wretched little creatures, like starved sumos, and impossibly young. One was visibly shaking. The other started to scream, and ran directly at a group of Laurie's lads, bent over to lift a hatch cover. The Jap swept up a belaying pin, wielding it as he ran, pounding diagonally past Laurie. Harry's sailors, the ones with the spikes and wrecking bars, and the ones with the tommy-guns, merely stood there, frozen in mid-step, transfixed, gawping.

Harry didn't see his Number One un-holster his weapon; he just heard the shot, sounding like a teacher's sudden wrap putting an end to some misbehaviour, and saw the little Jap thrown sideways into the scuppers, hit under the arm. His scream had somehow become a gurgle now as he tried to rise up, a hand scrabbling for the belaying pin that had rolled after him. He seemed determined to get up again, clawing, legs sliding and scrambling on the deck and blood pumping in pulses from his mouth and nose. And still he wouldn't shut up.

Bill Laurie stepped forward and was standing over him now. He shot the Jap once through the temple. Harry looked for the other one; he had jumped overboard.

The lads threw the Jap's body into the sea, and then set about sending the contents of the junk's hold after it. They worked swiftly and methodically. Meanwhile, Harry had stepped to the back of the bridge and was hailing the junk crews in the water, waving at them to come closer. None did.

When Laurie came back on board, the first thing he said to his captain was, 'We're going to have a bugger's own job sinking these damn things, sir.

You should see below decks. They're built like the insides of a bamboo pole. Sub-division after sub-division.' The junk was less than 100 feet long. 'She must have your Oriental's equivalent of nine water-tight compartments. If we're going to sink them, we're going to have to do that to them, sir.' He jerked his thumb over towards the burning junk, now drifting some distance away, and all but burnt down to her waterline.

'What happened to your other Jap?' asked Harry.

Laurie shook his head. 'Jumped in, sir, and tried to swim away. We yelled at the little bastard to come back, but he just opened his mouth and let himself sink. All the death before dishonour bollocks they say about them must be true. Mad buggers. Still, I suppose it makes it easier for us not having to worry about prisoners.'

They'd all heard the stories about the Japanese preferring to die rather than surrender; and about the atrocities they committed against those who surrendered to them. Mad buggers indeed.

Saraband went slow astern, pulled away from the junk and ran wide so she could begin firing on the other junks. Watertight compartments or not, they were going to have to try the gun. Just to make sure.

Harry watched while Purdie took five shots before he managed to score a hit. He'd need to do better than that. Harry hoped practice would sort him out. The result, however, was a satisfying, splintered mess, and a ragged cheer went up from the gun crew. But once the smoke had cleared, it became apparent that their 3 inch shells hadn't even dented the junk's ability to keep floating. After 24 hits, Harry told him to check fire. The junk was matchwood, but it was still bobbing away, taunting them.

Harry turned to the Oerlikon crew and told them to pack their pan with incendiary. After that it took three to four short bursts per junk to reduce the entire fleet to pyres.

All the while, the three clumps of survivors' coracles had been floating nearby, their occupants staring blankly at the pyrotechnics, watching as the rounds went home into what must have been their only means of earning a living, and likely the only places they had to live. Harry could only imagine what they were thinking, watching the towers of roiling black smoke rise vertically into an immaculate azure sky. Harry certainly knew what *he* was thinking; it was time to go, before some Jap saw them over the horizon and came to investigate. But there was something he had to do first.

He ordered *Saraband* to close the biggest clump of coracles, and he began waving again, pointing at himself, and then away into the offing, and then pointing at them, and at the remaining junk. After a lot of yelling, the people in the water finally seemed to get the message and started waving back and grinning, and more importantly, rowing in the surviving junk's direction. Waving and grinning. Pathetically grateful. Harry felt his throat tighten. Then, he ordered the casing and the bridge cleared and he dived the boat. As he went through the conning tower hatch, he noticed a small splash of vomit by the bridge voice pipes. It was Bill Laurie's. He knew because he'd heard him as he checked the casing was clear. It was alright. The sea would wash it away.

Nine

On the 1,000 mile journey back across the Bay of Bengal to their new base at Trincomalee, Harry found himself thinking about his former CO, Captain Charles 'the Bonny Boy' Bonalleck VC – the Great War hero, the drunk, and the madman.

The name had cropped up among Harry's sundry reveries as he contemplated what drove otherwise good people to do bad things. Like Bert Kershaw, his once errant warrant engineer. It must have started somewhere, and probably some time ago. The war, then the mobilisation, the gates to the citadel opening and the never-ending charge of infidels coming through, getting all dressed up in spanking new blue suits they hadn't earned, knowing nothing – their very presence seeming to sunder every tie and tradition that bonded his old world together. It probably started for him with simple anger at some falling standard in his beloved Royal Navy. And then, the realisation that all that new blood was bound to dilute the purity of the pool. In Bert Kershaw's eyes – the eyes of a lover, because the Royal Navy must truly have been his love – every additional affront must have been a personal wound. Until it all got out of control, and what had started as anger had become un-reasoning rage. He must have thought that when even degeneracy had reared its head, here was the final besmirching. But no; they went and appointed a schoolboy, part-time, kiddy-on, pretendy weekend sailor as his captain.

And then, carried off by his slow-motion temper tantrum, he'd gone and inflicted serious damage on his own boat.

The whole, vast unfairness of it all had driven him to what had effectively been sabotage. And that had been his *Jesus Christ, what am I doing?* moment.

Which was what Harry had been reflecting on; how some blokes, like Bert Kershaw, seem to have those trips already set in them. And when they broke, all the alarms finally went off, and they stopped. But others, like the Bonny Boy, for some reason – didn't.

While he had been busy lying on the beach at Beirut, word had wafted back to him of how the Bonny Boy had gone AWOL; had some kind of breakdown, had run away somewhere and was hiding. Then, when *Saraband* had touched at Columbo he'd had to report to his old chum Sam Bridger, now a full four-ringer captain and very grand indeed, with his own punkah-equipped office and a plaque on the door that said, 'Chief of Staff to Flag Officer, Columbo'.

'Do I have to genuflect, sir?' Harry asked after Bridger's flunky had shown him into the cool, wafting air of his sanctuary.

'Don't get smart! I have to take it down in a couple of weeks,' said Bridger. 'I'm getting packed off up to Kandy. Mountbatten's moving SEAC there from Delhi, and I've got my chit appointing me Eastern Fleet senior submarine liaison officer.'

SEAC stood for South East Asia Command and was the joint Allied command for this part of the war against Japan.

'Now I'd have to at least kneel for that, sir!'

'Shut up Gilmour and make yourself useful at the decanter,' Bridger replied.

Brandy with ice, and over the next hour Harry had finally received the latest, unofficial word on what had become of the Bonny Boy.

Apparently, he had walked out of the joint Allied HQ in Algiers just hours ahead of the arrival of a senior officer from C-in-C Med Fleet with an order to relieve him. No-one knew why. Rumour was that he had cracked up.

Whatever the truth, Captain Bonalleck hadn't left empty handed; he had disappeared with the mess petty cash and clutching a Yank travel warrant to Casablanca that he had forged for himself. But when he'd got there, instead of blowing the loot, he'd gone straight to the beach and 'walked into 'til his hat floated'.

'Nobody knows why. There was no note or anything,' Bridger told Harry. 'Anyway, that's the latest word doing the rounds. The impression

I got, however, was that nearly everybody seemed to be relieved. And I'm pretty sure you and I can guess why, can't we, Harry?'

Bridger and Harry had never had a blow-by-blow discussion of how the Bonny Boy had tried to kill Harry, first by sending his then command, HMS *Scourge*, on a patrol into a known enemy minefield, then tried to engineer the boat's loss to 'friendly fire' during Operation Husky. But both Harry and Sam Bridger knew it had happened.

Harry couldn't imagine how their Lordships would define such a series of events in the context of an inquiry, should they have ever been forced to conduct one. But from what rumours had wafted past his ears in recent months, it was plain their Lordships knew such events had taken place.

Lounging on his bridge hammock, the whole idea of it all made Harry laugh to himself, as the Bay of Bengal in all the tropic majesty of its boundless sea and vaulting sky lay stretched out before him.

At that moment, on the other side of Africa, other people were thinking about Charlie 'the Bonny Boy' Bonalleck too, even though they didn't know it was him – yet. And they weren't laughing.

The back office in the British legation at Casablanca was gripped by a fug of smoke and frustration. Its two occupants, the monocled Compton Dewar and the pipe smoking Alex Saumarez were silently reflecting on their recent, singular, lack of success. The bird had flown, right from under their noses. They should have known better; timing would get them in the end. Too languid by far; that was what they'd been. Just because everybody else moved in geological time in this godforsaken, fly-blown walk down memory lane, didn't mean to say that an inveterate shady dealer like Stroessner was going to chum along.

No; he had acted while they dithered.

If you went right back to the beginning – and both of them had, repeatedly, in their minds' eyes –they should have acted sooner.

Polite inquiries at Celine's as to who the mysterious British merchant navy captain was, the one who took his coffee and beignets there every day, had elicited only shrugs from the waiters. As if to say, 'who's asking?' Should they have offered a neatly-folded wad of francs, or even better, US dollars?

But then, conveniently enough, the captain had been there the next day, so that they could take a secret photograph of him with their Box Brownie from the back of the legation car. They had done something then, at least. Although what good the photo was going to be hadn't been clear to either of them, at that point.

Then it had been decided they would take a look at the spiv who seemed to be the friend of this mysterious sea captain. Alex, being the younger, said he would follow the spiv, ascertain his movements, before the two would select their moment and spot to pounce and badger him with questions – although what questions, hadn't yet been decided on. The following day, when Jerome the spiv had at last risen from his breakfast with the captain, and Alex had slid out of the legation car to follow, it had taken only 10 minutes for Alex to lose him.

That was when they'd decided they had no option but to enlist the help of the local *flics*, a move that was always going to be fraught with the prospect of low farce. And so it had proved.

Jerome – except at that point, neither Alex nor Compton knew his name – was promptly lifted roughly from the street and treated with the customary hospitality. A phone call later from the *gendarmerie* revealed Jerome's name, and that of Captain Charles Chaplin. Neither Alex nor Compton twigged right away. Only after the legation teleprinter had coughed out its reply to their original enquiry did the penny drop.

'The Board of Trade says it has no record of anyone by the name of Charles Chaplin holding a Master Mariner's ticket,' Alex had announced after returning to their office, crumpled paper in hand. Charles – *Charlie* – Chaplin. Both of them felt appropriately stupid. The news coincided with the non-appearance of said Master Mariner at Celine's the next day, and the next. Nor was Jerome to be seen. Another call to *les flics* had been required; could Jerome now be prevailed upon to reveal where *Charlie* Chaplin had got to?

Sitting in their office, in distinctly uncompanionable silence, the two hadn't had to wait long to receive the news; their captain had sailed 36 hours previously, aboard a Portuguese tramp steamer bound for Lisbon. And as the *les flics* had helpfully requested a full passenger manifest from the port authorities, they were also able to confirm that Stroessner's name was on it, too.

Only then had Alex and Compton done the right thing, and phoned that number in London, the one they had to use the scrambler for. One of the many, many questions London had asked was, did they have a description? 'Even better,' Compton had intoned gravely; the pressure lifting from his chest that he had at last *something* positive to communicate. 'We have a photograph!'

London had been strangely quiet for some time now, since they'd wired said image. So, all they had left to do was sit and puff and cogitate over what might have been, wondering just who Captain Charlie Chaplin really was. And how might their missing him have damaged the war effort?

'If at all?' Compton had suggested after a while, hopefully.

Ten

Saraband rounded Foul Point, its lighthouse two miles fine on the port beam, and Harry bent to take a fix on the southern tip of Elephant Island almost five miles across the mouth of Koddiyar Bay and the entrance to Trincomalee harbour, proper.

It was a beautiful morning, still too early for the full, cloying humidity, with a light breeze off the land, sweet with the scent of exotic blooms and spices. Once round the point, Harry ordered the deck party up and allowed them to lounge around, smoke and take in the scenery. There was still some distance to run before they came under the eye of Hood's Tower, up on the promontory overlooking the harbour's main channel.

It had been an uneventful trip across the 930-odd miles of the Bay of Bengal, from the northern tip of Sumatra to here, the north eastern shores of Ceylon. They had made nearly the entire voyage on the surface and hadn't been troubled by Jap air patrols nor sighted any wayward enemy U-boats. Even so, Harry had spent much of the three days it had taken, on the bridge. He still didn't have the confidence in his watch officers to leave them alone up there, especially at night. And anyway, his jury-rigged hammock proved really rather comfortable, rocking him to the fresh sea breezes instead of him having to lie on a sweat-sodden mattress in the oven that was down below.

And gazing up at the riot of stars each night had given him time to think, of lots of things.

For a start, he was going to make sure they dumped all their mattresses for their next patrol; sweat made them smelly and unhygienic. He had resolved to replace them with the dry rush mats he'd first encountered in Djibouti, that allowed what air there was to circulate around the body.

There was a long list of other housekeeping matters he'd drawn up; from the best drugs and salves and dressings they needed to stock the dispensary with, and what could be happily dumped; to the best types of gun ammunition for both the 3-incher and their Oerlikon. All discussed and noted with his first lieutenant; paperwork prepared for coming alongside at Trincomalee.

Then, there were the lessons he had learned; like his suspicion that the Japs were using Q-ships. He was certain that big, fat tub off Penang had been a rum 'un, and intended to write her up in his intelligence summary, lest some other poor bugger came up against her, and proved him right the hard way.

And thermoclines; he had discovered how useful they could be in the Mediterranean some time before. Here, in the enclosed warm waters around the Malay Archipelago, he couldn't help but notice that they abounded. Number One had brought it to his attention the first time they'd been driven deep by a Jap sub-chaser. Normally when you went down, the deeper you went and the greater the water pressure, the more it tended to shrink your hull, making you heavier. Which meant the trim had to be adjusted, and that involved the use of rather noisy pumps. But *Saraband* had descended into much denser water at just 80 feet, which had left her trim unaffected.

After that, every time *Saraband* had dived at first light, Harry ordered her down until they'd hit the first density layer, just so as he'd know where it was. Not just to help Number One keep his trim fine-tuned, but because the difference in temperature and therefore pressure between the layers played merry hell with any enemy hydrophone or other underwater detection device, and that meant below the layer was always a handy place to hide.

The main thing he'd kept reflecting on, however, lying in his hammock, up there on the bridge, was the crew.

Harry had had Number One draw up a crew bill for all those off watch while they were proceeding on the surface, allowing them up onto the casing in penny-packets to lounge around soaking up the sun and having a few smokes. So he'd noticed they had been quite chipper since leaving their patrol billet – that, and the general hubbub and laughter aboard, and the talk he'd overheard made it plain why.

After *Saraband's* first encounter with junks, she had gone on to have two more, each one resulting in a gaggle of sinkings. And as a result of all those loud explosions and all that destruction, her crew had become rather pleased with themselves.

Harry hadn't got it at first. He couldn't understand. After all, even for all the sound and fury, it hadn't been that much of an achievement. Just a lot of splintered wood and a few marginal cargoes. Also, he hadn't performed that spectacularly himself. Not once on this patrol had *Saraband* managed to get herself into a position to fire a torpedo, and it hadn't entirely been down to a lack of targets. And now she was bringing back a full load. Not a good look for a new skipper about to present himself for the first time to his new Captain S.

Yet the *Sarabands* all seemed full of themselves.

It was only after he had studied them more closely that Harry began to think maybe it wasn't complacency he was witnessing, but rather amazement. Astonishment even, at the fact they'd been able to achieve anything at all, together. That it just might be the dawning of a sense of ship's company, and what more they might be capable of. *So be it*, he thought. *Little acorns, Harry*, he said to himself. *Mighty oaks, from little acorns grow.* That thought had brought forth a dry chortle, at the rude awakenings they had yet to face.

And it hadn't just been the successful gun actions that worked their magic. There had been the warrant engineer and his change of tack. *That* had been a real weight off Harry's mind, when the old bastard decided it was time to stop playing silly buggers. It would have been a lie to say Bert Kershaw had been all contrition since his run in with the turning gear, but he had certainly become far more amenable in the aftermath, to the point Harry had been able to start having proper conversations with him, without feeling he was extracting information under duress.

The memory of the turning gear still made him smile. It had been a bad do all round. That Mr Kershaw had actually jammed the gear himself, made it even better.

Every time it came to mind, he laughed. Bill Laurie telling him the

101

warrant engineer had gone down into the space himself to fix it, the very tiny space, between the crank shaft and the bilge. And after it had taken several hours to complete, Harry deigning not to go aft to hear his report. He could only imagine the humiliation for the man. Yet he had only admiration for Kershaw when he came forward in person to report that the work was completed, and both engines were now back on line.

No actual apology had been offered, just an admission of responsibility and an assurance that all was now well, and it would never happen again.

For his part, Harry had decided that a rebuke was neither necessary, nor wise. There would be beating up to do, but Kershaw would certainly be administering it to himself. All Harry had said was a brief, 'Very well, Mr Kershaw. Carry on.'

And after that, everything had been sweetness and light, Kershaw not even objecting to being given a cameo role in the pages of *The Bugle*, courtesy of McTeer's skill as a cartoonist.

The Bugle was now up to its third edition, and through it McTeer had been making a name for himself as a bit of a satirist. Harry had decided to give him his head when it came to the cartoons he drew, even though some were close to the bone, especially the depiction of Harry – which had made appearances in every edition so far, in the background of every drawing, hands in pockets, watching everybody else, while pretending not to.

They were publishing once a week now, two copies for the for'ard ends, two for the stokers' mess back aft and one for the wardroom, all typed up by Cantor, laid out and etched onto the stencils by McTeer and the lot edited by Harry.

The second issue, immediately after the turning gear incident, had featured a cartoon of Kershaw celebrating his ability to fix almost anything and his tendency to be permanently slathered in oil and grease, entitled 'Box-up Bert' – 'boxing-up' being Jack's slang for getting something – anything – done and completed.

This cartoon took up half a page and showed two figures behind a discarded newspaper flyer with the headline, 'Betty Grable in Panty Panic Shock!'

The first figure was an unmistakable rear view of Betty, lifting her skirt. Facing her was Bert Kershaw in all his grubby glory, wearing only his shirt-tails, scratching his stubble and peering studiously at Betty's nether regions. The speech bubble coming out of his mouth said, 'If you wish it, I'll tackle it!'

The angle of Betty's head suggested she was looking at Bert Kershaw's nether regions and her speech bubble read, 'And if you wash it, I'll tickle it!'

The image also showed Harry in the background, his view the same as the warrant engineer's and his eyebrows having shot up through his cap line.

When Harry showed it to Mr Kershaw, to see if he objected to it, the warrant engineer merely sniffed and said, 'Fine, although I think that that McTeer lad is stretching it a bit.'

'How d'you mean, Mr Kershaw?' Harry asked, stifling his desire to start laughing again.

'I've never seen you looking that surprised before, sir.'

And at that point, Harry lost the battle.

*

Saraband cruised through the defence boom into the inner harbour, her deck crew now lined up, at ease, on the fore casing, all spruce in pressed whites, caps on. From the periscope stands, her new Jolly roger fluttered, with their little clutch of white trophy strips sewn on, representing all the junks they had sunk by gunfire. Pride of place, however, still went to the Jap sub they'd bagged off Socotra.

The huge natural harbour of Trincomalee opened out before them, its rim edged by low hills and thick jungle right down to the water's edge. In the inner lagoon was moored the Eastern Fleet in all its imperial glory; the imposing light grey floating castles that were the battleships HMS *Queen Elizabeth* and HMS *Valiant* and the battlecruiser HMS *Renown*, and then the aircraft carrier HMS *Illustrious*, with rows of spanking-new, American-made aircraft, now in Fleet Air Arm colours, ranged on her deck. There were trots of destroyers and a couple of new Crown Colony class light cruisers, sleek, fast looking creatures lounging under stretched white deck awnings. Harry, scanning the harbour, looked way over to the left and saw the distinctive slab-sided bulk of their new home, the new submarine depot ship HMS *Adamant*, flagship to their new flotilla, the Fourth.

When he studied her closely, however, the trots of S and T class boats alongside looked pretty full. He was wondering where *Saraband* was going to fit, when *Adamant* began signalling her pennant number.

Cantor stepped forward and read off the message from the blinking light.

'Captain S orders we come alongside HMS *Wu Chang*, sir,' he said. 'She's the auxiliary moored two cables astern of *Adamant*, sir.'

Harry's eyes followed Cantor's pointing arm, and fell upon a large, ramshackle-looking river steamer of about 3,000 tons, with extensive deck accommodation stacked two stories high, a single tall funnel and a ludicrously low freeboard. There was a spot free aft, and Harry, going aboard their new home, had the unusual experience of walking over the gangway at a slightly downward angle onto *Wu Chang's* deck.

'We filched her off the Chinese in '41, sir,' said an eager Midshipman who met him at the brow, and went on to sing the *Wu Chang's* praises as he steered Harry to her captain's office. 'She used to ply out of Shanghai, sir, up the Whangpoo river. And I know she looks a bit odd for her job, sir, but she's remarkably comfy, loads and loads of room. Really, you'll see. We love her.'

Harry had heard of Commander Maurice Kildare Cavenagh-Mainwaring DSO RN, the *Wu Chang's* captain. He'd had HMS *Tuna* early in the war and won his DSO for a number of singularly aggressive patrols in the Bay of Biscay. And of course, 'Ginger' – the captain's nickname – had heard of Harry.

However, Ginger wasn't the Fourth Flotilla's Captain S, so their business was purely practical; arranging for *Saraband's* periscope to be worked on, as well as all the other snags on Bert Kershaw's and Bill Laurie's lists. Then, there were crew billets to sort out, leave to arrange, stores' indents by the sheaves.

Harry's patrol report proper would have to wait until he was introduced to his new CO, the S4 himself, Captain H.M.C. Ionides. But Harry gave Ginger a brief run-down of their first war patrol into the Malay Archipelago, because being a fellow submariner, Ginger was dying to hear.

'Tinsides is down in Colombo, but he should be back tomorrow,' said

Ginger, once Harry had finished. 'It'll let you get a good night's sleep before you have to go and do all the formalities. He's a pretty fair bloke, I think you'll find, so I wouldn't worry about all that nonsense with your periscope and bringing back all your torpedoes. At least you showed willing, expending all your deck gun ammunition, eh!'

Harry just smiled and gazed around at all the opulent grandeur of the wardroom's very own open air lounge deck, all set up with wicker armchairs and an awning, now rolled back to reveal a vaulting sky that was becoming slowly suffused with subtle colours and the imminence of darkness. Two Chinese stewards in dazzling white patrol jackets glided nimbly in and out of the deck pantry's swinging doors with trays of drinks, heading for tables, each manned by little groups of officers, all in white too. And as twilight was starting to deepen, suddenly all the deck lights came on, and around the lounge, a garland of fairy lights, just as if they were aboard a cruise liner and not a warship.

As Harry was still staring, dumbfounded, more lights came, like rippling fire across the entire harbour, each ship blinking on; their lights twinkling from a thousand scuttles, until the entire anchorage was lit up like a peacetime regatta. By the time he'd taken in the entire, glorious vista Harry realised it was already completely dark. Tropic dark. No coolness in it. The night caressed him.

Ginger noticed his gawping. 'We're so bloody far from any Jap airfield here, nobody bothers to darken ship any more. Saves a multitude of banged shins.'

Ginger paused to savour it himself, then added by way of further explanation, 'The last time anybody saw a Jap here was when their carriers made their foray into the Indian Ocean back in 'forty two. The chances of them getting away with that again are long gone.'

'Good!' said Harry. 'Does that mean I can have a sparkler in my gin as well as a parasol?'

*

From Trinco to Kandy was 170 miles; a train down the coast to Batticaloa, and then in the back of a 3-cwt truck up a road that wound 1,500 feet up through the tea plantations to the Kandy plateau where the city lay in all its colonial, and even earlier, glory.

In the course of his journey, Harry had sat gaping as the train sped past beaches of almost perfect beauty and a sea of pristine azure. When his route turned inland and they started to climb, the humidity began to loosen its grip. The villages and jungle had given way to the terraced plantations, and the fetid jungle smells to the heady aroma of tea. He saw his first elephant, dragging a telegraph pole along the roadside, with a little boy perched behind its ears and a look of infinite resignation in the elephant's sombre brown eyes that seemed to watch him as his truck swept by.

There had been people everywhere when he'd got off the train, wherever he looked; milling with them; waves of dark skinned, smiling people. A shocking, horrible sight as nearly all of the men had teeth that weren't white, but red – from chewing betel nut. The colour didn't stop there; the women were in bright gaudy saris; crisp white shirts on nearly all the men, atop equally gaudy sarongs. And birds. Birds he had never dreamt of. The road up to Kandy, when his truck finally got to it, was busy with traffic all the way from the coast. Lots of military traffic. But lots of civilian buses, too, folk clinging to every outside space. And pedal rickshaws. The civilian stuff started to thin, the higher they climbed.

'One of the best things about this billet,' Ginger had assured him that previous night, while they sat under the riot of stars on *Wu Chang's* lounge deck, 'is that the place is a paradise. And the folk that live here are keen to share it. There are always stacks of standing invitations from local planters and any number of other well-meaning civvies for us submariners to come and spend our leaves with them. Take them, trust me. Get yourself out and about. See the island. There's an invitation we get regularly from one of the tea buyers in Kandy. He'd just forwarded us another. Grab that! Get up there! It's cooler up in the hills, and it's gorgeous. Kandy itself is one of their ancient capitals, from the fourteenth century they say. There's a temple that's even got one of Buddha's teeth in it, called, strangely enough, the Temple of the Tooth …!'

And on he had rhapsodised.

And now Harry was here, with Mr and Mrs Frater, in the bungalowed suburbs of Kandy, and all that that entailed. In the company of actual, real British women again. Women, in summer dresses, bare-shouldered and long-limbed, tanned and healthy and laughing, in that way men often forget when they haven't seen a woman in a long time.

The Fraters, an amiable, open and oh-so-generous couple in their early thirties; children running around your legs when they weren't being herded by amahs. Mr Frater, in his baggy white shirt and baggy linen trousers, prematurely balding, with a huge drooping sandy moustache and a sand-paper handshake who always managed to get discreetly in the way when you were looking at the shape of Mrs Frater's legs.

It must have been the third or fourth night that Colin and Diane Frater were having an 'at-home' for a clutch of fellow expatriate British civilians, middle-ranking SEAC staff officers and some Royal Army Medical Corps people from the big base hospital.

Later, Harry didn't really remember that much about the early part of the evening, the drinks on the verandah, the meal. When he thought about it, the only memorable part was when he was introduced to the late arrival, Dr Cotterell. She had just come off shift at the hospital, and was still in her khakis, with her hair tight back in a severe bun that gave her gaunt handsome face a skeletal look. Not even a suggestion of make-up.

When Diane Frater introduced them, Harry wondered what age Dr Cotterell was. Older than him, certainly – but what age was she? Mid-thirties? Older? No, probably not.

'Lieutenant Gilmour is the captain of His Majesty's submarine *Saraband*, and he's just arrived out here from home,' Diane Frater had said. 'So, we're making him feel at home here instead.'

He shook hands with the doctor. She had a firm grip and a thin smile. He noticed the grey flecking through her jet black hair. Harry asked where she was from and she replied, 'Cheshire.' Then, after a moment considering him, she said, 'So, you're another sub captain to add to our list of dinner guests up here in the hills. You know, you're getting younger every day.'

Harry, considering her, said, 'Thank you for the compliment doctor, but I can assure you, every day, I find I get a little older.'

Dr Cotterell gave a little snort and said, 'You know what I mean. You

107

have to be very young to do what you do. That's why it's the likes of you the navy asks. The younger the better, surely?'

'You don't think they rate experience, or skill?'

'When I say "young", it's a polite way of saying "daft", Lieutenant Gilmour. To go down in one of those things. You have to be daft. Let's face it, that's why the navy asks you.'

'Ah, it appears you know me so well, and on such a short acquaintance,' said Harry, with his best warm, engaging smile. 'However, on the other point, I can assure you the navy has never *asked* me to do anything.'

'Oh my. You submarine captains seem to do a lot of assuring, Lieutenant Gilmour,' said Dr Cotterell, with her own little trill of laughter.

'It's expected of us. Especially by our crews.'

And at that Diane Frater returned. 'My goodness you two seemed to have found a lot to chat about.'

Dr Cotterell turned to meet Mrs Frater's guileless smile with a full, frank expression on her face. 'Poor Lieutenant Gilmour, Diane. I fear it was more sparring than chatting.'

Then she turned to look at Harry. Her finely chiselled chin, jutting at him, looking for no sympathy, she said, 'I have just spent the last fourteen hours in a world made up entirely of wounds and their consequences, and where nothing has gone the way I've wanted it to. This is not unusual and causes me a great deal of frustration. So, when I come off duty after days like today, I'm afraid the first thing I look for is some poor sod to vent it all on. So Lieutenant Gilmour, I would like to apologise … no! No! Do not raise your hands and try to claim it doesn't matter …'

Harry had done just that, his hands up and the words already in his mouth to speak. But he shut up.

'… it does matter. However, you have been very patient with me, taken it all on the chin like a true gentleman and nary a snide retort. In fact, you have been refreshingly witty, which is more than I deserve …'

Harry gave a little nod and smile and was about to be even wittier. But Dr Cotterell was not finished.

'… and that is not all, Lieutenant Gilmour. You have also had the good grace not to notice my rank.'

'A crown,' said Harry quickly. 'You're a Major.'

Dr Cotterell silenced him with an arch look and continued, '… or that it is superior to yours, and thus burdened me with all your deference.'

She paused, regarded him coolly again over a bitten lip. Harry wanted to say something, but felt too bowled over by her frankness.

Then she added, as if after some thought, 'And as a result, for the first time in a long time, you've actually made me feel like a woman again. So, thank you Lieutenant Gilmour. Or would you mind if I called you Harry?'

Eleven

'Captain to the control room!'

The voice was that of Sub-Lt. Toby Verrell RN, who'd joined at Trinco as their new watch officer and number four.

Harry was out of his bunk and reaching to take the 'scope before Verrell saw him coming.

'What is it you see?' asked Harry, settling his eye in for a quick look before ordering the 'scope down. For the new lad to have made his sighting, called him, and still be looking at whatever it was, well, the bloody thing had already been up far too long. He'd have words later.

'I can't make it out, sir,' said Verrell. 'It looked like one giant junk, or maybe lots of smaller ones all lashed together. I think one of them might have a sail up.'

Which was more or less what it looked like to Harry. The distortions in the air however, made it impossible to gauge the range. Close, or far away? Bloody mirages.

'Down periscope!' he said, then, 'Asdic, anything in the water?' This fired off as he stepped over to the chart.

'No HE, sir,' came the muffled reply from down the passage.

They had dived as they entered the Nicobar Channel several hours ago, just before dawn. They were now heading deep into Jap-controlled waters and could expect regular sightings of Jap air patrols as well as sub-chasers of all hues. Harry's plan was to piggy-back on the three knot north westerly current that his sailing notes showed, ran through at this time of year and could take him down to the area around the One Fathom Bank lighthouse and the entrance channels to Port Swettenham. Hopefully, it would be a happy hunting ground.

The only thing was, the previous night had been overcast and black as the earl of hell's waistcoat, as his grandmother used to say. So there had been not a star for a sighting, and after first light, in the thickening hot air, not a landfall for a decent bearing, which meant that their progress thus far had been by dead reckoning and echo sounder. In other words, neither Harry nor Gowers, their Vasco, was exactly sure where they were. Not a good thing in these shallow waters, where you were never far away from soundings of 10 fathoms or even less.

Right now he was looking for Jemur Island, marking the right of the channel, to get a fix. He sent the periscope down. They would move away from whatever it was up there and try another sighting in two minutes.

Their trip back across the Bay of Bengal had been filled with activity as Harry took the time to constantly work the crew in all manner of exercises, from loading and reloading torpedoes to damage control and flooding drills. They had also held daily shoots against their gash sacks, each one gleefully blown to bits.

But up there on the bridge, during the nights in his hammock, there had been time to think. As there had been during the day, in his bunk, on his grass mat instead of a mattress.

Trinco; a new station and new depot ship, and a new Captain S. Harry had had his meeting with Tinsides, and an amiable cove he had indeed proved to be, with a big round head covered in grey furze shaved almost into the wood, and a crinkly smile. Tinsides explained how important their mission was here, disrupting Jap supplies up to their armies in Burma, and oil out of Sumatra. 'The roads up the Malay peninsula are … not good. So, everything needed by the Jap armies facing Bill Slim up north, usually has to go by sea,' Captain Ionides had assured him. 'You'll also be needed for quite a bit of cloak and dagger stuff. I don't like it any more than you probably do, but we've got this Force 136 unit Mountbatten is keen to keep sticking the Japs with, so we have to live with it.'

Bill Slim was the GOC Fourteenth Army in Burma, which was in the process of turning the tide up there, and Force 136 was … well, nobody quite knew. They were 'unofficial' and from what little Harry had heard, mostly a rag-bag collection of cut-throat burn-outs from the Med and Adriatic campaigns, teamed up with local Malay commies and anti-Jap nationalists. Harry wasn't looking forward to their company but refrained from telling that to Tinsides. 'We did it for Monty in the Med, so I'm sure it'll be fine here too,' he told the new boss, while grimacing inside.

At other times he would reflect gratefully on how the crew had apparently enjoyed the hill station rest camps, and that not one of them had fallen foul of the shore patrol, or reported back late. They had also seemed to revel in the fact that *Saraband* had managed to attain a certain fame in the short time she'd been in; all down to the talents of Leading Seaman McTeer. While Harry was away reporting to *Wu Chang's* skipper, Bill Laurie had taken a copy of McTeer's Betty Grable cartoon and stuck it up on *Adamant's* notice board under the banner heading, 'HMS *Saraband's back-afties cement Anglo–American co-operation!*' It had attracted quite a crowd. And the attendant laughter helped to drown out some rumours that had filtered east, the way these things always do, concerning *Saraband's* past. Suffice to say, by the time they sailed on this patrol, there had been a hefty demand for copies of the cartoon from round the fleet.

Also, the periscope was working again. 'A botched fitting by the builders damaged the seals,' the CERA in charge of *Adamant's* periscope shop told Harry. 'It's been waiting to happen. And impossible to repair at sea. But she'll be fine now, sir.'

So, a good run ashore, all in all.

Then there were the letters from home he'd think on. The one from Louis the bookseller back on Malta that made him smile; the ones from his mother, the smiles were less, and the ones from Shirley – well, what was there to say?

So he had been profoundly grateful for Verrell's, 'Captain to the control room!' shout, alerting him to whatever it was he'd just failed to identify through the haze. It felt that the patrol had started in earnest, and that he would now have other things to think about.

Harry stood up from the chart table and checked his watch. He'd given it a full three minutes instead; then he ordered the smaller attack periscope up this time. With all that bloody mirage about, and not having any sense of the range, he was only prepared to risk its thin tube of a head above the viscous warm slop of the current on the surface, and even then only for mere seconds. The image was still distorted in his view; then it seemed to break apart, and then assimilate again. What the hell was it?

'Down periscope,' then he ordered, 'starboard ten …'

Another few minutes, then, 'Up periscope.'

This time, all the random shapes in the eyepiece coalesced. 'It's Jemur,' said Harry, and ordered the 'scope down again. So, not a collection of junks, but the rocky outcrops of the island they'd been looking for after all, with its little lighthouse standing proud, and not a half-raised sail. He ordered Gowers to raise the search periscope and take a bearing. Gowers did so quickly, then compared it to their echo sounder returns, and just as quickly they had a fair idea where they were, in the channel, and ready for business.

The letters from his mother had been all about home and life there, as you'd expect. Except they were describing a world he did not recognise any more – and it wasn't just the rationing and the colourlessness of wartime that had enveloped the once vital little town he'd left behind, but the entirely new cast that seemed to have walked on stage in his absence.

The three evacuee children from Glasgow; still there, tales of their doings bursting out of all her close-written pages, alongside the familiar news of the house itself that she never tired of writing about; all the comings and goings and its face changing with each season. Except the place apparently was filled with laughter now, instead of all the shushing he remembered because his father was working in his study; or the hollow ticking of the mantle clock he remembered too, like destiny itself, marking the passage of his youth. And then there was all the stuff about his father. This figure who kept appearing, whom he didn't recognise. No longer the shattered, brittle man who seared himself into Harry's life like a dark and imposing memorial left over from the last great war. In his place was someone new; someone who would lift the youngest evacuee child onto his knee without her even asking, and who had written and staged amateur dramatics for all of the children, and their friends, who had even enjoyed going dancing again. And all that was before Harry had got round to contemplating the Hon. Shirley Lamont and her letters.

Shirley, the girl from home; the daughter of a long dead, impecunious, minor west Highland aristocrat. Shirley, whom he'd gone to school with, yet back then had never really noticed. Shirley, who was now an ambulance driver in Glasgow and who used to be the fearless possessor of a pre-Raphaelite explosion of chestnut hair, but since then … all sheared back and the embodiment of a spirit that had once been edgy and mesmerising and was now … what? Tethered? Closed?

There had been a letter, all those long months ago. A single page, a quotation from Emily Dickinson she had bent a little, to send her own message to him, that had wrung a yearning from his chest that he never imagined could be there. And then, what? A series of domestic essays that read like lists, recording the minutiae of her life; each one long, and rich in detail, communicating nothing. They'd made him feel like he'd been spun like a top, then left to spin away, off to God knew where.

He seldom went back to the box in his head where he kept all her memories. And now, he was unable to fathom the girl who was writing these travelogues. So there seemed little point in going back to constantly pick at them. There was a war on, after all. But every now and then …

The rest of that day, and into the afternoon watch of the next, nothing had broken their watch diving routine. Then, while he was poring over the chart again with Gowers, Verrell, who had the watch and was doing his regular all-round look, suddenly said, 'Two masts.' A brief pause as he leant back to read the bezel, 'bearing red two five, coming right up the channel.'

Harry stepped into Verrell's place, ordered 'half ahead' on the motors and ran *Saraband* out from what his eye told him would be the target's broad track, already thinking about how to get into an attacking position. Then he rang the alarm. The rushing slap of rubber flip-flops – new purchases from the bazaars ashore around Trinco – as each man ran to his fighting station; the bustle only ending when *Saraband* was all closed up and ready.

His second quick look – the attack 'scope up for just 15 seconds – told him what the target was. She was that fat slug of a not-quite-right steamer that had kept them down and wasting time at the start of their last patrol. The one he thought was a Q-ship. And here she was again, wheezing and puffing up through the shallows. Asdic reported the familiar clanking signature.

Harry hadn't sunk this tub the first time round because locals told him she had usually been the harbinger of better targets; so he had hung about, waiting for better targets; and look how that had turned out. What was it Teacher had told him, doing his Perisher? 'Always attack what you see.'

'Right you are,' Harry muttered to himself. 'Well, I can see you, chum.'

He got a few sideways glances from those who had heard him. The *Sarabands* weren't used to his commentary ways.

'Start the attack,' said Harry, and then he ordered the search periscope up, kneeling to grab the handles as it cleared the deck plates. The yeoman, Cantor, stepped in behind him to read off the bearing and range as Harry called them, and Verrell, their newly-designated fruit machine man, sat poised to start dialling them in.

It was hot in the control room, but not as hot as it was going to get. Everybody was still in t-shirts and shorts, apart from the officers in their baggy short-sleeved shirts. Nobody was wearing a cap. 'Ready tubes one and three,' said Harry. 'Make the depth setting six feet, if this bugger is what I think she is, she'll have a very shallow draught.'

The rating on the sound-powered telephone relayed the orders to the forward torpedo room.

'She's the rust bucket that messed us around off Penang last time,' Harry rambled on absently as he stepped to look at Gowers' plot. It was all there, all he needed to see. 'But I don't think she's just a rust bucket, I think she's a Q-ship, and I think we should blow the arse out of her.'

That got a few grins all round. Not least from Harry himself. It had just dawned on him that he was back in his old ways. His attack chat had returned. He hadn't planned to do it, but it felt right.

It was still quite tense in this control room though; none of the calm dance they used to perform on *Scourge* that he remembered. He had a feeling now of everybody concentrating too hard; still, that was better that than not at all.

Time for another look.

The target was still on the same course, no attempt at zig-zagging, coming inexorably on from the south east at what he estimated was eight knots. Harry read off the bearing and range. Verrell dialled the numbers and Gowers marked the plot.

Saraband was now sitting at almost 90 degrees to the target's track. Harry sent the periscope down and stepped to consider Gowers' work. He missed pockets to shove his hands into. Gowers' converging lines told him that even at just three knots, *Saraband* was coming on too fast. She'd be too close when the time came to fire her torpedoes.

Harry ordered the telegraphs rung for, 'slow ahead starboard, stop port,' and then he turned to Bill Laurie. He wondered whether to say anything to Number One about minding his trim but thought better of it. Bill wouldn't need telling. Another check on the plot. At this rate the range on firing would still be under 800 yards – 600 or less and he'd be too close to fire. The torpedoes wouldn't have enough distance to run in order to arm themselves. It was going to be tight.

'This is going to be a close one,' said Harry. 'Any closer and we'll be able to kiss him. It's times like this you wish these things were fitted with brake pedals.'

More grins.

Harry looked at his watch. 'Up periscope.' As he grabbed it, he said, 'Right, this is going to be my final call, Mr Verrell ... a DA as fast as you like when I read off the numbers.'

Jesus, she was close. But right where he'd expected her to be. Thank God his call on her speed had been right. If she'd been any slower she wouldn't be closing his firing point as obligingly as she was, and this attack would have been off.

'Bearing is ... that! Range is ... that!' said Harry, face pressed to the eyepiece, incanting to himself, *come on, son ... come son ... come on!* Willing Verrell to dial his calculations faster as Cantor read off the bezel numbers.

An eternity. What was the boy doing? Working it out with a pencil?

'DA is green eight degrees!' Verrell's voice was comically reedy and just a bit too loud. Harry touched the 'scope and Cantor turned him onto the bearing. He watched the bubbling bow wave curling off the target's blunt cutwater as it crept towards the graticule ...

'Fire one!' called Harry. The rating on the phone relayed the order, and *Saraband* went over the bump as her torpedo shot away. Harry kept the periscope up. He saw the bubbles rising from the torpedo's wake and he knew instantly it was going to hit. *Well, no point in wasting another one*, he thought. No point in even counting the running time. The torpedo was going to get there before he'd manage to ask Gowers to set the stopwatch. He could just stand here looking through the periscope and wait to see it detonate.

'Tell torpedo room, secure tube three,' he said, eyes still stuck to the 'scope. 'This one's a sitter. Hold on everybody. Strike down all glass ornaments!'

A most impressive geyser of water leapt into the air just forward of the target's bridge, and two huge sheets of wood went spiralling into the water from her well deck, as if in slow motion, revealing a large deck gun, possibly even a 5-incher. So, he'd been right – she *was* a Q-ship. He watched how the middle of her hull rose out of the water in a ridge, blown upwards by the blast, arching as though something vital had parted. Even before the roar of the explosion filled the boat, and the rapid physical buffeting hit them, Harry could see his torpedo had broken the enemy's back.

The ship settled, and her decks suddenly began to fill with running figures, tumbling up from below deck; far more than should have been the crew of an ordinary inter-island tramp steamer. Harry sent down the periscope. He didn't need to see any more.

*

Having sunk their Q-ship, Harry took it as a given the Japs would be behaving like a poked hornets' nest around the approaches to Port Swettenham, so he decided to withdraw to the northern end of his patrol billet and stick his nose in around Penang. Tinsides' staff officer, operations, a rather stiff RNVR three-ringer called Clarke with a pedantically-trimmed beard, had advised him during his patrol briefing that Penang was a place of 'special interest to us in the Trade'. His polite way of saying the place was a veritable home-from-home nest of Jerry U-boats. And he had stressed the 'Jerry' to make sure Harry knew he was talking about the real thing.

'There's half a dozen of them in there, we believe,' Clarke had intoned.

'And the Japs have equipped them with quite an extensive base … a repair dock, even their own canning factory to prepare European-style rations, because not even the Jerry crews could survive on the muck the Japs feed their own chaps at sea. And they even have a rest station up in the hills away from the heat. The boats are mostly type nines that've stopped off there on precious cargo trips between the fatherland and the empire. And because they've got the range, and they go after our merchant ships in the Indian Ocean, where our chaps should be safe, they're a bloody nuisance. Sir James always smiles benignly on anyone who manages to bag one of the buggers.'

'Sir James' being Admiral Sir James Somerville, C-in-C Eastern Fleet, their neighbour across the Trincomalee anchorage.

It was over 150 miles to run up coast to Penang, *Saraband* going flat out for a lot of it through the night, McTeer on her radar keeping them well clear of any trouble. The only traffic they encountered were fishing boats and the odd under-sized junk – none of them worth a torpedo, and not worth alerting the Japs to their movements by surfacing and sinking them by gunfire.

They raised the island through the periscope late the following afternoon. Harry spotted a Jap escort steaming out of Penang harbour. Harry's small Jap ship recognition wasn't as good as he'd have liked it to be. A *Chiburi* or an *Amakusa* class, he wasn't sure. Nasty little bastards anyway, according to the intelligence reports he'd read. Both about 900 tons, give or take, and 250 feet long. The *Chiburis* were the nastier, armed with three 4.7 inch guns and bristling with 25 mm cannon, some kind of mortar device and carrying at least 120-odd depth charges. Neither were fast however, being capable of less than 20-odd knots; just your basic, robust and all too efficient sub-killer. Before he ordered the periscope down, Harry took note that the tub had no unusual top-hamper, such as a rotating bedstead or aerial clusters. Good. This one at least appeared to have nothing resembling a radar or any device for detecting radar emissions. He stepped between the Asdic cubby and Gowers' plot, watching as the small escort slowed down and then came to a dead stop just to the left of the main harbour approach, now about two miles away.

He must have heaved-to to sit and listen, thought Harry, and immediately ordered *Saraband* to silent running, switching off all the fans and pumps, and just keeping the tiniest bit of way on her, on one motor, to help Number One keep his trim. With the fans off, it very soon became very hot in the boat and everyone was down to shorts or skivvies. Even though he was silently laughing at himself, Harry for some reason felt as captain he had to stand on his dignity and keep his shirt on. It was soon a clammy rag, clinging to him where it touched.

After a couple of hours of *Saraband* stalking her, sometimes to within 800 yards, the *Chiburi* – for that was what he'd decided the damn thing was – suddenly lit up her diesels again and moved off a few miles before stopping. She was obviously, blissfully, unaware of *Saraband's* presence. Harry had seen enough. If the *Chiburi* had been sent out to protect the port, then there must be something in there worth protecting, and sooner or later it would have to sail; either that or there must be something on the way here worth keeping the approach clear for. It was dark, so he withdrew quietly to seaward, so that he could surface the boat and get some fresh air inboard and a charge on the batteries. For all the listening the Jap had been doing, his kit couldn't be up to much. He certainly hadn't deterred Harry from his plan to return at first light.

As for *Saraband*, all the time they'd been shadowing the *Chiburi,* the crew had been closed up, all too aware they were standing off an enemy ship. Harry wouldn't have called the atmosphere in the boat tense, however. More like diligent. *Heavens above*, he thought, *is my rabble actually coming together as a proper crew?*

By the next morning, *Saraband* had circled Penang to seaward and was standing off the north end of the island when she dived. Harry kept the crew closed up as they motored across the mouth of the channel towards the Malaya coast. While doing one of his all-round looks he spotted two 'Jake' floatplanes performing a lazy-Z away to the north. Something was obviously coming. He ordered *Saraband* to close the coast.

'Bring me over the ten fathom line and then let's run north along it, Mr Gowers,' he said.

Gowers called the course changes to the helm and *Saraband* crept to starboard at a steady three knots.

'HE on green one six zero,' called Leading Seaman Meek from the Asdic cubby. 'Diesel engine. Still a bit of a way off, sir.'

'That'll be the *Chiburi* coming out to meet their new guests,' said Harry to the control room. 'Any HE to the north yet, Meek?'

There was a pause while Meek turned the Asdic head around. 'Yes sir. HE on red ten. Still very faint … sounds like multiple … reciprocating engines … diesel in there somewhere too, I think …'

'Start a plot, Mr Gowers,' said Harry, and he stepped to the chart table to see Gowers mark *Saraband's* position on the chart. 'You're sure that's exactly where we are, Mr Gowers?' he said, thinking, *That was fast*.

'Yes, sir,' said Gowers, not looking up, but drawing bearing lines to the two targets, fore and aft. 'The charts here are all Admiralty and very good. I'm using the echo-sounder to follow the shoal contours. It's surprisingly accurate, I've been finding.'

'Are you really?' said Harry, impressed, then said to the control room, 'Be aware, Mr Gowers is now flying the boat by echo-sounder, like an underwater bat. We're in safe hands. Good show, Mr Gowers. Carry on.'

Harry looked around the control room, in the dull yellow of the main lighting, seeing all the figures there, squeezed in among the pipework and cable runs. All of them bare-headed – not like home waters or the Med where nearly everybody seemed to love their hats – and lots of bare backs glistening with sweat, hunched over the helm, the diving planes, the trim board, the odd shoulder rocking in silent mirth. And looking back at him, Gowers with a frown and a smile on his face and Number One, the imperturbable Kiwi Bill Laurie, in a shirt just like his captain, rolling his eyes and smiling. This was *Saraband*, going into action. Her crew cool and concentrating, and confident enough to have a little laugh at themselves. He felt a sudden, unexpected surge of pride in his men and his boat.

Meek's voice came from the Asdic cubby, 'I have six targets, sir. Two diesel … light … sounds like escorts of some kind, running out ahead … and the rest definitely reciprocating … I can practically hear them wheeze, sir. The bearing is one five zero true. They're coming on line ahead … from the rev count, I estimate the speed at seven knots, give or take, sir.'

Harry listened with a quiet satisfaction. Meek was becoming an experienced Asdic operator, whose expertise he was learning to respect. He gave fate a private thumbs up for not lumbering him with one of those by the book, bare details and nothing more, men. Able only to parrot how many ships, their bearing, and if you asked nicely, a ventured guess on the engine type. Harry knew hands like Meek would be hearing so much more, and he wanted to know it too. Meek, a gangly hostilities-only man, didn't have the regular navy baggage of the monosyllabic reply and only speak when you're spoken to; he was a lad who was confident enough to share his knowledge, even with an officer.

Gowers already had Meek's calls down on the plot. Harry peeked at it. 'Time to have a shufti. Up periscope. Put me on the bearing Tully,' he said to the control room messenger. 'Three ten degrees.'

Up went the 'scope, and Harry read off the true bearing and brought the upper shape of the leading sub-chaser down onto the top of the lower shape and called, 'range is that!'

He didn't recognise the type. Maybe 400 tons, less than 200 feet long. A disproportionately big, boxy bridge structure, single squat smoke-stack and a pop-gun on the fo'c'sle. Maybe a 3-incher. It was the serried rank of bin ends he could see disappearing towards her stern that caught his eye. Even from this angle he could see there were a lot of depth charges on her long aft deck. But no unusual aerials, thankfully.

Someone did the sums and called out the range. 'Four thousand one hundred yards!'

He could also see the line of 'reciprocating engines' Meek had reported; a motley collection of inter-island tramp steamers, all rust and disordered deck cargo smudging the pure blue sky with smoke. From their bow waves he estimated Meek's 'seven knots, sir' was on the money.

'Down periscope,' he ordered. 'Four fully laden tramp steamers, three about seven to eight hundred tons, one just over a thousand. Rustbuckets. Each one would give a Lloyd's surveyor a nervous breakdown. A full salvo, I think, on an eighty degree track angle. Advise the torpedo room Number One, ready tubes one to six, depth setting … six feet, I think. The escorts are ranging ahead and to seaward, and the steamers look like they are heading to hug the coast more closely as they come on.' He stopped to pull his lip. 'So we go a little further inshore ... how close are we to the ten fathom line, Mr Gowers?'

'We're on it, sir, weaving in and out beneath our keel right now,' replied Gowers.

Harry looked at the plot. *Saraband* was at periscope depth, 32 feet. So, 28 feet below her keel right now, give or take. No going deep if the escorts came after them. But then even to seaward, the depth didn't increase that much.

'Starboard ten,' said Harry. 'Mr Gowers, give me a shout when I have three fathoms beneath the keel.'

He knew he was risking it, but it was one he decided was worth taking. *Saraband* nudged even closer inshore.

The little convoy came chugging on, watched by Harry who was putting the 'scope up and down every few minutes for mere seconds at a time. *Saraband* was so far inshore now, he was aware the targets were passing to seaward of a line of fishing stakes. So, not hiding behind the torpedo nets supposedly strung between. Which suggested there were no nets here. He didn't have time right now to deliberate that, because he wasn't half getting into a good firing position, and the range was closing too fast for him to hum and haw. The last look told him it was time to turn onto the track angle so he gave the order to port the helm.

Another look, and the bearing and range were called. 'What's my DA, Mr Verrell?' he said.

'DA is green nine, sir.'

Faster than your usual, Mr Verrell, he thought. *Well done.*

Harry swung the scope until the graticule was on green nine and watched as the bow wave of the leading vessel approached the datum line, still some yards to run.

Then the bow crossed the graticule. 'Fire one,' said Harry. The range to the first target was 1,800 yards, and the first torpedo should cover it in just a minute and a half. Even from here, he could tell it was going to hit. 'Down periscope. Start the stopwatch.'

But only 37 seconds passed before there was a colossal explosion. It shook the boat so badly they didn't actually feel her for'ard keel slice its way into the bottom mud, until the curve of her hull brought them to a juddering halt.

Harry called, 'Stop together. Secure tubes two to six. Rig for silent, secure for depth charging.'

The hum of fans died immediately, so that the roiling of the disturbed water outside could be heard in the boat. Then nothing.

'Meek, tell me what's happening the minute you can hear through all that din,' called Harry.

Their torpedo had detonated prematurely, and in these shallows the noise of it was still battering about.

'Last target in the line passing our bows now, sir,' said Meek eventually. 'One of the diesel targets is under helm, sir. Bearing red five and getting louder. She's coming back around the line. Dead ahead now, and closing … splashes, sir … depth charges …'

RABABAABUMM! RABABAABUMM! RABABAABUMM!

The three detonations reverberated through the boat, with the echoes battering back and forward for what seemed like an age. Harry waited in the noise along with everyone else, until it eventually petered out. Then he announced to the control room, with studied insouciance, 'Not evenly remotely warm. They're just frightening the fishes.'

'The diesel target is bearing red thirty now and opening, sir,' they heard Meek call. 'She's pulling away, sir. The multiple HE is now on red four zero and fading.'

Harry ordered the attack periscope up, just in case any Japs were still looking for them, but all he saw was the retreating fantail of the sub-chaser, rushing to catch up with her charges. When he did a quick all-round, he noticed *Saraband's* bows must be pointing between two fishing stakes a few hundred yards dead ahead, and both were skewed now at strange angles. That was when he knew what had just happened. All that intel bumf about the Japs stringing anti-torpedo nets inshore had just been proved true, because *Saraband* had just fired a shot into one of them.

'Well, bugger me,' said Harry, then remembering *Saraband's* dark past, and wishing he hadn't.

The tide eventually lifted *Saraband* off the mud, but not before the two Jake floatplanes had showed up and puttered for over an hour down their stretch of the coast, obviously still looking for whoever might have set off that explosion in their torpedo nets.

Meek reported the Asdic set was playing up. Not surprising really, since its head – the device that stuck down through the bottom of the hull to ping and to listen – had just been stuck face first into the mud. There had been seabed where Gowers' chart said there should not have been; but then tides and currents shoved the alluvial gloop wherever they wanted to, along this coast.

Harry ordered a quick burst of 'full astern, together' and blew the main ballast tanks, which popped *Saraband* off the bottom. Once they were swimming again, he decided they'd move over to the other side of their billet, and that night made a surface dash for the approaches to Belawan, formerly the main Dutch port for Sumatra. It turned out to be a good decision. Even before the sun came up, McTeer, on his radar scanner, picked up a contact coming out of the port, its return big enough to stick out through the background coastal clutter. The range was over six miles. With the sun at his back, Harry kept *Saraband* running on the surface longer than he would normally have dared, so that he could get a good look at her.

She was a modern Maru, a fast cargo–passenger job of at least 4,000 tons, with a huge single squat funnel and an extensive central superstructure to accommodate all her cabins. He guessed she was likely loaded with rubber and timber; vital war materiel which made her a real, honest-to-God sub skipper's dream. And if he had any doubts just what a prize she was, the presence of three escorts banished them. Two were non-descript sub-chasers like the ones he'd just faced. But the other was an actual destroyer, a *Mutsuki* class, if his imperfect Jap ship recognition served him. An old tub, 1920s vintage, about 1,500 tons but still capable of 34 knots flat out. Refitted, they apparently now only had two 4.7 inch guns, but up to a dozen 25 mm anti-aircraft cannon and in addition to the depth charge rails, they had four throwers. God knew how many depth charges the bugger was carrying. So, still nasty. Harry felt his throat tighten. This was going to be a fight.

All night he had been lying in his hammock on the bridge, worrying to himself – instead of sleeping, or even just enjoying the star show in the

124

heavens – about how he was going to paint yesterday's cock-up when it came to writing it up in *The Bugle*, without making himself look too much of a prat. Such were the pitfalls of a free press, he bemoaned to himself in the darkness. Was this whole bloody newspaper idea a rod he'd made for his own back? It wasn't that he minded looking a bit of a prat. God knows it wasn't the first time he'd made a bollocks of an attack. And anyway, in the Trade it was a tradition that everybody needed a good laugh at somebody's expense; especially if it was the skipper's. But bagging this bugger would get him out that hole. So he wanted this Jap; really wanted her, especially after yesterday.

The lookouts could see him smirking to himself just before he hit the tit to send *Saraband* to diving stations, and they felt the frisson of excitement from him as they dropped down through the conning tower hatch on their way to tell their mates that the skipper had the bit between his teeth again.

Harry dictated all the details of the targets, their speed and bearing, over Gowers' shoulder as he filled in the plot; McTeer provided the last range fix from the radar before they'd dived. Then Harry ordered the electric motors grouped up and rang the engine room telegraph for full ahead together.

'Target under helm,' announced Meek, who then read off the changing bearings. Verrell dialled them into the fruit machine. Just as Harry feared; the Maru was turning south, opening the bearing and the range. He needed to close that range fast. He parked his bum against the chart table and started pulling his lip as *Saraband* surged through the deep at a flat out nine knots, chasing his aim to get ahead of the Maru's beam as she nosed into the narrowing maw of the Malacca Straits.

The smaller sub-chasers were racing out and then in again on the target's beams, Meek announced, and the *Mutsuki* was sweeping ahead in long, lazy Zs. Meek said he was picking up the electronic echo of some kind of rudimentary sonar device pinging away down the destroyer's track.

Saraband continued her run in. It was getting time to stick the periscope up and take a look. Which meant he was going to have to put the brakes on.

He ordered. 'slow together', and the way started coming off. Stick your periscope up while going hell for leather submerged and all you'd get was a spectacular streaming wake from the periscope's head that shouted,

125

'Look! Here's a submarine!' You'd also be liable to bend the cylinder so you couldn't lower it again.

Harry got the control room messenger to put him on the bearing once more; he had seen how pleased the lad was at being given the responsibility last time, and he'd done a good, steady job.

However, as the 'scope broke surface, Harry was aware of a giant shadow passing overhead. Instead of doing a quick all-round look, he spun the periscope directly away from the target's bearing, following the shape. And there, its arse end disappearing to the east, was a giant 'Emily' flying boat, the Jap's equivalent of a Short Sunderland.

The aircraft was obviously heading on the outward leg of a sweep ahead of the Maru and its escorts. It gave no indication anybody on board had spotted *Saraband's* periscope. *This really must be some target,* Harry said to himself. He swung the 'scope back onto the Maru. She was zig-zagging on a tighter pattern to the destroyer, he could see that clearly now. From the bow wave, he reckoned she was doing 10 knots, and at that moment was running away from the track Harry wanted her to stay on. The range turned out to be well over 3,000 yards. He ordered the periscope down again.

'Group up, full ahead together, maintain heading,' he said, and went back to look at the plot. He pulled down the sound-powered phone. 'Torpedo room, control room. Set up tubes one, two, four and five. Depth setting … fifteen feet.' Then, after he'd hung up he announced, 'She's a big bugger, and from the size of the escort, she must be crammed with goodies. So, we're going to make sure of her. Four shots on the stopwatch, over one and a half lengths of her hull. One's bound to get her. Because I'm the captain and I say so.'

Everybody knew that by saying that, he was making them a hostage to fortune. You *never* predicted you were going to hit *anything*. Everybody knew that. But they could all see him smiling, so they all knew he seemed to think that *he* knew what he was doing. But was it wise? Especially after the last attack? There were some things you just didn't do on a submarine; like tempt fate. Hence, quite a few of the smiles that greeted him back were a bit feeble.

Harry studied his watch, then the plot. Meek called out the next zig, in the target's zig-zag. The Maru was coming back now. The destroyer was all over the place. The scene up there wasn't very disciplined, he thought.

Time dripped like the condensation from the hull.

The Maru was zagging back, and *Saraband* wasn't getting that much closer to the track Harry was aiming for. One more look at the plot. It wasn't going to work. The bloody thing was just too fast. It was going to get away. He ordered *Saraband* to slow ahead and stuck the 'scope up again. The 'Emily' was careering about miles ahead and the destroyer was actually masked now by the Maru, as was one of the sub-chasers. The other was off *Saraband's* port quarter now; they had penetrated its screen. But the range was hideous, and opening again, and the track was almost 120 degrees.

But every now and then you get a shot, and it's now or never; it's never going to get any better, there's no point in waiting and seeing. You just have to go.

'What's my DA, Mr Verrell?' he asked, very softly. 'Soon as you like please, Mr Verrell.'

The 'please' froze everybody. People were already starting to learn that their skipper was not a shouter, and conducted all his business with a quiet calm. However, if you wanted to know if things were actually getting 'sticky', as some would say; that there might be something to worry about, they were starting to learn that you listened for him becoming scrupulously polite, especially with his pleases and thank yous.

'DA is green one three!' said Verrell, breathless.

Five seconds passed, then, 'Fire one.'

It was Cantor, the yeoman's turn on the firing board. He threw the switch, and the light came on. 'One away, sir.'

'Three, four and five on the stopwatch, Mr Gowers. Down 'scope.'

Gowers counted down the seconds and sent the remaining three shots on their way. He checked a scribble on the plot and then back at his watch, calculating the running time left for the first torpedo. 'Two minutes twenty seconds to run on the first torpedo, sir,' he said.

'Group up. Starboard thirty, keep one hundred and eighty feet,' said Harry as he stepped back to the chart table.

Gowers started counting down the last seven seconds, but only got to three, before there was a reverberating thump of sound that filled the boat. Fifteen seconds later there was another one, just as loud.

Harry gave it a moment, until the disturbance in the water should have subsided, then he said, 'That sounded like two torpedo hits. Meek, what can you hear up there? Who's doing what?'

Meek took a few seconds. Leaning round the cubby, Harry could see him touching the bearing finder and pressing the headset to his ears.

'HE from the target has changed, sir.' said Meek. 'She's slowing right down, sir, bearing rate is decreasing again … It's like the way is coming off her … and I'm not picking up anything from the destroyer at all, sir … the two sub-chasers are under helm … sounds like maximum revs.'

Harry, without taking his eyes from the plot, asked, 'Is anybody coming after us, Meek?'

'No, sir.'

Harry said, 'Group down. Ahead together. Keep periscope depth. Let's go up and take a look, shall we gentlemen. See if we really have hit anything.'

The first thing Harry looked for was that bloody 'Emily', but it was still miles away to the south, a speck in the sky. When he wound the periscope head down, a strange sight greeted him. The Maru was veering, very slowly, and her lifeboat davits were swung out and he could make out a lot of activity on her deck. One of the sub-chasers was creeping up on her stern.

When he swung the 'scope, he saw the destroyer wallowing some way ahead, and there was a pall of oily black smoke billowing up from her quarter deck, flecked with the odd flash of flame. The other sub-chaser was alongside her and in the act of taking off the destroyer's crew.

Harry checked the 'Emily' again. He caught her in mid turn, a huge cross against the sky as she banked round, obviously having finally noticed what had happened to her charges and heading back. He looked back to destroyer just as the most enormous double explosions of water erupted up out the depths under her, ripping off the stern, before merging into a huge and mountainous fountain. Everybody heard it in the boat and knew the sound immediately for what it was – depth charges. The destroyer's bow jerked up suddenly until it was hanging at 45 degrees, jabbing the sky. Harry could no longer see the sub-chaser that had been alongside.

Harry said to the yeoman on the firing board, 'Mr Cantor, come and take a look at what you've just done.'

The yeoman stepped forward and took the 'scope. 'Bloody ... hell, sir,' he whispered.

'Whatever other damage the torpedo did, it must've knocked a couple of her armed depth charge over the side,' said Harry, as the yeoman looked. 'Turn it a little to your left and you'll see what you did to the Maru.'

Cantor did as he was told. Everybody in the control room was looking at him, and his hanging jaw, trying to imagine what he must be seeing. Suddenly the yeoman shot upright, as if the periscope had electrocuted him. 'Sir! You better ...' and he stepped back from the 'scope. Harry grabbed it, and was just in time to see the Jap transport, beam on, as her roll started to gather momentum, and she very sedately turned completely turtle and then stern first tipped up and slid beneath the surface, all in a mere matter of seconds. Knowing the flying boat was on its way back, he didn't wait to see any more.

'Down 'scope. Keep one hundred and eighty feet,' he said again.

*

On the other side of the world, someone else was taking his eyes away from a pair of lenses, having seen enough.

He was Claude Dansey's man in Lisbon. Nobody at the British embassy in the Portuguese capital liked him much, just as nobody in the entire Foreign Office back in London liked Claude Dansey much, either. Dansey was a creepy, bald little man in wire spectacles who gave off an aura of being capable of great deceit. Yet everybody in the Foreign Office had to get along with Dansey, because he was the man who ran Great Britain's foreign intelligence service. Just like Great Britain's ambassador to Portugal had to get along with Vernon Carmody, because he was Dansey's man.

Carmody already knew the man living in the corner flat of this little *rua* running up from the Praça Luís de Camões was the rogue Royal Navy captain whom he'd been tasked to find by his boss in London. His name, Captain Charles Bonalleck RN.

This joker had apparently had done a bunk from a very senior Allied liaison post, and no-one seemed to know why, or to where; and that was why they were so keen to find him, and were prepared to drag Vernon Carmody from his legitimate, important, espionage work to do the finding.

Well, now he, Vernon Carmody, knew where.

He had been easy to trace, once a photograph of him had been wired to the embassy. Except these days the man was calling himself Captain Charles Chaplin, not even disguising the fact he was British, thinking by just saying he was merchant navy and not Royal was enough to let him disappear. Carmody even knew all about the creepy half-chat who kept hanging around; taking the captain out to cafes all the time, like he was his manager. His name was Stroessner and he'd been a Vichy government flunky in Morocco. Daddy from Alsace and mummy, some back street houri from Algiers; apparently he'd jumped the dyke the second the Yanks had come storming up the beach, claiming he only owed loyalty to the future and not the past. Or so Carmody's informants had assured him. Here in Lisbon, Stroessner was calling himself Miller, and passing himself off as a Brazilian. Carmody hadn't liked the smell of him at all.

It wasn't just Carmody, however, who was sitting in there right now, on the other side of Charlie Chaplin's courtyard double doors.

'Come quick, *senhor*!' his little local watchman had hissed down the telephone over two hours ago; which is why Carmody was sitting here, in a flat across the narrow *rua*, behind the net curtains, in the shadows, squinting through a set of binoculars. Because this smart-as-a-tack schoolboy he'd long employed had arranged for the flat opposite to be watched all day, every day; this local kid who knew how to run a business and who could pass in English as well as Spanish and French, and who now ran a little network of street brats for Carmody. His brat-in-chief could be relied upon to hoover up lots of little snippets, especially from where other sweepers couldn't reach, or even be bothered to look. Carmody had always made a habit of bothering to look – everywhere. And that had turned out to be just as well in this case.

Because right now, looking through his binoculars, he was watching the man who had just been in that flat with his captain chum; walking out through those double doors and striding off down the *rua* with that Stroessner creep in tow.

Well, bugger me! thought Vernon Carmody.

It was the naval attaché from the German Embassy.

*

Saraband was back off Penang now, ordered there by a signal from S4 advising Harry to look out for a departing Jerry U-boat.

It was half an hour after sunset, and he was on the bridge, the aerial head for McTeer's radar set rotating sedately above his head; although he was more sensing it than seeing it, as he and the three lookouts were enveloped in that deep tropic darkness, the stuff in which you can barely see your hand in front of your nose.

They were at the entrance to the south channel and there was a warm breeze off the island, redolent of all manner of exotic smells. The lookouts were squinting through night glasses, although Harry doubted what good they might be doing. McTeer was their eyes, now.

Behind the thick cloud that covered the sky from horizon to horizon there would be a three quarters moon on the rise in about two hours' time – for all they would see of it. The air was full of the thrum of the diesels running on full battery charge and from where Harry was standing, out of the breeze in the lee of the periscope stands, he could practically feel their reverberations rippling the hot syrupy air against his cheek.

It was worse downstairs. Yet despite the oppressive heat there was a buzz. Everybody knew by now they were after another U-boat. Harry had passed the word. No point in keeping stuff like that a secret aboard a submarine. Who were the crew going to tell? And keeping the lads informed always seemed to add an edge to routine tasks. He had learned that early in his career. Everybody was waiting to hear if he was going to make another prediction, like he'd done for the Maru.

Silly buggers, he thought. *They're getting cocky now*. Which, of course, he knew was par for a crew getting back on their feet. They would need to get knocked over again a couple of times before they could be declared truly steady.

The latest edition of *The Bugle* had just come out, and he'd featured in it.

McTeer had immortalised him in a cartoon, with a silhouette of the Maru sinking in the background and a queue of *Sarabands*, each identifiable in their caricature, and each clutching a betting slip and a wad of bank notes, waiting for their space at the captain's table. Behind the table was Harry in full uniform, apart from a gypsy woman's scarf tied round his head; and he was hunched over a crystal ball, asking, '… so you're after the first three placings in the three thirty at Uttoxter next Tuesday?' And there was a growing pile of bank notes at his elbow.

All of it under a headline: 'Captain plans career after navy'.

When Number One had seen it, at the editing stage, he'd arched an eyebrow. Harry had said, 'I know, Bill. But look how much they're prepared to pay me!' McTeer, working the Roneo machine at the opposite end of the wardroom table, had had to stifle a guffaw. Harry knew what Bill Laurie was driving at; familiarity breeding contempt, and all that. But he'd thought, *what the hell!* It was one of those things about the Trade; if a crew knew their captain could handle a bit of piss-taking, then they could be confident he could handle a hell of a lot worse. Which was even better.

'Bridge, radar.'

Talk of the devil. It was McTeer, his tinny voice coming up through the pipe.

'Captain here,' said Harry.

'Surface contact, bearing green three five, sir. It looks like an escort, sir. Maybe even a destroyer. Looks like she's just departing George Town. Range … eight miles, sir. She isn't moving fast, sir.'

They were just three miles west of Pulo Aman, so whatever their contact was, it was right up the other end of the channel and seemingly intent on just hanging about.

Harry stopped the charge, sent the boat to diving stations, but only ordered her trimmed right down, so that just her conning tower was above the limpid sea; then he began nosing her up into the maw of the channel. An escort hanging about at the entrance to George Town could mean she was scouting the way for a departing U-boat.

If it was a U-boat, and the one he'd been told to look out for, then it would merit a full salvo.

He leant to the bridge voice pipe. 'Control room, bridge. Order forward torpedo room to ready tubes one to six. Make the depth setting ten feet.' That should be about right to hit a Type IX right in the guts, he decided.

Saraband crept on into the darkness. As they closed the escort, Harry ordered the diesels killed, and they went onto motors. He didn't want the thump of main diesels reaching the ears of any keen lookout aboard the Jap. Because the Jap was stopped, now.

Bill Laurie was on the bridge with him, officer of the watch.

'He's probably sitting there listening for the likes of us trying to sneak up, submerged,' Harry said.

Bill nodded, realised nobody could see him in all this cocooning darkness, and said, 'Yep. Sure you're spot on, sir.'

McTeer's tinny voice from below announced they were passing the Jap now, just over a mile to starboard. They must be just where the channel began to narrow. He could see the chart clearly in his head now, and suddenly the reality of the picture in the darkness around him hit home; as if it had just popped up when he wasn't looking. And right then he knew he had taken his eye off the ball; lulled by the night into seeing nothing, when there was everything to see. From being afloat on a wide, wide sea, he suddenly felt as though he was stuck up a drainpipe, unsure of what was coming down it.

No U-boat had appeared, and the darkness didn't feel quite so secure any more. How had he allowed himself to get into this? For the first time in a long time, he started to feel afraid. *Time to get out of here*, he said to himself.

'Gentlemen,' he said quite softly. 'Clear the bridge now, please.'

His polite tone and the precision of his speech sent chills down the lookouts' spines. They were down the hatch in seconds, passing wraiths, disappearing back to hell. Harry bumped into Bill Laurie in the dark.

'Oops, sorry Bill,' he said in a way that gave Bill the willies, too. 'I think we'll dive now. When you hit the deck plates, take us down to sixty feet, please. Do it as quietly as you can, no klaxons and of course, venting tanks notwithstanding, eh? I'll lock up behind us.'

Venting tanks – allowing the air out of your ballast tanks to let the water in – was always going to cause a racket. But then there was junk traffic about, and there was a port nearby after all. There was bound to be the odd rattle and clank echoing across the otherwise silent water to distract any listener. He was hoping whatever racket *Saraband* was going to make wouldn't automatically yell, 'submarine!'

The last thing Harry noticed as he was closing the hatch, was that the sky above had suddenly cleared, and was suffused with moonlight reflecting off the burnished plate of the water.

They were creeping now, meagre knots on one motor, through the narrow gap between the old Fort Cornwallis on the island, to port, and the town of Butterworth rising up from the mainland shore. Harry risked the attack periscope. The contrast looking through the 'scope was disorienting; from the diffuse red light of the control room to the stark, mono-colour relief of the world above, in moonlight. Looking one way, with the moon up he could make out the Queen Victoria Memorial Clock Tower standing proud, and the other way, the colonial town, all picked out as sharp as a set of black and white post cards you might send home. He described the view, mainly because it was starting to feel too tense in the control room.

Forgivable, really, on the crew's part. He'd just sailed them blithely into something he hadn't worked out how to get out of. Thus breaking rule one of safe submarining. How on earth had he allowed himself to get them into that hole? Too busy maundering on to himself about how his shambles of a crew were shaping up, and not paying enough attention to the fact he too had been away from his game for too long. McTeer's cartoon didn't seem that funny any more.

Once clear of the narrow, Harry ordered half ahead together, and a few more revs on the counter. They began pulling away out of the north entrance to the channel. People were breathing again.

Then: 'HE bearing green six zero,' said Meek. 'Diesels. Coming out of George Town, sir. It sounds like a U-boat on the surface, sir.'

Harry looked at the gyro-repeater above the chart table. *Saraband* was heading for open sea on 340 degrees. The target, if it was a U-boat, was passing abaft their port quarter. A box immediately formed in his head.

'Starboard thirty. Group up, full ahead together. Keep periscope depth,' he said. This time he selected the search 'scope. He waited until the turn

134

was completed, then ordered the motors grouped down again and back to slow ahead together.

Everyone could feel the way coming off *Saraband* up through the deck plates. Harry kneeled, spread the search 'scope handles and called, 'Up periscope.'

Harry could see the moon dapple on the surface through the up-swivelled lenses as he followed the periscope up from his crouch. When the head broke surface he swivelled the head down again, and there it was, the U-boat, beam on, passing from their starboard to port at about 12 knots by her bow wave. Definitely a Type IX by her sharp silhouette.

'Bearing is … that!' He said, then twisted the stadimeter, bringing the top image down onto the lower one to the split image. 'Range is … that!'

Cantor, who was behind him again, read the bearing and the angles off. The range was just over 2,700 yards.

'Tell the torpedo room, full salvo,' said Harry, still looking through the 'scope, risking it being up for so long. The bloody Jerry was going to turn starboard very soon and if she was going down the channel, and then all he would be looking at was her arse. He stared at the sharp, black shape slicing through the barely rippled, silvered sea, willing it not to turn.

'Firing on the stopwatch, five second intervals …' he said, '… for a one and a half ship length spread … Mr Verrell, how's my director angle looking please?'

Polite. Things were getting tense.

Verrell called it, and Harry simply said, 'Lionel …' which was all it took for Cantor, peering at the bezel above Harry's head, to turn him onto the bearing.

A heartbeat, then, 'Fire one!' said Harry. He watched the bubbles rise through the 'scope as the first one shot away. He shouldn't have, but he couldn't bring himself to order the 'scope down. He was risking them being spotted even before the full salvo had been fired. This was reckless. But then, *there's nobody else up there to see,* he argued with himself. Before he had finished his little internal debate, five seconds had passed and torpedo two was out and running. He did a swift all-round look. As if to justify the fact his periscope head was still sticking up out of the water. Not even a junk.

Before he'd come back on his original bearing, another torpedo had gone, and the U-boat was still holding her course. Three gone now, and there! That was the fourth. Then five. Enough. *Get it down, and let's be ready to get out of here immediately the last one fires,* he told himself.

'Down periscope,' he said.

And in the hair's breadth of time between the words and *Saraband* bumping as the last torpedo launched – between Harry delivering the order and getting ready to pull his eyes away from the lenses – he saw the U-boat's silhouette start to shorten. And as he did, there was Meek, right on cue, to confirm it. 'Target under helm, sir,' came the quiet, certain report from the Asdic cubby.

The U-boat was executing her course change, turning away to enter the north end of Penang channel; away from *Saraband's* spread of torpedoes; showing Harry her arse.

Gowers, at the chart table, had already begun counting down the torpedoes' estimated running times on his stopwatch. He was mid-chant when Meek piped up again.

'I have new HE, sir. Off the starboard bow ... bearing red five. It's still a way off, but closing, sir. Sounds like it could be the Jap escort, coming our way, sir.'

'Keep sixty feet,' said Harry. 'Group up, full ahead together. Starboard thirty ... Poulter,' he called to the helmsman; he had decided it was time to get out of here. 'Bring us back on to three one zero.'

The control room was silent as they felt the boat fall away beneath them, into her turn. Harry hadn't the heart to tell Gowers he could shut up now. None of their torpedoes were going to hit. He also lacked the heart to come away with a smart comment. The U-boat had been a sitting target, if a bit far away when he'd fired. Until some Jerry, just like him, standing in a pool of his own sweat in his red-lit control room, had ordered another routine touch of the helm.

Well, he'd said *Saraband's* crew would need knocking on their arses a couple more times before they finally settled. Here was one more time. Behind Harry, Gowers came to the end of his torpedo running counts. None had ended in any confirmatory explosion.

Twelve

Gowers was officer of the watch, so Harry told him it was his job to bring *Saraband* in through Trincomalee harbour and alongside *Wu Chang*. Gowers had been skulking about pretending he wasn't there for the whole trip back across the 1,100 miles from the Malacca Straits. Him and the rest of the crew. From a hopeful start to their patrol, the *Sarabands* had descended back into a dull lot, individually doing their jobs instead of performing as crew. Harry couldn't remember the last time he'd heard laughter in the boat.

After missing the U-boat with their full salvo, *Saraband* had only one torpedo left in her stern tube, so when Harry had reported their failure, Captain Tinsides had recalled them early from patrol. After seeing that 'Emily' flying boat, Harry had been careful to make sure there was no homeward-bound slacking among the lookouts. He'd had to look up the four-engine Kawanishi HK8 to get all her vital statistics, and just as she looked like a Sunderland, they'd confirmed that she was as deadly, with an operational range of almost 2,000 nautical miles and a depth charge load of over 5,000 pounds. So for the first couple of days, when on the surface, he'd been on the bridge. Which was why he had missed the general lumpishness aboard until they were well on their way.

So, he'd missed the Jerry. So what? They were like surly children, this lot, in the way they refused to muster even the remotest scintilla of the fortitude his last crew had. Christ, the *Scourges'* cheerfulness in the face of adversity had been tantamount to bloody belligerence!

Just thinking about *Scourge* made him remember that afternoon at the officers' beach bar outside Algiers, when he and his officers, Nick Farrar, the Jimmy and the Vasco, Miles Harding, had got hog-whimpering with a signals detachment from Eighth Army. How they'd had to carry the usually fastidious Farrar back on board. When he looked at his officers now, he felt like weeping.

Caudrey he could almost forgive; a hostilities-only wavy-navy boy who was starting to show the odd flash of competence but most of the time was intent on keeping his head down and hoping it would all go away. And the new boy, Verrell, in for a career and full of misplaced energy, most of the time too busy being eager to pay attention, who hadn't a clue how to handle the crew.

Then there was Gowers. Another regular officer who had all the technical skills for the job; a good navigator whose plots were a joy to behold. But when it came to sharing a wardroom with him – from what Harry had seen so far, he appeared to have all the personality of a plank of wood. And he was another dead loss when it came to handling Jack.

So it wasn't a happy Harry who dropped down into the control room while *Saraband* was securing alongside. He was on his way to grab his personal paperwork before going looking for a tender to take him over to *Adamant* to make his patrol report to the Captain S.

When he hit the bottom of the conning tower ladder, he could see there was a bit of a scrum at the forward bulkhead door, just ratings joshing and joking, the usual going ashore fever. No big deal. He held back, waiting for them to clear, so that he could get to the wardroom and grab his stuff. Which was when it occurred to him, he could grab boat's camera while he was at it and drop it off at *Adamant's* dark room; he was headed there anyway.

It was while he was rummaging for it among the charts that he heard the words. The context, the reason they were spoken at all was lost in the general hubbub; but the words themselves, those words, they got through alright. Like a diving klaxon.

' … get Yeoman Yid to send a signal …'

'Who said that?' Even Harry didn't recognise his own voice, it was so loud. And shocking.

Because shouting wasn't a habit that was ever encouraged in the Trade. For a start, since you were all jammed in so close, you really didn't need to shout. Then there was general tendency to do things quietly on a boat anyway, especially if you were dived, for obvious reasons. So most folk usually made a moderate tone the rule on board, whatever the boat was doing.

So the bellow that had just exploded from the skipper froze everyone in the compartment, being more like something you'd be liable to hear on a sailing ship quarterdeck in a gale, than in a submarine.

Harry scanned the faces, all of them staring back at him, stunned. He knew right away the culprit from the terror in his expression.

'You!' bellowed Harry, an accusatory finger pointed right at the lad; a leading seaman in his white going-ashore rig. The sailor was transfixed.

'Cox'n!' called Harry.

'Sir!' Garbutt was there in an instant.

'Place that man under close arrest. Charge, conduct contrary to naval discipline. And get him off this boat immediately.

'Aye, aye, sir!'

'Hand him over to *Wu Chang's* regulating PO until I decide exactly what I'm going to do to him. And get someone to throw his dunnage after him. He's not coming back.'

The *Sarabands* had never seen their skipper so angry; never even thought about him in terms of his true, arbitrary and absolute power over them. It was generally accepted he was a stickler for doing the job right, better than right, even. But apart from that he was a fairly easy-going bloke who liked a laugh. In the control room that hot, clammy afternoon, all that changed.

'It wusnae like he blew his top,' McTeer confided later to others not there. 'It wuz worse than that. Yuv nevvur heard cold fury the likes o' it in human voice a'fore.'

'The rest o' us werr lucky ta get out alive,' confirmed another. 'It was, "tin hats, boys!" and duck!'

'Flash signal to *Saraband* … do not piss off skipper … urgent!'

Bill Laurie buttonholed Harry in *Wu Chang's* wardroom when he came back from seeing the Captain S.

'Young Caudrey has been to see me,' said Bill. 'He's the divisional officer for the rating you had arrested, sir.'

'And why hasn't he come to see me?' said Harry, flat and not at all willing to be reasonable.

139

Bill said, 'Let me get you a gin first, sir. Your hand's empty.'

When he returned with two tumblers full, he said, '… too scared probably, sir. Anyway, he asked me to intercede on behalf of …'

Harry interrupted, 'His rating is terribly sorry … didn't mean it … he has greatest respect for PO Cantor … and an unblemished record so far.' Then he paused and stared hard at Bill. 'I don't care, Number One. You put up with that and you end up with Hitler. That sailor will not serve aboard my boat. The matter is closed. And as for Caudrey, if he wants to continue to hold the King's commission, he'd better start showing he deserves it. Tell him he's to report to me if you see him first. "… asked me to intercede …" *He's* the rating's division officer! Not you. What a load of bollocks … spineless little wretch.'

Caudrey got his bollocking a short time later, standing in the skipper's berth Harry had been assigned on *Wu Chang*. Harry explained to him in unambiguous terms how he was failing to assume his responsibilities as an officer, and that if he wished to remain as part of *Saraband's* crew then he must start conducting himself in an assertive and officer-like manner with immediate effect. At all times.

Usually, after delivering such a rocket, Harry liked to sweeten the pill with a little homily about how he knew his culprit had it in him and with just a little more application he'd be a star. Not this time.

But that wasn't the end of the matter. Caudrey had had something to say. Given that the ashen-faced youth had taken his dressing down like a man, Harry gave him the chance. Caudrey then proceeded to present extenuating circumstances for his rating's outburst. Some nonsense about lad's upbringing in the East End. Harry wasn't that interested. There was stuff about communities in conflict, bad influences, all that bollocks; and how the rating was filled with remorse.

Out of mercy, Harry cut him off. 'Did he start singing to you, Caudrey?' he asked.

'Sir?'

'Did he not give you the old, "can I come back next trip sir, on your great big ship, sir? I'll polish your brass, and kiss your arse, can I come back next trip, sir?"'

Caudrey stared back, blankly.

'Caudrey. I've met sneering little shits the likes of him before. The only remorse your rating has is for himself. He didn't try the, "daddy was a Blackshirt, he made me do it!" line on you, did he? No? You astonish me. The fact is, I personally detest everything about him and his so-called "outburst", and I'm the captain. But more importantly, that kind of poison rots away at a crew and I will not tolerate it even starting. He's dismissed from his ship, and that, for you, is the end of the matter. I will, however, also leave it at that as far as he's concerned. We're about to sail on patrol. I don't have time to get wrapped up in charges. If he comes back to you saying he wants to pursue it, *you* are not to become involved. Because *he*, believe me, will rue the day. You are dismissed, Mr Caudrey. I'll see you on board.

After giving Caudrey his dressing down, Harry headed for the hills.

*

The Fraters' invitation to Harry to spend his patrol leave still stood. So it was back to Kandy, up in the central highlands.

Back, with the specific intention of not just renewing his acquaintance with the Fraters, but also seeing that woman whom he hadn't been able to stop thinking about. The doctor woman.

And now he had her all to himself, for a moment. Aperitifs before lunch, on a beautiful, cloudless afternoon suffused with the benign heat of the mountains, so different from the cloying, oppressive humidity of the coast.

'I'm told you're a bit of a submarine ace,' said Dr Cotterell, sitting perched against the Fraters' verandah rail. She was wearing civilian clothes today in the shape of a thin cotton print dress, and a very fine shape it made too, thought Harry.

'I don't know about "ace", doctor,' said Harry, all shy and self-effacing on the surface, but thinking impure thoughts underneath. 'I've been responsible for the sinking for a certain amount of enemy tonnage, sure. But I haven't done anything particularly remarkable, apart of course from surviving. And that's just been dumb luck. Which has almost run out, should have run out, on several occasions.'

However, even he could see from her demeanour that Dr Cotterell wasn't much impressed with his 'aw-shucks' act. 'I've said you should call me Victoria, Harry,' she said, after a significant pause. 'Otherwise I shall start to refer to you as "sub lieutenant".'

'That's not my rank. Victoria.'

'You're a lieutenant. And you're on a sub. So how am I expected to know that? Harry.'

Harry met her arch smile, and smiled back, knowing enough not to push it. He'd been thinking about Dr Victoria Cotterell since they'd met here, right here, during that last leave, when she had arrived straight from performing surgery at the base hospital, still in her army fatigues. He had been thinking about her a lot. On the bridge during *Saraband*'s 1,100-mile transit out to her patrol billet; and on the transit back to Trinco; and in numerous quiet interludes in between. The older woman, austere as an Arctic iceberg, and as remote. Composed, contained, tall-ish, sleek rather than just slim. He got butterflies in his rum-a-tum-tum just being with her. And that was before he looked into those pale blue eyes.

'But surely that must be a good thing,' she said, returning to the subject. 'Sinking lots of tonnage and surviving. Your crew must be very pleased with you. You must be very pleased with yourself.'

Harry did an immediate flashback to his crew, in the control room the day before yesterday, and the horror and the cowed fear he remembered on their faces in the control room as the silence had closed in after his bellowed commands; the, '… off this boat!' And the, '… he's not coming back!'

'"Pleased" is not a word I'd use in either context, Victoria.' Then he risked giving a slight, self-deprecating laugh. 'The relationship between a submarine crew and a submarine captain is … a bit more convoluted that that.'

Her arched eyebrows said he hadn't got away with it. 'My! That sounds fascinating. I'd love to hear more.' She paused to sip her gin. So did he, and then as if to show just how much more she *really* wanted to hear, she asked instead, 'How are you finding Serendip? Have you seen much of our island paradise?'

Harry, who had arrived by train and 3-cwt truck the day before, had woken up before lunch after sleeping for a solid 18 hours. So he said, 'No, but I am assuming that any place with an old Arab name like Serendip, and an ancient Greek one before that, must have a lot to see.'

She frowned.

'Taprobane,' said Harry. 'It's what the ancient Greek geographers called this place, before the Arabs gave it a name.' And that was when he decided, *now or never*, and, *why the hell not?* 'However, I'd love to have someone who knows the place to show me around. Would you mind being that someone, Victoria?'

'My, we are a clever boy.' A pause while she considered him, then: 'Are you asking me out on a date, Harry? Or just for me to extend a courtesy?'

'A date, Victoria.'

'Certainly not!' She raised her eyebrows again and the pale blue eyes flashed in a way that made Harry immediately want to do indecent things to her.

'Oh. Well then, I apologise if I have been in any way inappropriate. Victoria. Unreservedly apologise.' He paused long enough to frown at her contritely, but only long enough for it to fade to a smile. 'But if I were merely to ask if you would extend a courtesy … What then?'

She couldn't help herself laughing now, all too aware of their fencing again. Then she gave an airy shake of her bobbed hair, which although it only swept to her jaw line managed to shimmer most engagingly.

'I might,' she said, equally airily. 'I'm off duty tomorrow afternoon at three thirty. If you check with the hospital reception then, I'm sure they'll be aware of my availability, Mr Gilmour.'

*

He ordered Caudrey to take them to sea, under his eagle gaze. The lad acquitted himself well enough, giving clear, concise orders, not faffing about, and they managed not to hit anything in the crowded anchorage.

When they got to open water, beyond the swept channel, Harry took over for their first trim dive. There'd be no sounding the klaxon for diving stations for this one, this was a purely housekeeping evolution, to get the feel for how the boat was stowed for the next patrol. Fore and aft … where her centre of gravity lay … to help the first lieutenant work out how to balance her at depth.

'Open up for diving,' Harry ordered down the voice pipe.

Opening up for diving was an activity undertaken well before you actually dived a boat. It allowed you to ensure that all the boat's systems were lined up correctly so that when the time came to order, 'open main vents,' she would dive, and, more importantly, would be able to surface again. So it was the cue for Number One, whose responsibility the all-important trim was, and the outside ERA, or wrecker, as he was affectionately known, to tour the boat checking everything was functioning as it should. They checked the vents, the machinery for letting the air out of and the water into the ballast tanks; the fore and aft hydroplanes that acted like wings and flaps on an aircraft, sending the boat bow down or bow up; the trim tanks and valves that allowed ballast water in penny packets to be pumped to and fro to finely tune the boat's attitude in the water at whatever depth.

Harry stood back and watched it all unfold with an intensely critical eye. When Number One was satisfied, Harry ordered, 'keep periscope depth', and down they went, Number One keeping an eye on the dive board and on the angle on the planes, manned by Cox'n Garbutt and his 2nd Cox'n, Petty Officer Newbold, while watching all the time the all-important 'bubble', which acted like a spirit level and told him whether he was heading up or down, and all-importantly, when he was level and had caught his trim.

Harry could sense the different atmosphere in the boat just from watching them all go about their business. He wouldn't have called them a happy lot, but there was a new seriousness about them that he approved of. They must have had a good run ashore. Small steps, but going in the right direction. He was curious now as to how his other plans for them were going to unfold.

Saraband continued her transit on the surface, for which the crew were grateful. The dry season before the onset of the south west monsoon had had them in its oven-like grip ashore. But at sea, the air was marginally better. And Harry ordered the boat to run with gun hatch as well as the conning tower hatch open. Because cooler on deck it might be, but down below it was still bloody hot, especially in the engine room with both diesels going. Which explained why there was a new fashion craze aboard – a printed native sarong wrapped round your waist and a pair of sandals locally made out of rubber tyres was standard dress now.

144

First night out, Harry had *The Bugle*'s editorial team round the wardroom table at work on the next edition. He insisted everyone wore a shirt or t-shirt if they were sitting at the wardroom table. There were some standards you just could not let slip.

Although not officially on the team, Bill Laurie was there to lend moral support and act as a sort of second opinion on what was within the general bounds of naval propriety – bounds that were often very loosely interpreted aboard *Saraband* when it came to her newspaper. Also, since he was her first lieutenant, Bill Laurie liked to keep a weather eye on everything that happened on *Saraband* – especially this newspaper lark. And one thing his eye told him now was that there seemed to be some kind of conspiracy going on between the skipper and that rascal McTeer.

He hadn't long to wait to find out what it was.

'Now,' said Harry, which Bill had learned was usually the harbinger of one of the skipper's bright ideas. You didn't have to be long in the Andrew to realise that skippers' bright ideas were usually anything but.

Harry continued, '… I have been feeling life on patrol has been rather dull up 'til now in the wardroom, so I am instigating an officers' Uckers league. But I want to involve the entire boat in the excitement, and I'll be looking to you, Mr Laurie, to organise the fun.'

Here we go, thought Bill, 'Of course, sir. Be happy to.' *Like bollocks!*

Harry outlined his idea: Each officer would stand alone in the league, a team unto himself, *mano a mano*, as the Spanish say,' said Harry. 'But not quite. Because each officer will be acting as champion for his division. Apart from me, of course. Since I don't have a division. I will be the joker in the pack.'

Divisions were an old navy tradition. Even back in the 18th century, the navy realised Jack needed more than just discipline to keep him a jolly tar. So, once aboard his ship, every rating was assigned to one of the ship's officers, who would then be responsible for his welfare, personal affairs and general all-round well-being. You were then said to be in that officer's division.

'Every time an officer wins a game, members of his division will each receive an extra gulpers,' continued Harry. Gulpers was a traditional measure of rum that through the centuries had taken on the mantle of legal currency aboard a King's man-o-war. 'Also, to further encourage Jack in supporting his divisional officer, each division will have to come up with new team chants, a team song and regularly updated verses, to be sung at appropriate moments throughout the lead up and during each game. All will be published in *The Bugle* and there will be a weekly hit parade, which I shall adjudicate using a strict points system. There will be extra points for excessive filth and gratuitous grottiness. And the winners here will also be awarded an extra sippers each.'

Sippers resembled gulpers, but a smaller measure.

'Now, have I forgotten anything McTeer?'

'Eh, naw, sir.'

Harry looked for any kind of reaction from Bill, but the first lieutenant just sat there nodding sagely. 'McTeer will be co-ordinating the song, and the chant contests, getting the entries in, keeping a score,' added Harry. For all this had been planned aboard the depot ship before they'd sailed, when Harry had summoned the rating to his cabin to explain.

'Everyone was looking far too glum last patrol,' he had told McTeer. 'So I've come up with something I hope will get their blood up a bit. Take their minds off war and being far from home. Make them want to tear each other's throats out instead. That sort of thing. Now, I know I'm asking a lot from you, a lot of extra work on the paper that will likely encroach significantly into your Egyptian PT, but what do you say? And what do you think of my plan? Now be honest. No bollocks. That's an order.'

McTeer sat with a face composed like granite throughout his captain's exposition. He had known what he'd been thinking alright, but was he really about to say it out loud?

'An order, sir?' he'd said instead.

'That's right McTeer. An order.'

The young sailor had had to look away; had to take a moment to think about this. He was a lad wise for his years, a lad from a hard background who knew how to stay ahead of the game. He knew his skipper was out manipulate his crew, but then he was part of that crew and he knew it needed manipulating, although that was probably too big a word for him to have ever used. 'Yanking their chain' might have been the phrase he'd have alighted on. There had been times in his street life when he had done

146

the same himself. Had to, to save his own skin. So he wasn't above doing it again. And he was quite prepared to doff his cap to a master. So, when he'd looked back at Harry and saw that face, all serious of purpose, he thought to himself, *okay, well you asked for it.*

'See you, surr. You're a right bad bastard, surr.'

'Why thank you McTeer,' Harry had said, suddenly grinning. 'From you, that's an accolade. Now are you up for it?'

'Oh aye, surr. Ah wuddnae miss this fer the world.'

'Good man. Tell Mr Garbutt, an extra tot for you, and if he gives you any gyp, refer him to me.'

The next edition of *The Bugle* was devoured and both copies per mess got so worn out so quickly, an extra print run had to be rolled off. The song and chant entries began to pour in within hours.

After nodding sagely at the wardroom table, Bill had later added, equally sagely, 'That's a lot of rum, sir.'

'I know,' said Harry. 'But I had a chat with Tinsides about the crew. Geeing them up a bit. Anyway, I think *Saraband* will be good for it. We might just have to put in for a couple of cracked jars. It's not as if they're going to get the rum while we're on patrol. They can wait 'til we get back.'

Indenting for cracked jars – that is, jars of rum ration – was one way of getting extra rum, especially if you had a depth-charging written up in your patrol report.

*

Saraband was headed right down the maw of the Malacca Straits for her next patrol billet. In his patrol briefing Cdr. Clarke, the Fourth Flotilla's staff officer, operations, had told Harry to expect heavy enemy traffic up the straits. 'Slim's having a right old ding dong with the Japs in the mountains east of Dimapur,' he'd said. 'It's right on the Indian border. They're trying to bash through, and he's not letting them. The Japs have two armies up there, and they're positively soaking up any materiel they can lay their hands on. So the more you sink, the less Johnny Jap has to play with. Where are you planning on opening your innings?'

147

Harry knew the charts by now and told Cdr. Clarke he'd go immediately down to One Fathom Bank, which lay right on the main shipping channel, at a choke point barely more than 10 miles wide, between Port Swettenham and the Aroa Islands.

'Good choice,' Clarke said, and with that the briefing had been over and off they had sailed.

The transit was fairly uneventful, apart from one of *Saraband*'s persistent little technical problems becoming aggravatingly worse. From the start she had been plagued by high pressure air leaks. Mostly, they were irritating little snafus which you didn't really notice running on the surface, but every time you dived, you inexorably built up the pressure in the boat. Until now, *Saraband*'s warrant engineer had been going after them like the man who paints the Forth Bridge; no sooner did he finish, than he had to start all over again.

As a running fix, Acting ERA Priestly, their temporary wrecker, had suggested that every so often, when dived, and when there were no Jap escorts about to hear, they ran the compressors in short bursts to draw the extra pressure out boat. And Harry had approved, if only on the grounds that it would certainly prevent the poor sod who had to open the conning tower hatch on surfacing from being fired out of the boat like a champagne cork.

Also, the Uckers league had got off to an uproarious start, with Caudrey inflicting a drubbing on Bill Laurie, much to both officers' astonishment, and simmering hatred between the two divisions. On that day the boat had been no place for a church fete, with each side belting out their deeply offensive and salacious anthems, while over it all PO Cantor's clipped and precise, move by move, BBC-style commentary came through the boat's address system. He had quickly become the voice of the tournament.

So, on the whole, Harry was a happy man, as they slipped past Diamond Point on Sumatra, and headed into the straits proper. Apart from the issue of Priestly. His repeated requests to S4 to have Priestly promoted to substantive petty officer had fallen on deaf ears. Which was a bloody pain as the man was a gem at the job.

Anyway, so to war.

Again.

What followed were three days of frustration.

There seemed to be a permanent air cap over the One Fathom Bank area; either small floatplanes or one of these damned, hulking great 'Emily' jobs. Then, there were the escorts. It seemed to Harry that the Japs had commandeered every local tug or tender, or indeed anything that floated and had an engine, and stuck a pop-gun and a handful of depth charges on it, and sent it out to do battle with him personally. The cumulative effect was that the enemy kept *Saraband* down. Down, however, being a relative word in this case, given that there was seldom any more than between 25 and a dozen fathoms beneath her in the channel.

The targets were there alright. All around, continuous reports of HE, big and small; escorts and transports; singly and in small convoys. Except that during daylight, putting up the periscope was an invitation to all those Jap planes, and at night, the tropic night, the periscope was all but useless in the impenetrable darkness. Not once had Harry been able to steer his boat into anything resembling an attacking position.

Even when they had come up at night to recharge their batteries and get fresh air into the boat, they kept getting driven down again. McTeer on the radar alerting him, 'contact closing, range two miles, bearing …' Twice, three times, four times a night. And then those bloody HP air leaks. And never a sizeable target; the Japs just weren't moving the big transports at night; instead, they sneaked them into small ports along the way, before sundown. Ports like Swettenham, or bays where they could corral them with escorts until dawn, and the Jakes and Emilys were back in the sky.

Which was why, after three days of this, Harry took *Saraband* back up the straits in the direction of Pulo Perak to look for better hunting grounds. Relief aboard spread fast. Everybody was too exhausted by the constant round of tension and frustration to lapse back into their usual despondency.

Harry had marked a spot on the chart just off Perak, and about half an hour into the last dog watch, not long before nightfall, Gowers announced *Saraband* was there. Harry sent up the 'scope for an all-round look, then turned on the bearing to where the island should have been. It wasn't. Gowers looked crestfallen when Harry told him, which pissed off Harry more than the island not being there. If he'd got it wrong, he'd got it wrong.

Or there might be some other explanation. Why could the stupid arse not just stand by his decisions instead of taking everything so personally?

Harry ordered *Saraband* a little further down the bearing and put the 'scope back up again. Out of the corner of his eye he could see Gowers fiddling with the echo sounder instead of concentrating on the plot. Harry focused on what horizon he could see. It was the fishing stakes, suddenly coming into view then vanishing again, that gave him the clue. That bloody heat haze on the surface again. When Harry turned back to Gowers. The navigator was fiddling with tracing paper now.

'Mr Gowers,' said Harry.

Gowers looked up. 'Sir?'

'I think a haze might be hiding the island … what are you doing, Mr Gowers?'

'I'm recording the depths, sir. On this tracing paper. Another couple of readings and I can place it over the chart and see where it lines up.'

Of course, that was what he was doing. His navigation by soundings on the chart trick. He'd done it before. Every time he was ready to dismiss Gowers, he went and did something like this. 'Good work, Mr Gowers,' said Harry. 'Carry on and let me know when you've got a fix.'

Ten minutes later, Harry knew exactly where he was, so he ordered the compressors run for a few minutes to get the pressure down from the bloody HP air leaks, then he ordered, 'Surface.'

It was Number One's watch, so Harry followed him onto the bridge. There was a quarter moon due up in an hour, which would give enough light to burn through the gauze of heat that blanketed all around and blocked out all the star light, enveloping them in the usual immaculate tropic darkness. Their faces to each other were mere pale smudges, even when jammed so close together on the bridge.

'Where did you get the idea for the Uckers league, sir?' asked Bill.

Harry pondered the wisdom of answering, given the four lookouts around them. But, with the hot breeze blowing weakly onshore at their back, and if he kept his voice down against the diesel thump of the engines piling on battery amps, he decided to spill the beans.

'It was a doctor up at the base hospital in Kandy,' he said. He didn't mention that the doctor, or rather the surgeon, was a woman. 'I said, "doctor, my crew aren't exactly a laugh-a-minute bunch, and the doctor diagnosed the bleedin' obvious. Just like you did before. The war's five years in and most of the blokes fighting it these days aren't the regular soldiers, sailors and airmen any more. They're civvies in uniform. That lot downstairs are no more Trade than I was when I started. But at least I was surrounded by teachers from the start. Not for them, though. It's just been, "there's the deep end. Jump!" They're still bricklayers, kitchen porters, factory workers, except now they're in a blue suit. And they don't know how to wear it.'

Bill thought about this for a while. 'I still don't follow with the Uckers,' he said. 'If they get any more worked up there could be violence, you realise that, sir?'

'Nah,' said Harry. Bill couldn't see him smile. 'It's good for them. They need something to take their mind off the grim bloody fact that they're at war, and the factory whistle isn't going to blow and they can all go home at five. I don't know why I didn't see it earlier. It'll be like supporting their local football team, and they'll get to make a lot of noise for a change. Plus its already got Kershaw out the pit back there and into civilised company for an hour or so.'

Harry had arbitrarily ordered that *Saraband's* notorious warrant engineer was henceforth a divisional officer for all the back afties for the purposes of the league.

The night wore on, the quarter moon began to rise, and the world around them began to take on a dim shape. Then the voice of McTeer's deputy came up the pipe. 'Surface contact, range four miles, bearing one seven eight.'

Harry nodded to Bill, who hit the general alarm. Harry waited. Then he heard McTeer's voice; McTeer at his action station, on the radar. 'Multiple contacts, sir. One big-ish, the others smaller. At a guess, auxiliary sub-chasers, plus a medium-sized transport of some sort. Closing fast, sir. Range less than three miles now, sir.'

Harry ordered down the voice pipe, 'Ready tubes one, two, four and five.' He wasn't going to waste time getting the TBT up, he was going to use the small night sight on the bridge wing, and yell back and forth to Verrell, below on the fruit machine.

'Can you see anything yet, Number One?' he said to Bill, who was standing next to him, glasses stuck to his face, still peering into the night.

All binoculars were trained aft, the direction of the target's approach. 'No, sir,' said Bill. But the starboard lookout called, 'I can see a bow wave, sir. Bearing green one six zero, sir.'

'Starboard thirty,' Harry ordered down the pipe. 'Bring us on to zero seven zero. Mr Laurie, ring for half ahead together.'

Saraband turned away from the targets' track and began moving slowly to the north east. Below, Verrell at the fruit machine was dialling in the bearings being fed to him from McTeer's radar plot, as Gowers worked his slide rule, calculating the targets' speed from the ranges McTeer was reading off. The team were doing it by themselves – no Harry standing over them – because they knew how to now, and had somehow got it into their thick civvy skulls what was expected of them.

Harry ordered the course changes to turn them back the way they had come. *Saraband* was now bow on to the enemy's track. He ordered slow ahead together. He didn't even try looking for the target himself. His night vision. He let Bill be his eyes. The moon was on their beam, and on the targets' quarter now. *Saraband* was safe from being silhouetted, while the moon played shadows over the main target's shape.

'She's a queer looking bugger, sir,' said Bill, night glasses stuck to his face. 'A bit like a tanker's shape, but too boxy … the central structure's too far for'ard … and … well, stone me, sir. She's got aircraft as deck cargo. Definitely. Those are planes on her.'

'How big is she, Number One?'

'All the shadows, hard to say. Big-ish, sir. Maybe five or six thousand tons …'

Harry stepped to the voice pipe. 'McTeer, the captain here. What's the range now to the big bastard?'

'Two thousand two hundred yards, sir,' said McTeer

It was time. Harry bent to the sight and peered through the lenses as he traversed it until there it was a nice surprise, the enemy's bow wave. Slowly her bulk coalesced in the shadows. Yes, even he could see her now. The rough outline of her; she was a whaling factory ship. He remembered the type from a newsreel he had seen of the Southern Ocean fisheries. This must be a Jap one, obviously converted now for other use. An aircraft transport? Why not? She'd have the flat deck space. But his mind needed to be on matters other than ship identification.

'What are the escorts doing?' he asked, from his crouched position.

The port lookout called it. 'I have eyes on only one, sir, directly astern of the target.'

Harry stood up and spoke down the pipe. 'What's my DA, for a one and a half ship length spread, Mr Verrell?'

Verrell, who'd been dialling it all in, updating with every call from radar and Gowers, replied within a heartbeat. 'DA is green nine.' No shout, no squeaky voice this time.

Harry bent again and placed the bar of the sight on the bearing, and waited. His mind was full of nothing but the vague moon shimmer on the water. He heard himself order, 'Slow ahead together.'

And then the target's bow crept into the edge of the sight, its bow wave a little beard of paleness moving towards the bar, closer, closer …

'Fire one!' said Harry, without moving from his crouch. He felt *Saraband* go over the hump as the torpedo launched. He raised his head slightly and could see the iridescent trail of bubbles, churning up a wake of green phosphorescence just below the surface, running true at 45 knots like a horizontal rocket trail; then he bent again to the target. The bar was over its boxy superstructure now. Bill had been right, it was too far for'ard for a tanker. Definitely a whaling factory ship.

'Fire two!' he said, but this time didn't raise his head, just kept watching as the target's hull continued its progress across his sight. 'Fire three … Fire four !'

He stood up. He wanted to shout, 'Starboard thirty!' then turn *Saraband* around and put as much distance between her and where she'd fired from before the sub-chasers spotted them. But he said nothing. They were too close to the enemy now. The last range called up to him before firing was 1,500 yards. Being bow on though, meant *Saraband* was showing no profile to the enemy. But if he turned now, the Japs would have a shape to look at, to catch the eye of even an unwary lookout. And if the lookout looked down he'd see the torpedo wakes. There was still time for the bastard to turn and comb his salvo.

So, accustomed to the dark now and with the moon to help, he could make out the shape of another sub-chaser, emerging from the shadow of the transport ahead. That was two he could see, and if he turned, two who could see him. *Saraband* continued to creep closer to the transport's track, still going slow ahead together. When he did finally order the turn, it was going to take precious minutes to get some decent way on her. He hadn't even bothered weighing the option of diving. This close, the racket and the green phosphorescent plumes his venting tanks would shoot up would look, and sound, like the Blackpool illuminations. So, he continued to wait, and wait, and …

There was a sudden gout of water up the target's flank, like a fountain being turned on, then in an instant a dull, a smothered bang. Seconds later, another. The shape of the enemy transport seemed to distort in the darkness, shorten, like she was slewing, then there was a huge jet of something pale. The high-pitched scream an instant later explained it, escaping high-pressure steam, coming right out of her boilers, shooting up out her smoke stack into the night.

From the corner of his eye, Harry saw two more trails shooting into the sky, rockets from the sub-chasers. Flares, probably. Now, it was time to dive. He hit the klaxon twice.

'Clear the bridge!'

As the lookouts went tumbling down the hatch, he was aware of *Saraband*'s tanks venting over his shoulder, and then suddenly every steel edge and plate and bridge fitting was there, in front of him, fixed in chemical light. A flare. The dazzle made him blind as he too went down the hatch, feeling for its stirrup to drag it shut behind him, fumbling for the securing clips, to seal it.

He hit the deck plates and in the red light of the control room he could see again; he began issuing orders in stream. 'Keep one hundred feet.' He remembered 20 fathoms beneath them from his last look at the chart. They were in a bloody paddling pool. 'Shut off for depth charging … Starboard thirty. Bring us onto three two zero. And group up, full ahead together. Run at this speed for three minutes. Asdic? What are the escorts doing?'

Saraband sank fast in a diving turn.

'HE closing fast on our port beam, sir,' said Meek's voice from the cubby.

'Two of 'em, sir. The other one's coming in on the port quarter … further out … first one's closing …'

And suddenly everyone was aware of the repeated creaking sounds in the boat, coming from outside; the sounds of the transport, bulkheads starting to fail. They noticed it because rising out of it came the gut-churning, sewing machine screeching of high speed propellers.

RICKA-CHICKY-RICKA-CHICKY-RICKA-CHICKY!

Running flat out was going to gobble up a lot of battery amps they might need later, if the Japs decided to gang up on them. But at least if this sub-chaser was coming on hell for leather, whatever he had for a listening device would be picking up bugger all right now, and speed was the best way to get away from where they'd fired their torpedoes; because all that phosphorescent wake they'd churned up would still be hanging in the water, pointing back to exactly where they had been.

For some reason, in all the action, Harry couldn't remember whether this crew had been on the end of a serious depth-charging before. Well, they were about to be, now.

'The closer high speed HE bearing is increasing, sir. He's going to pass astern …' Meek's words were interrupted by a series of distinct splashes that everyone could hear. Depth charges entering the water.

'One hundred feet,' called Bill from the dive board.

Saraband had already come onto her new course, but she was still going flat out.

RABUMM-DAH-RUMM-BUMMM!   RABUMM-DAH-RUMM-BUMMM! RABUMM-DAH-RUMM-BUMMM!

The detonations seemed to go on and on, and then stop suddenly. You could feel the boat quiver and bump. Gaunt faces, eyes wide, everybody caught in the sharp angles of the control room's red light.

'Six,' said a voice from the control room door. It was Cantor, standing there ready to step in and place Harry on a periscope bearing when needed, counting the number of depth charges.

'Cold. Cold. Not even remotely warm,' said Harry as the reverberations echoed to nothing. Experience told him the Japs had dumped their pattern well away from *Saraband's* egg-shell hull. He'd still have a few more crucial seconds to build the distance since nobody, not even Meek, was going to hear anything in that water until the turbulence had settled. Out the corner of his eye he could see weak smiles passing across the faces now. If the skipper wasn't bothered …

He counted the beats in his head. Not three minutes yet, but long enough now.

'Stop together, group down, slow ahead starboard,' he called. 'We won't push our luck in case Tojo has kit he can hear us with,' he announced to the control room. 'Shut off all fans. Absolute silence in the boat. Number One, how's your trim?'

Harry needed to know. They weren't deep, but even at 100 feet the water pressure compressed the hull enough to make their boat just that little bit heavier. Adjusting trim required them to run a noisy pump.

Before Bill could respond, Garbutt called from the fore-planes position. 'Sir, going through eighty feet we hit a density layer. I felt it on the wheel …'

A thermocline. Variations in water temperature and therefore density; it occurred everywhere in these waters at nearly all depths, and it was damned handy to know when you hit one. The denser the water, the more buoyant the boat.

'Trim is holding fine, sir,' said Bill.

They wouldn't have to run the pump.

'Good show. A bit of luck to us,' said Harry.

The other good thing about a density layer was that it tended to deaden any sound trying to pass through it, stopping anyone who might be listening on the surface from hearing what was happening below. Another piece of luck.

With all the fans shut down, the heat hit them like the opening of an oven door.

'Passing over the twenty five fathom line,' said Gowers.

'Zero bubble, keep one hundred and twenty feet,' responded Harry. No other sound could be heard. He wondered whether, if he listened really hard, he would start to hear the sweat droplets hitting the deck plates.

Saraband slid slightly deeper, still holding her course.

'High speed HE,' whispered Meek, 'bearing red one seven zero … bearing rate is increasing, sir … she's passing astern port to starboard …'

Harry stepped to look over Gowers' shoulder. He wanted them to get away from all these islands and shallows, and to run out to the north west. But he needed to keep the sub-chasers dead astern; not to present whatever echo-sounder device they might have with a big, beam-on target for their pings to ping off. 'Starboard ten,' he said, all too aware that would take them back towards shallower water.

'More HE, coming up fast on red one eight zero,' interrupted Meek. 'They're a way off, sir, but moving quickly.'

Not what he wanted to hear.

Meek started again. 'Two are definitely sub-chasers, but there's another, bigger ...'

Meek was cut off by another pattern of depth charge detonations. They sounded loud, very loud. But no shock waves hit them.

'So cold, they're positively freezing,' said Harry, automatically, still concentrating on the plot. None the less he got a little ripple of laughter. 'Now, now. Stop tickling the girls. Silence in the boat.' The laughter stopped, but when he glanced up, he could see the shoulders rocking.

Meek's 'bigger' was something he definitely hadn't wanted to hear.

A slow game of cat and mouse began to develop, the first sub-chaser now joined by the other two. From Meek's commentary, they appeared to have formed up and were conducting a sweep, east to west, passing *Saraband's* stern. *Saraband* was still creeping along at two knots on one motor, one propeller turning, to minimise noise. All her tele-motor systems were shut off now too – the hydraulic pumps that turned and moved the rudder and the dive planes. All those were now being hand cranked. To cut noise.

They were still in shallow water, and the way these damn sub-chasers were forming up, it was taking them to the west of *Saraband*, cutting them off from that 30 fathom line, where the seabed fell away and deeper water beckoned.

Harry had a plan. It should have been a good one, but he hadn't been paying attention to what Meek's 'bigger' target was getting up to.

'Meek,' said Harry, still looking at the plot. 'The instant you hear splashes, sing out. I want to know the moment those buggers start sending down their next depth charge pattern.'

'Aye, aye, sir.'

He didn't have long to wait.

'Splashes now sir. Multiple splashes …'

'Group up. Full ahead together. Steer three one five degrees,' said Harry. He was pointing his boat back out to deeper water and running for it. They all felt *Saraband* move beneath them as her propellers bit deep, and she accelerated to nine knots, the noise of her propellers cavitating all drowned out now in the rippling detonations of the Japanese depth charges going off well behind, off her port quarter.

Whatever hydrophones or echo sounders the Japs might have would be deaf, now.

At the same time, however, the noise of the charges was also drowning out the sound of the other advancing escort, now a mere few thousand yards away and coming up *Saraband's* port side. Harry let rumbles fade, then ordered the motors grouped down again, and *Saraband's* speed drained away until she was back creeping along at two knots.

Meek was halfway round his all-round sweep.

'High speed HE off the port beam, sir,' he called. 'Another target … the big one again. She's close, and closing, sir … coming right at us, sir.'

They had been acquired. The minute Meek said, 'coming right at us' Harry knew it. In the gap between the rumbling echoes of the depth charge fading and Harry shutting down *Saraband's* dash, the Jap skipper must have heard them. If he had some kind of new detection kit aboard, the stuff the flotilla intelligence officer was always banging on about, it would have been easy. Because *Saraband* had just dashed right into the Jap's arms. The Jap skipper must have had a hunch and had known to work westward to cut off their escape; and his hunch had paid off. There was nothing Harry could do about it now. Because there was no going down into the cellar to escape; no going deep. Twenty-five fathoms were all there was. They really were in a fucking paddling pool.

RICKA-CHICKY-RICKA-CHICKY-RICKA-CHICKY!

Here he comes, said Harry to himself. *Here he fucking comes.*

RICKA-CHICKY-RICKA-CHICKY-RICKA-CHICKY!

The sound grew; a teeth-on-edge crescendo, punctured by the splashes.

158

Most of the crew were too young, too inexperienced, to know this was the moment for your heart to congeal and your throat tighten. But Harry knew, and so did the cox'n, and in the engine room so did Bert Kershaw, and up for'ard, Jowett, the torpedo gunner's mate. All of them waiting for the first click; the sound of the first depth charge's trigger, flipping that half heartbeat before everything went to hell.

… *click!*

The pattern straddled them aft. The noise was indescribable, and instantaneous blasts thumped into them like trains colliding. The very air seemed to fuzz before their eyes and the steel plates and formers bounced and seemed to buckle as the shock waves rippled through the hull; a vision of distorting reality before it all went black as light bulbs shattered, and fragmented glass added to the rain of cork hull insulation and paint flakes that filled the turbulent air.

Harry had instinctively known to hold on; others had not. When the emergency lighting flickered on, bodies were strewn across un-seated deck plates; cuts and gashes leaking blood like dark soup in the red light.

'Another six … that's twelve,' it was Cantor's voice, coming from by the aft control room door, where he had wedged himself, crouching; still counting the depth charges. The racket of the Jap warship's propellers could be heard racing away still, as the echoing churn of the sea around them started to calm.

'Helm!' Harry was shouting, 'Starboard thirty! Come on to two nine zero! Group up, full ahead together!'

Time to run while the Jap was deaf; before the waters calmed and he came back again.

The engine telegraphs rang, people started getting up off the deck, *Saraband* slewed; but it wasn't the engine telegraphs that started ringing back, acknowledging. It was the sound-powered telephone. Harry grabbed it, pressed it to his ear. 'What d'you mean, *can't?*' he said, but hardly anyone else in the control room heard him for all the screaming sounds filling the space.

Warrant Engineer Kershaw kept it short and to the point and Harry, despite his brain feeling like a pea that had been rattled in its tin, had the sense to listen. Then all he said was, '… I understand, carry on Mr Kershaw, but get someone up here quick … we've got HP air leaks all over the place.'

The engines and their mountings had suffered serious damage, possibly the propeller shafts too. The boat was flooding, aft, but the engine room crew were getting that under control. Flooding? *Jesus Christ!* he thought. But Bert Kershaw said it was under control, so ... he'd worry about that later ... when there was time for a proper damage report ... too much to do now, up here, to save the boat.

A posse of grease-smeared figures came out of the gloom, padding fast, wielding huge adjustable spanners, looking for the HP leaks.

Bill was shouting at Petty Officer Garbutt, the cox'n on the dive planes; their bow angle was all to hell! Standing beside Number One was Priestly, manning the trim board, his hands dancing over the valves, trying desperately to make corrections while Bill's eyes stayed fixed on his 'bubble' with a look of daemonic concentration. Harry, puzzled, didn't understand the shouting – until he felt how unstable *Saraband* had become beneath his feet. It was Meek's voice that shook him out of it. The Japs were coming back, from two directions. Then it dawned on him what Bill Laurie and Eddie Garbutt were yelling about. Number One was fighting for his life, and everybody else's, to regain control of that bloody elusive bubble.

He didn't have to look at the chart again; he knew how far they had to run to the 30 fathom line. They were too late. He turned to Gowers. 'What's the seabed, Mr Gowers?' Calm, polite; it was how the crew knew things were getting sticky. Of course, Harry already knew the answer, but he needed to be sure.

'Sand and mud, sir,' said Gowers, his face gawping, breathing heavily through his nose.

'Put us down on it, Number One,' said Harry. Then he ordered 'Stop together.'

He turned and smiled to the control room, his face looking strangely innocent for being washed in red light, 'we don't want to be rolling around all over the place, especially since we've got all this mess to tidy.'

It only took a few moments until they felt it, like falling on and then rolling over on a mattress.

They were resting on the seabed.

Suddenly everything was quiet, and still. Even the screaming had stopped;

all the HP air line valves shut, and the leaks isolated. Harry could hear himself … hear everyone in the control room … breathing.

'Multiple high speed HE, bearing red three zero, sir,' intoned Meek, knowing everybody wished he would just shut up. 'Bearing rate is increasing fast … another contact, sir … HE on green nine zero … he's under helm, sir … it the big chap … he's not in a hurry, like he's listening for us … first contact … three of them, line abreast … getting louder and moving really fast now, sir … going to cross our bows, close in … port to starboard …'

They could hear them now, like the subdued hissing of a coming squall …

… *ricka-chicky- ricka-chicky- ricka-chicky- ricka-chicky* …

… nowhere near as loud as before, yet, and not sounding like they were coming right at them. Harry could still hear people breathing, which was a good sign. Nobody was actually holding their breath yet. Just waiting. Counting the seconds they had left …

Harry decided to pass the time profitably in trying to work out what was going on upstairs; what the Jap skipper in the big one was up to. Before he did that though, he put the phone to his ear again and cranked.

'Ah, Mr Kershaw. Captain here. We're about to get stonked again, as I'm sure you can hear. When they're done, could you take one of your ERAs and go through the boat and tell me just how badly hurt we are? Excellent … hold on now, here they come.'

He hung up the phone, wedged himself on the other side of the chart table to Gowers, and turned and winked at him. Gowers grimaced back.

Now, the Jap upstairs …

… Harry decided he must have heard, or guessed, *Saraband*'s last dash for deep water, and had run directly over her track, dispensing charges. Meanwhile the other three sub-chasers had swept east to west well astern of *Saraband* … so big Jap must have signalled them to form up and come back round again so they could straddle what he must have have guessed would be *Saraband*'s track for her next dash, which he'd be guessing she'd make amidst all the bangs and wallops of his own, last pattern.

Harry nodded to himself, even risked a pull at his bottom lip. Not a bad guess by big Jap. If *Saraband* hadn't been sitting here on the bottom right now, she'd have been …

… there were the splashes …

… motoring right into it.

The roaring cataclysm all around them, the whole steel fabric of the boat bucking and twisting under each successive blow; it wasn't quite as bad as the last lot … if you were a connoisseur of that sort of thing. Or at least that was what Harry was thinking to himself, with one part of his brain, while the other resolutely forced itself to stare down the fear. Jesus, but that bit never got any easier. Especially now, it suddenly occurred to him, even amidst all this mortal chaos, that he'd been thinking about someone else … someone whom he couldn't stop thinking about … whom he *really* wanted to see again … so much so that he really didn't want to die … not here, not after everything; not now … *please*.

Well, fancy that, he thought. And funnily enough, those thoughts tided him over all the falling cork and paint, and the whole world going dark, and the roaring, roaring, roaring, until the lights came on again and silence crept back.

When Harry looked around, he saw two LTOs, the torpedomen who handled all the electrics aboard. They were working their way along the passage leading aft, replacing light bulbs. Bert Kershaw came past him, nodded, then carried on for'ard, moving through the boat, carrying out the damage checks he'd ordered.

Harry passed the word; anyone not working was to lie down on a bunk, keep quiet and stay out of the way. The less moving about the better. Not that anyone felt like moving. The heat was making the air almost unbreathable. Also, there was a stink in the air. Something chemical, burning. Harry could feel it searing in his throat. He looked at his watch. They hadn't been submerged that long, so the air shouldn't be getting choked with carbon dioxide for some time yet. Not that you'd smell that. But there was something wrong with the air.

It made him think about the batteries; they must be damaged. Their glass cells, all that rattling. But he didn't want to think about that, was frightened to; so he thought about their charge. When they'd dived after attacking the transport, it had been quite early in the night; they'd had no chance to get a good charge back on after spending the day submerged. And since they had dived, he'd ordered a couple of high-speed dashes. He swallowed and it hurt. Turned out, he didn't want to think about how much charge they had left, either.

Instead he thought about what big Jap was doing. With their Asdic dome in the mud, Meek would have no idea where the big Jap was right now. Or his pals. Were they coming back to finish them off?

Kershaw appeared at the for'ard control room door and broke that train of thought too, gesturing Harry to follow him. Harry stepped over lifted deck plates, Priestly on his knees, working on tele-motor hydraulic lines in the space below.

Kershaw had slid into one of the wardroom banquettes and was taking a wedge of a notebook from the pocket of his shorts. The shorts, and a bandana round his neck, were all he was wearing – those and his cap. Harry sat opposite him. The LTOs had replaced the light bulbs here, and they hunched over the table in the little yellow puddle of light.

'We've got battery problems,' Kershaw said, his breathing laboured. 'There's no chlorine gas, so far … but it's bad …' he paused as he sorted the limp sheets of notepaper. 'A lot of the cells are cracked … I don't know how many yet, but the electrolyte in them is leaking into the sumps …'

There were over 100 cells in each battery, and each cell weighed more than eight hundredweight. They were all packed tightly together and rested on wooden slats in battery tanks that were covered in acid-resistant bitumastic. Each tank had a sump, so that any of the electrolyte that leaked – basically diluted sulphuric acid – ran into the sump and could be tested to see how much neutralising alkali should be dumped in to soak it up.

Submarines always carried a lot of alkali because as every submariner knew, if any electrolyte made it into the bilges and mixed with salt water, the result was chlorine gas. And chlorine gas would kill them all, quickly and nastily.

'… None of it is in the bilges yet, but these fumes … the electrolyte is obviously getting too low in too many cells, while we're still putting electrical charge across them … that's what's generating the bloody fumes. So I need to cut out all the damaged cells, sir, and I need to do it now otherwise the bloody fumes are going to start choking people. Except we don't have enough cutting out leads for such a big job. But we do have a very long main charging lead. Do I have your permission to start cutting it up, sir?'

'Permission granted, Mr Kershaw,' said Harry.

Kershaw nodded. 'And could you order all power not required to be shut down, right now …?'

'Done, Mr Kershaw … Number One!' Harry called in a rasp. Bill came stumbling from the control room. 'Turn the lights out, Bill, emergency lighting and torches only. All pumps and motors shut off too. Pass the word.' He turned back to the warrant engineer, 'Anything else, Mr Kershaw?'

'I haven't got started yet,' said Bert Kershaw, laboriously flattening out his notes. His face looked flat, skin drawn, smeared with oil and strain and belligerent concentration.

The grim tally began.

The damage from the shockwaves from the first depth charge pattern that had wreaked such havoc on *Saraband*'s glass battery cells hadn't been confined to the easily breakable.

The main holding down bolts of both diesels had been slackened or twisted. There were 60-odd of these high-tensile steel bolts and they secured each 50 ton diesel to the boat's main frames. The forces at play to do that had probably exerted a serious effect on the engines' alignments, and if that had happened, then it could have meant whiplash damage to the propeller shafts, so that either or both might be out of alignment, too. He would only know after they'd fired the engines back up.

Then there were the main shaft stern glands; both had started to open under the pummelling, allowing tons of seawater into the boat. The glands' packing effectively sealed both propeller shafts where they went out through the pressure hull, and they were all that stood between the sea and engine room. Kershaw reported that he'd put a team on tightening and securing them, but they would need to be loosed again before *Saraband* could start either engine or motor, to prevent over-heating on both the shafts and glands. And when they did start up, Bert Kershaw said he couldn't answer as to whether the glands' packing would still hold the water out, or fail completely.

Then there was the question of why Bill Laurie had suddenly lost the trim. It hadn't just been because of all the tons of seawater they had shipped aft, or the tele-motor pumps getting knocked out and feed lines between the trim tanks rupturing. While stripping out bent piping, one of the stokers had discovered the aft dive planes were more than 12 degrees out of phase with the main plane indicator. The sheer pressure from one of the blasts must have bent the entire mechanism, so what Terry Newbold, the 2nd cox'n, had been reading on his dials had borne no resemblance to the angles his aft planes were actually at. The warrant engineer reckoned they could manage to batter the planes back into a semblance of synchronisation, but they'd only find out if it had worked when they turned the system on again.

A litany of lesser catastrophes followed, until Harry wasn't really taking it all in any more.

It was the Japs who snapped him back to attention.

Rah-bumm-duhdumm-dumm-dumm!

Both men looked up. Depth charges, but a long, long way away. The patterns went on for what must have been two or three minutes.

'They must think we're out there, still trying to run away,' said Harry.

The warrant engineer scrunched his eyes, sucked in a laboured breath, and started again. 'As I was saying, sir, the temperature in the engine room is now over eighty nine degrees Fahrenheit ... because we shut off all the coolant circuits when we dived and went right to silent running ... the freshwater cooling system is now practically boiling. I'm going to start spelling some of my lads before they conk out with heat exhaustion. And talking of water, just to let you know ... the ready use drinking water tank is almost exhausted. We'd need to pressurise the main water tank to blow any refill back across, but that's going to cause a racket. So I take it we're just going to have to go thirsty ... sir.'

'I'd say it might sound like Johnny Jap is far enough away for us to risk it, Mr Kershaw,' said Harry. '*But* ... I don't know if he's left anybody hanging around upstairs, waiting to see if we really are still here and about to break cover. So yes, we're going to have to go thirsty for just a bit longer.'

Saraband sat on the bottom; to any passing fish, a dead carcass. Unless the fish got too close, and heard the vague scufflings and thuds of her crew as they went about patching up their boat through the long night. Teams patching pipes and cables; others measuring and sawing through the charging lead, while others sat soldering makeshift connectors onto each end of the cut lengths. And all the while the air grew hotter and more fetid, and this time, the carbon dioxide levels *did* start to climb.

No-one felt like food, so the galley remained shut and Jimmy Scobie, the cook, helped sweep up all the broken glass with a hand brush and pan. Harry picked his way through the boat, stern to bow, talking with all his crew, telling them that once all the repairs were done, they'd be having another shot at making a run for it. 'Last man back to Trinco is a big girl's blouse,' he'd say, and it usually got a grin. Only one or two asked what would happen if the Japs came back. 'Meek's got a rod with one end stuck to the pressure hull and the other in his ear, listening for them,' he replied. 'If they do, I'm thinking about firing McTeer out a torpedo tube to go and offer them a square go. I'd warn them he's from Glasgow first, of course … just to keep it fair.' That got a grin, too.

The line about Meek and his rod was true. It did work, after a fashion; you could hear a passing ship quite clearly if it was close enough. No bearing, of course. An hour into the afternoon watch on the following day, Meek's voice echoed down the passage to where Harry was lying on his bunk, eyes shut to stop the sweat stinging them, thinking how his tongue felt like a dead husk in his cracked mouth.

'Captain to the Asdic room.'

Harry levered himself up through the viscous air, and crept aft through the control room.

'I've got HE, sir,' said Meek. 'Somebody's up there, moving about. No idea what bearing, or what it is, but it's getting closer, slowly … sorry, it's just the rod I've got, sir,' making his excuses for lack of anything more, and brandishing the said device impotently. 'Best I can tell you.'

'Thanks, Meek,' said Harry. 'Good job with your rod … which I'm sure is what all the girls say.'

Meek went from glum to giggling. And was that a blush? Harry went out into the passage and started stooping to whisper to anyone he encountered, 'Pass the word … there's somebody upstairs … total silence in the boat.'

The sounds came past, never close enough to hear in the boat without a rod, then faded.

Later, the sound came back again, then seemed to stop.

At about what would have been time for the watch change at the end of the first dog, Kershaw came stumbling from aft. The first Harry knew was when he saw the spindly legs go past his bunk, to sit at the wardroom table. He got up and joined him.

'That's us,' said Kershaw, using his bandana to mop his greasy face. 'She's as good as I can make her here. Engine room's ready when you are, sir.'

'Well, it'll be getting dark soon, upstairs,' said Harry. 'But wait, before you head back aft, Mr Kershaw. I need a word …'

He passed the word for Number One, and for Caudrey too, in his capacity as guns 'n' torps.

The four of them sat round the wardroom table, brows furrowed, each one exuding all the energy of wet face flannels. Only Kershaw wore his cap.

'We're going up in ten minutes for a shufti,' said Harry. 'There might be a Jap in the vicinity. If there is, we're going to fight it out with him. On the surface. Deck gun and Oerlikon. Tommy guns from the armoury too, if we get close enough. Torpedoes, if I can get our bows round fast enough. So I want everybody closed up and ready to go. We've all heard the stories about what happens if you surrender to the Japs, so I don't need to say any more on the matter. I want you to explain all that to the crew. Understood?'

Everybody understood; nodding 'Aye, aye, sir'.

'Carry on.'

*

Harry was back in the control room, *Saraband* closed up and ready to surface; everybody at their diving stations. There should still be enough light on the surface for a good all-round look. Harry wondered what the weather was like. Stupid question for this time of year; hot, cloudy and humid as hell.

Harry stood in the control room with the sound-powered telephone pressed to his ear. 'Engine room, captain. Righty-ho Mr Kershaw, close your breakers. Let's get some power in the motor circuits and get ready to go … Number One, stand by to blow all main ballast, let's get her out the mud … Surface!'

Harry looked forward and saw all the faces of the gun crew, and the shell handlers pressed under the gun tower hatch. The noise of the vents

167

blowing was loud in the boat. If a Jap was up there with ears in the water, he'd be hearing them now alright.

There was a jolt, and it was obvious they were free floating again.

'Full up on the bow planes, Cox'n,' said Harry, 'group down, half ahead together.'

Mr Kershaw listened hard for any whine on his shafts; he had a man with his hands on the shaft glands too, feeling for them heating up. They had tightened and loosened engine bolts in a bid to fine tune the engine alignments, and loosed the tension on the gland packing. No water was coming in yet, and the heat from the glands wasn't building too fast.

Saraband was moving. There were creaks, groans from the hull.

'Thirty-five feet,' called Number One.

Three feet to go. Harry said, 'stop together', stepped forward and ordered the search periscope up, opening the handles as it rose.

'Thirty-two feet.'

'Keep periscope depth,' he said, then pressed his eyes to the lenses … nothing. Just what looked like clouds. He knew what it was instantly; the search periscope had flooded.

'Down 'scope!' he said, stepping back. 'Get the attack 'scope up!'

The big 'scope slid down as the attack 'scope rose. Harry got his eye on the smaller 'scope's lens, followed it up, and saw it break surface on a glum day with a sea as fluid as mercury. With all the way coming off *Saraband*, there was no periscope feather. Harry's all-round look was swift. He was aware there might be that bloody haze on the water again, masking even something close by, so he scanned high in case there might be a mast top. But there was nothing.

Then, two things caught his eye, moving fast from the corner of his vision, dark objects that had suddenly broken the surface, disturbingly close. His breath stopped, then he released it and began laughing in a way that un-nerved the control room.

'Dolphins,' he said eventually, not taking his eye off the lens. 'Two dolphins … now bugger off before you get the fright of your lives! Surface!'

And up they went, into a beautiful Malacca Strait sunset.

Thirteen

In the normal run of events, all Vernon Carmody should have had to do was report back to London that their missing person was here in Lisbon. *Captain Charles Bonalleck RN, currently a.k.a Charles Chaplin, Master Mariner, Elder Dempster Line rtd… . now residing at … blah, blah.*

And his job would have been done. One more missing person found. He'd have been quite happy – nay, more than happy – to let someone else worry about what to do next.

In the normal run of events.

But he now knew that this RN captain they were looking for, *a.k.a Charles Chaplin, Master Mariner, Elder Dempster Line rtd.* had been receiving Kapitän zur See Paul Trott und Boedicker, the German naval attaché, and that had changed everything.

Carmody was a spy, not a policeman. The 'why?' and the 'what did it all mean?' were always more important to him than the mere 'who, what, where?' that your ordinary copper needed to know.

What Carmody had needed to know now was – more.

To achieve that end, he had just the device; something called a Poulsen magnetic wire recorder, from the American Telegraphone Company of Springfield, Massachusetts.

His local foot-soldier schoolboy had smoothed the way for the tradesman Carmody usually used, to enter the building where Captain Bonalleck lived and 'fix' the electrics. A respectable purse of escudos for the concierge had allowed that to happen, and essentially all the tradesman had to do was put the device in a broom cupboard and run a wire from it to the ceiling light fitting in Charlie Chaplin's living room. When Charlie went out, the concierge let the tradesman in, in return for another purse, and the tradesman twined a wire around the light flex and dropped a sound-powered microphone down into the lamp-holder.

Carmody had had the whole set-up put together by some refugee from the Spanish civil war, who knew about these things but whose circumstances in Lisbon were now much reduced. It never ceased to amaze Carmody what otherwise respectable people were prepared to do for money, if they had to.

This way, he was going to be the proverbial fly on the wall every time the German naval attaché and Stroessner came to call.

There was however, one drawback to the telegraphone device. To get just one hour of recorded conversation required more than 7,000 feet of wire. The fact that the magnetic wire was only a thin 37 gauge steel filament, or 0.004 of an inch, made it easier; but that was still a lot of wire for the machine to hold. And an hour meant you really had to target your conversations.

The schoolboy of course had had the answer to that too; he had his own little gang keep the flat under their beady eyes from the time Charlie Chaplin got up until he went to bed, and if anyone showed up who resembled the little Box-Brownie cameos of the Hun attaché or the half-chat flunky that Carmody had snapped earlier, the gang members immediately sneaked into the building and upstairs to the broom cupboard and switched on the telegraphone. It was a set-up that always ran smoothly on account of yet another purse finding its way to the concierge.

As a result, Carmody now had in his possession a considerable mileage of 37 gauge steel filament, and it hadn't made cheery listening.

'Essentially,' Carmody was now explaining to the British embassy's deputy head of mission, 'your Captain Bonalleck, né Chaplin, is negotiating to sell to the German naval attaché specific details of the operation and conduct of the Allied convoy system in the central and north Atlantic. Does he know he is selling it to the Germans? No. He thinks his customers are the Brazilian navy. Should such a nicety concern us? No, it bloody well shouldn't! The man's a spy. And all we need to do now is decide what we're going to do to him.'

'A bad business indeed,' said the deputy head of mission, a bland man in a morning suit, with too much pomade for this early in the day. 'But whatever it is we decide, it cannot involve upsetting the Portuguese government. You do understand that, Mr Carmody?'

'Ah, Mr Whittam, I think I can say with some certainty that "we" will not be doing the deciding,' said Carmody. Left to him, he knew exactly what he would do … get this rogue captain to feed Jerry a parcel of bollocks, then throw him under a bus. But then the higher up you went with these matters, the more due process ended up getting in the way. He often thought there was something to be said for totalitarian dictatorships … only in some departments, of course.

*

The Bonny Boy was mulling things over, sitting in his *apartamento* with the lights out, in an easy chair, smoking a Cuban cigar. Matters had begun most promisingly with *Senhor* Miller; the cabin he had funded for him from Casablanca to Lisbon had been most comfortable for a ship that was definitely not a trans-Atlantic Cunarder; the 'temporary' *apartamento* was adequate, the flash dago had even managed to track down a typewriter for him, with an English language keyboard.

He liked the idea he could type for himself, didn't have to rely on others. Admittedly, he was never going to be a touch typist. No. He was a strictly a two-fingered man, and truth be told, not all that good even then. But he'd started doing his own typing a long time ago. He learned early in the navy what all those ratty-faced PO Writers were up to – running off to tell everybody what you were putting in your reports.

Just as well he did, since he needed those typewriting skills now more than ever. No giving dictation to some stranger. Nobody was going to tamper. The deal was that he would write them a convoy manual, and in return … well, they had promised him the world. After all, he was going to save the Brazilian navy, the Marinha do Brasil, a lot of face as a result. No more Yanks telling them what to do all the time.

So, he expected them to be true to their word, because he was going to demand his pound of flesh this time. All his life, the little people; the lesser people, had been filching his just desserts – belittling his skills and

171

achievements; inserting themselves between him and the recognition he deserved, and taking all the credit that was rightfully his.

Well, all that was stopping here and now.

He'd decide exactly what the Marinha do Brasil were going to get out of him, and when. And that would only be after the goodies started coming his way.

Except *Senhor* Miller, and now this capitão de mar e guerra of the Marinha do Brasil … all these bloody dago names … what did he call himself? The top dago? Capral? Anyway, it seemed to him they were both back-sliding these days. Suddenly, straight answers were becoming few and far between. And where was his invitation to the Brazilian embassy? If he was going to be coughing up so much for the buggers, the least they could do was give him a reception!

But when he thought a bit more about that, then maybe not a reception. It could attract too much attention. He could see the argument that the dagoes wouldn't want it to get out where they'd got all their expertise from so fast. And it would be bad for him too. Of course it would. The last thing his new persona needed was to be recognised as his old one. So, alright, he'd pass on demanding a reception. But surely a meeting with the ambassador. A quiet glad hand for all his good work. Some kind of offical headed vellum, setting out in print all the lovely lolly they were going to shower on him.

Because there was going to have to be cash *before* delivery from now on. No loot, no deal.

And he was expecting other displays of gratitude. For example, what options were they going to present him with, regarding his future? Did he want to live in Brazil? It was an awfully long way away, and anyway, here, Portugal; it was growing on him. Maybe a nice villa by the sea could form part of the package? With a servant or two? They said they were going to be generous, after all. Well, let's see it, *Senhor*! Otherwise no manual. It's either pay up or go a-begging to the gringoes again, *Senhor*!

He'd sort 'em! He'd fix ' em! For a start, this easy chair he was sitting it wasn't even his own easy chair. It was the *apartamento's* … the rented *apartamento's*. A man should have his own easy chair. And he was going to have his own damned easy chair!

Fourteen

Down in Columbo, the south west monsoon had broken, deluging the place in rain and humidity. It was all over the radio, as if it had come as a total surprise rather than being the same thing, something that happened every year. Up here in Kandy, however, it was in the high 70s Fahrenheit, and sunny, so Harry continued to be pleased that *Saraband* hadn't had to go all the way down to Columbo for her drydocking.

He was walking from the Fraters' bungalow to the hospital, dressed in civvies; a pair of cream linen bags, a white cotton shirt and pair of tennis shoes, and a panama hat borrowed from Colin. He was also carrying a knapsack with a US Army poncho in it; it might be dry now, but by 3.30 this afternoon, the daily downpour could be expected. Harry still hadn't got over it, how you could practically set your watch by the cloudbursts during monsoon.

The city was 1,600 feet up on a plateau in the island's central province, nestled in a series of wooded hills around an artificial lake, with British colonial houses mingling with architecture dating back to the 15th century and an earlier pre-colonial kingdom.

Dr Cotterell had taken him round the city on his last leave. To the Temple of the Tooth, the island's holiest Buddhist site, which was said to hold one of the deity's actual teeth; to the sprawling, 17th century royal palace, and through the warren of old town streets to dine on a meal collected from all of the different food stalls and eaten at a communal wooden bench under a giant peepal tree.

He had been trying not to think too much about her during their transit back from patrol, knowing he intended to come back up here for his leave anyway, telling himself it was also for the clear air, and the beauty of the place, and the Fraters' company. But there had been a note from her awaiting him when he got to the Fraters' last night; she'd asked them when he was expected back again, apparently, and they had told her. 'Come and see me tomorrow,' the note said. 'I need to talk to you.'

As he strode in from Randles Hill, he was not letting himself get excited. *Saraband* wasn't in as bad a shape as he and Mr Kershaw had first feared. No significant hull damage and the diesels themselves were intact. The floating dry dock at Trinco could handle all the pipe work, shaft and engine re-alignments, the gland packing and the battery cell replacements. And the periscope shop on *Adamant* was seeing to their main search 'scope.

Also, the post-patrol debrief with old Tinsides hadn't been as strained as he had feared. They had missed that damn U-boat. But apparently, bagging the transport was a real feather in *Saraband*'s cap.

'She's been carrying 'Oscars' up to Langkawi,' Captain Ionides had told him. 'Oscars' being the Allied code name for the Jap Army Air Corps' Nakajima Ki 43 single-engine fighters. 'They've been trying to strengthen their air defences up around there … not any more! Hah! Hah!' And then he had topped up his gin. 'The C-in-C is very pleased with you, Mr Gilmour,' Captain Ionides added. 'Very pleased indeed.'

Harry hadn't needed to ask why C-in-C Fleet was so concerned about a gaggle of pop-gun fighters; coming into Trincomalee anchorage that morning there had been two more huge fleet carriers there, which had not been there before. *Indomitable* and *Victorious*, it turned out. Land-based fighters would be a threat to their air groups.

He'd also had had a very good chat with Bill Laurie before everyone buggered off for their lie-down.

They had sat on the *Wu Chang's* top deck, tucked away in a corner at a table under one of the lifeboats. 'I want to put quite a few of them up for promotions,' he had said, which was partially true. Really he wanted to hear what Bill had to say about his dirty stinker of a plan to hold some of the crew back; because they had performed so well after that bloody awful depth charging, and he needed them. Bill knew what his skipper was up to even before he told him.

'I think that is a pretty rotten scheme, sir,' he had said, swirling his pink gin like dental wash. 'On the face of it. But …'

'It all came together out there, Number One,' Harry interrupted. 'Don't tell me you didn't notice. I know you did. They stopped being …' Harry found himself lost for all the disparaging epithets he had wanted to say, to describe his crew – or rather, the crew they used to be. Instead, what he said was, 'That kicking we got out there, they're a proper crew now. They know they can take it. They know just how bloody marvellously they performed, and …'

'… and they're full of it, sir,' Bill had interrupted, in return, smiling. 'So right up themselves, you can hardly see their boot soles. And it'd be a shame to break it up.'

'Precisely,' Harry had said, smiling back.

'They wouldn't thank you, if you did,' Bill commented, his grin now even broader.

'I don't know. McTeer might put a scorpion in my underwear drawer if he suspected,' said Harry, agreeing none the less.

So he was really looking forward to his leave. And to what Victoria Cotterell might have planned for him next.

Victoria wasn't in civvies. No light summer dress, waiting to stroll on his arm down the avenues. She was in scrubs and a surgeon's cap, undone, was perched on the back of her head so you could see how tightly her hair was tied back. She looked like she'd been being all bustly a moment ago, but was perfectly calm now, ready to receive him in a corridor between wards.

The hospital was bright and busy. She lightly grasped his baggy shirt front, and said, 'Come with me, I want to introduce you to someone.'

No 'Hello, Harry!' or 'How have you been?'

The next thing Harry knew, they were striding purposefully down the corridor to French windows, flung open at the far end. 'That story you told me about the Italian pilot you knew …' she was saying as she walked.

'Fabrizio?' said Harry. He had been interned with him in neutral Spain, early in the war. Fabrizio crash landing after attempting to shoot up a British battlecruiser in his single-engine Macchi fighter, and Harry there after being washed off the deck of a diving submarine.

'Yes, your Fabrizio,' she said, turning to give a smile. 'He sounded like a classic tale of survivors' guilt … and you talked him down off the ledge, so to speak. I remember thinking what a nice man you were. And I think I might have another one for you to work your magic on.'

This wasn't what Harry had been envisaging at all.

They stepped out into the sunshine. The lawn was dotted with pyjama-clad servicemen in various stages of recovery, some lounging in deckchairs and a couple in wheelchairs. It was one of those scenes you didn't want to be in, as a fit and healthy man, to be walking through intact; there but for the grace of God, and all that … Knowing your presence was a reminder to every one of them, looking at you – because they *were* all looking at him.

At the far end of the lawn, by a low hedge, a young man sat in a loose-fitting dressing gown. The thing Harry would most remember him for was the mop of blonde curls; like tow, really. A bit too long for Army regs. Or anybody's regs. That and the thousand-mile stare.

'This is Lance Corporal Bain, of the Royal Marines,' said Victoria, inter-rupting the stare.

Bain was more boy than young man; you could tell he was gangly from the way his legs splayed, and a boy from the total blandness of his unformed gaze. A thin smile, not reflected in the eyes. All Harry saw there was an utter lack of curiosity.

'Hullo,' said the boy. He didn't hold out a hand or even make to stand up. Harry wasn't in uniform so the question of a military response didn't arise. He didn't know it then, but even if he had been an admiral in full sail, Bain would not have reacted any differently.

After an exchange of pointless niceties, Victoria led Harry away. As they walked, she talked, mostly looking at her feet as she did so.

'He came here a couple of months ago,' she said. 'I didn't have anything to do with him initially. None of his wounds required surgery … mostly blast effects, detached retinas, a bit of hearing loss, some light shrapnel. The physical stuff healed quick enough, apparently. It was when he … I don't know … failed to return to the normal world … that they got me involved. The grande damme of the hospital. There was a push to just RTU him anyway,' she said shaking her head at man's … Stupidity? Inhumanity?

176

RTU meant returned to unit – at least Harry got that bit.

'But that was out of the question. He couldn't, wouldn't even dress himself,' she was saying as she stood aside to let him go back inside the hospital.

When they got to her office – she had an office, Harry noted, impressed – she said, 'There's a bit of an escarpment behind the hospital. The hill just drops away to a road. It's not much, but the drop, it's over sixty feet … which is a killing height. He's never talked about doing away with himself, or shown any inclination in that direction, so we let him go, because he goes there most evenings just to watch the sunset and it seems to calm him. He just sits there, smiling.'

She considered Harry for a long moment, then said, 'Do you think while you're here, you could go out there and just talk to him … about anything. The weather … how Mr Churchill isn't going to win the general election?'

'Isn't he?' asked Harry.

'Churchill? Good God, no. Not if the soldiers out here have anything to do with it. And they've all got a forces' vote. You haven't answered my question. Please don't say no. If you say yes, I'll let you take me out to dinner tonight, and this time it can be a date, if you like.'

This was all very strange for Dr Cotterell.

Kandy, since April, had become the headquarters of South East Asia Command, which ran the war against Japan, from Burma to south west China, Malaya to northern Indonesia. Everybody who was anybody out here, from Mountbatten downwards, was in Kandy; the town was the biggest concentration of Allied top brass east of Suez, British and Empire to the good old US of A. And there was no end of potential suitors for a woman, even if she was of a certain age, and especially one who brushed up as coolly and elegantly as Victoria Cotterell did.

And what a pain in the arse they all were, she had decided. Most of them were married, especially the ones who said, 'ah-hah! But dontcha know, east of Gibraltar every man's a bachelor,' and then thought themselves terribly witty.

There had not been a man in Victoria's life for some time now, and she'd decided she wasn't going to sully any memories by letting anyone here break her duck. Until Harry Gilmour had come along and spoiled everything. What age was he? Ten years younger? Less than that? But enough for the whole idea to be ridiculous. A bloody boy! Why wouldn't he just leave her alone? The fact that she really didn't want him to leave her alone, was neither here nor there.

Harry went along that evening to the escarpment, and there was L/Cpl Bain, sitting with the setting sun bathing his bland, boyish face. He couldn't remember what they'd talked about afterwards. Drivel mostly, as Harry did the talking.

When he returned to the hospital Victoria was waiting for him, looking … gorgeous.

'So, what did you say to him?' she asked over dinner in one of the town's smarter hotels; referring of course, to Bain.

'I commented on how nice the sunset was,' said Harry. 'I certainly didn't ask him about home. It's not something we … well, you know … it just makes being wherever we are, harder … talking about home. I asked him what his plans were. That got an answer. "Oh, that's nothing to do with me", he said, which is all too true. It wasn't that he didn't want to talk … he just didn't.'

'It's as if he's down a hole, and won't … can't … come out,' she said, all pensive. And then all of a sudden, her mood lightened and poor L/Cpl Bain was forgotten and their evening really took off.

While he walked her home, however, she asked him, 'You will go and chat to him tomorrow again, won't you?'

Fifteen

It was Able Seaman Tully, McTeer's number two on the radar, that called up the fix on Kabosa Island, right where Gowers' had said it would be. Not that Harry could see anything from the bridge, it being two hours to sunrise, not to mention the monotonous, visibility-crushing downpour that had been engulfing them for the entire night.

The five-day transit from Trinco to the Mergui Archipelago had been one long buffeting by the monsoon weather, with *Saraband* continuously dogged by a long, endless, Bay of Bengal swell, interspersed by a daisy chain of sharp squalls. There had been no smokos on the casing this trip, and the bird bath had been a permanent fixture beneath the conning tower hatch.

The rain however, was warm, and Harry had allowed all watchkeepers, if they reported five minutes early, to bring a bar of soap up and bask in a free shower without wasting a drop of their own precious fresh water supply. And the crew had passed the time with two more bouts in the Uckers league; all spoils to the winning division delayed until their return to Trinco. Caudrey, to the dismay of everyone but himself and his division, had once again demonstrated that he was the boy to beat. And Harry had to live with the fact that he really was the worst Uckers player aboard, if not in the entire Eastern Fleet.

Saraband dived just before the sun showed itself and they crept round the top of Iron Island with the intention of lurking in the middle of the north-south channel for whatever might turn up.

For three days, nothing.

Three days at periscope depth, sweating standing up, sweating lying down, sweat running into your eyes, from your armpits, down your sides, off the end of your nose, your crotch a swamp. And if you were on the dive board, you were showing everyone else how to really sweat, with the constant touching and adjusting to keep the trim against a relentless swell that you could feel even at 32 feet, the depth between hill and trough amplified by the shallowness of the seas beneath them.

Cdr. Clarke had briefed Harry before they sailed as to why they were given this billet in the island chain that garlanded the narrow isthmus at the top of the Malay Peninsula. Things weren't going too well for the Japanese army up on the Indian border, and with all the subs now operating out of Trinco – while Harry had been on leave, *Maidstone* had arrived with another flotilla – they weren't going too well for the Japanese navy down here, either. Yet the Japanese still desperately needed military materiel moved north in quantity and in a hurry.

'Big transports are providing too easy targets for our boats, so now they're requisitioning all the large junks and small coasters the length of Malaya and are trying to sneak them inshore through all the islands. They've decided small, and more, is better,' Clarke told him. So he had better pack more gun ammunition.

Finding this new armada of enemy transports however, was proving very difficult. You could see bugger all in the rain and mist. Visibility was seldom over three miles. The rain was also interfering with their radar, causing all sorts of clutter the harder it fell. This was monsoon season, after all. Then there was the fact that hundreds of little islets and rocky outcrops littered the channels and patches of open water; and all the bigger islands were all steep-sided and jungled. Ideal for radar reflection.

Then, Cox'n Garbutt had his first cases of prickly heat; the red, bumpy rash that appears when your pores get blocked and the sweat leaks in below the skin … and drives you mad with itching. Cox'ns being traditionally designated the sick-bay attendants in the Trade, it was down to him to treat them, so out came the calamine lotion bottle. Harry, if he was in the wardroom, could hear Garbutt's consultations from the petty officers' mess.

'If you think I'm puttin' my hands anywhere near that … Ya can slap it on yerself, son, and do it here where I can see ye. I'm no' having' ye scandalising the rest of crew with any unnatural practices!'

Twice *Saraband* had tried to see into Port Owen, the harbour on the east side of Tavoy Island, to see if any junks had made it past them and were tucked into the anchorage there; and twice bad visibility had thwarted them. Then, just over an hour into the forenoon watch on the fourth day …

'Captain to the control room!'

They were at periscope depth, a mile or so off the eastern approach to Iron Passage.

Harry took over the 'scope from Verrell, the watch officer. Verrell said, 'I can't make her out, sir. I thought it was one of those islets. But when I checked the chart, there shouldn't have been one there, and when I looked back, the islet wasn't there either … it'd moved …'

Harry couldn't make the target out either, at first; was about to send the 'scope down because he'd had it up too long … and that was when he saw the shape of a tumble-home stern amidst all foliage, and the churn of a single screw on the surface of the choppy water.

Foliage.

It was some kind of small transport, covered in tree branches; like they were woven into the hull, right down to the water line. Obviously, a new trick to make the tub disappear against the backdrop of the islands. She was fast approaching their port beam, maybe 1,000 yards off, going the other way. He called the bearing, and then checked for the range. Nine hundred and twenty yards. Not bad for a simple visual guess, he congratulated himself; getting blasé because he could make her out now behind the camouflage. A coaster, well over 300 tons, steel-hulled with a bridge and smokestack aft. Borderline as to whether she was worth a torpedo, but worth sinking.

'Port thirty,' he called, bringing *Saraband* round so she would start to run parallel to the target's course, 700 yards off her port quarter.

'Stand by for gun action,' he called, and sent the 'scope down, checking his watch. A stampede erupted behind him. Deck plates were lifted in the for'ard passage just at the wardroom, opening one of the magazines *Saraband* had added for extra 3-inch shells; the lower hatches on the conning tower, and the gun tower, just above the wardroom, were opened and the gun crew and ammunition handlers jumped into place.

'Gun crew and magazine handlers standing by, sir,' said Verrell.

'Number One, take us up.' He paused while Bill Laurie got them going, then issued the orders, 'Surface! Gun action! Target is a coaster bearing red three zero, range seven hundred … initial aiming point is the wheelhouse, aft.'

Harry heard the main ballast blowing, and when he looked for'ard he could see the cox'n's hands holding down the forward hydroplanes on 'hard a'dive', holding the boat down against her blowing tanks and increasing buoyancy.

He ordered, 'Up periscope.'

The 'surface; gun action' drill he had taught them was working like a ballet, and he wanted to see it all, as it happened. *Hold her until you can barely hold her no more …* he had told them. '*… then reverse the planes … hard up … and we shoot up like a cork. One minute, a flat un-threatening sea, the next, there's Saraband, blazing away at you.*'

Harry felt the planes reverse. He turned the periscope back onto the target's bearing. She was tootling along at eight knots, no more, about 30 degrees off their port bow now – perfect for a shoot. If he turned the 'scope a nudge he could see *Saraband*'s bows break surface.

'Fifteen feet,' called Number One. The gun tower wasn't yet clear, but it and the conning tower hatches were thrown open, water tumbled down as the gun crew went up in a rush, shells following them. Harry had to wait until the gunners had cleared the conning tower. Then he sent the 'scope back down again and ran up after them.

'Bang!'

The first round was on the way before he'd got his eyes over the bridge front. Like he'd said; a ballet.

Their first round blew the wheelhouse to matchwood. And the world celebrated with the rain suddenly ceasing, as though someone had turned off a celestial spigot. Yet the coaster kept on motoring along, course unchanged. So Caudrey changed target, from the deck to the waterline below what was left of the wheelhouse, where the engine room would be, and to the rudder. Half a dozen more rounds went into the coaster's hull. She juddered with every detonation. Then she slewed, and all the way came off her. Harry ordered 'check fire,' stepped to the voice pipe and began ordering *Saraband* round with the intention of boarding her and finishing her off with a few demolition charges. Up until now the coaster had been like the *Marie Celeste*, with not a single crewman visible. However, as she started to settle by the stern a sudden rush of bodies appeared on deck; three Japs and the rest Malay. They all immediately dived overboard; the shore was only a couple of hundred yards off.

Harry ordered *Saraband* round again at slow ahead together, this time to head them off.

'If you can bring back a couple of prisoners,' Cdr. Clarke had told him, 'it'd be much appreciated. But don't endanger your boat getting them.'

Harry took a good look around. Below, McTeer was searching the skies with his radar. *Saraband* wasn't in any danger right now. Harry ordered Verrell onto the casing with two of *Verrell's Raiders* armed with tommy guns. Back before they had sailed, and after Harry had been advised of his mission, he had officially appointed Sub-Lt. Verrell as *Saraband's* new Boarding Officer. If they were going to be operating inshore against junks, there would be times when it was easier to board them and sink them with charges, rather than waste shells. So Verrell had been given the job of selecting and training up a suitable band of known hooligans to be his boarding party. Not surprisingly, the next edition of *The Bugle* had a cartoon of Verrell trying on eye-patches before a movie poster for a new blockbuster – *Verrell's Raiders*. The name had stuck, and boy, was young Toby proud of it!

The first Jap they approached was striking out powerfully for the shore, another was a few yards ahead. Both were going in a straight line. The Malays, Harry noticed, were all swimming at an angle; well, nearly all of them.

One of Verrell's men was now standing on a deployed bow plane, holding a boat hook. Number One, who was on the bridge, was calling their approach down the voice pipe to Poulter on the helm in the control room.

The first Jap broke stroke and rolled onto his back. All they saw bobbing on the surface was a fine-boned skull, hair cropped tight, and fresh, clean-shaven face. When the Jap saw how close they were, and that he was facing imminent capture, the face set with a grimace of utter hatred. Harry watched as he suddenly kicked himself shoulder clear of the water and then just let himself sink. Gone. Straight down. *Saraband* was so close, Harry could even see the bubbles coming up from where he had disappeared.

'Well, fuck me!' Harry heard the rating on the bow plane exclaim, as he looked back at Harry on the bridge with an expression of astonishment.

The incident had so distracted all of them from what was going on a few dozen yards off to their right that nobody noticed a group of Malays had caught up with the other Jap. When Harry looked up, they had just fallen upon him. Harry, and then slowly, everybody else on deck and on the bridge, turned to watch the slow motion tableau unfold. Four of them systematically swam around until they'd each got a firm hold on the Jap, and when they had, they calmly, and with minimal fuss and froth, proceeded to drown him.

All the while, treading water on the edge of this execution, several other Malays were waving and grinning at the British submarine, their message clear. 'The beach is just a stone's throw away, it's okay, we've got this, we don't want to be rescued. We're going home.'

Suddenly Verrell shouted, 'Sir!' And was pointing aft. When Harry looked, there, in the water, was a figure, trying to swim, but unable to do so. Harry ordered, 'Slow astern, together,' and *Saraband* backed towards him. They crept up until the figure was practically rolling against the port saddle tanks. Verrell's team sprinted back past the conning tower. One of them anchored himself on the casing and gripped another rating's arm, allowing him to step down onto the curve of the tank, bend over and roughly pluck the figure from the water.

It was the third Jap they had seen emerge onto the coaster's deck, and his shoulder was obviously dislocated. He also looked to have flash burns to his other shoulder and upper arm, and the back of his head appeared scorched and crusted.

Looking at the wretched figure, who was obviously dazed and with no struggle left in him, Harry observed to his Number One, 'Oh dear, the cox'n will be pleased.'

Bill Laurie laughed, trying to imagine the expression on Cox'n Garbutt's face when he learned that he was going to have to nurse a wounded Jap. It wasn't going to be a smile. Still, they had their prisoner.

*

The rain had started again, but that was good. It was coming down in sheets, like a shimmering gauze, from clouds so low they had created a grey twilight in the late afternoon. Nothing better to cloak *Saraband's* approach into the shallows of the Port Owen anchorage.

The break in the monsoon after they had sunk the coaster gave Harry this idea. Port Owen on Tavoy Island wasn't a port as such, more like a lay-by for passing convoys, where they could nip in, top up their fuel from the small base and settlement there, or hide behind the shallows and the islands at its entrance for the night. The island was, after all, right at the top of the archipelago and a natural crossroads for north–south shipping.

And *Saraband's* crew was so binged up and raring to go, Harry had thought now was the time. He had risked the sprint north on the surface; the weather was so bad not even a suicidal Jap would be up in an aircraft, and the visibility so broken that as long as they kept trimmed down he was sure he would see any surface contacts before they saw him. When they reached the sound between Tavoy and the mainland, *Saraband* dived and they had snuck in for a peep through the periscope. He was glad he'd made the effort.

They were right on the line for safe diving when he sent the search periscope up and the first thing he had seen was a large junk and what looked like some kind of armed motor launch, coming down the channel between Tavoy's off-shore islets and the island proper, heading into the natural bay of the main harbour. The chop on the surface was so messy, he had risked keeping the 'scope up for an all-round look. Nothing to seaward, but when he'd circled the 'scope back to look into Port Owen proper, it had been a treat to behold. A strange looking transport, more like a mini liner, but he'd estimated no more than 800 tons. Big enough to merit a torpedo. Then another coastal steamer, old, with her natural draught smokestack towering aft, and two more substantial junks of 200 or 300 tons each. All heavy laden. All anchored, fore and aft, tucked in for the night.

Even on this cursory glance however, he knew that if he was to get in amongst them, he'd have to go in on the surface. But then, he had studied the charts before they'd sailed from Trinco; the pre-war Admiralty charts for the archipelago when Malaya was still very much British empire. So he knew once he'd crossed the line he was creeping along now, he could forget any option to dive. He was barely going to have enough water under his keel going in with tanks fully blown as it was.

He had then sent the periscope down, and painted a picture of what he'd just seen to the control room. They'd been abeam Clyde Point at the entrance to the bay, with the islets north of them. He was unable to see if there was any more shipping lying round the eastern lip of the bay, escorts, for example.

That was the risk.

He had decided that if he was to take them in, he would need to circle north of the islets and come down the main channel. The water was deeper there, and he could get closer in submerged; he'd also be able to see into the blind side of the bay.

He had been thinking aloud, and knew they were hanging on his every word. Bill Laurie had been smiling, guardedly, to himself; Harry had seen it from the corner of his eye, had known Bill was feeling the mood in the control room too; that they were raring to go. A load more loud bangs before bedtime – nothing better to take your mind off the rain and the sweat.

He had a brief conversation on the sound-powered telephone with Jowett, the torpedo gunner's mate; tubes one and four to readiness, he'd said, torpedo settings the shallowest they'd take.

And now they were in the channel with the islets off their port beam, creeping down it at periscope depth, periscope up. That was how Harry knew the rain was on again. There was less than a few feet between keel and seabed at this depth, and Gowers, reading the echo-sounder, told him the water was getting shallower with every ping.

Caudrey already had his gun crew under the gun tower hatch and the Oerlikon men queued up in the passageway waiting to go up the conning tower.

'Stand by for gun action,' said Harry, his order now superfluous; the crews were already champing at the bit. 'Surface!'

And up they went, hatches flung open, dollops of sea coming down as the crews ran up each tower. Harry was right behind them.

He burst into a world of grey; the rain-dappled sea, the air thick with rain, the insipid light despite the time of day, and a strange sight on the casing. Harry had already briefed Number One that when they came up, he was to keep *Saraband* trimmed low in the water – and they were. What he hadn't anticipated was the effect; each thick rain drop hitting the casing exploded, causing a mist to form so that every man on the gun team, pale wraiths in shorts and singlets and most with caps jammed on to keep the rain out of their eyes, looked to be wading on some sub-surface plinth. He stood mesmerised for a moment, before he heard Caudrey, up behind him, saying, 'No targets in sight, sir!'

Harry looked up. It was true. They were suspended in a saturated grey haze, moving slow ahead together so that there was barely even a bow wave creaming back to show where the real world began. Anchorage noises drifted towards them; halyards slapping, voices, the sound of a derrick being worked. They were right in the enemy's lair, now.

A head appeared in the conning tower hatch, coming up without asking permission. Harry was about to turn on him, when he saw a flash of white in the rating's hand.

'Number One says you might need this …' the words came from the pale face set in the big black hole, holding up *Saraband's* White Ensign.

'Thank you,' said Harry, snatching it. 'Now get below.' Then he turned to one of the lookouts. 'Jones,' he said, handing him the ensign, 'do the honours. We can't have Johnny Jap not knowing who is kicking the crap out of him.'

The young rating stepped aft, smiling, and ran up the colours, before briefly coming to attention and snapping off a salute. Harry all the while thinking, *Number One, you big Kiwi lunk, whatever would I do without you?*

And then shapes began to loom, off the beam, the end of a wooden pier. And then the shape of a hull. It appeared like some raised villa, windows, a balcony, cantilevered over the water, wooden scuffed paint, and then the shape of a tumble-home and a stern post and rudder. It was one of the junks. Four hundred yards off, no more.

'Enemy in sight fine on the starboard bow, Mr Caudrey. Engage,' said Harry, tapping his guns 'n' torps on the shoulder. Caudrey had the common sense not to shout his orders over the bridge front. Harry looked down at the crew. Purdie, the layer, raised his arm to show he understood, while Duncan Disorderly, the loader, was already cradling the next round like it was his baby, beamed back at him. Everybody had heard the shore voices, and knew their voices would be heard too. Purdie fired the gun.

Bang!

The sound deadened so fast in the thick air; it was as though it never happened. And then the junk's rudder disintegrated.

The breech worker already had the shell case out and Duncan Disorderly had rammed the next one home.

Bang!

The next round went in under the waterline, where the big junk's engine space would be. Harry saw the splash and the splinters of wood blossoming from the hole it had made. In the time it took to register, the next round was on its way. When he looked up, figures were running about the junk's deck. Only one of them was looking back at *Saraband*, slack jawed as if he was watching some Kraken wake from the deep. Harry couldn't tell whether he was a local or a Jap.

He looked away, peering now into the curtain of rain, straining to see where the other ships were; listening to Gowers reading off the echo sounder and calling up the voice pipe the depth under the keel, like a chant. With each fathom, he ordered tiny course adjustments back down the pipe to the helmsman below, drawing on his memory of the plot as he conned them deeper into the anchorage. And all the while there was the noise of the rounds going into the big junk's hull, and then above it all, the sounds of alarm from the shore.

Slap! Slap! Slap! Slap!

A heavy calibre Jap machine gun, pumping bullets out of the grey; zipping beads of light, the grey leeching all colour from them. He knew immediately it was tracer, hosing through the air, way ahead, across their bows. The man firing, firing at nothing at all.

Then, like a curtain going up, the intensity of the rain slackened, and the visibility opened to 1,000 yards or more.

Harry could see the entire anchorage now. And there, tucked in under the eastern lip of the bay, two, or was it three, large motor launches, all painted dull grey and trotted up, making them difficult to pick out in the still hazy air; and all armed with what looked like heavy machine gun mounts well for'ard on their bows. Motor gunboats. Figures were standing on their decks, all staring across the water at *Saraband*, frozen with incredulity

'Check fire!' It was Caudrey, shouting in his ear, down to the gun crew. 'New target! Junk bearing green ten! Commence firing!'

When Harry looked round, he saw the origin of the roaring that he had been hearing but not really registering. A pillar of crimson flame, like a firebox blow-back, jetting out of one of the first junk's holds. He couldn't begin to guess what manner of cargo they'd just set ablaze, but the junk was doomed.

Harry turned all the way, and there were Tupper and Crick, manning the Oerlikon, eyes on him like gun dogs.

'The gunboats!' said Harry, looking right into Tully's glittering eyes and pointing, his arm outstretched. 'Red twenty. Engage!'

Twenty-millimetre shells instantly started pumping out as Harry leant back to the voice pipe. 'Number One, order Jowett to flood number four tube, and stand by to fire.'

He stood up again and looked round the anchorage. Tracer was coming at them now, three arcs from guns somewhere on the shore. Tully's Oerlikon shells were splintering the decks of the gunboats for'ard, so as no Japs were able to run to their own guns. Caudrey's deck gun was still pumping 3-inch shells into the hull of the second junk, and there, dead ahead, was the two-funnelled outline of the transport he'd seen, anchored against the shore at the head of the bay; his mini-*Queen Elizabeth*, all rusty but not abandoned. All those figures running about her decks; he couldn't work it out, but then he didn't have the time now. Another course correction into the pipe. He bent to the fixed torpedo sight on the bridge front. The range was getting too bloody tight, torpedoes needed at least 600 yards to run before they armed.

'Helm. Port five,' he said, then, 'and ring for stop together … and Number One, order the engine room to clutch out the motors and engage diesels, but don't fire them up yet.'

The transport slid into the sight's reticule. What was that? He looked up as one, then two flaps fell out from where the transport's superstructure reached into the well decks, to reveal two big deck guns, trained fore and aft, 5-inchers, he estimated. Another bloody Q-ship! The fore gun began to train round. Jesus! It hadn't even occurred to him the bastard might be another Q-ship. He bent to the sight again. This would have to be quick.

'Steer green five!' he yelled, loudly so it would carry down the pipe without him having to lean up to it, his guts clenching, hoping there was enough way on *Saraband* for the rudder to bite, to just swing her round that little …

… there, just on the mark, thank Christ … 'Fire four!'

A second past, then two, then … the departing torpedo coming out the top starboard tube stopped *Saraband* dead in the water, and her stern began to slew. The torpedo was running so shallow he could see a wave creaming off her as she went … and then into his line of sight was the transport's forward deck gun, now fully traversed and pointing at him. There was a flash, followed almost immediately by a deep resonating *BOOM!* and suddenly there was a terrible screeching, tearing sound, ripping through the air directly above his head as the shell went shooting over, way over, to splash hundreds of yards astern in a towering blast of water.

He had looked back instinctively, not meaning to; meaning instead to order number one tube flooded too, to get ready to fire another shot into that damn Jap. He jerked back in time to see his first torpedo's wake disappear right between the twin funnels and a huge fountain of water expand directly into the air, solid like one of those sausage balloons being inflated from a gas bottle, just as he remembered it from childhood fairgrounds. The noise of the explosion, and the pressure, like a punch, arrived at the same time, shimmering the sodden air. The middle of the transport arched slightly, as if it was forming a shallow roof pitch before sliding slowly back, until the angle was inverted, and the sound of tearing steel filled the air between the sounds of shooting.

He could see immediately their torpedo had broken the Jap's back.

He looked around the anchorage and saw only mayhem.

The first junk, aft, was burned down practically to her waterline. The second was settling by the stern, with crew huddling forward on her deck.

Great gouts of steam were venting from the Q-ship's exposed engine room as her two halves began to settle – separately – onto the anchorage floor, and Tully was still pumping rounds into the gunboats, whose for'ard ends were being turned into matchwood.

'Clutch in diesels. Full astern, together!' Harry yelled into the voice pipe. Then to Caudrey he said, 'Check fire. Clear the casing.'

Tracer from the shore continued to seek them out, but the gunners were still firing wide, or long.

There was no room, no water, for them to turn, they would have to get out of this bloody cul-de-sac arse end first. Not something he'd done much of, on this boat. Well, never too soon to learn. He leaned to look directly aft through McTeer's cat's cradle radar head, fixing on a spot on the roiling water where he could throw her hard a'port and run straight out of the southerly channel. Diving as they went.

There was suddenly a cacophony of pings, clangs, ricochets from down on the forward casing, and a scream.

'Duncan's hit!'

Rounds punched through the bridge front steel, one pinging off the for'ard periscope stand, going God knows where. Harry felt the wind of several rip past him, pinging, sparking on their way out the other side.

'Clear the bridge! Now! Everybody, down the hatch!' He hardly recognised his own voice. He was crouching behind the stands now, shoving Tully and a lookout towards the gaping maw of the hatch.

The rounds were hitting the casing below, falling short into the water. Looking aft, he could see their stern yawing dangerously to starboard, towards the shore. He wasn't going to stand up now, so he yelled his order to, 'stop port!' to correct their shear, hoping to be heard down the pipe, or even just through the hatch. And then he felt *Saraband* respond, and he breathed again.

He was aware of the rain battering harder. The persistent machine gun chatter still filled the air, but he sensed it was drifting, falling short. He stood, and saw they were cloaked in rippling sheets of rain again, masking them from the far end of the anchorage. But when he looked to starboard, he saw there, 100 yards or so away, standing huddled under trees a score or more of islanders, locals, in their colourful sarongs, mostly women and children, all waving and grinning.

He stood up and raised his cap, and waved back, and then he stepped to the voice pipe. He ordered stop together, then, 'full ahead together, port thirty.' Briefly, he went to the aft end of the conning tower and lowered the ensign. When he did, he brandished it for a final wave, and the locals cheered a little ragged cheer as Harry leant forward and hit the tit twice to dive the boat. Then he too disappeared down the hatch.

Sixteen

'Hello, captain.'

The Bonny Boy didn't recognise the voice, but he knew its sound, intimately. The whole clipped, glib, received pronunciation of it. Official England, to the tip of its public school toes. It sent the death chill into his guts. Did he walk on? Did he turn and see who had addressed him? The man, whoever he was, must be sitting at that street café table he just strode past.

The avenue was bright and sunny, the broad pavement of the Avenida da Liberdade dappled by tree shadow and the Monumento aos Restauradores to his right, rising so cool and solid. The world around so normal, while his own froze to brittle.

He opted to turn.

A man was sitting, clad in a dark blue suit that looked too heavy for the warmth of the day, in fact for these latitudes at all. He was wearing a homburg hat that looked equally inappropriate. The down-turned droop of his face was so bland, it designated him a nobody, yet the Bonny Boy couldn't look away.

'Have a seat, captain, I want to talk to you,' he said. The Bonny Boy had no idea who this man was, had never met him, and if he had, would probably have forgotten him. Except right here, right now, he was the most frightening person in the whole world.

'I don't know you,' said the Bonny Boy. 'How dare you accost a chap going about his business? Like some street beggar!'

'But I know you, Captain Bonalleck,' said the man. 'Allow me to introduce myself. I am Vernon Carmody.' But he didn't get up or offer his hand.

Instead, he flourished a long, slim folder. 'I have a ticket for you. How would you like to go on a trip? This evening. To meet some old friends.'

'I have no idea who you are talking about, nor have I ever heard of you. So, I suggest you cease harassing me or I'll call a policeman.' But the Bonny Boy didn't move.

'Oh, if you called a policeman, I think we both know he'd end up harassing you a lot more than I ever could. Sit down. Please. There, I asked nicely.'

Something oily and enticing in the voice made Charlie Bonalleck wince. It was enough to un-freeze him. He turned on his heel and began to stride quickly up the pavement.

Oh bugger, thought Carmody, *I knew he'd try and play silly buggers*. He tilted his head and raised his hand, like he was hailing a taxi, which in a way he was. *I bloody knew it!*

The pavement wasn't crowded, yet the Bonny Boy didn't see where the man in grey flannels and white shirt had appeared from, with his military-precise haircut and hand raised slightly as if he only sought to detain him for a moment. He certainly didn't see the other man, in bags and a sports jacket, slide out of a car by the kerb and step smartly up behind him.

'Get out of my way, you ruffian!' barked the Bonny Boy. But the flannels man didn't move, just smiled, and looked to be on the point of saying something. The Bonny Boy was caught between curiosity as to what it might be, and an impulse to push the impudent lout out of his way. And then the thought occurred to him that this cove was English, too. Of a different class, of course, to that man he was purposefully striding away from; coarser, definitely an 'other rank' … *oh dear* … were the last words his mind formed before he was aware of the white hankie coming from the side and clamping onto his face. He tasted, smelled, a sharp chlorine-like … And then nothing.

The pavement might not have been crowded, but there were passers-by; two women, an older man, another man. They turned, seeing a commotion. A man on the ground. Hands to mouths. 'Oh! Meu dues!' Two men bending to help, and another coming from the street café, saying in stilted Portuguese that the man had just collapsed. 'The poor old man! Someone call an ambulance!' 'I have a car right here!' 'Will you take him to the hospital?' 'I'll help, I'll help!'

And suddenly the slumped, inert figure was being hefted into the back of a black Citroen by the two younger men, everyone else standing, impotent, by the kerb. The older man, in the dark blue suit that looked too hot for the day, was saying in his stilted Portuguese, 'I was sitting right there ... I saw it all ... that young man was asking him the time, and he just collapsed ... the man ... he just folded onto the ground ...' He was obviously a foreigner. But then, the whole city was crawling with foreigners these days. It was the war. 'So kind,' he continued, '... so kind of those two men, to take him to the hospital. I think it might have been a stroke. Or his heart ... I hope he'll be alright.' He only stopped when the passers-by started to melt away. Nothing left to see. All of them agreeing that the young men were very kind to help.

*

Down near the river, on the R. de Belem, at another street café, diagonally opposite the Jardim Afonso de Albuquerque, another man sat on his own. There was nothing nondescript about him, however. His lightweight suit was perfect for the warm day and you could practically see your face in his polished wing-tips. The tie was maybe a bit more jazz-age than you would expect for a man of his years. But he was wearing a hat, as gentlemen of his generation tended to do. He sipped his coffee and read his newspaper, the *Frankfurter Zeitung,* the only German newspaper that remained relatively respected; Goebbels' liberal fig-leaf to a sceptical world.

Kapitän zur See Paul Trott und Boedicker, the German naval attaché, was not in a good mood as he waited for that fawning wretch, Stroessner.

The Kapitän didn't like Stroessner, nor did he like being forced to consort with him, or with his 'source', that preposterous – and the Kapitän was sure, dangerous – Captain Chaplin. But he had been ordered to by those SD thugs who seemed to run the German embassy these days. The Kapitän was an Imperial German Navy veteran and didn't take kindly to many of the new attitudes that passed for manners now.

195

Stroessner's source had become a problem over these last few days. Demanding, like a petulant child; and the Kapitän suspected that he had been lying to them through his teeth. He also suspected Chaplin was quite mad. Nor did the Kapitän think that what this Captain Chaplin was offering was at all as fabulous as the ill-informed SD goons were trumpeting. After almost five years of war the Kreigsmarine had become pretty adept at working out the Allies' convoy procedures. At best, this lunatic's secrets were likely to add little more than a few new curlicues to the existing, long-tested body of intelligence. On the other hand, there was a good chance that all they would get were red herrings, blind alleys and diversions. The possibility that this Chaplin fellow that had suddenly been so 'fortunately' thrown into their lap was just there to toy with them, and muddy the waters, did not seem to have occurred to the great SD, or to give Himmler's spies their full vain-glorious title – the *Sicherheitsdienst des Reichsführers-SS.*

The Kapitän shook his paper and turned a page. And that was when he saw Stroessner ambling down the street, like someone who could afford to take his time.

Well, he couldn't. The Kapitän was going to have it out with him once and for all. They were either going to get that fabled damned document Chaplin said he'd written, but was refusing to part with, or he was walking away. No more meetings, no promises or 'pretty pleases' for Chaplin, and certainly no more cash. The petulant Englishman was either going to hand over what he had promised or Kapitän zur See Paul Trott und Boedicker was walking away. If the SD wanted Chaplin's work they could carry on cajoling him, or even better, just hit him over the head and take it.

The Kapitän had been about to fold his paper at Stroessner's approach, but was glad he had not.

Two local police cars came screaming down the road, bells ringing, horns blaring. It was quite a spectacle and the Kapitän used his paper to peer over. He watched as Stroessner turned to see what was up and then recoil as the first car mounted the pavement, streaked past him, and then slewed to a halt in his path. The other car was tucking in behind him. Simultaneously, both cars' doors flew open and a tumble of uniformed officers hit the street, mobbing and milling around the stunned Stroessner, whom they had obviously come to detain.

The entire scene happened sufficiently far away for the Kapitän to remain seated and observe. The implications were obvious. Stroessner didn't dabble just in espionage. It now looked like he might also be involved in petty criminal activity too. The idea came as no surprise to the Kapitän. The notion that the local police were arresting Stroessner at the request of the British never occurred to him. As far as he was concerned, all it meant now was that Stroessner no longer existed for him. And once he had apprised the SD of what had happened, neither would that Chaplin fellow. He was done.

Later, the SD goons finally did come to the same conclusions as the Kapitän, regarding the impertinent Captain Chaplin. Two of them were dispatched to his apartment where they kicked the door down, intending to beat his secrets out of him. But Chaplin had not been there. Neither had his mythical document. The SD goons finally established that, but only after they had ransacked his rooms, practically to the bare brick.

What they didn't guess was that Vernon Carmody had been there before them, and that their man had already been bundled onto the scheduled BOAC Short Empire flying boat service to Falmouth, which had departed four nights previously from the Tagus estuary; spirited away along with his typed document, which travelled in a diplomatic bag in the hold.

Seventeen

After the attack into Port Owen, Harry ordered *Saraband* right down to the bottom of her patrol billet, to a small box between the mouth of the Pakchan River and the bottom of the Forrest Strait.

'Time we made ourselves scarce about here,' he told Gowers when ordering him to get them to the Nearchus Channel and then to lay a course south through the island tangle. Logic dictated the Japs would be keeping their transports home with a sub about, so the only thing they'd be likely to encounter for the foreseeable future up around Tavoy would be sub-chasers.

The rain eased considerably for the voyage south, nearly all of which *Saraband* made on the surface, day and night. For Gowers' course threaded them through a warren of channels, weaving in between scores of uninhabited islets with not a fishing boat sighted, or a settlement passed. The leaden skies also stayed clear of aircraft. If the waters hadn't been so shallow, frequently without enough depth for *Saraband* to dive in, you could have hidden a fleet here, thought Harry.

All the while, Cox'n Garbutt tended to AB Duncan and the wounded Jap. The Jap responded well to his treatment, but Duncan's medical needs exceeded anything Garbutt was capable of, so he kept the lad comfortable and stable as he could.

Two machine gun bullets had gone into poor young Duncan Disorderly. One through the top of his right lung and the other had shattered his left hip.

The fight to save him during the hours they spent making good their escape from Port Owen had sucked from the boat any excitement following the attack. Instead, it felt tense, subdued aboard. When he spoke to crewmen,

Harry felt a sort of resentment from them, not at him, but at the unfairness that Duncan was lying there when he should have been getting on with laughing and back-slapping over their victory, along with the rest of them. It was not unusual; Harry knew that. Civilian sailors. It was all fun for them, this war lark. A real hoot. Until it wasn't. Until the reality of war intervened. And it didn't get any more real than seeing your mate with two great holes blown in him, and the big cox'n up to his wrists in his body, all bloody, and effing and blinding under his breath trying to save him.

The instant he'd come down the hatch, Harry had told the cox'n to throw Duncan on the wardroom table to work on him. First, Eddie Garbutt had gone about stopping all the bleeding from the lad's chest and the ragged tear in his hip. Yeoman Cantor was one of the few with the fortitude to get in among all the snotters and gore to help him. So did McTeer, before he had to go on radar watch. They began by cleaning and then pressing and packing the hole in his chest with dressing after dressing, bandaging it tighter than a drum. Then they did the same for the burst-open pulp at the top of his left leg. The chest wound, however, was sucking. Harry, when he looked in on the wardroom, saw the bright ruby bubbles trickling on Duncan's alabaster skin, the lad too young for anything you'd call chest hair.

'He's got a tension pneumothorax,' Garbutt had explained, jabbing at an open first aid manual that lay propped open on one of the banquettes, its pages all red finger smears. 'There's a hole at the top of the lung that has collapsed it … that's stopped the lung itself bleeding, more or less … but every time he breathes, air is still getting into the pleural space. It's compressing the other lung and the heart. I've got to do something to release the trapped air, sir. I just need to sit down and read this …' And he had jabbed again at the manual.

Garbutt had read quickly, enough to tell Cantor how to first 'aspirate' Duncan's morphined-out body, while he delved deeper into the surgical procedure necessary to save Duncan's life. Garbutt had never imagined having to carry out anything like this. First aid was one thing. This was another. Gowers, strangely calm and unruffled, had held Duncan steady while Cantor began the aspiration procedure, inserting a needle into the air-filled space in the lad's chest. He had then fitted a very thin rubber tube to it, and using a syringe, began sucking air out through tube.

In the galley, Garbutt meanwhile had produced a thicker tube from the medicine cabinet. It was a chest drain, with a tiny non-return valve that was going to allow air out but not back in. Harry and Garbutt stood together while Garbutt rinsed the device with disinfectant. As he turned to go back to his patient, Harry had put one hand on his chest and with the other handed him a tot and told him to, 'gulp it.' Garbutt had smiled thinly, and complied. Then, Harry had followed him back to wardroom, and watched as the cox'n's steady hands first swabbed the spot, then wielded a scalpel and without a tremor, deliberately cut through Duncan's skin and sub-cutaneous tissue and inserted the tube through the chest wall. Almost immediately he bent close, and nodded to himself; he could hear a fine whistle of escaping air. 'There,' Garbutt had said, straightening up, his face unusually pale. 'That stays in place until the air leak has resolved and his lung re-inflates.'

'Ooh. "Resolved",' Harry had grinned, relief suffusing his face. 'Getting all medical on us now, Cox'n?'

And Garbutt, not grinning, had replied, 'Fuck off, sir.'

*

Over the following days, in the islands north and west of the Pakchan, *Saraband* encountered and sank three more sizeable junks, each one sent to the bottom by Verrell's Raiders going aboard and planting demolition charges. The chases and the kills all proceeded in a matter-of-fact way. Not even the epic news from home – the top headline in the weekly war news signal broadcast from Rugby – that the second front had finally opened, caused much of a stir.

Harry included it in the latest edition of *The Bugle*, but both McTeer and Cantor objected to McTeer's latest cartoon going in. 'It was drawn before Duncan copped his,' Cantor had explained to Harry, 'the lads that've seen it think it's taking the piss out the cox'n.'

McTeer's scribble was a faux "Bateman Cartoon", with the entire crew, and especially their wounded Jap, looking on in shocked horror while the cox'n, centre stage, brandished a saw at the Jap's leg. One end of that leg had a throbbing toe on it, and the other, a dotted line drawn around it at the hip, obviously marking where the saw was to cut. The cox'n, incredulous at the collective outrage, was saying, 'Well, he did ask, can you stop my in-grown toenail from hurting?'

Harry showed it to Garbutt, who couldn't stop laughing. The cartoon went in.

'Let's go north again,' Harry said at dinner round the wardroom table, after a second day of nothing turning up. Between the two flotillas now operating out of Trinco, he knew from radio traffic that there were currently six British boats operating on billets up and down this coast right now, from the Andaman Islands down to the bottom of the Malacca Straits. If one of them was doing well in one billet, it stood to reason business for boats elsewhere would get squeezed.

The drain was now out of Duncan's chest, but his hip wound was worrying Garbutt. It had become infected, so the cox'n pumped him full of this new wonder drug called penicillin, which was supposed to deal with all that. The pus had stopped coming, but the boy was running a fever, and he'd had to stop giving him morphine because it wasn't really working any more in doses that weren't likely to kill him. Harry had given up his bunk for the lad, hoping that tiny bit of extra space and privacy might help.

They set a course north after Scobie had cleared the table.

Neither sunset nor sunrise is a drawn out process in the tropics, and so Harry, after spending the night charging batteries and sniffing about the bottom end of the Celerity Passage for any brave junk master trying to sneak through, was heading west in the first light, through the Jubilee Channel. He intended to spend the day dived and nosing between The Sisters and Bushby Island. There appeared to be a break in the monsoon, no rain and good visibility, although the humidity clung to the bridge and the rising sun showed no sign of breaking through the banked-up cloud.

That was when the starboard lookout saw the two junks coming through the tangle of islets between Bushby and Domel Island.

Harry ordered the deck gun and Oerlikon crews to close up, and Verrell's Raiders to assemble under the torpedo loading hatch. The two junks puttered on, as if whomever they had on watch was napping. *Saraband* slowly turned bow on to them, making her low shape even harder to see with the light-suffused horizon behind her. It was shaping up for another regulation, by-the-book junk action.

Harry studied them through his binoculars, then looked to the sky, then back to the junks. His hunch was that there would be no Jap pilots in the air yet, and probably not for some time yet. Sub-chasers were another matter. He told the lookouts to keep their eyes glued on every channel and passage that led into this stretch of water, for anything coming down.

He concentrated on the junks. The smaller one, about 200 tons, he estimated, looked odd. No masts or derricks. Just a wheelhouse aft, and … those canvas-covered humps that had what looked like sticks poking out of them; that's how Harry recognised them for what they were. The sticks were two twin-mount gun barrels. He squinted. Machine guns, he reckoned; heavy, but not cannon, thank God!

Caudrey was on the bridge beside him, his binoculars on the targets.

'Get your boys up, Mr Caudrey,' said Harry, not taking his eyes off the two puttering junks, angling across their bows at a leisurely shamble. 'Concentrate your fire on the starboard junk. Rake her stem to stern, she's the one with all the fire power.'

'Aye, aye, sir,' said Caudrey. His commands, in a low voice, and the stamp of feet followed. In under a minute the first rounds were on their way.

If the starboard junk was the escort, Harry found himself wondering what the other bigger tub was carrying. He estimated her at 300 tons, just another scruffy trader. He was still studying her when he heard Caudrey order the Oerlikon to check fire. He looked up.

The smaller junk's deck was wrecked, the wheelhouse a set of splintered posts and the gun mounts dismounted, their four barrels pointing in all directions but back at *Saraband*. And she had turned, and was obviously headed for the sandy strip that bearded a nearby islet. No figure could be seen on her deck; whoever was conning her was down below, clinging to whatever cover her splintered timbers were offering. The 3-inch deck gun sent another round into her hull at the waterline. The junk lurched but didn't slow in her headlong rush to beach herself.

'Mr Caudrey, tell the deck gun to check fire,' said Harry, turning to the other, bigger junk. 'Then send a shot over our other friend's bows.'

The deck gun crew traversed their weapon and the warning shot went out. Something in Harry's head said he should take a look at what she was carrying before he started shooting at her. He stepped to the voice pipe. The junk's engine was cut, and she began to drift.

'Cox'n, the Captain here,' said Harry. 'Send Mr Verrell's party onto the casing, and Cox'n, go with him. We have a trading junk off our port bow. Go aboard her and tell me what she's carrying, before you let Mr Verrell blow her to kingdom come.'

'Aye, aye, sir,' said a tinny voice coming up the pipe.

This junk had been heading south. All the important junk traffic they'd encountered so far, had been heading north, carrying supplies to the Jap armies still trying to batter their way into India at Imphal. Yet this one must be important too, if it had an escort.

While he watched, the junk began to pirouette in the current as *Saraband* edged toward her. She was only 20 yards or so away now, and one of Verrell's men was already on the deployed diving plane with a line, ready to jump. There were figures in the junk's wheelhouse, he could see bobbing heads.

Suddenly, the junk's engine sprang to life. He shouted down to the casing, 'Mr Verrell! Get one of your tommy-gunners to rake the wheelhouse! Now!'

Harry watched as one of the ratings dropped onto one knee and took aim. There was a quick *brrrp!* Then another, and another, and splinters flew around the frames of the wheelhouse's glassless windows. In the middle of the bursts, he heard a scream. Then suddenly, a man in the dirty sand-coloured fatigues of a Japanese soldier burst onto the deck, brandishing a rifle. He was yelling some gibberish with great gusto as he too kneeled to take aim. Harry didn't have to say anything. There was another swift, clipped *brrp!* from over his shoulder and half of the Jap's head and chest disappeared, and what was left of the torso jerked upright before toppling into the scuppers.

Someone in the wheelhouse must have cut the engine again, because the churn at the junk's stern stopped, and once more she began to drift. *Saraband* bumped her and the man on the plane was across the gap and securing the two together, and Verrell's Raiders were across too, running up either side of the huge hatch for the wheelhouse, shouting for whoever was there, to come out.

Three locals leapt eagerly into view, two of them no more than boys, and the other an older man in a shirt and trousers, all waving their arms in the air trying to make a point; the point being, 'Don't shoot! We surrender!'

The older man began talking in local dialect and vigorously pointing at the hatch cover. Cox'n Garbutt, having donned a shirt and his petty officer's cap to show his rank, shoved his way to the front, and Harry could see his jaw jutting as he fired questions at the man. It was obvious to Harry, even from this distance, that neither understood a word the other was saying. The cox'n fingered his holstered sidearm. Meanwhile, Verrell was sending his men down a hatch into the junk's engine room, and another into what must have been crew accommodation. When Harry looked back to the cox'n, he was standing by the hatch cover, and Harry watched as he wrenched it back; Harry thinking, *oh for God's sake get a move on. Let's get the bloody charges set and get out of here.*

On the junk, down below in the thick dark and basting heat, they had heard the first report of a cannon firing with a listless resignation. Then the *bump-bump-bump* of a quick-firing gun. The unbreathable air and their fatigue beyond tiredness, and their thirst, meant it all sounded far away and nothing to do with them. But the sounds persisted and were obviously coming closer.

And then, abruptly, they stopped, so that the hissing between the two Japs on deck could be heard quite clearly. The few who retained the ability to discern nuances wondered whether what they were hearing was anger, or fear. The others no longer cared.

Then there had come the stamping and banging of the fight in the wheelhouse. They had all heard that. And then, those repeated *brrrps!* Really close. And more stamping on the deck, lots of stamping, and then suddenly there was sunlight, or what passed for sunlight for those deprived of it for so long. It seemed to explode above them. Someone had ripped the canvas hatch cover off. Who would do that? Nobody ever did that. And now there was a big grizzled head looking down at them all, as they cowered in the bilges. A white man's head, with a bashed peaked hat jammed upon it, the likes of which none of them had seen in a long, long time.

The first thing that hit Cox'n Garbutt was the stench. Like a hefty belt from a hot, sour, wet blanket, right in the face. And the dark. He couldn't see anything at first. And then the figures swam into view. Difficult to make out, because they were all tangled in a heap.

Women. European women. All of them in what must once have been floral print summer dresses, nice frocks, blouses. All rags now. And not really women; rather, wraiths of women. Women piled like stacks of cordwood, with all their shape gone, just sagging skin and hair with its lustre turned to string. All the big, big globular eyes staring up at him, and all the gawping mouths.

The cox'n mouthed something to himself. Then he took a deep breath, swallowed hard, and said in a deep, reassuring tone, 'Nobody's to be frightened. You're all alright now. The Royal Navy's here.'

*

Harry sat at the wardroom table with Bill Laurie, Gowers, Warrant Engineer Kershaw and the cox'n. It had been well over an hour since they'd discovered the big junk's cargo; 77 European civilian internees, all of them women. They had been held in a camp outside Rangoon since the city fell to the Japanese in 1942, and were only now being transported to God knew where. The only person who possibly could have told them had been the remaining Jap, who had been hiding in a void space beneath the tiller flat.

While the crew had been busy trying to work out what to do with their boat load of survivors, he had sneaked up on deck and dropped over the stern transom, intending to swim for the nearby shore and the cover of the jungle. One of *Saraband's* ratings, straight from helping the women into the fresh air, heard him hit the water. The sailor walked back to the wheelhouse where he'd stacked his Thompson gun, collected it and walked back to the transom. There, with everyone watching him, he flicked off the safety catch, and the weapon to single shot, knelt to take better aim, and fired four rounds into the swimming Jap. One of them blew the back of the Jap's head off, so there was no doubt.

205

Despite all Harry's strictures about never shooting survivors in the water, nobody said anything. Not even Harry, who had watched it without a blink or a comment.

Many of *Saraband's* crew had by then seen the hell that was the junk's hold, and those that hadn't had certainly smelled it.

The thing now was, what were they going to do with these 77 women? Most of them English or Australian, two of them American, the rest either Dutch or French. All were suffering from malnutrition and almost certainly, internal parasites; there were tropical ulcers as well as a text book's worth of tropical diseases; several of the women were too ill or just too infirm to be moved from the junk's hold, and anyway, there was no room aboard *Saraband* to carry them all to safety.

Harry had appointed Verrell in command of the junk, and then gathered his other officers to review what had been done already; Bill Laurie taking notes.

'Eight of the women are nurses apparently, sir,' said Bill, looking down his tally. 'And three of them are fit enough to help us with looking after the others. One of them is a nursing Sister. After this, maybe you should have a chat to her, sir. Sister Margaret Buchan, sir.'

Harry nodded. He was going to need all the help he could get. The practical stuff was all done. He had ordered Caudrey to get all three of the .303 Browning machine guns, and their ammo boxes up and moved onto the junk, plus boxes of .45 calibre ammo for the Thompson guns. If any Jap air turned up, they were going to fight it out; that was his short term answer. What happened after that … well …

Soup. Thin soup, and lots of it. That was the task assigned to Scobie. These women needed food, but even Harry knew enough not to hit them with beef and potatoes right away. Their stomachs wouldn't be able to take it. He would kill more than he'd save. The savoury aroma of the two huge pots Scobie already had on the go filled the wardroom.

An inventory of all the drugs and dressings on board was being compiled in the petty officers' mess. How to use them, how to prioritise who got what? He hadn't a clue. For that job, he really would need the Sister. Garbutt and Cantor and a couple of ratings had already done their rounds, dispensing water. And right now, all the women who were able were being helped into the fresh air. His first plan was straight up, good old-fashioned Royal Navy wisdom; when in doubt, clean. If they got most the women out the hold, then they could make a start on the squalor. Because if the hold was going to be the only place to stow the women, they should at least clean it for them.

Then, it had been Warrant Engineer Kershaw's turn. He had made an inventory of the junk's seaworthiness, her engine and fuel. The hull was sound, if not particularly sanitary, and the diesel in remarkably decent nick, he said; but her tanks had just enough fuel to get her 200 miles, probably. *Saraband*, on the other hand, had more than enough in her tanks for herself and the junk, if getting back to Trinco was the plan. He left it at that, not wishing to speculate any further.

The lists read out, Harry said, 'The only thing left to settle then, is what we do next.'

All faces stared back at him, grim, blank. No fucking help whatsoever.

They were over 1,000 miles from Trinco, still deep in enemy waters. They hadn't seen any enemy aircraft so far this patrol, up here in the Mergui Archipelago, but that didn't mean there weren't any. There were certainly sub-chasers. What if one of them was to turn up? Or, more likely, lots of them? *Saraband* couldn't fight it out with a mob of sub-chasers on the surface and hope to survive. They'd have lots of deck guns, and *Saraband* had only one, plus an Oerlikon. Normally, the simple answer would be to dive. But right now she couldn't dive, because there was no room aboard for 77 sick and hurt women, and if she didn't dive, sooner or later some Jap would put a hole in her pressure hull, and then she wouldn't be able to dive anyway.

He did not even have the option of radioing old Tinsides for advice, not that he could imagine the S4 would have any more bright ideas than he'd had. No, if he radioed now, the Japs would hear him; he'd be telling the Japs where he was. After their little party in Port Owen they must know a sub was operating in the area anyway.

'I'll speak to Sister Buchan now,' he said. God, this was a bloody mess. Was he really going to leave them? Going to *have* to leave them?

He met her on the casing, where she was just standing forward of the gun, gazing blankly at the sea and sky. She had one spindle of an arm clasped across her flat chest, and with her other hand was dragging heavily on a cigarette that had been passed to her by one of the junior ratings. Sister Buchan somehow managed to look pale, despite her weathered skin that sagged like sails in a doldrum. Harry guessed that her hair had once been blonde, but it didn't really have a colour any more. Guessing her age was impossible. She was wearing a smart ratings' t-shirt and shorts.

'Your young sailors have been most kind, Captain,' she said, in a strong voice that jarred with her sickly appearance. *Jesus*, thought Harry, *and you're supposed to be one of the fitter ones.*

It had been Garbutt that had passed the word, the minute he'd come out of the hold. Some of the poor wretches weren't even decent. In the messes, fore and aft, packs had come out. In a flash, best dress whites, favourite t-shirts, sarongs, had all appeared, stacked in a pile on the casing by the open torpedo loading hatch. Cantor and the able women had helped to move the pile into the junk's hold and passed out the new clothes to the women, many of whom accepted the items with tears in their eyes, nodding and bowing as they were so used to doing for the Japanese, so that Cantor had had to turn away to hide the tears in his own eyes.

Harry stood nodding himself, no words coming. What could he say? He had no idea what to say.

'I hope the girls aren't upsetting your boys too much with their crying,' she added, after another drag. 'Going all blubby on them, them being so young. But, as I'm sure you'll appreciate, it has been some while since anyone has been kind to us at all.'

'Jack's a generous chap at the best of times,' said Harry, glad of something to say at last. 'Now, what do we need to do? Your girls need medical help, and we don't have much of that on a submarine.'

Sister Buchan smiled a most enchanting smile at the word 'girls', then said, 'Can you show me what you do have?' She threw the tiniest remnant of the cigarette over the side. And so began the work to patch and mend the best they could.

Harry retreated to the bridge, having cadged half a packet of cigarettes from the wrecker, Priestly. He didn't normally smoke, but today …

'Your rewards shall be in heaven,' he had said, as he snatched the control room's box of matches tucked behind the 2nd Cox'n's aft dive plane panel, on his way up.

Both *Saraband* and junk were underway again, heading north west to the islands that formed the Nearchus Passage. The weather had improved, with a strong breeze from the south west driving scudding clouds and opening patches of blue sky. That breeze made it idyllically warm. The radar head turned methodically behind him, searching for aircraft, and the lookouts, with the captain on the bridge, religiously attended to their business of hunting the horizon.

Harry dragged a lungful from his cigarette. What was he going to do with these women? The islands that framed the passage were their last chance to dump them, once they'd been bandaged and fed. But even before he had finished asking the question; before he had even considered what would happen once they reached the Nearchus, he knew the answer. All that remained was to break it to the crew.

Thirty yards away, the junk was struggling to keep up with *Saraband's* nine knots. On her deck he could see a couple of dozen of the women up there taking in the clean air, much of their listlessness gone already. They were chatting to the sailors in the wheelhouse and manning the .303s. Down below on *Saraband*, he knew Sister Buchan was now tending to young Duncan, who was still lying in the Captain's bunk.

There was no point in putting it off. He'd made his mind up. Or rather, the Royal Navy had made it up for him. As captain, he had one responsibility. His command. He would answer for that command at his peril. The KR&AI said so in so many words. But what had Admiral Cunningham said after the evacuation of Crete, when they were losing a lot of ships? 'It takes three years to build a destroyer, but three hundred years to build a tradition'.

He slid down the conning tower ladder. He lifted the address system mic.

'This is the Captain. Clear the lower deck. All hands not on duty, muster in the control room.'

All of the shuffling had died down, and all the eager faces were fixed on him, furrowed brows, craning to see, wondering what the hell was going on now.

Harry always believed in getting to the point right away, the whys and wherefores could follow later.

'We're not leaving them,' he said.

There wasn't even a murmur. Not a word, not a shuffle. But he knew right away he had said the right thing.

In all the years he had served, he had never come close to working it out; how you could tell what was what on a boat. Almost as if you sniffed it in the air, because God knows you could sniff everything else.

'The chances are that means we'll have to make a fight of it ...' he went on. But he knew he didn't have to. They were with him. The entire Imperial Japanese Navy could come steaming over the horizon, and this crew still wouldn't leave these 'girls' behind. He finished his gibber for form's sake of course, but he knew everybody's minds were made up already. They were taking these girls home, and if the Japs wanted a fight over it, then they had come to the right shop.

*

It was just after 1300 hours, local time, when the first dot appeared in the eastern sky, picked out by one of the lookouts, not *Saraband's* radar. They had been running on the surface at the junk's maximum comfort speed of not quite eight knots, a depressing performance given that Harry had wanted to put as many miles as possible between them and any Jap air patrol before nightfall.

Saraband went immediately to Diving Stations, not that there was much closing up to do as most of the gun crews were already sat around their guns, smoking, drinking the endless supplies of tea sent up by a diligent and uncomplaining Scobie, in between his boiling up endless vats of thin soup.

In fact, it turned out to be two dots. Or so McTeer said, once he had got himself in front of the radar screen. Closing from east south east at 3,000 feet, just below the cloud base, it seemed to Harry. Pretty soon they were close enough for him to identify them as a pair of 'Jakes'. He knew each could carry up to 250lbs of bombs – not much, but enough in the hands

210

of a pilot who knew how to place them – and a pop-gun for the observer in the back to blast away with, and which posed no more than a serious risk to their paint work.

Harry watched the aircraft circle; it was as if they couldn't make up their mind which direction to attack. No attempt to come right at them from opposing angles to catch *Saraband's* gunners on the hop, and split their fire.

The first 'Jake' dropped its nose and began to dive, but she was still miles off their beam, sneakily choosing to come in on the junk's side. Harry watched as it descended almost to sea level, watching her come in through the junk's masts.

'I do believe the bugger thinks the junk will mask him from our fire, sir' said Caudrey, his brows furrowed in disbelief.

Harry smiled and shrugged at him. What they were watching didn't say much for the professional acumen of the Jap pilots. He stepped to the voice pipe. 'Ring for full ahead together.' Then he leaned over the bridge front. 'Purdie!'

'Sir!' said the gun layer, already on his feet, straining to see what was what.

'When we pull ahead of our friend,' said Harry, pointing at the junk, 'I'd like you to start dropping rounds in front of the Jap, fast as you like.'

'Aye, aye, sir,' said Purdie, overseeing the rounds coming up and going into the ready use magazine. *Saraband* was already pulling clear of the junk's bow now, giving everybody on her deck a clear view as the Jap bored in at a mere 150 knots, and at a height of no more than 50 feet. What was the Jap trying to do? Did he think he was going to skip his bombs into *Saraband* with everything she'd have firing at him, and no wing man coming the other way to distract her?

Harry was telling Crick, on the Oerlikon, to hold his fire for the moment, when the deck gun barked and the first round went on its way. The next was on its way before the first round hit the water, throwing up its familiar spout, just too far to the right for the Jap to fly through, and too far ahead to drench her pilot. The second did the same, but Purdie corrected for the third, and the fourth he held back until he had seen the third hit. Another adjustment and …

Harry was watching through his binoculars, transfixed. He was looking directly into the Jap's big radial engine cowl, aware of the two wing bombs, and a third suspended between to two big floats, when suddenly the aircraft disappeared behind a pillar of water, and then the next moment appeared through it, spirals of water being flung in great arches, disintegrating what had looked like a solid mass. At first, he wasn't sure what he was looking at, but then like a slow motion film suddenly speeded up, the Jap's left float was torn away in a flash of movement, but the aircraft itself continued on in slow motion. Until that is, it just stopped in mid-air, and fell into the sea in a Catherine wheel of bits of wing and fuselage.

A cheer went up from the gun crew, and from over the water, from the junk.

Harry looked at a beaming Caudrey and said, 'Anyone would think that shower of yours down there did this gunnery game for a living, Mr Caudrey.'

Caudrey couldn't keep his face straight enough to reply.

Above them the other 'Jake' continued to circle, then it too began to descend. Down she came in a long, slow dive, dropping down for 1,000 feet at least, until she was stern on to them. And then she stopped diving and levelled out. Coming on, but still too high to see whether she was aiming for *Saraband* or the junk. Harry called across the water between the two.

'Mr Verrell! Close on me, please. Come to twenty yards.'

'Aye, aye, sir,' Verrell shouted back, waving and grinning and having a whale of a time. The junk slid in deliberately, and on came the Jap.

'Right you are, Crick,' said Harry, craning his neck up to see the Jap advancing on them at the ridiculous height of over 2,000 feet, if McTeer's range calls were to be believed. 'Time to engage the enemy. Commence firing.'

The distinctive *bum-bum-bum-bum-bum-bum!* of the Oerlikon spoke out, the tracer rounds marking their own arc while the empty shell cases began their clatter on the deck. Crick walking his deflection firing across the 'Jake's' front, then moments before it must cross *Saraband's* and the junk's sterns, three little dots separated from Jake and began their own giant downward parabola.

Harry said into the voice pipe, 'Poulter, port twenty!' Then, standing up, he called across, 'Mr Verrell! Hard-a starboard, please!'

Submarine and junk veered elegantly apart, and everyone on deck watched as the three bombs came angling down in a perfect V. 'Duck, everyone!' Harry yelled, in his best Force 10 bellow. And everyone's heads on *Saraband* and the junk went down as the bombs hit the water between them, harmlessly, and only two detonated. When the spray had subsided, and the *tings!* and *clunks!* of the shrapnel stopped, they all stood up and watched as the Jake peeled away and headed east again.

Only another hour until night. Harry wondered whether the Japs had any more air strikes on the way. However, if the pilots flying them were going to be as good as those two, did it matter? *I suppose any good pilots you have left are on your carriers, fighting the Yanks,* he thought to himself, trying not think, *what if it's that bloody 'Emily' that turns up next?*

Eighteen

The motor gunboat that came out to escort them in for the last dozen or so miles, had all its people on deck, waving as she came up in a great sweeping turn to match their progress. Her skipper yelled his congratulations, which was all very well, but a bit too theatrical for Harry's liking, until he explained he had a newsreel cameraman on board and a couple of newspaper photographers who were keen to get themselves onto *Saraband* – and the junk – to get some 'candid shots' of the crew and the damsels they had rescued.

'Bugger off!' Harry had called back, surprising himself at his own outrage. The bloody presumption of the bastards! These poor women weren't going to be looking their best, to say the least, even after several days of Indian Ocean cruising under the tender ministering of every man jack aboard his submarine. Who the hell did they think they were? Bill Laurie had a wry smile at his outburst, but Sister Buchan, invited onto the bridge for *Saraband's* entry into Trinco, had said, 'Thank you, Captain,' in his ear.

To make matters worse, the C-in-C had ordered all ships in the anchorage to 'man ship', so that even the battleships and the carriers had their matelots out in force in their whites, lining their rails, giving their three cheers, on cue from the flag, as *Saraband* and her charge made their progress up to *Adamant*. Except that, before they got there, *Saraband* was relieved as the junk's escort by the Admiral's barge, which had then proceeded to conduct Mr Verrell's first command up to the Admiral's landing stage and the convoy of ambulances that waited there. All under the rolling film of the newsreel cameras.

Sister Buchan got to stay aboard *Saraband* and managed to miss it. 'And thank you for sparing me that, too,' she had later whispered in Harry's ear.

The other person to miss it all was their Jap prisoner, now much recovered after the tender ministering of Cox'n Garbutt, who'd done his duty by him as if he he'd taken the Hippocratic oath himself. Harry had stowed the Jap aft in the stokers' mess, with Garbutt at first going back every day to change the poor wretch's dressings. The Jap spoke no English, and *Saraband's* black gang no Japanese, but basic communication was soon established and it had quickly become apparent that the little bugger was no threat to the boat, and indeed, keen to make himself useful.

'I never had my brasswork so gleaming,' Kershaw later told Harry. 'Every time you looked round, there was little Charlie Chan polishing and scrubbing. He's a better bloody hand than half the lot I have already.'

It would have been a lie to say the stokers loved the little Jap, but none of them liked the way the pongos roughed him up when they took custody of him at *Wu Chang's* gangway.

Much later, in Tinsides' day cabin, after Harry had delivered his verbal patrol report, the Captain S had suddenly gone all grim on him. Up until that moment, he had just been formal. Which was not like him. Usually he was all bonhomie, with lots of pink gins flying in from all angles, especially for one of his captains who had come in with a lot of new bunting on his Jolly Roger. Harry thought maybe he was just pissed off too, with all these cameras and C-in-C Eastern Fleet staff meddling at his elbows. He watched as his boss poured him his first bumper of gin and dripped the angostura into it. Then, after he had handed it to Harry, Tinsides stepped across to his desk and lifted a signal flimsy, which he also handed to Harry before sitting down.

'I'm really, really sorry Harry, to be bringer of such bad news.'

The Captain S had never used his first name before.

Harry looked at the flimsy. It was a signal from Northways, the FOS's converted mansion block HQ in north London, and marked 'personal to Lt. Gilmour, Fourth Flotilla'. It reported in simple naval-ese, with deep regret, etc. that his father had died; date, cause and place filled in; heart failure, at home; a 'peacefully' was added by the SSO – senior staff officer – who had dispatched it.

Harry looked at the words, he had never imagined this was how he would hear such news.

'Commander Clarke wanted to forward it to you on patrol, but I overruled him,' said Captain Ionides. 'I didn't want you … distracted. Oh God. What a terrible thing for me to say. But you know what I mean, I hope? It was my decision, anyway. Only you know whether it was the right one, I suppose. Drink that up, Lieutenant Gilmour. And that's an order. There's another on the way.'

Harry obeyed. He heard the Captain S explain how it was too early for any mail from home yet, regarding the death. But the covering signal informed him that any letters would be expedited. This was followed by a brief homily on his own personal experience of bereavement, about how you never really get over it, just learned how to deal with it. Which was kind of him, thought Harry. He didn't have to bother.

Then he moved on. 'Now, this rescue business, Mr Gilmour.' Business indeed, no more first names. 'I'm sure you're no more enamoured than I am of having all these reporters and cameras everywhere …'

'Sir,' Harry said, nodding.

'Oh, and congratulations, by the way, on a very fine job. I'm to tell you everybody back home thinks you're a credit to the service. Etcetera.' From the roll of Tinsides' eyes, Harry could imagine, and felt a deep, nameless depression creeping over him.

'Our job is done now, though, isn't it, sir?' He said, then shut up, silenced by the baleful look Tinsides gave him.

'You're just going to have to get on with it, Mr Gilmour. And do as you are expected to do. One of the press photographers is from the UPI, and three of the women are American. Surely I don't have to paint you a picture? Someone from the flag is going to meet you and tell you what to say. We are being leaned on, Mr Gilmour. Now, I don't want to hear anything from you except, "aye, aye, sir".'

UPI – United Press International, one of the big Yank wire services. Their sad little story was headed stateside, coast to coast. For the good of the Allied cause, hands across the ocean, this is for all the folks back home. Harry wanted another gin before he went anywhere. However, there was one more thing he had to ask.

216

'When we encountered the women, sir, most of their clothes were in rags,' said Harry, swirling the gin reflectively. 'My crew emptied their kit bags to make them decent again. When they indent for new uniforms, can you tell the depot ship pusser not to charge them for lost kit, please, sir?'

The newsmen wanted the Captain, and Cox'n Garbutt, the man who had lifted the hatch cover, They also wanted Verrell, and Verrell's Raiders – they loved Verrell's Raiders, and young Toby Verrell loved telling all about them. Harry did his duty, smiled when he was supposed to and talked into the microphones as though was reading an official signal. He was so stiff, he made Sister Buchan laugh. Cox'n Garbutt merely stood, face and posture like an Easter Island monolith, behind his Captain. In contrast, Verrell did his bit with a million-candle-power smile and a line in repartee stolen from the Hollywood public relations manual, and he made everyone laugh.

When all the interviews and the hanging about and waiting for the cameras was done, Harry went in search of Duncan Disorderly, to see how he was doing. There was an infirmary ashore, but they didn't have him. He had to pin a busy sick bay attendant to check their paperwork. 'Oh, we did have him, briefly,' the attendant managed to tell Harry after consulting a pile. 'Not much we could do for him down here, they've moved him up to one of the big base hospitals. Like bleedin' hotels they are, sir. Is he alright? Oh yes, they'll have him re-upholstered jig-time. We'll signal the depot ship which one he's in.'

Only then did Harry sit down and write his patrol report. Then he checked with Number One that the boat had been scoured clean, and had been formally handed over to the depot ship's hands for maintenance and replenishment, and that the leave bills had all been posted. He hadn't even had time to think about his father, or the news; he didn't even have time for a drink with Cdr. Clarke or *Wu Chang's* Cdr. Cavenagh-Mainwaring, or any of the other flotilla COs, if he was to make the train to Batticaloa. And then, a truck up to Kandy.

*

Harry had walked out of the dark and into the spill of the light from the Fraters' porch lantern, and Colin Frater had immediately leapt up from his lounger and met him on the steps.

'Give me that,' he said, grasping Harry's grip. 'Vicky says you've to go up to the hospital the instant you arrive.'

So he did.

He tapped on the glass of her office door, and stepped into the darkened room. He could see her standing at the open French windows, her back to him, very still, looking out into the night towards the jungled mountains. He walked up behind her and gave a little cough. She didn't stir.

'It's Harry,' he said. They might like each other, but their relationship was nowhere near his being free to reach out a hand to her, yet.

She turned, and in the pale glow of the city's lights in the background, her face looked funny. Puffy.

'Victoria?' he said.

She seemed to snap out of some vague reverie. Then she said, in a very simple voice, 'Bain's dead.'

'Sorry? What?'

'Bain. Our Lance Corporal. He's dead. He jumped off the cliff. He went for his evening walk and when he didn't come back, we went looking for him. And we found him lying at the bottom, dead. All burst and no two bits of him pointing the right way.'

Then she took the two steps between them and buried her face in his shoulder, held on tight, and began to wrack with sobs. Harry gripped her just as tightly, but the tears that ran down his face were silent. They held each other in the darkness for a long time.

When she finally eased her grip on him, she leant back to look into his eyes, dry now, all his tears gone. She said, 'I don't know why it was him that got to me. Why poor, lost, young Lance Corporal Bain?' She gave a wan smile, then with one hand reached back and pulled the pin out of her hair. Then she looked at him in a way that brooked no misunderstanding.

He never told her that his father had died too. Not then, not later.

*

'You have a lot of nasty scars about your person,' said Victoria, absently stirring her cup of tea. They were sitting under a tree in a café yard in the

218

centre of town. It was the next morning, but the location made their tryst look innocuous. 'And by a lot, I mean I've counted them.'

'Industrial injuries,' said Harry, smiling his sated smile and sipping his tea.

'Well, as your medical adviser, I'd advise you look for another industry,' she said. 'I prescribe lots of rest and pampering. In a little cottage on top of the Andes. Which should be just the right distance from any wars or seas. You're far too beautiful for any more wear and tear.'

*

'Is there the girl you left behind?' she asked, walking along, swinging his arm, his hand in hers. 'Whose schoolbooks you used to carry but who you now write endless declarations of love to, and she responds on paper dipped … nay *saturated* … in Chanel Number Five?'

'I'm not sure,' said Harry.

'That's a trifle enigmatic, even for you Gilmour,' she said, stopping and standing back to stare. She had taken to calling him Gilmour all the time now; as if to see whether it would irritate him. Harry played along.

'I thought I did,' said Harry. 'But I'm not so sure any more. She writes, but her letters read like a newspaper column.'

'Really? Do tell.'

Harry told Victoria about Shirley. Not everything, just enough. A girl from his home town, yes; that she was now an ambulance driver and very much a young woman who knew her own mind.

'Good for Shirley,' Victoria said, and banged the table.

He told her that he had believed there to be a passion between them – no details though, he was a gentleman after all. But that instead she had told him that she wasn't his girlfriend, and that she had no intention of waiting for him. Then he told her about the letter she had once sent to him back on Malta, the one that quoted Emily Dickinson.

'She'd already made it plain, "I've no intention of wearing widow's weeds for you!"' said Harry, mocking her tone. 'And then she went and wrote me that letter.'

219

'Women, eh?' said Victoria, as if dismissing their chat, but knowing deep down what Shirley must have been thinking. The fear. The impossible pain of losing him. Bandaging herself tight, now, so that maybe it wouldn't hurt so badly when it happened, leaving no part of herself open, or unprotected. Giving nothing away now, so there would be nothing out there for loss and grief to steal from her.

She never said any of that to Harry, of course. But she held him extra tight that night, and buried her face in his chest so the scent and strength of him might blot out the whole world. It had been a long time since she'd felt like that with anyone.

*

Another day spent together. As they were drinking after dinner ports in one of the big hotels, Harry said, 'You don't wear a wedding ring. You're not married, I take it?'

She smiled over her glass.

'Or is there a husband somewhere, you're not owning up to?' pressed Harry. For all the times she had accused him of being 'enigmatic', she had seldom parted with any titbit about her own life away from the here and now.

She considered a moment, then, 'Oh, I have had hundreds of them …'

'And where …?' interrupted Harry, meaning to ask '… where are they now?'

But she wouldn't let him. 'I'm a black widow,' she continued. 'I eat them after mating.'

'You haven't eaten me yet.'

'That's not what you said this morning.'

*

And then there had been that moment on their second day, when she told him, 'You have a boy sailor called Duncan. With the hole in his hip. And one in his chest. But that's healing nicely. We have him up here now, you know.'

Harry didn't know; had only been told by a Fleet sick bay attendant that the lad had been moved to a base hospital immediately.

'He must have been admitted when you were arriving. I popped in to take a look at him when I heard,' she said. 'He's doing well, by the way, considering. That wound, and all that time without proper treatment. He should've died you know. But he didn't, did he?'

'The cox'n's got a bit of a vocation, I think,' he replied, relieved the news about Duncan was good.

'I don't think your cox'n saved him. I think you did.'

Harry looked at her.

'The only reason your boy didn't die was because he didn't give up. Except at his age you usually don't have that kind of fortitude of your own. Someone has to *make* you. I reckon he didn't give up because he thought that would be letting you down. You, and the crew that I take it you've made in your own image. It's an interesting phenomenon. I see it all the time up here in the recovery wards. Boys that shouldn't make it, but do.' She paused to consider him. 'You know, I'd love to see you on your boat, in command, doing your captain things. I bet you'd be great to watch. I bet you're funny, as well as …' and here, she lowered her voice, *basso profundo*, '… commanding!' Then she changed her tone, became more girly. 'Not that I ever would, darling. You'd never get me down in one of those things, not even if it was to save my virginity.'

And that made Harry laugh.

They didn't always spar, for all they seemed to enjoy it. Harry was mesmerised by Dr Cotterell; another exotic creature war had thrown in his path; he'd never have encountered a woman like her on the steamer to Dunoon, or walking along Byres Road from his digs to lectures. If he had … he shuddered to think. Except now, her reticence and distance didn't intimidate him as they would have intimidated the daft young undergraduate he once was. Instead, she made him laugh. And he loved the fact that he didn't have to care who she really was. It was the war, of course; the indifference the war seemed to allow him; that had made him feel he was a stronger man, living a more real life. It was like being in a romantic novel – and that, in itself, also made him laugh, out loud.

He went to visit Duncan the next day, taking him some Yank chocolate. Hershey Bars. A Matron confiscated them, but he and Duncan managed a laugh when she swore blind they would be waiting for him when, 'the boy is well enough.'

And what about Victoria? Of course, there had been several men in her life; Victoria, the daddy's girl of a Manchester industrialist. All the money, and all the moral support to be whomever she wanted. She could have been a debutante, but she had wanted to be a doctor, at a time when there weren't any female doctors. But then she'd always been a wilful girl. Also, she had never had the time for most of the men in her circle, who, it seemed, never really had any interest in her as a person, only wanting to divert her in their direction.

There had been one man, however, who hadn't been like that. But he had been married. Victoria never told Harry about him. She'd put the memory of him in a box long ago. And now there was a war on, and it seemed she wasn't the only one putting things in boxes these days. Including poor young L/Cpl. Bain, whose box had turned out to be too heavy to carry anymore.

'Did he ever say anything to you, Lance Corporal Bain, when you talked to him … when you used to sit and watch the sunset together?' she asked, sitting down on another morning stroll, on another day. 'Something that might have given you a clue as to why he did it?'

Harry thought.

Bain had never talked about anything. Sometimes it felt that every time he and Bain sat together on the cliff top, it was like walking into the pages of that Herman Melville short story, *Bartleby, the Scrivener*. The boy had always been physically there, living and breathing, but the person inside seemed to recede further and further every time he met him.

'One day he came out with something really rather strange,' said Harry, eventually. 'He said that when he was tuning between frequencies on his radio, he'd started listening to the static. He said he'd never really listened to the static before, but then it had come to him what it really was. He said, "It's the sound of all the blokes who'd ever copped it in a war. All callin' out at the same time." It's a pretty disturbing image, don't you think? I remember the hairs going up on the back of my head. Then he told me how he couldn't work out whether they were laughing or screaming, and how it was getting him down.'

They both sat and contemplated that for a moment, until Victoria gave herself a shiver and sat upright. 'Look not too long into the abyss, lest the abyss looks into you,' she said, frowning; all arch and school-marmy.

'You took the words right out of my mouth,' said Harry, thinking to himself, *fancy having a girlfriend who quotes Nietzsche to you.*

Nineteen

Dead ahead, fine on *Saraband's* bow, was a low confection of white cumulus, sat there in pristine isolation; a tiny, finite chunk billowing up over the southern horizon.

'Sumatra,' said Harry.

'How do you know?' asked Captain Saundby, with his now familiar petulant abruptness.

The four lookouts positioned round the bridge were all well within earshot, and all bristled at the bloody cheek of anybody, let alone a bloody pongo captain, questioning a Royal Navy captain on his own bridge. Even Caudrey, who was the watch officer, thought it a bit off. And all were doubly sniffy when the pongo added, 'You said only half an hour ago we still had fifty miles to run.'

'It's a meteorological phenomenon,' said Harry, with extreme patience. 'Land causes the moist warm air close to the surface of the sea to rise into cooler air, where it condenses.'

'Yes, but the fifty …'

Again, with extreme patience, Harry interrupted Captain Saundby, '… so it goes without saying the clouds must be higher than the mountains below them, hence we can see them from much further away.'

'Oh, I see.'

It had been a long few days, transiting across the Indian Ocean with this man, but they were almost there, at last.

Up until now on this deployment, *Saraband* had avoided cloak-and-dagger ops, so un-beloved of submariners. But alas, when Harry had come back down from Kandy to begin preparations for their next patrol, he discovered their luck had run out.

Thankfully Cdr. Clarke had briefed Harry on his own, so Harry had been free to ask questions without fear of offending whatever 'joe' he was being lumbered with.

'*Saraband* is to take a party of three down to Pulo Weh, which is an island right off the north of Sumatra,' Clarke had said, barely concealing his amusement that *Saraband* had at last been roped in to doing her share of shite-shovelling.

'Your joes are an army captain from that Force 136 lot, with a Royal Marine to carry his pencil case, and a local,' continued Clarke. 'The local is an Indonesian national who used to work for the Dutch colonial service and now works for us, and the job is as simple as kiss my hand. You drop them off, and five days later you come back again and pick them up. In between times however, you must *not*, under any circumstances, *attack*, or become involved with, in any way, *any* enemy shipping. Is that understood?'

'Understood,' Harry had said, understanding very well; if you attacked enemy shipping you automatically alerted the enemy that there was a submarine operating in their area. There was nothing quite like it for stirring up a coast, which was exactly what you didn't want if you were trying to sneak in and pick up a parcel of joes from a beach.

'Your main joe is Captain Eric Saundby,' Clarke went on. 'He's a Royal Engineer, and a word to the wise … you might find him somewhat lacking in the social graces.'

Harry could tell Cdr. Clarke had enjoyed telling him that, in a friendly, gleefully malevolent sort of way.

'The marine is a Corporal Dutton, he's a radio operator, so you'll be carrying his set too, and the local, you are only to call him George … something to do with his personal safety. He'll be going in with a set of forged papers and the clothes he stands up in. As to what they're going to do when they get there, nobody tells us anything. Johnny Jap has been building up the island as base, so one can only assume our chaps are going in to make an inventory of what the Japs have actually put there. The wafus say the last time they flew over the place they were tucking a new fighter strip in between all the mountains, and they'd built bunkering tanks around the main port at Sabang … so it'll be that sort of thing our playmates will be taking snaps of, I suspect. But as they say, ours is not to reason, etcetera.'

'Wafus': Jack slang for the Fleet Air Arm, and anything connected to it.

And that had been it. His leave over, the idyll he'd spent with Dr Victoria Cotterell in the mountain, downgraded to a memory. Standing there on the bridge beside Saundby, he recalled the true moment of transition from leave to war as that afternoon they'd spent conducting landing drills with the Captain and his little gang off the beach at Dutch Bay, and the comedy of errors with the inflatable life raft donated to the operation by the RAF.

He also recalled the moment he'd started to have a bad feeling about this op. The sealed orders. They were handed to him by Ginger, at the last moment, just as he had been about to go up *Saraband's* gangway, with a verbal instruction that, 'Tinsides says you have to open these in Saundby's presence.'

The orders said Harry was only to drop off George, initially. Then, when he went back for him five days later, George would report back to Saundby what he had found ashore, and if Saundby was happy with that, all three of them would disembark, and *Saraband's* role in the operation would end. If Saundby wasn't happy, then nobody was going anywhere, the op was off and *Saraband* was to take them all back aboard and get on with her patrol.

The fact that Saundby was to be the arbiter of whether the op went ahead or not, didn't give him much of a warm glow.

Saundby; as short as a schoolboy, with his small, neat face and questing nose, and his nondescript hair brilliantined to the contours of his scalp – so short that only his head seemed to reach above the bridge front. And his wide, bright eyes that appeared to miss nothing.

Less than an hour later, *Saraband's* radar picked up the trace of the Sumatran mountains, and they had dived to await nightfall and their run into the Bengal Passage between Sumatra and their designated landing spot on the south side of Pulo Weh.

Now that the monsoon had blown through, the humidity had lost much of its malignancy and the night air no longer cloyed at those on the bridge; was once again something breathable and fresh. Down below though, in their hot, steel pipe, every breath still felt as though you had to suck it through wet muslin, despite the diesels drawing down all the fresh air they could, the condensation still dripped and what clothes you chose to put on, you didn't wear them, they just stuck to you. There was mildew everywhere, and on everything that didn't move.

Harry and Bill Laurie sat round the wardroom table with Capt. Saundby and George, maps and charts spread before them in a confusing pile. Since Saundby had insisted on wearing his uniform shirt, with epaulettes, three pips and regimental badge, Harry and Bill had put on drill shirts over their skivvies, so as not to let the side down. Only George, in his pale linen shirt, looked cool. Harry and his officers all liked George. He was a real gentleman, and his English sounded as if he'd learned it in a Surrey conservatory.

The insipid light from the little wall shades meant they had to peer at the maps. Saundby had a pocket magnifying glass. They laid their plans.

*

There was still almost two hours of daylight left, and *Saraband* had dived much earlier to close the coast. Right then, they were at periscope depth in the Bengal Channel, but the water was deep here, and they still had over 270 fathoms beneath their keel. They were also less than a mile off the southern coast of Pulo Weh. Saundby was studying all the cartography he could find for an alternative landing spot.

Gowers' excellent navigation had brought them right up to within half a mile of the original, for a quick periscope look to check all ashore was as it should be. When Harry had stuck up the search periscope and blasted it to full magnification, there had been a perfect view of the beach and the paths leading off it, up a gentle rise into the surrounding jungle. On first sight it looked like a lovely spot for a holiday. He had then sent the periscope down.

'I think I needed to take a look too, Captain.' It was Saundby, at his elbow. Being impertinent again, haranguing a submarine captain in his control room and demanding to look through the periscope.

'Certainly, Captain Saundby,' Harry had said. 'But in the Trade, we only tend to keep the periscope up for a few seconds at a time in case anyone sees it. I shall send it back up again in a few moments.'

Saundby stood bouncing from one foot to the other, waiting, clutching a crudely-folded survey map of the area in one hand. The rest of the crew sat staring fixedly at whatever valve or gauge or bend in a pipe was in front of their faces. Harry said later he could practically feel the collective seething.

He had sent the 'scope up again, aligned it on the bearing, and gave Saundby a very brief instruction on how to use it. He had to order it down a touch, so that Saundby could see through. The man stuck his face to the eyepiece, and fiddled with one hand.

'Oh!' he said. 'That's close! How remarkable!' And had begun to walk the 'scope back and forward, chuckling. Until he stopped. 'Oh! No, can't have that!' then he was on the move again, pausing briefly to take his face off the eyepiece and check his map, look back again and check again.

Harry had to step in and fold up the handles, before calling, 'Down periscope!'

'I *beg* your pardon!' Saundby snapped. 'I was looking through that!'

'I said, Captain Saundby, that we only keep the periscope up for a few seconds at a time,' said Harry again. 'Now, what seems to be the problem?'

So here they were, Saundby muttering something about it being like Piccadilly Circus, obviously much put out. Harry had put the 'scope up again to see for himself, and immediately spotted the problem. At the top of the main path there were a handful of native *bashas* – or grass huts – with people milling about, doing chores. It was out of the question, putting anybody ashore right under the noses of a village. People talked. So now he was doing a more meticulous sweep round the shallow bay, and he saw at its far end a stubby headland jutting out, with steep sides and garlanded by thick bush, masking the run of the coast ahead. He sent the 'scope down. He wanted to look at Saundby's map, but couldn't bring himself to ask, so brittle was his grip on the anger bubbling away down below.

So *Saraband* motored slowly on along the coast.

'We have to find another place to land right away!' announced Saundby. Both he and Harry knew most of the rest of the coast was steep and jungled right to the water's edge. Even if they did manage to land George from the dinghy at any spot there, he'd never be able to cut his way through the undergrowth. Harry looked at his watch, and said, 'just give it a minute.'

The minute passed, then another, and another, Saundby persistently tapping his map with a chinagraph pencil, and chanting to himself, 'there's nowhere else here, there's nowhere else here.'

Finally, Harry ordered, 'Up periscope.'

It broke surface, and he could see they had just cleared the headland, and lo, as he had hoped, it opened onto another, much smaller beach, well hidden from the one with the settlement. 'There,' he said to Saundby. 'That should suit our purposes admirably.'

*

Saraband withdrew to about four miles off the coast to wait for nightfall, and for Saundby, Dutton and George to prepare. Harry was sleeping when the control room messenger shook him awake. Asdic had reported multiple HE approaching from the south east.

It turned out to be a small convoy. Three steel-hulled coasters, each one between 200 and 300 tons, and one of those bloody *Chiburi* class sub-chasers. The last intelligence report he'd gone through had reported there was an improved version of the type on the loose now, equipped some form of updated hydrophone kit. The convoy should have been an ideal target for *Saraband*. But Harry had been ordered not to engage any enemy shipping. He thought about conducting a dummy run against them instead, but dismissed it immediately; he had been ordered not to 'become involved with, in any way, with *any* enemy shipping', either. He watched them hungrily as they slipped by, and then after he'd ordered the periscope down, wondered at himself, and where the bloodlust had come from. Probably being cooped up for a week with Saundby had done it. He went back to sleep.

When it was dark, they had come up and headed back inshore on one diesel, the other cramming on charge. Harry handed the approach to Gowers, standing over his shoulder just in case. He'd watched Gowers earlier, meticulously taking all the bearings to each hill and outcrop onshore, backing them up with soundings, drawing up a precise plot to get them as close in to their selected landing beach as the Captain might wish, marking

229

exactly the spot where they'd want to drop their passengers. All without being asked. The chap continued to confound him. Timid and self-effacing so as to be almost not there as an officer, and utterly professional as a navigator.

Harry interrupted his progress only once, to halt their advance to the shore and cruise up and down with still a good four miles to go. The three quarters moon wasn't due up until midnight and he'd agreed with Saundby earlier it'd probably be better to have its light to help them get ashore and off the beach, just to be safe. Also, Harry wanted as much charge on as he could get. It was that niggle at the back of his mind. He didn't like having bad feelings.

Then the allotted time came. Harry could see the silvery glow rising between the dark humps of the island as he stepped to the voice pipe. The moon was coming up.

'Control room, Captain here. Break the charge, engine clutches out, standby motors.'

He had decided to ghost in on electric power; no point in waking the surrounding countryside with rumbling diesel thump. Gowers called down their new course, and crouched over the binnacle, taking continuous bearings, mapping in his head their sedate progress in towards the land.

The moon, clear of the island's ridge tops now, bathed everything in its shimmer, picking out the lines of *Saraband's* hull, trimmed down; Harry could even make out the broad strand of the main beach, and the settlement's *bashas*. He watched them slowly eclipsed by the stubby headland, and then the much narrower strand of their landing beach appear. He had told Gowers to lay them within 900 yards of the shore; close for *Saraband*, but it would still give their party a strenuous pull.

Suddenly Harry was aware of a crudely slapped about Al Jolson at his side, face all blacked up, and his thin lips glowing pale. 'Right. That's us then,' said Saundby, grinning like he was about to take the kids out on a pedalo.

Harry hadn't heard anyone come up onto the bridge. He had been listening to Gowers announce that they were right on position now, and call down for 'stop together'. Bloody man, creeping about. But he just smiled, leant to the voice pipe and said, 'Control room, bridge. Tell the cox'n it's time to get going.'

What happened next had been well choreographed beforehand. Harry, looking down on the casing, saw the torpedo loading hatch open and the bodies tumble out, followed by the collapsed crumple of the inflatable. Harry watched the inflatable hefted clear of the hatch and then last man was out, and the hatch door was slammed firmly shut. He never liked having deck hatches open at sea, the deck was too close to the water, especially when they were trimmed down, as they were now.

There was a sudden hiss as the inflatable's CO_2 canister was yanked and the beast ballooned to its rightful shape; it would have skittered over the side and been gone if the cox'n hadn't already had its painter in a double hitch round one of the deck cleats. Harry smiled to himself; it was always a joy to watch a man who knew what he was doing at work.

'Well, best of luck Captain,' said Harry, turning to look at Saundby peering over the bridge front.

'Yes, indeed. See you in three hours then,' and the little man gave Harry a firm handshake and was off down on to the casing. He was last into the inflatable, picking up his paddle with one hand, and waving with the other. Harry watched the three of them pulling away into the flat black of the listless sea, Saundby and Dutton rowing, and George, sitting straight-backed in the stern, steering with a third paddle, their progress marked by tiny little explosions of green phosphorescence. He watched them onto the beach, a little jumble of jostling figures as they carried the inflatable up to the tree line, and then were gone.

Back at 0400, indeed. That was the plan. Dutton would stay hidden with the inflatable and Saundby would see George inland, and on the path to whatever rendezvous these secret squirrels had planned. Meanwhile *Saraband* would lurk about close in offshore until Saundby and Dutton returned to the beach, and called them in like a cab off a rank with their little torch by repeating the letter U in morse; dot, dot, dash; repeat.

Harry turned to Gowers and said, 'Well done, Vasco, now take us back out again. Three miles should do us.' Then he ordered that Scobie should send him up a flask of coffee and a sardine sandwich.

Harry was too tense to let his mind wander far from the operation at hand. He tried stretching out on his hammock arrangement, but he was too restless and just spent the time leaning over the Oerlikon bandbox rails, watching the trickle of their green glowing wake as they nudged along with barely steerage way, killing time, the diesels cramming on amps. The niggle in his head had turned into a dread they'd be surprised by one of those Jap *Chiburis* and forced down for an entire day with only a short charge on.

The three hours dragged by, and then it was time to head inshore again. Harry ordered *Saraband* to Diving Stations, her gun crews closed up under the gun tower and conning tower, the forward torpedo room closed up and two tubes flooded, Number One on the dive board ready to take them deep, and Gowers with a plot that marked the shortest course to the 100 fathom line. There was now only him and three lookouts on the bridge, and behind them, the radar head turned with a monotonous regularity, sending out its pulses to probe the night while McTeer sat hunched over its screen watching for anything bouncing back. Harry wanted to be ready for anything.

The charge was broken, clutches pulled and the motors engaged, and in they glided.

Harry intended to risk going into within 700 yards of the beach this time; it would leave only between 10 and 20 feet under the keel, but with less distance for their passengers to row, they'd be out of here far quicker. Harry was crouched over the binnacle, checking bearings to the shore, when …

'Signal flashing, five points on the port bow, sir!' It was one of the lookouts. Harry looked up, then looked at his watch.

Dot dot dash … dot dot dash … dot dot dash.

' … the letter U, sir! Repeating, sir.'

The signal right enough, but it was at least a quarter of an hour too early, and because the moon was still above the loom of the island, he could see it was much nearer to *Saraband* than the surf line.

'… I can make out shapes on the water, sir,' the lookout was saying, night glasses pressed to his face. 'It's a dinghy, sir … two figures sitting upright … one's rowing … one of them's waving now, sir.'

Harry picked up the hand-held Aldis lamp from its hook by the binnacle and flashed the response, the letter D … *dash dot dot.*

*

232

Harry and Bill Laurie had the two adventurers round the wardroom table for a de-brief. Signals exchanged and understood, Harry had conned *Saraband* at slow ahead right into the path of the inflatable so that Dutton, with just a couple of strokes of his paddle, had brought them alongside *Saraband*'s deployed bow plane, and Saundby had merely stepped aboard. The cox'n and a rating had hauled the inflatable up behind them and let the CO2 out, before bundling it back down the torpedo hatch behind them.

Dutton, the Royal Marine, now sat up straight before him, and only talked when spoken to, conscious of exactly where he was, although he couldn't help his grin. Saundby on the other hand was like an animated schoolboy, hands gesticulating, words tumbling out.

The row in had been, 'like being on the Serpentine,' said Saundby. They had hit the beach without a hiccup, dragged the inflatable up the sand and George had stepped out, 'without even getting his feet wet.' Finding the path had been, 'a piece of cake, with all that moonlight', and Saundby had handed George over to 'his chums', waiting for him up on the main trail that led to the main port town at Sabang. He had been back on the beach with Dutton again within the hour. However, they'd got tired of waiting and thought they'd paddle out at their leisure to meet *Saraband* halfway. Harry didn't mention that that had been a pretty damn fool thing to do, as neither of them knew what currents there were, or what was the set of the tide. They could have ended up anywhere along the entire stretch of the Bengal Passage. But as Harry had seldom seen anyone so pleased with himself as Saundby, he decided not to prick his bubble. Instead, he ordered Scobie to put a tot in their coffee and then told them both to get cleaned up and have a lie down. They now had five days to kill.

*

And sure enough, five days later, they were in with the shore again, 20 minutes early for their midnight rendezvous with George. The moon was well clear of the shadow of the island, and just that much brighter. God, but Harry was glad the wait was over. But he wasn't happy.

Saundby was on the bridge with him, in all his war-paint, fidgeting.

Harry had to say one thing for him: he'd never once broken security the whole time he'd been on board. Harry was no more the wiser about what Saundby, or George, or Dutton for that matter, were there to do on Pulo Weh than when they'd first walked up the gangway.

After heading back out to sea, *Saraband* had spent those days, first slowly moving down the Sumatran coast, looking in to ports down the eastern edge of the big island for potential targets once she was free; then creeping back again. Harry had even marked one; a railway bridge crossing a river mouth on the approach to the port of Sigli, so close to the open sea it was prime for a gun action; made even more so by the fact that there appeared to be a busy timetable on the line, from all the goods trains he'd watched pass through his periscope. From Saundby's exhaustive collection of survey maps, he'd learnt that the line ended at the north's main town, Banda Aceh. So, he'd promised himself to look into its port, Ulee Lhoe, on the way back up the coast. When he did, mere hours before, he'd seen something there that had made him feel even more twitchy about this whole op.

Then there had been the nights; all spent on the bridge, fretting.

Saraband spent the nights well out in the Malacca Straits, one diesel pushing them along at never more than three knots, the other cramming on charge. Harry passed the time watching the stars, or the marine life. On the first night, he saw two whales, rising and diving, making their way north. Like on all previous sightings of marine life, he had no idea what kind they were, and it annoyed him. Dolphins were always there.

That was when the thoughts started intruding. Harry, the master at putting things in boxes; well, now it seemed like the boxes were getting full up, stuff was bursting out of them all over the place. He thought about his father, gone now. Dead. And all the things he'd never get to say to him. To ask him. And his mother; a sudden vision of her all alone in that big house. Sitting forlorn in the big kitchen. Until his common sense self overcame this maudlin version and suddenly the echoing emptiness was populated again with the three clattering, yelling, laughing evacuee children, as he knew it would be. Agnes, little Maggie … and then he couldn't remember the little boy's name. But he knew they would be there, sharing her grief, just as he was not.

Then there were all the thoughts about Shirley. What his mother had said when Shirley dumped him … when had that been? Two years ago? Three? … about how, whatever future he had before him, it would be less without her. What the bloody hell was that supposed to mean? Shirley Lamont; just one more bloody thing in his life that just wouldn't stay in its box.

And then there was this Cotterell woman. What in God's name did he think he was doing with her? Having fun? Certainly, she was fun. But she was so much more than that. A very real, up-and-down, squared-away, three badge, Grable-bodied woman; no girl, she; who might be sitting there in front of you right now, laughing at your jokes, but in reality was so utterly remote, so utterly un-knowable.

The 'Grable-bodied' bit was a McTeer-ism, a tribute to his favourite cartoon subject, the Hollywood actress Betty of that name. She of the famous legs, not to mention her … other attributes.

Thinking about Betty Grable reminded him of that big Wren, Mandy Trevanion; the one who'd helped run his Perisher. What was it she'd said? Something about how they were all probably for the chop, so what was the point in being glum when you had so little time left for parties?

Dr Cotterell took him to parties alright, and what with SEAC having all but taken over Kandy, to their huge dances. Which was marvellous. After all, wasn't the whole idea of Dr Cotterell to help him forget about the war? Except she had done something else entirely. Being with her, looking forward to being with her, had instead focused his mind on living again. The prospect that he might die in this war was something he had stuck in a box long ago so he didn't have to think about it. But now Dr Cotterell had let it out.

He considered the purposeful way he had been trying to blank from his thoughts the chop list of boats operating out of Trinco. Even though you couldn't help but hear. Even though every time he came in from patrol now, once he'd filled in all the paperwork, he'd headed straight for the hills; hadn't hung about in the wardroom to hear the details.

Four boats had still been lost whether he was paying attention or not. Out of just the dozen or so that had been out here when he had first arrived.

Seeing that *Chiburi* had reminded him too, how lucky he and *Saraband* had been. All their patrol billets so far had been at the top end of the Malacca Strait, or even further north. The Japs sent mostly their second division anti-submarine stuff up north. All the Jap heavy stuff, the *Chiburis*, and their big fleet destroyers, they were mostly deployed further south around Singapore, or the Musi River estuary, protecting all the oil traffic coming out of the refineries around Palembang. Harry didn't fancy coming up against those bastards. Each *Chiburi* could carry up to 120 depth charges. The thought of all that explosives coming down on you was enough to make anyone's knees turn to jelly.

He knew that just serving on submarines made death a very real prospect. Just being on a submarine was dangerous. The secret was not to care. But Victoria Cotterell was making him care.

Then Scobie interrupted him, bringing up sandwiches and flask of coffee and he went back to watching the stars and the dolphins, while he ate; until all the thoughts started leaching back into his consciousness, and the whole tumbling mess began churning through his mind all over again.

On only a couple of occasions did McTeer, in the radar cubby, call up a contact, forcing him back to work, to steer *Saraband* out of the way.

Then, earlier today, he'd loitered the boat at periscope depth at the mouth of the breakwaters leading into Ulee Lhoe port. There had been a cluster of junks and a large steel-hulled ferry, all good gun targets. And two smaller vessels, like fishing boats; modern design, almost identical, with strange looking deck hampers he couldn't identify, all snugged down with canvas covers. The boats were trotted up against the far wharf, and while he watched, several deckhands emerged and began casting off. Puffs of smoke to show diesels firing on boat boats, and them beginning to move out into the harbour.

It was when he was in the act of sending down the periscope that he'd seen the Japanese sailor suit, in the wheelhouse door of one of them. What was a Jap sailor in uniform doing on a Sumatran fishing boat? He hadn't hung around to find out. Were they really patrol craft, and was the deck hamper concealed weaponry? Or was it just all that crap swirling round his head that was making him too twitchy? He hated having crap swirling round his head. Up until now, he had been rather good at stomping on it.

Too late now, they were off the landing beach, and ready. The gun crews were closed up under the hatches, and the cox'n and his lads were under the torpedo loading hatch with Dutton, his radio and the collapsed inflatable. Up on the bridge with him were four lookouts and Caudrey. And of course Saundby, who fidgeted.

The moon wasn't up yet, and there were scattered clouds that would mask it off and on when it did rise. The Midnight deadline came and went. The firm arrangement was *Saraband* would wait only half an hour. If George didn't show the first night, they'd be come back at the same time the next night. Harry looked on as Saundby kept staring at the second hand on his watch, clicking round, second by second, for the entire half hour.

Harry watched his own second hand approach the half hour, then with a few seconds still left, he said, 'Right. We're off. We can come back tomorrow,' and he bent to the voice pipe to start firing off orders, thinking, *what a bloody anti-climax.*

He was already saying, 'Clutch in motors, half astern together. Pass the word to the cox'n, casing team to stand down', when one of the lookouts yelled, 'Signalling light on the beach, sir. Off the starboard bow.'

Harry looked up. It was their code alright. But then it stopped. When it started again, the light had moved. Meanwhile, with every second passing, *Saraband* was slowly edging away seaward. Harry said to Caudrey, 'Is it me, or is the light coming from too far up the beach?

Caudrey said, 'It is, sir. In fact, it's in the treeline, sir.'

It was also coming from the wrong place. They had arranged for George to make his signal from closer to the stubby headland, closer to the path off the beach, where the strand was not so wide, and so a shorter distance to drag the inflatable.

Harry had expected Saundby to explode, to demand they turn back. But the rules here were really very simple and had been explained to Captain Saundby in precise detail. Saundby was in charge of the op. But Captain Gilmour was in charge of the submarine, and that meant he could call the entire thing off at any time if he felt his submarine might be endangered.

Harry was about to explain his reasoning; how he had no way of knowing what was happening on the beach, so everything was going to be done by the plan, but when he looked at Saundby, the man was frowning in the direction of the flashing torch too, the letter U in morse; dot, dot, dash, coming at them out of the night, repeating and repeating. Saundby obviously didn't like it either; the fact that it was late *and* in the wrong place.

The next day dragged by. *Saraband* loitered at 80 feet, well out in the channel, at watch diving. Harry told Scobie to lay on a special dinner for the crew, tinned lentil soup, steak and kidney pie, roast potatoes and tinned carrots, and rice pudding with raspberry jam. Jack never ceased to amaze Harry. Here they were, 10,000 miles from Blighty, on the other side of the world, only five degrees above the equator, the temperature in the boat bubbling around the high 80s Fahrenheit, and they weren't happy unless they were eating like it was a wet afternoon in Great Yarmouth, in March.

When *Saraband* went inshore that night, she was early again. Harry and Saundby had had several conversations about how this was to go down, Saundby endlessly trying to rehearse scenarios as to why last night had happened as it did … 'maybe he was just late to the rendezvous, was still running to get there …' then, '… maybe his watch stopped and he re-set it wrong. He was just late …' then, later, 'maybe he's hurt. Maybe he's sent someone else to bring help …' Harry said, 'You have to stop this, Captain. We can "maybe…" until we're blue in the face, and we still won't know what has happened. So we just play it by the plan and see what transpires.'

'What d'you think, Bill?' Harry asked Number One, to one side.

'I think he's in a blue funk,' Bill replied.

This time going in, Harry wanted to be ready for anything. *Saraband* sat beam on to the beach, with not only the cox'n and his casing team up, ready to launch the inflatable, but the deck gun crew up too, with a round up the spout, and Tupper and Crick manning the Oerlikon behind him.

Midnight came and went. Harry was thankful for the lack of moonlight, there were still almost 40 minutes to go until it was due to rise. Saundby, all blacked up again, was back on the bridge. And he wouldn't leave Harry alone, every few minutes back and forth, arguing now about the wisdom of proceeding; finally uttering the so far unutterable – that maybe the Japs had caught George, made him talk, and were luring them all into a trap. Harry had been thinking just that for some time.

The night beyond was still, the island loomed dead ahead, a depthless black shadow, distant jungle screeches and the susurration of waves on the beach wafting back through the heavy air. Were the enemy waiting there for them? The only thing that stopped Harry from shutting the whole thing down right now was the scene in his head, of being in Captain Ionides' cabin, trying to explain to the S4 why he'd done it. Were his concerns real, or was all that shite that'd been rushing through his head making him flinch from shadows?

Right on the half hour, Harry saw it himself before the lookout called, 'Signal light on the beach … !'

The letter U, not quite where it should have been the first time, but close enough. Repeating now. Harry thought to himself, *If you were on the beach, why did you wait half an hour exactly before signalling? Again, like last night?* But he dismissed the thought. Instead, he looked down into Saundby's goggling white eyes, staring transfixed at the shore. *Bill Laurie was right, the poor man is scared fartless.*

Saundby said, 'What if it's not him?'

There was no time for this now. Harry had made his decision. Now, Saundby had to make his. Harry said, 'Captain Saundby, you have to decide now whether you are going to go ahead with this operation. As you know, I do not have the authority to order you to go, but unless you make your mind up right now, I'm putting to sea, and we are leaving and not coming back. Do I make myself clear?'

How would Saundby account for any decision to abort?

But all Saundby did was nod, then turn and climb down onto the casing. There was a brief milling about as the inflatable burst to life again, and Saundby went first, Dutton's radio set was lowered to him, and then Dutton himself stepped off the bow plane and onto the bobbing shape, and they cast off.

Harry was aware of Number One at his elbow.

'You have to hand it to the little fellow,' Bill said, his grim face pale and thoughtful, in the darkness. 'Scared out his skin, yet he still went. Takes a lot of bottom to do that, sir. Don't you think?'

Harry nodded, smiled, then said, 'For God's sake don't say anything about bottoms in front of McTeer. Or I shudder to think of what cartoon will be waiting for poor Saundby when he comes back.'

But what he was really thinking was, *My God, have I just brow-beaten that man into going to his own death?*

They watched the little black smudge on the water creep towards the beach, until it was lost in the loom of the land. Then they waited.

*

What they were waiting for was *dash dash dot dot*, for 'zulu', indicating that Saundby and Dutton had met up with George, he was OK and the mission was OK, and *Saraband* could bugger off and get on with her patrol.

Nothing. Minutes dragged by. Harry let the others on the bridge scan the beach, he kept his eyes seaward, and up and down the coast. For anything that might be coming their way. How long did it take to walk up a beach, say hello, inquire how everybody was doing and flick your torch on?

Then the original signal came again, from the right. The letter U, again and again. What the hell was going on? The lookout had called it, and Harry had turned to see the blinking light.

Then the lookout called again, 'Object in the water!'

Harry stepped to the side of the bridge. Even with his poor night vision he could see that it was the inflatable, but even at this distance he could see only one figure sitting upright in it. This wasn't good. Not good at all.

'Gun crews close up and stand by,' he said, over his shoulder and over the bridge front. No shouting. He took care never to forget how far voices could carry over water.

And then the entire bowl of the shallow bay exploded; from the steep slope of the stubby headland to port, to the hills rising above it as it swept east. Harry saw the tracer coming first, before the chatter started. Four firing points, all converging to where they must have assumed *Saraband* was, except she wasn't, not quite. Heavy calibre machine guns, the noise of their bursts running together to weave a solid din, tracer marking the parabola of their fire, arcing over Harry's head, all of the lines converging

240

out to sea and to his right, the red tracer rounds landing, skittering over the surface of the matt black of the water.

Harry stepped to the bridge front and called down to the gun-layer, 'Purdie! Open fire on the signalling light! Now!'

A deep crack from the shore, to the east. A bigger gun. And in a moment, 100 yards or more further out from the beach than *Saraband*, a gout of water where the shot had landed. Some sort of field gun, Harry guessed. An army gun, whose gunners could not conceive a submarine would be so far inshore. But he could not imagine it would take too long for them to be disabused. The tracer bursts were now ranging back, seeking their target closer to the shoreline. It was getting decidedly dodgy here.

'Clear the bridge!' yelled Harry. The risk of voices carrying ashore seemed less important now. 'Check fire, Purdie! Clear the casing!'

Another deep, resonating crack, and this time Harry felt the waft of an artillery round go screaming over his head. *Saraband* needed to dive, right now. There was enough water under her, even this far inshore. Just. The last tracer burst fell short. They had been bracketed. It was only a matter of time. Harry looked over the bridge wings, and there was the inflatable, still coming on, the single figure paddling like fury, making ground with each stroke, but oh, so slowly.

Harry's mind clarified, like a tumbler of neat gin. He needed to step to the conning tower hatch, hit the tit to dive the boat and drop down. Of course, the instant he did, that man in the inflatable was dead. Or worse, a prisoner of the Japs. He had as good as sent him out onto that beach, so was he now going to abandon him there?

Ting! Ting! Clang! Ting!

Machine gun bullets hitting the casing; had that been one hitting the deck gun?

Harry hid behind the periscope stands, not feeling particularly brave, wishing he could duck, except he needed to be standing up, to see how the inflatable was doing. This time, when he peeked round the stand, he could see a second figure in the water, kicking and swimming behind the raft, holding on with one hand, helping to propel it with his feet. They were so close now.

But this was just two men against the lives of his entire crew, and his submarine. If he'd had a direct line to his Captain S and could ask him, right now, what he should do, Harry had no doubt what the answer would be. But the orders he needed give, that would leave these chaps behind, stuck in his gullet. He could not speak them.

'Are you alright, sir?'

He spun, and there was Gowers' head in the conning tower hatch.

'Yes,' said Harry, suppressing a flash of irritation at such a stupid question, but knowing immediately that Gowers was right to ask. How much more stupid would they have looked down in the control room waiting for orders while he, the captain, was lying up here with his head blown off?

Gowers said something down the tower that Harry didn't hear, then he leapt up onto the bridge and crouched behind the thin plate of the bridge front; probably no protection at all from a burst of machine gun fire.

'They've almost made it, Mr Gowers,' said Harry, risking another look.

Ting! Ting! Ting!

Just as another artillery round went tearing over.

Gowers just nodded and slipped off the bridge. Harry didn't understand what he was doing at first, then it dawned on him; Gowers was going to pull their two chums aboard. Harry had not ordered him to, but he was doing it anyway.

Harry had to look, despite all the *zzzzing! zzzzing!* going past his ears.

Gowers, in his shorts and shirt, standing on the ballast tank, one hand wedged in a vent, reaching into the inflatable for its painter, the man inside too exhausted to fumble for it himself. All the bangs and flashes and rounds in the air; Gowers calmly wrapping the line round a fairlead and then dragging each man out the raft and propelling him by his backside up onto the casing.

Harry shouting, 'Never mind the bloody raft!'

But Gowers had just been casting it off; then Gowers propelling Saundby and Dutton up the bridge ladder; both men retching and coughing, hardly able to breathe; done, spent, bundled down the conning tower hatch, Saundby head first. Gowers followed them as Harry sounded the dive klaxon and jumped after.

When he hit the control room deck plates, he could see immediately that Number One had her not running for the open Indian Ocean, but on 165 degrees and heading for the 100 fathom line and the Malacca Straits.

Harry said, 'Maintain your heading, keep eighty feet.' Then he turned to Gowers, who was leaning panting against the chart table. 'Mr Gowers. Bloody good show!' he said, and gave him a thump on the shoulder that made Gowers wince. 'Bloody marvellous, Mr Gowers! Bloody marvellous!'

Twenty

'High speed HE, green four zero, closing fast,' Meek's voice from the Asdic cubby was tight. Harry listened as the leading seaman trotted out his narrative of what the sounds in the water were telling him; two ships, almost certainly destroyers or large sub-chasers, barrelling in from the straits. Harry ordered every fan shut down, the boat to go silent, the revs cut until she had barely steerage way in the deep. Hoping, willing the boat to become a black void in the water.

Meek talked them through the enemy's passing, like some course-side commentator at the Grand National, but without the rising excitement. Harry stood stock still in the red-lit control room, feeling the sweat trickle on his flanks, willing the two speeding ships to have no new-fangled thing in the water, able to listen and to hear; grateful for every mad rushing rev on their propellers that might saturate the deep with their own noise and not *Saraband*'s. And when they were gone, he ordered *Saraband* back to life, and her continued creep to the east of Pulo Weh.

Saundby, with two huge tots in him, was at the wardroom table, at last able to speak: his breath back and his head coherent again. A huge mug of sweet tea, glaucous with condensed milk, sat steaming before his sunken head and sagging shoulders. Despite the treacly heat that clung to everyone else, Saundby still needed a blanket round those bare shoulders. The brilliantine was gone from his hair, it was the humidity that now plastered it to his head.

'What in God's name happened?' asked Harry.

'… we were already dragging the raft up the sand, and I was hissing at him, "George! George! We're bloody here!" But the torch just kept flashing … it was coming from some rocks, boulders in the sand, a rocky outcrop, I dunno … so I told Dutton to stay with his set and I crawled towards them, still hissing at the poor bugger, hoping nobody else would hear, not that there looked to be anybody about … and then I heard his bloody giggling … you know, George, like he used to do … like a girl. Then he was all, "Sir Sawby! Sir Sawby! Here! You must come here!" Like he couldn't speak English like a white man any more. Like some bloody coolie. It made my bowels run cold. I told him, you come here, help us with the kit. But then he says, "… no, no. Both you come to me, I'm hurt, I'm wounded, I need help, two must come!" And I thought, bugger this! I was back at the raft as fast as I could skitter, bundled Dutton in and we pushed off … and the rest … well … thank you for waiting Captain Gilmour, by the way. Thank you, from me, and from Dutton. For our lives.'

'Don't mention it,' said Harry with a wan smile. 'Just out of curiosity, why was Dutton in the water pushing and not rowing? Would that not have been quicker?'

Saundby looked up through the steam of his tea. 'His idea. Said if only one of us sat up, and then caught a burst, the other could climb in and keep going. Seemed as good an idea as any at the time.'

'You were lucky,' said Harry.

'No, Captain Gilmour. We had you,' said Saundby, with not a trace of any other meaning.

Harry thought about the two odd craft in Ulee Lhoe, with the bloke in the Jap sailor suit in the wheelhouse. If the Jap navy had been to seaward off that beach, they would all be dead now. He wondered whether those boats had been part of a plan that hadn't worked. The two destroyers streaking away astern of them now; were they turning up too late? And why? A Jap army so arrogant it thought it didn't need the navy to help it spring the trap? You could only hope so.

Anyway, they must have pinched George early, got him to spill the beans, and then just sat in wait for the submarine to come back. He wondered how they had got the word out of him; torture? Or maybe the promise of something better; an entire Indonesia free of Dutch colonial rule after

Japan had won the war? Then why had he as good as warned Saundby by talking all coolie? It didn't much matter anymore, he supposed. All he knew was that he would not be in George's shoes right now, for the world.

Back at the chart table, looking at Gowers' course to take them out into the straits, he didn't like their rate of progress. Three knots submerged wasn't going to get them very far, especially as this place was going to become a hornets' nest after first light; the entire Jap navy and air force knowing there was a sub about, and looking for it.

He guessed they'd probably already started. But then the night belonged to submarines, didn't it?

He had Meek do an all-round search; nothing, just the ordinary sounds of the deep out there now. So he ordered *Saraband* to the surface. Instead of slinking along at 80 feet, they'd stay up and go flat out under the cover of darkness, on both diesels, heading for the Malay coast, where nobody would be expecting them, and then worry about topping up the amps in the last hour before sunrise.

When Harry got onto the bridge, the cloud had covered everything. It was another one of those tropic nights; all creation gone, just impervious, depthless black. Harry had already decided against turning on McTeer's set; he didn't like the risk that some big, important Jap job out there might be the one with a new gizmo for hearing his radar beams pinging round the compass. So, the lookout was now just down to Mk I eyeballs, and not much good they were going to be on a night as immaculately dark as this. Nonetheless, the diesels were clutched in, and off they went on the bearing.

Harry was dozing on his hammock at the back of the bridge, when he became aware of one of the ratings shaking him. 'Sir! Sir!, Mr Verrell says come quick!'

Verrell, with the best night vision on the boat, was watch officer. He was at the bridge front. He pointed into the void when Harry came up, and said, 'Flashes of phosphorescence on the starboard bow, sir. Could be dolphins, or a wake, or a bow wave …'

Verrell knew by now that he was on safe ground, even waking Harry for a dolphin's splash. There was no such thing as a false alarm as far as Captain Gilmour was concerned.

246

'There!' said Verrell, his arm shooting out again, almost fine on the port bow. Even Harry could see the greenish, glittering streak that appeared to be ripping at a sharp angle across the water towards them. It looked … incredibly close. But how could you tell in this black void? No point of reference, no depth of vision … Until a thrum louder than their own diesels rippled in his ears, and you could actually feel air being pushed on your face. Harry bent to the voice pipe, and said in a voice rigid with urgency, 'Starboard fifteen!'

Saraband was already running at full ahead, together, and everybody on the bridge felt her heel under their feet, as she bit into her turn. Harry hit the alarm and called for the deck gun crew to close up under the gun tower. As he said his instructions into the pipe, the rest of the bridge crew saw a great looming presence coalesce in the dark; steel hull plates, their welded ridges, the smell of different diesel and somebody else's ringing telegraphs, all sweeping past at tremendous speed. No-one was in any doubt, it was a Jap warship – had to be, because no other warships operated in these waters – and she had almost rammed them.

Harry grabbed the arm of the nearest lookout, it was AB Boyle, a child, but he knew he was rated on the Oerlikon. 'Boyle!' he yelled in the lad's ear. 'Get on that gun and stand by to engage!'

Not going hard a'starboard, Harry had kept *Saraband*'s stern tucked in, so the Jap went scooting past without even a graze, but it had been close. From where he stood Harry had the impression of towering sides, suddenly dropping to a long sweep of deck at *Saraband*'s own bridge height, and a high, boxy bridge; a single funnel, much further aft, 25 mm anti-aircraft gun mounts, a blur of a face, and then the long, long stern and the run of the depth charge racks. He could have thrown a naafi bun at them, and hit.

He watched the blunt stern, the churning, glowing wake and her hull under helm, as she swung away fast. She'd seen him too, and was obviously intending to run out, and then come back again and ram. It was another bloody *Chiburi* class, no doubt about it.

He knew without telling himself, if he tried to dive now, the *Chiburi* would catch him on the way down; driving her speeding cutwater right through *Saraband*'s pressure hull, then finishing off the mess with a depth charge pattern as she swept past. Nor could he try to run away, the bloody Jap could outpace him without drawing breath. They were locked in a dance, the Jap turning, turning to get a run at them, and *Saraband* waiting to dodge at the last moment, until it got light enough to have to fight it out with guns. He called his orders into the voice pipe, 'Diving Stations! Starboard thirty. TGM to close up for'ard torpedo team … flood tubes one and three, and flood the stern tube. Set the torpedo depths to five feet.'

Chiburis only drew 10 feet.

Behind him, Boyle was wrestling open the Oerlikon's ready use magazine, hauling out the rounds. Harry tapped another of the lookouts. He couldn't make out the face in the black dark. 'Go and load for him,' was all he said, pushing the lad towards the bandbox. When he looked up, he could see the slashes of green light on the water, curling back towards them. The way the *Chiburi* was coming round … he thought, *don't do what the bugger expects, turn towards him!*

'Boyle!' he yelled. 'Stand by to commence firing! Wait for the order then aim for the target's bridge, when you can see it.'

A faint, 'Aye, aye, sir!' came back as the rating struggled to bring the weapon to readiness.

But Harry was already ordering the course change, slewing *Saraband* back to face her tormentor. One high speed pass, and Boyle could rake the bastard, then they'd see where they were. He watched the *Chiburi's* curling bow wave as it bent to come right at him, *Saraband's* jumping wire practically splitting its image in his eye. There was no point in firing a torpedo, they were too close now. Then he ordered *Saraband's* helm over, and as he felt her heel, the Jap was on him. Her forward deck gun went off, a 4.7-incher, its boom deafening *Saraband's* bridge crew, and the rending scream of the round as it went over their heads; *Saraband* too low for the Jap's barrel to depress far enough to hit her.

The touch he had ordered on *Saraband's* rudder was going to take her clear; Harry could see now he'd called it just right. They went skimming past each other at a closing speed of probably 30 knots at least. The sheer of the *Chiburi's* tall bows, rushing past so close now he felt could reach out and … He yelled, 'Boyle. Shoot at their bridge, when you bear!'

The bows had passed now, the bridge, big and boxy, was there and was passing now too, and then the *bump! bump! bump! bump!* of Boyle firing, and Harry felt the recoil up through his feet; he watched the sparks and flashes of the exploding shells, shattering the Jap's bridge glass, tearing the frames; a door splintered, all in tiny flashbulb moments, each detonation felt as a pressure blast rather than heard. And then the Jap bridge was gone into the dark too, and Boyle checked his fire.

But Harry was looking at the space between *Saraband* and the *Chiburi*, how it was opening up like they were being peeled apart instead of zipping past. He couldn't work out what the Jap skipper was up to, and then he could. Decisions being made in the flash of a gun. *This bugger knows what he's doing.* Harry's mind racing at a million miles per hour … *he's realised he's missed his chance to ram again, but he's determined to get a good kick at me on the way by* … and at the same time thinking, the Jap skipper must be still alive on that shattered bridge of his, and if he was, he must be pretty mad by now.

For Harry could see the enemy skipper had thrown his helm hard over, and was about to show his blunt aft end to *Saraband*; and as he did he was going to roll depth charges, all probably shallow set in the hope that when they dropped they'd be sufficiently under *Saraband*'s retreating stern, that their detonating would blow it off. Harry ordered *Saraband*'s helm reversed, so as she would instead turn in towards the *Chiburi*'s wake, and as she did, he watched the Jap's careering stern coming sweeping in to hit *Saraband* a glancing blow. He was thrown bodily against the bridge wing; the lookouts knowing better and clinging on; Verrell on his backside, and the terrible, un-nameable sound of tearing steel. Blurs appearing against the vague, moving, blacker darkness, dragging itself down *Saraband*'s flank; were they faces? Japanese faces? Then a sudden silence instead of the tearing, rending metal and only a green, dancing churn on the water as the two shapes, unseeable in the night, sped apart.

Boyle had started firing again, into the space where he thought the Jap might be, above all the roiling phosphorescence. Harry didn't stop him; the rounds were hitting something; who knew, he might set off a Jap depth charge. Except, right now, he'd had an idea for something more substantial to fire at the Jap.

'Mr Verrell!' he yelled. 'Relay my orders down the pipe!' And he stepped aft to stand by the Oerlikon, watching Boyle's tracer arc out in bursts. It was only when he got there, he realised how badly *Saraband* was rolling; he clung to the gun mount. Then he called an order to reverse *Saraband's* helm again

This one was going to be on the turn. 'Stand by stern tube!' he called. Verrell repeated. Turning, turning; gauging the deflection for his shot, his own director angle, by his eye; by the fire arc of Boyle's shooting. The Jap's shadow was speeding away. 'Fire stern tube!' he called. And Verrell repeated … and there it went; an explosion of glowing green bubbles, and the tell-tale trail running into the dark. Harry raised his hand to tell Boyle to check fire. The two of them, the captain and the young rating, breathing hard, staring into nothing, and then that bloody great orange flash that silhouetted the entire aft end of the Jap as it seemed to rise and separate from its huge forward mass, still in shadow and carrying on into the night; and then just flickering and darkness, and the enormous great bang that followed.

Harry reached up and helped Boyle out of the Oerlikon mounting, their bodies no more than dim shapes to each other in the dark; once he'd got him on the deck plates, he put his arm round the lad's shoulder and started leading him forward towards the conning tower hatch.

'Boyle,' he said. 'Have you ever considered taking up this fighting sailor lark professionally?'

When he turned to look down into the lad's face, all he could see was teeth glittering up at him, out of a featureless bundle. And all he heard was Boyle saying, 'Aye, aye, sir,' sounding as dazed as he looked; and then he was handing him down the hatch, calling, 'Double tot for Boyle!' Before he stood up, wondering what the hell he was going to do about the total fucking mayhem that had just befallen his boat.

Twenty-One

When *Saraband* passed the boom and entered Trincomalee, the rails of practically every ship in the anchorage were lined with sailors. They weren't there manning ship, with orders to cheer her in, it was just curiosity that had sent them all there. Everybody had heard the story and wanted to see for themselves; that *Saraband* had been chewed up by a Jap destroyer. Actually chewed up, in the literal sense of the phrase.

Alas, as she made her way up the anchorage to where the depot ships *Adamant* and *Wu Chang* lay, only those aboard the few ships moored to port of her got a good look at the damage. And they later confirmed, chewed up pretty much covered it, from just abaft the deck gun, all the way aft. Although words such as sliced or slashed or gouged might have served just as well.

For there on *Saraband's* ballast tank were the wounds inflicted by the *Chiburi,* where, when the Jap's stern dragged itself along the submarine's flank, her high-speed port propeller had sliced and torn a terrible, uncoiling series of slashes through *Saraband's* thin steel ballast tank plates. Wounds that *Saraband's* crew were intensely proud of. For those who chose to look closely enough, there was the smug expression on each one of her casing crew's faces. Then there was their immaculate turn-out, all pristine white, caps on jaunty, bags o' swank. Chests bursting with pride that their boat could have taken such punishment and not just survived it, but that they had had gone on and sunk the fucking bastard that did it to them! Which was why the sailors lining the ships on her port side started to cheer her as she crept past, without having to be asked. McTeer was already working on a series of celebratory cartoons under the title of *Take That! Tojo!*

As *Saraband* came up, the signaller on *Adamant's* bridge wing made her number and ordered her to berth on the main depot ship instead of her usual home, trotted up alongside *Wu Chang*.

'A nice gesture,' Harry observed sarcastically to Bill Laurie, standing on the bridge beside him.

'But a pain in the arse,' finished Bill. All *Saraband's* crew's shore gear was on *Wu Chang*.

But the courtesies weren't over. Captain Ionides, the flotilla boss, was waiting on the brow for Harry, waving and beaming at him; and instead of Harry coming aboard *Adamant*, he came running down the gangway onto *Saraband*; no pipes, no ceremony whatsoever.

'We'd given you up for lost,' he said, pumping Harry's hand. 'Right, show me all the holes!' And with Harry holding one of his hands, old Tinsides was down on top of the port ballast tank, leaning out to gaze down through the giant tears in it, his face a mask of horror as he watched the green water lap through all the ripped and bent stringers and ribs.

'Dear, dear … dear, dear …' he kept repeating, incredulity leaking from every syllable. 'Somebody's broke your boat, Mr Gilmour.'

Then they were back up the gangway and onto *Adamant*, and Tinsides was leading him below to his day cabin. 'I'd already drawn up the signal reporting you overdue, presumed lost. It was just waiting its activation day. I tore it up when I you finally signalled your damage. Although looking at the state of you, it's a wonder you made it as far the boom.'

'Sorry sir,' Harry replied, 'I should have let you know earlier, but I thought it best not to acknowledge your last signal. I didn't want to let any Jap listening in to know where I was until I was too far away for them to do anything about it.'

The day after the *Chibuki* had torn them up, *Saraband* had received a signal from S4, to proceed to position 3 degrees 20 minutes north, 96 degrees 53 minutes east, just off the port of Tapaktuan on the west coast of Sumatra, with orders to act as a guard boat to rescue downed aircrew.

Harry remembered looking at it, not having a clue what it meant. It took Saundby to explain what it was about, the two of them sitting at the wardroom table, *Saraband* groaning and screeching as she limped out into the Indian Ocean, going the other way. 'Your Fleet Air Arm are going to launch a big raid on Medan. From carriers out in the Indian Ocean. It was why I was to be put down on Pulo Weh, to watch in case any Jap fighters were going to be there to pick them off on the way by. Obviously your boss wants you on this position,' he said tapping the signal flimsy, 'so you can grab any lads from planes damaged over the target able to make it back out to sea.'

Harry never saw Saundby and Dutton again; he found out later they'd sneaked up the gangway onto the depot ship, ashen-faced and in hurry, saying goodbye to no-one, after Harry had gone off with the Captain S.

When Tinsides and Harry got to the Captain's day cabin, his steward already had two bumpers of pink gin waiting.

'When Japanese radio broadcast they had sunk a submarine slap in your patrol area, we were worried,' said Captain Ionides, lowering himself into a big floral-patterned easy chair. 'Then when you failed to acknowledge our signal, well, we all thought that was it. So, it is very good indeed to see you back Mr Gilmour. We all had a little cheer to ourselves in the ops room when you flashed your number and announced that the rumours of your demise had been greatly exaggerated. Cheers! Bottoms up!'

Captain Ionides hurried him through his basic patrol report then took him back to the beginning and walked him through the whole story, blow by blow; he wanted to know all the details, especially how he'd managed to coax his boat all the way back to Trinco.

What did Harry remember?

He remembered being on the bridge thinking it was too late to worry about any damage; that they needed to get as far away from here as fast as possible; and ordering full ahead together, and a course that would take them well north of Pulo Weh and out through the Great Channel and into the Indian Ocean; the barrelling along at 13 knots – the best they could coax out of her skewed hull – and all the groaning and clanking from the shredded tank; and the list on her that didn't seem to be getting any better.

Then there had been the hurried briefing he'd had with Kershaw. 'The bastard hit us at rib fifty seven,' he said, 'at the back end of number three tank, then sliced us through tanks four, five and six. All the way in fact, to rib a hundred and seven. All those tanks, open to the sea. But there's very little damage to the pressure hull. I've a couple of sprung welds aft, but nothing we won't lash up quick time. And a few broken gauge faces and lamps from the depth charges he rolled as he went past.'

The depth charges? Oh, yes. There had been three of them. Of which Harry had had no memory at all, until Kershaw mentioned them. And then he did. The huge icebergs of phosphorescence leaping out the blackness of the sea, right at the spot where *Saraband* should have been if he hadn't ordered her helm reversed. He must have blanked them at the time; too many other things, more important, to think about.

Then there had been the re-storing of everything that could be moved, and the pumping fuel and water, topping up the starboard tanks to try and cure the list to port. And at first light sending down the leading stoker in the Davis escape set to inspect the extent of the damage, and him coming up, his face ashen, telling Harry all he needed to know. At least they could still dive. The forward dive planes still worked, and after all, you could argue the port tanks were already flooded, Harry had ventured to Kershaw, who looked at him like he was a remedial-class schoolboy.

Diving and surfacing however, had to be taken very slowly, Kershaw had told him; especially the surfacing. A too vigorous blowing of the starboard tanks could roll the boat, and that, 'wasn't recommended', Kershaw had said.

And off they went, on their way home, which would have pleased everybody but for the excruciating discordant symphony of the port tanks' metal working and tearing, the entire way across the Bay of Bengal.

When Harry had finished the full version of his report, Captain Ionides told him to get all his torpedoes unloaded and empty the boat of stores. 'Before I even ask them, I know what the fleet engineering office is going to tell me,' he said. 'The floating dock over there is for running repairs only. This is too big a job. So, I'm telling you now, you'll likely be going round to Walker's yard at Colombo. There's a solid month or more of dock yard work in that boat of yours before we get you back to sea. I hope you've got a good book.'

Then, smiling again, the Captain S rang for his steward and ordered more pink gins.

'But before all that, I have better news for you, Lieutenant Gilmour,' he said, taking a signal flimsy from the desk and handing it Harry. 'Or I should say, Lieutenant *Commander* Gilmour. Yes, that's right. You've been promoted ... no need to look so thunderstruck, man. It doesn't hurt, you know.'

Harry stared at the words on the flimsy. It was true. He was now a two-and-a-half ringer. This was no acting rank. It was, 'with immediate effect'.

'Thank you, sir,' he said, not sounding the least sincere.

But Captain Ionides merely sat there beaming at him. 'And well deserved, too, Lieutenant Commander. Now, you'll be wanting to wet your new half ring. I know Ginger has already taken the liberty of commandeering next door's wardroom veranda deck for tonight.'

'Ginger', Cdr. Maurice Kildare Cavenagh-Mainwaring DSO RN, had become one of Harry's very good friends since he had first arrived at Trinco. So, of course he had planned a party. Harry would have done just that for him, if the circumstances had been reversed.

Except that for 1,000 miles, when not worrying about getting his boat back, Harry had been thinking about nothing else but seeing Victoria Cotterell again. Now, just when she was so close, a wardroom party had pushed her further away.

There was a stack of post waiting for him in his cabin back on *Wu Chang*. Letters from his mother – he could tell by the handwriting – and ditto for one from old Lexie Scrimgeour. God, he hadn't written to the old bugger in ages. He was Sir Alexander to the rest of the world; the Edinburgh financier whose yacht he used to crew on, who had presented him with a sextant when he volunteered back in 1939; who had promised him a job when he came home – although Harry had always been careful to say 'if' up until now; like all sailors being loath to tempt fate. Saying 'when' seemed to be another marker that the notion he might survive this war was intruding more and more. And then there were two from old Louis, the Valetta bookshop owner. Harry was going to save them, to savour, for later; a long later. Louis' letters could always be relied upon to be wry, witty, rude, even offensive – but always wise.

Then there was this other one, posted in New York, in a hand he didn't recognise. The address simply read, 'Lt. H. J. Gilmour RNVR, c/o HM Submarines, Portsmouth, Gt. Britain', re-addressed to 'c/o South East Asia Command'.

He sat down on his bunk. Could this be from her? What was she doing writing to him now? He felt a thrill catch in the back of his throat. After all, that was where she had gone, wasn't it? America. His Kitty. After she had married that US Army Air Force supply bloke; while *Scourge* was stuck operating out of Algiers, and she had still been back on Malta. Kitty Kadzow, the émigré Polish nightclub singer. He tore it open, not knowing what he hoped to read there.

But it wasn't from Kitty.

He read the opening lines, didn't quite understand ... stuff about Canada ... and going home now ... he flipped to the end.

'Jesus!' he whispered to himself. 'Fabrizio!'

And an avalanche of memories came rushing in on him, overwhelming him. His time in that hotel in Palma d'Mallorca as an 'interned belligerent'; one of the many officers and gentlemen of the Allied and Axis forces held there by the neutral Spanish authorities; mostly crash-landed aircrew who had come down on the Balearic islands rather than risk ditching in an unforgiving sea. Waiting there until their own people could repatriate them and they could start fighting the war again.

He was already laughing, just seeing the name, remembering how neither the young British nor Italian pilots had been particularly interested in getting back to the war again; the parties they used to have.

And Fabrizio.

Sottotenente Fabrizio di Savelli of the Regia Aeronautica. His particular friend. Whom he'd had to kidnap to get him out of the clutches of two Gestapo goons who had turned up in Palma looking for him; something to do with his family back in Italy, involved in some treasonous plot against Mussolini. And how he had managed to sail poor Fabrizio away to Gibraltar on a stolen yacht, as his prisoner, to spend the rest of his war in a PoW camp, instead of ending it against a wall in Berlin.

And now Fabrizio was writing to him. A long letter; effusive, at times hilarious, describing his PoW life working on a farm half the size of

Lombardy, in Manitoba; how he was getting to go home now. Thanking Harry for his life, and the British Empire for liberating Italy; and inviting Harry to a wedding, if he could make it. If his war was over yet. Because Fabrizio was getting married to his darling Sybilla. Did Harry remember her?

Remember her?

How could any man ever forget a woman like Sybilla Cruz Soriano? That raven-haired temptress from the upper tiers of the upper crust of Mallorcan society, who had once flirted with Harry at one of the many 'at homes' thrown by the joint mess of the Regia Aeronautica and the Royal Air Force, but who had only ever really had eyes for her Fabrizio.

Fabrizio: if ever there was a chap who had earned the right to go home.

There was a family address in Rome. He would write back later.

Then, there were two letters from his mother. He read the first, posted before his father had died. Then he read the one posted after. It was everything he had expected. He knew her so well. Even so, his eyes filled when he got to the bit he was hoping would be there; how his father had asked for him before he died. She even advised him not to regret all the things he would never get to say to his father now. 'He understood more than you know', she had written. 'And he missed you.' He felt the warmth trickling on his cheek at that, and didn't bother wiping it away.

It was only when he had laid his mother's letter aside that he discovered there was one from Shirley in the pile, stuck between two others because it was so thin; obviously not one of her usual travelogues. He had no idea what to expect from it.

She had been to see his mother, she wrote, after she had heard about Duncan, his father. It was all very sad. Many people always had had a lot to say about him, little of it flattering. But she remembered what her own father had said about Duncan Gilmour. He had known him on the Western Front; her father in his horsey regiment, and Duncan a stretcher bearer. Both Argyll lads, finding themselves on the same sector more than once. She wrote, 'My dad said your father was the bravest man he'd ever known. Hating everything he ever had to do out there, but doing it anyway.'

Harry lay down, and rested the letter on his chest for a moment while he let that sink in. These bloody letters from home were supposed to raise your morale, not wring your heart out. He started reading again.

> … *We're all dancing to a new Glenn Miller tune, 'Don't Sit Under the Apple Tree With Anyone Else But Me'. I sang it to the sea yesterday, when I caught the steamer to go and visit your mum. I wanted the sea to carry it to you wherever you are, far away. Because I realise now, I don't want you sitting under the apple tree with anyone else but me. So you had better not, Harry Gilmour, or you'll be getting the third degree … when you come marching home! I'm so sorry my letters have been so cold and horrible. I just got frightened. But I'm not any more. So when you read this, imagine my arms around you, because in my dreams that's where they will always be, my love …*

He laid the letter on his chest again, fighting the urge to crumple it; and then he said to himself, out loud, through gritted teeth, 'After everything … now you tell me.'

*

On *Wu Chang's* veranda deck that night, with the sun well down and the lights of the fleet glittering as if all laid on for their party, Bill had just finished topping up Harry's tumbler.

'You're looking a bit glum, sir,' he said.

'A letter from home, Bill,' said Harry, not really paying attention, gazing across the assembled throng of officers from the depot ship and all the submarines in from patrol; milling beneath the fairy lights, all bent on a good time.

'Not a "Dear John" I hope,' said Bill, giving him a sideways look.

'The exact opposite,' said Harry.

'What's up with your face, Gilmour?' It was one of the T-class skippers, over from *Maidstone*, interrupting, already half drunk.

'Woman trouble back home,' said Bill, laughing. Harry threw him a look, he wasn't in the mood to be joshed.

'Back home, Gilmour?' said the red-faced T-class skipper. 'What about your angel in the clouds?'

'What?' snapped Harry, but his flash of anger was completely missed.

'Your bit of stuff up in Kandy. Everybody knows!' said red face, laughing heartily now. 'And now there's one back in Blighty, too? You're a dirty bugger, Gilmour …'

'Dirty *lucky* bugger,' said a voice in the growing crowd around him.

'… nothing but a philly-danderer …'

'It's *philanderer*,' said Harry, not amused.

'I know that. But just because I can't say philanderer properly, because I've got a speech impediment, and you've got a new half ring, doesn't mean you're allowed to poke fun at me!' The big red face was still laughing. 'Very bad form to poke fun at a fellow officer!'

'I'll say!' said one officer, standing right by his elbow. 'He's a rotter!' said another.

Then the shout went up, 'Rag 'im, bag'im and scrag 'im!'

And that was how Lt. Cdr. Harry Gilmour lost his trousers on the night *Wu Chang's* wardroom wetted his half ring.

Twenty-Two

On the other side of the world, in a panelled office ante chamber, sat a gangly, fusty man of indeterminate middle age. Greying skin, with a sag to his face and a thin moustache on his thin upper lip, grey tinged with nicotine from a pipe that had seldom been far from his mouth for decades. At a first glance, he looked bland; at a second, you would see the implacable planes to that face. He was wearing a suit of a cut so old it might have belonged to his father, the waistcoat displaying the chain of a fob-watch, which he suited.

The main door opened, and a very young man, who had contrived to look just as fusty, stepped round. He was wearing glasses with lenses as thick as milk bottle bottoms. 'They'll see you now, sir,' he said.

And as the older man stepped into the main office, the younger one said, 'Detective Chief Superintendent Skellern, of the Special Branch, gentlemen.'

The main office was partially panelled too, with windows overlooking Whitehall and walls hung with a couple of Georgian-era oil paintings. Green leather chairs around a big, ancient table. The windows still sported their patterns of blast tape, not so necessary these days, since British propaganda that V2 rockets being launched against London were nearly all over-shooting their targets. Thankfully the Germans obviously believed it, because most of the bloody things were falling in rural Kent now. And anyway, it wouldn't be long until the Allied advances across Europe would push the rocket launch sites back, beyond London's range.

Behind the office's big table sat several gentlemen, all looking suitably venerable and at home in their surroundings. All were civil servants; a permanent under secretary from the Home Office presided.

He wanted to begin by saying, '… for the record …' and then introduce Skellern and what he had been up to, for the stenographer; explaining how he had been given the task of interrogating Captain Charles Bonalleck VC of the Royal Navy for the past few weeks, at a special centre the government maintained at Ham, in the London suburbs, called Camp 020. But then there was no stenographer, and there would be no record of this meeting.

'We might as well cut to the chase, Chief Superintendent,' said the permanent under secretary. 'We've asked you here to give us your personal observations of the interrogation, before we read your report, which, by the way, we are all extremely grateful for. So, what can you tell us about Captain Bonalleck?'

'He's off his rocker,' said Skellern. 'I'm not saying he's *always* been off his rocker. I strongly suspect until not that long ago he was just plain bad. But he's a nutter now. I speak of course without any kind of psychiatric expertise, but from the point of view of a lifetime as a police officer.'

'Of course,' said the permanent under secretary. 'And thank you very much for coming straight to the point. But could you extrapolate a little, please?'

Skellern did.

Having subjected the accused to extensive questioning, he believed that Bonalleck had had no idea he'd been involved in selling secrets to the Germans. Indeed, was convinced he had been dealing all along with the Brazilians, who were, after all, allies. So he was just oiling the wheels of co-operation really, or so he had insisted.

'Despite the evidence I presented him with,' said Skellern, 'he refused to budge. It was all lies and fabrications I was telling him, a conspiracy got up by his enemies.'

'And who did he claim his enemies were, Chief Superintendent?' asked Home Office.

'Apart from me? Oh, everybody,' said Skellern, with a sardonic laugh. 'Except the King. I don't recall him naming the King. He had a specific bile however, that he directed at some junior officer called Gilmour, whom he claimed was being egged on to spread rumours about him. None of it made sense.'

Skellern's narrative continued; one long reiteration of how the subject

261

refused to believe he was being accused of treason, or the evidence present, and in return the constant, persistent insistence that *he* was the victim; the target of some vast but always vague conspiracy.

Eventually Skellern returned to the main allegation and began to sum up. 'So, as far as I can discern there never had been any intention to betray this country on the part of Captain Bonalleck, only to exact some kind of revenge on this amorphous "them" he seemed obsessed with.'

'Did he mention any previous attempts at exacting this revenge? Any other treasonous activity he might have got up to? Any other acts of sabotage in pursuit of his cause?'

'No', said Skellern, with considerable professional certainty. 'As far as he is concerned, he has done nothing wrong. Not now, not ever. He's convinced of that, and I am convinced he's convinced of it.' He paused and looked around the table, knowing that stuff was going on here he wasn't being told about. Then he said, 'In this specific case, I am certain the subject had at no time knowingly tried to establish any link to the Germans. He is part of no network that needs to be tracked down. Whatever he got involved in was a scam of opportunity that blew up in his face. I am not saying that excuses him. He is almost certainly at heart a bad man, and most assuredly a deeply stupid one. Something he also refuses to accept, of course.'

The permanent under secretary looked at his own dossier. In it was paperwork from the Commodore, Western Approaches, and from Admiral Max Horton, the C-in-C, Western Approaches, dating back to his time as Flag Officer, Submarines. There was also a note from the Prime Minister's unofficial man in the Med, Wincairns.

In his entire career, the permanent under secretary had never encountered such a depth of establishment fury as was evinced by these documents. This affair had intruded deep into the territory of England's grey suits, and it was almost as if a red mist had descended upon its denizens. The incredulity that someone so garlanded by them once, could have been capable of what these witnesses accused him of. The spying for the Jerries stuff was truly bad. What on earth had the man been thinking about? But it was just high farce really, compared to this madman's vendetta against some obscure reserve officer. Starting with the rumours he had spread to discredit him, through each escalation until he was actually conspiring to get the young man killed in action– and prepared to sacrifice an operational submarine to do so. Senior British officers just didn't do that sort of thing. Decorated heroes of the empire simply could not be allowed to have done them, ever. That this individual had been guilty of such actions was a betrayal of the nation's fundamental myths. That was the consensus, and that was why they were out to get him. They were going to expunge him from history. The corporate hatred for this lunatic had already gone beyond legal bounds. And probably beyond rational ones, too. No rule of law was going to save Captain Charles Bonalleck now.

The permanent under secretary did not need it spelled out. It all sang out to him from between the lines. Which was why all these papers were destined for the furnace. The civil servants had had their instructions on how to wrap this matter up; all that remained for them was to make sure there were no loose ends. He was a mad dog, and mad dogs needed putting down.

Skellern was again thanked for his trouble, told to leave his report and all its copies with the assistant, and to forget the matter. Before he left, however, Skellern had a question. 'I'm no naval expert, gentlemen,' he said, 'but from what I saw of the stuff he was trying to sell, it was pretty thin fare. Was there really any danger he was going to do serious harm?'

'No, Chief Superintendent,' said the permanent under secretary. 'Not selling that stuff.'

The Bonny Boy had already been charged under the Treachery Act, 1940, before Skellern had started on him. But the policeman's report and conclusions would make no difference to the eventual outcome. *That* had already been decided. There had been some talk of judicial process requiring Captain Bonalleck to be tried at the Old Bailey, albeit behind closed doors. There would be a hearing, he'd be duly convicted and then handed over to the hangman at Wandsworth prison. But closed doors wouldn't stop the Old Bailey press mob getting wind of something happening. Especially if there was a death sentence involved. Yet there must be no chance of anything surrounding this whole sorry affair ever reaching the public domain.

There had been consternation, until someone pointed out that under the Act, members of the armed forces being charged could be tried by court martial. And court martial proceedings could be held in complete secrecy.

Captain Bonalleck's court martial was convened at Camp 020; a bare statement of the evidence of his activities in Casablanca and Lisbon was reviewed and he was offered the chance to address the charges. No mention was made of his other activities. However, throughout the hearing the Bonny Boy refused to co-operate with the court, calling it all a sham; insisting they couldn't fool him so easily; endlessly denouncing his oppressors in a shrill, hectoring and quite mad voice.

A guilty verdict was duly returned, and a sentence of death by firing squad passed. On the night before he was due to be shot, he was visited by a padre.

'This is silly, padre,' he said, in a very rational voice. 'And with all due respect, you're even sillier for allowing yourself to get involved. Nobody is going to shoot me in the morning. They're just trying to frighten me. To stop me finally speaking out. I've done nothing wrong. Treason, for God's sake! I am a holder of the Victoria Cross. I have laid my life on the line for this country. How can I be guilty of treason? No serving British soldier will ever pull a trigger against me. Because I'll refuse the blindfold, I'll look them in the eye and tell them! Then they'll know! Then they'll know!'

Captain Bonalleck never actually explained to the padre what he was going to speak out about, or what the British soldiers would finally know. Instead he trailed off and began rocking on his cell cot.

There was a brief whispered conference outside his cell. Then, with just over an hour until his appointment in the sand-bagged gym, an officer had entered the cell and offered him a stiff brandy to prepare him. He drank it down, complaining it must have been a bloody cheap one by the funny taste.

The six soldiers who made up the firing squad were marched into the gym. They hadn't been there when the Bonny Boy was carried in on his chair, a black hood over his head. All they saw was the seated figure in front of the bank of sandbags. They couldn't see that the hood covered slack jaws he couldn't close, and the drool he couldn't stop running from his mouth, or the eyes that rolled in his head. They couldn't see the elaborate strapping that held him upright in the chair. There would be no direct appeal, no getting to look his executioners in the eye.

All the firing squad cared about was the little white target, pinned to the prisoner's shirt over his heart, and all they knew was that they were going to shoot a traitor. No-one recorded what they thought about that.

The order to fire was given, and their shots made a tight little grouping, not that they would ever be able to check them, for the pulp their six rounds had made of Captain Bonalleck's chest.

*

A couple of weeks later, Admiral Horton was dragging Commodore Shrimp Simpson round a golf links just outside Londonderry. The weather was miserable; a thin drizzle that permeated every item of waterproof clothing. Shrimp was an indifferent golfer, but his admiral was fanatic, and so every visit to his subordinate had to include a round. Their conversation ranged wide, until it eventually got round to something that had been on Shrimp's mind for a while.

'Has anybody ever heard anything more about Charlie Bonalleck, sir?'

Admiral Horton said nothing until he'd teed up his ball. 'The Bonny Boy?' he said.

Whack! His ball went shooting off, straight down the middle.

The admiral knew exactly what had happened to the Bonny Boy, but what he said was, 'No. He walked off that Yank transport plane at Casablanca and vanished into thin air.'

'Oh,' said Shrimp.

Shrimp Simpson had known the Bonny Boy for his entire career in the Trade, and never particularly liked him. But ever since what he had tried to do to that young RNVR officer, Harry Gilmour, Shrimp had developed something closer to hatred. For Shrimp had once been the young officer's CO, and he never forgot one of his own.

Shrimp considered the admiral's reply for a moment, then he said, lining up his own shot, 'I suppose he realises if he's going to spend the rest of his life in hiding, when he eventually dies, there'll be no obituary in the *Daily Telegraph*.'

'Indeed not,' said the admiral. 'The unkindest cut of all.'

Twenty-Three

Harry was lying on his bunk, thinking about nothing when the control room messenger coughed loudly from beyond the curtain.

'Sir, excuse me sir. Mr Gowers says you should come to the bridge, sir,' said the lad. 'Says to tell you, sir, we're there.'

Harry swung out of his bunk. 'Thanks, Smudger, tell him I'll be right up.'

Harry emerged into a flawless day, and even before Gowers could say, 'Good morning, sir', he saw it, standing proud on the horizon, the peak of Murray Hill, which at almost 1,200 feet presided over the tiny island.

'What you see, sir …' said Gowers, turning to him with a grin and an uncharacteristic flourish, '… is the physical manifestation of that point on the chart where you said you wanted to be. Ten degrees and twenty five minutes, south, one hundred and five degrees and forty minutes … and a bit … east. In other words, we've arrived. I give you Christmas Island, sir.'

They had not quite arrived yet, probably another hour or so to run before they would be entering the island's anchorage at Flying Fish Cove, but still, it was sight to see; just like the day. He took in the huge vaulting turquoise sky, empty of any cloud apart from a few cottony wisps low in the south east, and the deeper blue of the vast, empty Indian Ocean. Looking along the horizon, he said, 'You realise, Mr Gowers, that rich people lavish fortunes on cruises to see such visions, and the navy lets us see it for free.'

Behind them, *Saraband's* wake stretched out in an untidy to-and-fro across the blue face of the world. It might be a nice day, but they were still only a little over 200 miles south of Japanese-occupied Java. They might be in waters rarely visited by either side's navies these days, but Harry didn't want anyone left in any doubt their boat was back at war. Hence the standing order for *Saraband* to steer a zig-zag routine, the full bridge watch, and McTeer's set doing its endless sweep of sea and sky.

The passage down from Trinco had marked the end of a long, mad interlude for *Saraband's* crew. Their boat had been out of the war for months; most of the time spent in Walker's Columbo drydock where they had the men with the skills and enough materiel to effect a proper repair on the damage that had been inflicted on her. Her crew had spent the time ashore.

It had been a strange time for her captain, too.

His enforced leisure hadn't started right away. Two days after limping into Trinco, after that last patrol, there had been some running lash-ups to complete, to hold her together, before she had to sail again, heading for Columbo under her own steam.

In one way, Harry recalled, that work to get her ready had been a relief; because it had stopped him rushing off up to Kandy to see Victoria. He wasn't sure he should go, after that letter from Shirley. Juggling thoughts and emotions between two women had never been a natural state for Harry; whereas others might revel in it, it was the sort of thing that made him uncomfortable; upset the balance of his peace of mind.

And having to lash up his crippled boat then get it round to Colombo had meant he'd more immediate things to worry about. Harry remembered standing around on *Saraband's* bridge on that day they finally entered the Wilson's drydock, feeling totally spare, while the yard's pilot had squeezed her neatly through the dock gates; and then having stepped ashore, being impressed by how quickly they began draining it down. He had stood with Walker's ironworks' manager, the noise and bustle of the yard going on around them. It had been like a burlesque reveal, the murky harbour water slipping off his boat's flanks, to expose, foot by foot, the true spectacle of her damage. The slashes down her port ballast tanks were too big, too real; immaculate in their symmetry, a perfect record of the path the Jap's turning propeller had taken along her side.

'Bugger me, Captain,' the manager had said. 'She looks like a bliddy toast rack.'

Not another bloody Jock, Harry, from Argyll, had said to himself.

Other dock yard workers had been standing round too. As well as most of the *Sarabands*. A foreman welder, an Englishman this time, had said to the cox'n, 'Ah've heard the King's ordered you back to Blighty. He needs a place to park his penny farthing collection.'

The boat was Walker's responsibility after that; nothing more Harry could do. But that was not what he had told Victoria on the phone, making excuses for not being with her. 'Doesn't matter,' she'd said. 'I've got leave coming.' And she had booked herself into the Galle Face Hotel on the Colombo maidan. She arrived the next day, and having unpacked, she invited him round for afternoon tea.

She looked glorious against the pillared, empire grandeur of one of the great iconic hotels east of Suez. Not a woman to be toyed with. But by then, Harry had pulled himself together. Victoria was here, now, and none of the nonsense that Shirley's letter had churned up in his head was her fault. Victoria had feelings too, he assumed.

So they'd spent an idyllic two days, right on the Indian Ocean. Then the phone had rung. There had been a big battle up at Mektila in northern Burma; a crushing victory for Fourteenth Army. But now the casualties were coming in; the Curtis Commandos were stacking up over Kandy airstrip, all of them full. She had better get back up there.

She had booked the room for a week, so Harry stayed. He left it to Number One to move the crew back up to Trinco where they were turned ashore to do their worst. Some immediately got on the bus for the rest camp up at Diyatalawa, others had preferred to stay near the beaches. The lads who had remained around Trinco had the most opportunity to run amok, and they'd made a passable attempt at it. So much so, the wardroom and the senior rates' mess had to set up a standing, joint 'apologies committee', with a duty roster of officers and petty officers charged with visiting the scenes of their fellow sailors' crimes during the previous night, to unruffle feathers before victims sought redress through more formal channels. Everyone agreed the effort had helped to keep *Saraband's* defaulters' list down to a manageable level. But then *Saraband's* crew, being mostly 'hostilities only' ratings, had never had the chance to develop the true Jack's capacity for creating mayhem ashore. No-one had died and there had been no critical injuries, to crew or bystander.

Eventually, Harry did go back up to Kandy. He stayed with the Fraters, who were happy to see him again, but he didn't get to see much of Victoria. She was working or sleeping; and in the odd moments he did see her, it was like meeting someone who was present, but not. A visitor from a strange and parallel place. In the end he didn't give her the twisted chunk of phosphor–bronze he had recovered from the bottom of *Saraband's* mangled port tank – a chunk from the edge of the Jap's propeller. A war memento; but by then he had realised she probably would not appreciate such things.

After that he had travelled round the island on his own, daily rediscovering why everybody said it was a paradise.

On a stop by in Trincomalee, on his way back to Kandy, he went for a drink with Bill.

'The beer's rationed for other ranks, which is a bloody pain,' Bill told him. 'So, I try and keep a good store of knocked-off or dodgy beer chitties. I distribute them to the needy, which is all of them, of course.'

'That's a bit dodgy itself,' Harry said.

'Better that than them drinking the local muck.'

'The arak? I've heard it gives you some hangover.'

'You heard wrong, sir. You don't get hangovers from arak, its full nervous breakdowns … blindness … that sort of thing.'

Harry had decided it was best to leave 'that sort of thing' to his Number One.

Then had come the dispatch rider at the Fraters' house, with a telegram for him. 'Report immediately to flag.' So off he had gone, within the hour, no chance to say goodbye to Victoria; no chance to say anything. It had been so anti-climactic, just slinging his kit into the back of the 3-tonner and heading off down to the rail junction. Extended leave obviously over.

A briefing from some anonymous staff officer that lasted less than 10 minutes and an order to report back aboard *Saraband* at Colombo, store and arm for a war patrol then sail 'with utmost dispatch' for Christmas Island.

'I thought the Japs had Christmas Island,' he'd said.

'They did,' said the staff officer. 'But the Australians have taken it back. You've to report to the PNO on the island to receive further orders. Carry on.'

The Principal Naval Officer. Not even a rank or a name or a hint about what those further orders might be.

Given that the orders included the words 'with utmost dispatch', *Saraband* ran for most of her passage from Colombo on the surface. She suffered only one slight delay, and that happened crossing the equator. In the tradition of the Trade, *Saraband* crossed on the surface then returned under the line submerged. When Harry had ordered *Saraband* up again, King Neptune was waiting; Cox'n Garbutt in a cardboard crown, with a huge adjustable wrench for a trident, hiding between the two conning tower hatches; there to welcome all those who had not yet officially 'Crossed the Line' into the 'Brotherhood of the Sea'.

Nearly all the *Sarabands* were novitiates, including Harry. 'Neptune' sat on the gun and presided, and Harry couldn't help but notice he had never seen a man fall to his task with such relish. His 'constables' presented each nervous victim to the King before lathering his face with oil sludge and shaving him with a steel rasp. They were then tipped into the boat's own inflatable, on deck and filled with seawater, where they were ducked, 'with much ceremony' – read, a roughhousing. Needless to say the 'constables' had paid particular attention to the captain.

And now, here they were at Christmas Island.

There were two River-class frigates in the anchorage, and a big 10,000 ton general cargo ship that was sporting a White Ensign; so a Royal Navy requisition job. Harry wondered what all that was about. He wasn't long in finding out. As they came into the anchorage, the signal light on the transport began to flash. *Saraband* was to trot up on HMS *Bonaventure's* starboard side, and her CO's presence was required aboard by the Captain S14.

So the general cargo ship was called HMS *Bonaventure*, and if she had a Captain S aboard, then she must be depot ship to the Fourteenth Flotilla. Which he had never heard of.

Going aboard her, Harry was treated with all due ceremony; met at the brow by an officer of the deck and piped aboard by a senior rate, all tricked out in their whites. On the way to S14's day cabin he saw why Fourteenth Flotilla had no other boats trotted alongside. Her boats were all on deck;

270

X-craft midget submarines. Six of them, on cradles where *Bonaventure's* cargo hatches should've been. He recognised the little tubs, looking more like spare boilers for a battleship than warships themselves; he'd seen them in all the newspaper coverage of the attack on *Tirpitz,* in that fjord in northern Norway, when was that? A year ago?

Captain S14 turned out to be a short little fellow, radiant in his whites, with a cheery face, called Bill Fell. Harry hadn't heard of him either, but then as Captain Fell informed him; if the Trade was a close-knit community then the midget submarine world was buttoned-up all the way to hell. And he, Bill Fell, had been in midget submarines right from the beginning. But welcome, anyway.

'So, you're here for the fun, Lieutenant Commander,' said Captain Fell, when they had both sat down at his dining table, gins in hand.

'What fun's that, sir?' said Harry.

'Sneaking into Singapore harbour and sinking a Jap battleship,' said the Fell, with a big idiot grin. Then he reached across for the rolled-up chart in front of him and began to outline the plan. He would introduce Harry to other officers involved in the wardroom that night.

Before Harry left, Captain Fell said, 'No shore leave for your chaps, I'm afraid. We're not long back on Christmas and the engineers haven't been over the island to check for mines or booby traps. But as you'll have seen on the way, there's not much you could dignify with the description of a beach here, it's all just bush – and there's no women on the island, and there's no beer either. Beer in the messes though, and I've allocated your crew space on our mess decks while you're alongside, if they want to shift their kit.'

Harry decided to have a quick look at the Fourteenth's order of battle, arrayed there on *Bonaventure's* deck, before he returned to *Saraband*. He buttonholed an oily-looking figure in loose overalls that were more grease than cotton, who was scratching his head while halfway up a ladder, looking like he wasn't quite sure what he was supposed to do next; a fatal look in any military surroundings, as any military man will tell you.

'Excuse me, d'you mind giving me a quick look at one of your boats?' asked Harry, dressed contrastingly in his whites, his two and half rings on each epaulette.

The grease-smeared figure looked down. 'Of course, sir. A pleasure. Follow me up.'

On what passed for a casing on the midget sub, the lad – for he was really quite young – began expounding. 'This is *XE-Ten*. The *XEs* are a modified type of the earlier *X*-craft. She weighs in at about thirty tons, is just over fifty three feet long, with a beam of almost six feet and a draught of five feet. Would you like a tour inside, sir?'

Harry went to the tiny deck hatch and looked down. She had the familiar submarine reek, but all else was … miniaturised. He went to step down inside, but really it felt more as if he was pulling her on.

The space below was like being in the interior of a medium bomber, without any perspex canopy to see out. The lad in the overalls said, 'That's the first lieutenant's seat, handy for the ballast and trim controls and the hydroplanes, and electric motor controls. And that seat there, under the two periscopes, is where the CO sits. For'ard of him is the ERA's position on the helm. The rating diver slobs about wherever he can, until he's on, and then he goes through that little watertight door into the W and D position – that's the wet and dry to the uninitiated, sir – which he then seals off, fills up with seawater and exits out the top. And when he comes back, he shuts the top lid, pumps out the sea water and he's home.'

This all felt wrong to Harry. Four of them in this? For how long? He didn't dare ask, he just gave a wan smile, and said, 'Tight.'

'Well, we've got to make room for what's behind the fore and aft bulkheads, sir. Back there we've got a four cylinder forty two horse power diesel which drives us along at six and a half knots surfaced, on a good day, and behind it a thirty horse power Blackman electric motor which can cough out five and a half, submerged. We carry enough fuel for an operating range of about five hundred nautical miles, but I'm not sure we could carry enough grub for that, sir. Behind the forward bulkhead there's the battery, Q tank, and where we keep all the tinned soup. And that board at your shoulder is why we get to be called a warship. That's all the releases for the two charges we can carry as saddle loads. About five and a half thousand pounds each. That's about four tons of amatol in total, give or take. Quite a bang when they go off. They don't half make a mess of anything sitting above them.'

Harry said, 'Thank you,' then had to struggle to get out the damn thing. When he got back aboard *Saraband*, he had no idea how he was going to dhoby all the oil stains off his good whites, especially the shoes. Needless to say, none of his officers, or Scobie, his ears flapping at the galley door, gave a damn. All they were interested in was hearing about what the hell they were all doing here, with all these midget subs that everybody could see on their cradles, and what latest escapade their Lordships had devised to cut short their young lives.

*

If you drew an imaginary triangle south from Takong Island to Batam Island and then east to Bintan, *Saraband* and *Sittang* were about halfway along its hypotenuse, right in the entrance to the Singapore Strait. They had both carried out their crew transfers in the pre-dawn light of the day now gone; their respective charges, *XE10* and *XE11* both brought alongside and their passage crews brought off, and their attack crews sent aboard.

The tows stretching back from each boat to the midget subs were taut, and no more, as they crept along at steerage way to the launch point, just under 25 miles from the Angler Bank at the entrance to the Straits of Johore, between Singapore Island and the mainland proper, with a further six miles to where *Shosei* was moored just this side of the Sembawang naval base.

Shosei was a Kongo class battleship, designed by an Englishman, Sir George Thurston, for the Imperial Japanese Navy two years before the outbreak of the Great War. Indeed, the first of the five Kongos had been built at Vickers in Barrow, so that the Japanese could study the construction technique. However, *Shosei*, like her sisters, had been much worked upon and improved since. She still mounted her original eight 14 inch guns, but down the years her hull had been lengthened to 730 feet, and she had been fitted with that tell-tale feature of a modern Japanese capital ship – the armoured pagoda mast. Her tonnage had been increased to just under 32,000 tons, her boilers from coal-fired to oil and her new four shaft geared turbines could now deliver a top speed of 32 knots.

She might be old, but she was still a formidable ship. At the briefing they'd been told her presence here had everything to do with the deteriorating situation up north in Burma, and the developing threat to the entire Malay peninsula.

Harry looked back into the impermeable darkness of another tropic night. He couldn't see Percival, *XE10*'s skipper, but he knew he would be standing out there somewhere, perched on the tiny boat's casing, one arm round her extended periscope and clutching his Aldis lamp, waiting for the signal to slip the tow.

It would be the same aboard *Sittang*, with her charge.

And there it was in the night, the tiny blinking red light; red, so its light wouldn't travel far.

'Acknowledge,' said Harry to Cantor, standing right beside him, just a darker shadow against a dark background, 'Make, "Slip tow now, I am standing by to recover. We'll have the kettle on when you return."'

Harry called down to the aft casing team to stand by to reel in the hemp line the instant it went slack. He had no intention of letting the damn thing foul *Saraband*'s propellers. It was too dark to see any activity on the casing, but he could hear them bustle. Then came the call from aft, out the darkness. 'Line slack! Am recovering now!'

And it was done. Percival would have ordered Morton, his ERA to apply a spurt of throttle so the tow slackened and then he'd have stepped forward to pull the cotter pin from the big crank shackle that held the towing line, and *XE10* would have been free and on her way.

'*XE10* signalling,' said Cantor. '"There better be a tot in it", sir.'

'Cheeky bastard,' said Harry, Cantor knowing he didn't mean it, because he could see the gleam of his teeth in the dark, grinning.

But he did mean it, really. Lieutenant John Percival RN had been the lad in the greasy overalls who'd shown him round the XE craft on *Bonaventure*'s deck that first day, and impudently had never let on he was her skipper. The first Harry knew he'd been practised on was when he was introduced to Percival in *Bonaventure*'s wardroom that night, when all the officers involved in Operation Samaritan were introduced by Captain Fell – Operation Samaritan now being the sanctioned name of this little show.

Harry had shaken Percival's hand and said, 'I met someone earlier who looks just like you, you know, except dirtier.'

'My scruffy brother, sir,' he'd replied. Harry had recognised the impish grin too; it was one he used often himself. Copied, in fact, from someone he had known long ago and been grateful to, and admired. Peter Dumaresq, whose bones probably still lay aboard the cruiser he had commanded, somewhere at the bottom of the central Med.

That Percival had reminded Harry of Peter Dumaresq, would be an impression rammed home time and again during the long tow Harry's boat was about to undertake, hauling Percival's midget sub to the waters off Singapore. It was also why Harry decided he liked John Percival right away, which alas gave him much time to fear for the lad's safety in light of the plan he was about to hear.

Like all good plans, this one had been simple – in its description. Executing it would another matter.

Fell had opened the briefing by telling all assembled that another submarine would be joining from Trincomalee the following day. HMS *Sittang* from Eighth Flotilla, previously based on HMS *Maidstone*. With *Saraband*, they would form the towing team to transport two XE craft from Christmas Island to within striking distance of their target. 'The tow could prove to be the trickier part of the op,' Captain Fell had told them, tapping with his pointer at the tiny bottleneck of the Sunda Starits, between Java and Sumatra. Tides, currents and Jap patrols were discussed; the choice of whether to transit surfaced or submerged to be left to the towing sub captains.

It would be assumed they would proceed dived during daylight hours from then on, their speed of advance negligible. So, surfaced at night, they were expected to crack on. Which was why several days had been allocated for the tows to practice with their XE craft in the deep waters here, before setting out.

Then when they reached the IP out in the Singapore Strait, *Saraband* and *Sittang's* part in the attack would be over. Then they would just wait until the XEs emerged again, and bring them home. The midget subs themselves however, if towing them back presented problems, were expendable. Getting the crews back was the main job.

'We don't really like to dwell on that aspect,' said a cheery Captain Fell. 'We X-craft chaps get quite attached to our little chums, you know, just to see them cast adrift to fend for themselves in a cruel world.'

But everybody knew they'd never be left *to fend for themselves*, they'd be stuffed with demolition charges and sent to the bottom.

The midget submarines' long approach from the IP – the initiation point – was timed for them to arrive at the entrance to the Straits of Johore just on first light. There, the XEs would dive for their run up. It was only six miles to where *Shosei* lay, but it would be a fraught passage. The waters were very shallow, and there'd be a lot of traffic, most of it light, which was worse; small boats, close to the water's surface, easier for someone to lean over the gunnell and see the dark shadow passing 10 to 15 feet beneath them. There was also a problem of there being sufficient water under *Shosei*'s keel for the craft to get under her and drop their charges.

The battleship lay on the south side of the Strait, on the inside edge of a curve in the channel, close to the north end of Seletar island. The Royal Navy knew these waters intimately; they had been their own back yard until 1942. The bottom here was gravel and at low tide there could be as little as three feet of water left under *Shosei*. Percival and his fellow skipper on *XE11*, Lt. Mark Varley RN, would only know when they got there.

Because the op was tide sensitive, both craft would have to arrive on target as close to the same time as possible, so they were to try and remain in contact throughout the run in. *XE10* would take the bow end of *Shosei* to lay her charges, and *XE11* the aft.

And that was it. *Saraband* and *Sittang* would try to hang about at the rendezvous point, enemy activity permitting, until their watches told them the X-crafts' fuel had run out and they weren't coming back.

The drills with the towing had been bloody tricky; co-ordinating your speed using the telephone connected by a wire rove into the manila towing line; surface signals using Aldis lamps, and emergency dived ones using the lamps through the periscope; and practising how never to permit sudden jerks on the manila towing line in case you parted it.

'When we started off at this game, we used chain,' Captain Fell had explained during one calamitous exercise off Flying Fish Cove. 'Which was great unless the weather was bad. Then, if the bloody thing parted, especially at the towing end, the chain went straight to the bottom dragging your X-craft with it. Bad business all round.' Then it was time, and they were off.

Perversely enough, the sweaty-palm-inducing passage through the Sunda Strait went off without a hitch. Harry had devised a plan with *Sittang's* CO, Lt. de la Pole, a comically pukka-posh Dartmouth lad whose mouth was so full of plums he could hardly speak properly. He'd brought *Sittang* out from blighty to join Eighth Flotilla while Harry had been up in Kandy, so they hadn't met before, but he turned out to be really a rather nice chap, self-deprecating and very funny. He was also, Harry quickly discovered as their op unfolded, extremely competent.

They had decided they would run through the Sunda Strait at night on the surface, using the Java side, and the fast running tidal current there. With the tide about to turn in the early hours of the morning after another tropic night, they turned east around Panaitan Island and ran into within six miles of Labuhan on the Java coast to start their run north. Radar told them there was some junk traffic in the Strait, but presumably because of the tide, not much on their side.

They weren't expecting anything big; the Strait was so shallow, with shifting banks out in the middle the further it narrowed, so that big ships usually avoided it. They'd both agreed to set their revs for a towing speed of 11 knots; between that, and the speed of the body of water they were swimming in, they would, 'shoot through faster than Errol Flynn through a harem gate,' according to de la Pole.

The peak of Krakatoa painted on their radar screens on the port beam. Then it was Siangiang Island, and they were closing the narrowest point, the 15 miles that separated Cape Tua on Sumatra and Cape Pujat on Java.

Harry let Lt. Percival up on the bridge to watch – his *XE10* right then was being commanded by her passage skipper, a young RNVR Sub-Lt. called Starkie. The red Aldis lamps flashed to and fro, between *Saraband* and *Sittang*, and between them and their charges. On *Saraband's* bridge, only commands passed between Harry and Cantor. There was no chat, no conversation. If they were spotted, there could be no crash dives here; submerging with a tow was a delicate process that couldn't be rushed. It was all to do with coordinating your trim. And anyway, there were barely 10 fathoms beneath their keel, so nowhere really to crash to. No-one on *Saraband's* bridge mentioned the prospect of having to yell to their casing party to slip the tow and abandon their charge.

And then they were through. Just like that, and a course laid for the eastern cape of Pulo Belitung and the Karimata Strait, and when they were through there, they were halfway to the target.

All the way north, Harry watched Lt. Percival and the easy way he had with his crew; the quiet, understated way he talked them through their drills, the good company he was at the wardroom table. All the while Harry trying to imagine what it would be like for the lad and his three comrades to get into that boiler tank they called a submarine and go off to war. The full-sized jobs were bad enough. And yet Percival and his crew all seemed genuinely excited and eager. He seemed such a nice chap, Harry found himself really hoping he wasn't going to get killed.

And now he was looking into the impenetrable darkness into which the two cockleshell *X*-craft had been absorbed, conjuring up how Percival would be sitting there on the casing, arm around the retracted periscope, legs dangling down the boat's hatch, conning his command as she sailed off into mortal peril, just as he had done himself so many times before. He found himself thinking of Shrimp Simpson, his old Captain S in the Tenth and wondered whether the same ineffable thoughts passing through his own mind right now, had passed through Shrimp's every time one of his crews departed. Which was one of the reasons Harry had hatched a plan with de la Pole, that instead of just hanging about IP waiting for the *XEs* to return, *Saraband* would follow a couple of hours behind them in to the entrance of the Johore Strait; wait, submerged, for them coming out, and then to escort them back to the IP where they'd pick up the tows; just in case anything went wrong.

*

XE10 and *XE11* were now at the entrance to the Johore Strait.

Both *XEs* had dived before the sunrise, and began creeping their way up the Strait, *XE10* leading, *XE11* 100 yards behind. Percival and Varley had marked sets of waypoints on their charts to take bearings on, and then time their run to the next one, running true along a planned line of approach. Percival watched the first one pass their starboard beam, then activated the periscope hoist to bring his attack 'scope down before starting his stopwatch. They ran on for 15 minutes exactly, ERA Morton holding her steady on their pre-set course, Steele maintaining the revs on her motor. Then Percival got the 'scope up again and Steele leant forward to turn him on to where the next waypoint should be. And there it was. Percival called the bearing, dropped the 'scope again, and started the stopwatch once more.

And on they ran, until Percival did an all-round look after a waypoint, and there looming over him was a large merchant ship running down the strait towards him; a huge cargo-passenger, maybe 18,000 tons, hogging the fairway.

'Stop motor. Flood Q. Put us on the bottom, Dave,' he said to Steele. There was a bump, and a bounce and then a grinding as *XE10* came to a halt. 'We were about to get run over by a bloody great Maru,' Percival looked around, grinning. 'Let's hope "Varlet" Varley sees him in time.' But he had to speak up, as the noise of the Maru's churning propellers and her wake filled the boat. It was mid-morning now, and when *XE10* started off again, they knew they were coming up on the anti-submarine boom.

Leading Seaman Kirk, their diver, was already sitting in the 'W and D', suited up, ready with his huge cutters to go out and cut it. The drill was you motored dead slow up to the boom net, coming to a dead stop before you hit and alerted the surface that something was down there. The diver went out, made his cuts and bent back the wires to let you through, tapped the lid and off you went, the diver re-joining on the other side. This could be a long and tedious process, especially if the waters were murky and the visibility bad. But Percival had noticed, looking through the retracted search 'scope, he could see quite clearly underwater, the visibility being excellent. Checking his watch, he stuck the scope up, just to confirm their approach, and he saw the boom defence boat that opened and closed the net, hadn't closed it behind the big Maru.

XE10 motored through unmolested, with her diver still sitting safe and dry. Percival hoped "Varlet" Varley would make it through, too. They were ahead of schedule; which was just as well, because the boat was starting to get hot now, and the air none too fresh. It could have been worse, but because Percival had made the entire night run in, sitting on the edge of the hatch, night glasses stuck to his face and his legs dangling in the boat, and because the sea had been calm and the night very dark. As a result, lots of fresh air had been allowed to blow through, clearing the reek the passage crew had left behind.

Alas, Percival and his crew had their own reek to contend with now. The condensation had started to drip, making the air hard to breathe and the sweat to form rivulets all over their bodies. On they crept.

Just before noon, when he stuck the 'scope up for another all-round look, there was *Shosei*, off the port bow, right where she was supposed to be. A huge, improbable steel castle. Percival said, with a chuckle, 'Enemy in sight, chaps. Dave, take the bearing and range.'

Steele leaned forward to read the angles of the 'scope's bezel as Percival pointed the periscope at their target, then took his slide rule to translate the numbers into yards. 'Bearing two one eight, range twelve hundred, sir,' he replied.

Percival sent the 'scope down. 'Start the attack,' he said, and fleetingly wondered if *XE11* was still right behind them. She wasn't.

Varley had managed to follow *XE10* through the open boom net, but a quarter of a mile further on, as he had the periscope up to check another waypoint, he'd become aware of a different noise in the craft, louder than all the ambient traffic they could hear. He swung the periscope for an all-round look, and almost immediately a shadow passed across his vision, then the bluff tumble home of the back end of a harbour tug, coming full astern directly at him. He hit the hoist switch to drop the periscope, and said to Kendall, his Jimmy, 'Stop motor, Number One, put us on the bottom.'

Kendall pulled the breaker and flooded Q, but before they had even started down there was a sickening clang and *XE11* rocked on her beam ends. The thick glass panel above Varley's head went into total shadow as the tug passed over them, then they hit the bottom. They couldn't have dropped any more than 20 feet. *XE11*'s crew held their collective breath. Some Jap on the tug must have heard the clang and looked over the side. They couldn't have missed *XE11*'s dark shadow on the bottom. But the tug carried on, and nothing happened. Varley ordered Kendall to bring them back up to periscope depth and he tried to take a look. The periscope hoist sounded laboured as it sent the 'scope up, and when he looked through it, he knew from the opaque lenses it was full of water. When he tried to lower it, it jammed fast. They were blind. And as far as *XE11* was concerned, that meant Operation Samaritan was over.

Back on *XE10*, Percival had lined them up to go under *Shosei* just abaft her "B" turret. According to the stopwatch, they should be just going through 200 yards to the target. It was time for a final look before dropping down to their attack depth. *Shosei*'s draught was 32 feet, and an *XE* craft's draught was five and a half feet, which meant they needed to find not much less than 50 feet of water if they were to successfully place their charges. Even at high tide that was a big ask in the Johore Straits.

Percival sent the periscope up, and almost immediately brought it down again, hissing urgently, 'Stop motor, flood Q, put us on the bottom. Now!'

His glass panel went dark too. Kirk, looking aft, saw the shadow pass over Percival's face.

'A bloody crew boat almost ran over us,' he said, a pant in his voice from the fright he'd got. 'Full of bloody Jap matelots. The bugger standing at the tiller, steering only had to turn the other way and he would have been looking right at me. I could see their faces, Christ! I could see their bloody gold fillings, laughing. One even had his hand trailing in the water.'

His voice trailed off as he calmed down. They all felt the bump as they hit the bottom. ERA Norton looked at his depth gauge through the sweat stinging his eyes. 'Forty-seven feet,' he said.

Several long moments passed. Percival said, 'I don't understand how they didn't see us.' Not addressing their main problem; which was, was there enough water under *Shosei* to get the charges in?

Eventually Percival said, 'Well, we're here now. From what I glimpsed, we're on target. So see if you can bounce us along the bottom Number One, slow ahead. Keep going until the sky darkens,' he added, jerking his thumb up at his deckhead glass panel. No more calling Sub-Lt. Steele, 'Dave' any more.

XE10 started bouncing along the bottom. The glass panel began to darken, then there was a bump, and a grinding sound of gravel beneath the keel, and steel against steel above. 'Stop motor!' called Percival, but he hadn't had to. Steele had already pulled the breaker. There wasn't enough water; they had hit *Shosei* and the seabed at exactly the same time.

'In breaker, half astern,' said Percival. The motor made a whining sound; it was turning but they weren't moving. Percival felt his guts congeal, thinking, *Dear God. Please tell me we aren't going to be jammed under this battleship on a falling tide.* 'Stop motor,' he said, pulling himself together. 'Put a couple of puffs of air into the main ballast, Number One. Hard dive on the bow planes. Full ahead on motor.'

XE10 sprang to life, rocking herself deeper under the steel hull above. 'Full astern now, Number One!'

They moved. They definitely moved. But they were not free.

They tried it again.

Then again.

Then ... they shot out from under *Shosei* with such force that Steele struggled to control her trim, to keep her submerged. Everybody was panting hard now. *XE10* hung there, with less than 10 feet of water covering her. There was no getting under *Shosei* here. But Percival wasn't worrying about that; right now all he could think about was how some dumb Jap up there must look down now; and see them. But they didn't. Because they were deep in Singapore harbour. No enemy submarine could reach them in here. No fleet submarine, that is. Because no Jap was thinking about midget subs, even though the Jap navy had their own versions; and the idea that an enemy one might enter here was a joke. It could never happen.

'I'm taking us back out. Half astern for thirty seconds, then we'll try again, further down the hull,' said Percival.

On the third attempt, just abaft the aft funnel, they succeeded in getting under the Jap battleship. Resting on the bottom, Kirk did all the final circuit checks on the release board and pronounced *XE10* ready to drop her charges.

Percival said, 'Well gentlemen, without further ado, like Santa, let us leave our presents under the tree and retire.' Very apropos, as Christmas 1944 wasn't far off.

Both charges were fitted with six hour time fuses. Kirk opened the cock on each board to activate them. Then he pulled all the release levers in sequence. *XE10* lurched slightly to starboard, then stayed there. 'Port charge has gone,' said Kirk, studying his board, 'and according to the board, so has the starboard one.'

Except, from way *XE10* was lying, everyone knew it hadn't. Kirk re-set the board and pulled the starboard levers again. Nothing. Percival considered puffing some air into the tanks, taking her up a smidge then bouncing her back again to shake the damn thing loose. But there wasn't enough room under *Shosei* as it was, and in a very short time, the tide would turn. Percival, his face crimson, said, 'I hope you chaps know that I'm having some considerable difficulty maintaining my sangfroid? Because if one more thing goes tits up, I'm going up stairs, stabbing every Jap I find until I get to her bloody seacocks and then sinking the bloody bitch myself, by hand!'

Everybody chuckled, including Percival.

'There's only one answer, sir,' said Kirk, holding up the craft's big adjustable spanner. 'I'm going to have to go out and hit it with this.' He meant their reluctant charge, not *Shosei*.

Percival was inclined to agree, 'Well said young Kirk. It's getting far too sweaty in here and its high time some bugger did something.'

Kirk, still in his diving suit, being sweatier than the others.

After they had cleared the boom without him having to go out the craft, he had thought about taking it off; but seeing as the boom would be probably be shut on the way back, and he'd need to go out and cut a hole anyway, he had decided to keep the suit on.

Morton fitted Kirk's clear faceplate to the suit's helmet, and Kirk got himself comfortable in the W and D. Its hatch was sealed and Kirk opened the valve to fill the compartment, giving a thumbs up through the peephole. Morton watched him stand to open the casing hatch, and then all heard a couple of dull thuds.

Percival immediately got to his knees so he could look through the search periscope without raising it. He immediately saw the problem. 'There's not enough room,' he said, sighing. 'Kirk can't get the hatch fully open. It keeps hitting the Jap's arse.' Looking down the length of *Shosei*'s keel plates was like looking down a green tunnel. He could see over a dozen yards into the gloom. And there, silhouetted close up was Kirk, struggling to get out. Percival looked round the rest of the crew for a long silent minute. 'Everyone put their hands up,' he said, 'who thinks there should be a law against God taking the piss.'

Then there was a sudden banging from above, and when Percival looked into his glass panel, there was Kirk's mask in it, and his thumb, well and truly up. He was out. For the next few minutes, a series of metallic clangs echoed through the boat, and scraping sounds. If the Japs fitted hydrophones to battleships, they were all surely dead. And then they felt *XE10*'s extra buoyancy. The charge was free. Percival checked the periscope again, and there was Kirk's helmet, and his finger, gesticulating aft, away from *Shosei*'s very close hull. At first, Percival didn't get what he wanted. Then it dawned on him.

'Kirk wants us to slide from under,' he said. 'And then pick him up when we're clear. What a smart chap, eh? Aren't we glad he's on our side!'

Percival ordered slow astern to clear the charges, then put *XE10* on the seabed. He waited a few minutes, then using the retracted periscope to look through the clearing billows of mud, plotted his path to escape from under the battleship. A couple of puffs of air into the tank, and off they motored, slow astern, scuffing the bottom, towards the shimmering light. They were going to get away; this was going to work.

Then they all heard the cracks; a ripple of them, echoing through the hull, without anyone realising what they were. Like whips, but heard through cotton wool. It was only after the *bang!* that Percival knew. The little judder of a shock wave confirmed it. It was a grenade. And the cracks? They must have been rifle fire. It didn't take much to realise the Japs must've been shooting at Kirk in the water. After getting away with it all the way to here, they'd been spotted.

XE10 emerged from under *Shosei* into a benevolent cascade of light and shadow through her glass panel. When Percival stuck his face against the panel, he could see round its edges the shadows of boats, gathering, milling. There was no Kirk. He ordered the helm hard over, and as *XE10* bent into her turn, he ordered full ahead. There was nothing he could do for their diver now, but he was going to try to run. Sitting pinched and crouched in air that was more like a slick of heat, nobody said a word, the only sounds they made was the labour of their breathing. They felt their boat gather way. Then total shadow covered the glass panel and there was a sudden *clang!* Metal on metal, then a scraping sound; something being dragged along the hull. Another *clang!* More dragging. Percival turned to look at his fellow crewmen, the tension on their faces turned to puzzlement. And then suddenly *XE10's* gathering way stopped abruptly and the stern seemed to kick up.

'They're dragging grappling hooks,' said Percival, knowing instantly what had happened, his flat tone dripping resignation. 'And they've got us by the arse.'

He closed his eyes and he could see the hooks entangled in their rudder; their prop guards. He didn't have to look. And he could also see, opening up like a giant black hole beneath them all, their captivity at the hands of the Japanese. The lecture they'd had on what would happen if they were ever taken prisoner. The memory of that tall, jolly Commander giving it in the wardroom. Him saying, 'The first thing that's going to happen is they're going to give you a doing. So expect it.' All delivered in a matter-of-fact tone, with a chortle in his voice. Percival took a deep breath. It was time to go up. No point in putting off the inevitable. He snatched their little wallet of Aldis codes – *XE10* carried no radio – and he ripped the pages out as he shuffled on his bum to the W and D watertight door. The scraps he crammed down into the drain tray, then he shut and sealed the door and opened the valve to flood the space. He looked around to see what other damage he could do to his boat before he surrendered it. But the whole gimcrack lash-up was so basic, it seemed hardly worth the bother. The noise he was hearing, the air flooding into their ballast tanks, for some reason made him think he was lying in a coffin, still alive, being trundled into a crematorium's furnace.

'Open the lid, Dave,' he heard himself say, 'upsa-daisies chaps. First one to the Tokyo Ritz gets the penthouse suite.'

Percival was last out, dragged the final foot or two by the scruff of his shirt. He couldn't see Steele or Morton. There were too many Japs all over the casing; guns, rifles, rattan canes. He could hear the blows though, through all the yelling in Japanese. There was a big whaler, and a motor launch alongside them. Out the corner of his eye, he saw Kirk's body being hauled aboard another launch not 30 feet away, his suit all punctures and leaking blood. As he turned his head back, he was just in time to see the first rifle butt coming at his face. He'd been thinking what a nice day it was turning out to be, all the usual clouds had cleared to reveal blue skies, and then the blow had landed.

The only other thing he had been aware of later, as they dumped his beaten body into the bottom of the launch, was the engineering sounds coming from *Shosei's* hull. 'They're firing up the boilers', he'd said to himself.

*

Having set off several hours after the *XE* craft, *Saraband* was motoring with barely steerage way at 60 feet, in a tiny patrol box three miles north Nongsa Point on Batam Island, bestride the *XE's* route from the Johore Straits. This was the forward rendezvous point agreed with de la Pole, where Harry would wait for them to come out and then escort them back to *Sittang* where they'd re-attach the tows – always assuming everything went well. It was very shallow here, seldom more than 100 feet of water, and right now less than 40 feet beneath their keel.

It was late in the afternoon. If everything had gone to timetable, both *XE* craft should have laid their charges by now, and be creeping back to open sea. They would be expecting *Saraband* to be waiting with a friendly Aldis greeting flashed through her periscope. If anything was wrong, if they found themselves in difficulty; *Saraband* would take the crew off and scuttle the craft, then they'd all go home.

Harry, wearing only his skivvies and a towel round his neck, was sitting eating a bowl of tinned pineapples with condensed milk for breakfast at the wardroom table, breathing in the aroma of fresh coffee from the galley that was managing to top the usual submarine reek. The crew were at breakfast too – this being submarine time, when the working day began at nightfall.

He was looking forward to his coffee when he heard one of Meek's stand-ins on the Asdic set call, 'Sir, I have some strange HE on three five two degrees.' The bearing to the entrance to the straits.

'Pass the word Meek,' called Harry and he stepped to the Asdic cubby. The lad was sitting in just in his skivvies too, his meagre teenage frame sheened with sweat, and his rowdy hair matted under his headset. He was frowning and tuning the set back and forth. 'It's really something small, Sir, and not very fast.'

Meek came up, no better dressed, but grumpier at being called away from his bacon and powdered egg. He slid into the seat, and took a matter of seconds to pronounce the contact one of their *XEs*.

'They're early,' said Harry, looking at his watch. 'Far too bloody early.'

In the control room, he issued orders to close the target, slowly. Gowers drew a plot and Harry conned *Saraband* to creep up on the *XE's* projected course so as to be there when she arrived. They waited, the control room watch keeping an eye on the clock because it would soon be time for *their* breakfast and nobody was in the mood for these novelty acts in their grannies' wash-house boilers keeping them from it.

Harry ordered *Saraband* up to periscope depth. He was about to order up the 'scope when Meek's voice, urgent, intruded.

'Muliple high speed HE, sir. On red four zero. Closing fast, sir. There's a lot of them, sir. Three at least. Big. Sounds like destroyers. Fleet destroyers, sir.'

What in hell's name were three Jap Fleet destroyers doing coming barrelling out of the Johore Strait right now? They couldn't just be after him; not even a submarine would be worth the candle. Not for them. If he'd been spotted, it would've been escorts; *Chiburis*; and an 'Emily' flying boat, or even two.

Harry hit the general alarm. Breakfast was going to have to wait.

Fleet destroyers coming on fast; that meant 30 knots, maybe even 35 knots; they'd be on him in minutes. It was only three or four miles to the mouth of the strait.

'Put us on the bottom, Number One,' Harry said to Bill on the dive board, then. 'Rig for silent. Shut off all unnecessary pumps and fans.'

Saraband fell away beneath their feet. They gently bumped the sand and mud at 87 feet.

Meek's monotone recorded the approach of the Japanese warships, coming on to cut across *Saraband's* bows. Such was the silence in the boat, the noise of their speeding screws started to be heard through the hull; a faint machine whirr.

'There must be some flap going on,' said Harry *sotto voce*, 'for them to be tearing about like that.'

A few sage nods in the control room. The noise began to recede, and as it did, Meek piped up again, 'The bearings are opening out, sir. They're under helm. Moving from line-astern to … it's like they're setting up to carry out a sweep … running east, fast.'

Harry stepped to the plot, where Gowers was marking it. He knew deep down now, what must have happened. The Japs must have sunk, or God forbid, caught one of the *XEs,* and those destroyers were running out to tackle the midget subs' support. There'd be more coming. He was certain now. And *Saraband* was caught in exactly the wrong place – in enclosed waters, no depth beneath her keel, right in the Japs' backyard and there'd be nowhere to run, if they didn't run now.

'The high speed HE is opening fast now, sir. Running almost exactly due east,' said Meek. 'I'm picking up the weak contact again, sir. Bearing red sixty, and close … still running very slow, sir.'

'Periscope depth, Number One,' said Harry. And up they went. As they did, he started musing aloud. The control room breathed a collective sigh of relief; everybody wanted to know what the hell was going on upstairs.

'I think we can assume its all gone tits up,' said Harry to no-one in particular. 'And it is my considered opinion we get the hell out of here, right now. All dissent will be crushed ruthlessly.'

A little wave of chuckles wafted round the control room. Sub-Lt. Verrell actually rocked with silent laughter, so as the sweat dripped off the end of his nose. 'But it's only gentlemanly we go up and grab whoever's still aboard our little chum before we skedaddle. Yeoman, bring me the hand Aldis would you.'

He got a true course for the *XE* from Gowers and ordered the helmsman to lay *Saraband* on a parallel heading. Then he ordered up the periscope again. He checked the sky first, and there heading away to the east was the unmistakable backside of an 'Emily'. A quick look round the surface. Nothing. Not even the retreating sterns of the Jap destroyers. He had been hoping for the *XE's* periscope.

'Where away, Meek?' Harry asked, sending the 'scope down again.

'Right on our port beam, sir. Wheezing away, crawling along. Very close. If you banged on our hull he'd probably hear you.'

'I might bruise my knuckles, Meek. Cheek of you …' a few more snorts round the control room … 'and anyway, acoustics is your job. Give him a ping. One ping only. If we're that close we might even take out an eardrum. Serve the bugger right for making the duty watch late for brekkie.'

'One ping, sir.'

Meek was going to use his Asdic set on 'active'; instead of just listening to all the noises coming out the deep, he was going to have the set fire out a pulse of energy which must inevitably hit the *XE* and bounce back confirming it was there. It would also alert the *XE* to the fact that someone very close knew they were there, in no uncertain terms.

Everyone heard the pulse go out, and come back almost simultaneously.

Harry ordered the periscope up, expecting to see the *XE's* 'scope looking back at him. The periscope head broke surface into a dimming sky; what passed for a brief twilight in the tropics. But there was nothing else to see.

He heard Meek say, '… he's blowing his tanks, sir.' And indeed now he could see a ruffle on the long swell, and then suddenly there it was; a miniature casing, water sluicing from its flanks and a periscope stand bent at 45 degrees with the head snapped off.

Harry ordered, 'surface.' And he watched as the *XE's* hatch opened and a head appear before *Saraband's* rising dropped the *XE* below his view. Harry was right behind the first lookout on the bridge, hoping yet not letting himself admit he was hoping; knowing it was a pretty shabby thought to have in his head, but knowing it was there anyway. And then he was up and looking at the waving figure on the *XE's* casing not 30 yards away in the swiftly gathering darkness, and feeling the sinking in his gut anyway, the shameful sinking, as he recognised it was Varley, not Percival. No time to dwell though.

'Don't bloody come any closer,' he yelled across the narrow water on which both boats were now rolling. 'You dent my boat with that boiler of yours and I'll throw you back!'

*

He sat with Varley round the wardroom table, Laurie topping up Varley's mug of coffee with rum. *XE11* hadn't needed to come alongside *Saraband* to transfer her crew; they were all fit young men who'd needed a good stretch after being cooped up for so long. They had all merely slipped of their craft's casing and swam; Varley going below and opening all the sea cocks before he followed. Only he had paused, standing dripping wet on *Saraband's* extended for'ard hydroplane, to watch as his command slipped stern first beneath the swell. Now he was explaining how that Jap tug had knocked off his periscope, and how the op had ended there and then for *XE11*. Then he described how he'd just dumped his charges in the fairway in the hope a lucky strike, and then how they had begun their long, laborious and blind creep back out to sea, only to be interrupted by the most terrible commotions.

'We could tell there was a flap going on,' he said, staring into space. 'All sorts of stuff started churning up and down the straits. And then we heard a lot of depth charging … back towards the boom. But we had nothing to take a shufti with, and I was buggered if we were going to surface amidst that lot. All we wanted to do was scram. But all we had to navigate with was the chart, my all too fallible ability to estimate our speed as relating to the state of the tide, and a stopwatch. So I just kept as near to the centre of the fairway, hugged the bottom and pressed on. You wouldn't believe the stuff that went over us.'

They discussed all the possibilities, but there was only one real explanation; *XE10* had been detected and either sunk or forced to the surface. That there were now lots of Jap warships putting to sea suggested the latter.

'If that's the case, it means John must have blabbed ...' said Varley refer-ring to his pal, Percival. '... told the Japs there were people waiting for us, that we had support.' In a tone that said it could not be true.

'Of course he did,' said Harry, pulling his bottom lip as he always did when he was thinking hard. 'Because he knew we'd be here. Which means he must've known something else ...'

'*Shosei's* putting to sea,' said Varley, smiling, relieved that this must have always been Percival's plan, and not treachery at all.

'How long does it take to raise steam on a battleship?' asked Harry.

*

On *Shosei*, her captain had asked the same question, and ashore, so had the admiral and his staff responsible for the sea defence of Malaya. *Shosei's* engineer's best estimate had been 15 hours, at least. Do it faster, he'd been told. If the British can sneak in once ... We need to get *Shosei* to sea and to a new, safe anchorage.

Down in the battleship's boiler rooms there was hive of industry, her black gangs hard at work for the past six hours, ever since that liberty boat had motored over the top of a lurking enemy midget sub emerging from underneath's *Shosei's* hull. The shame that such an event had been allowed to occur! Right away, tugs had been dispatched to tow *Shosei* away from where she'd been attacked. Who knew what the British had left beneath her? Nudged out and into the fairway, she had anchored, and divers had gone down to check her hull for limpet mines. Nothing. But back where she'd been, they had found the two giant charges lying on the seabed. *Shosei* had then been towed further away, and a huge area around her former anchorage cleared. The admiral said the charges must be allowed to detonate; for the noise of the blast to convince anyone over the horizon that they had been successful. Meanwhile they would hunt down the enemy task force.

It had only been a few days since *Shosei* had been to sea, for gunnery practise. So her boilers weren't completely cold. First, her chief engineer had ordered water to be pumped into the de-aerating feed tank, in order to reduce the amount of oxygen in it, then the feed water to be circulated

291

through the entire cycle of the boiler; all while he checked and adjusted the water chemistry. About four hours in he was ready to begin the light off procedure, inserting huge lit tapers to ignite the boilers' fireboxes. Once going, he'd ordered the cycling of the water increased, watching as it heated up to the correct psi of pressure.

Later still, in the engine room, it was time to start the electric turning motor and begin rotating the engine shaft. Once it was going, he ordered the valves opened to begin sending steam through the high pressure and low pressure turbines, turning them too, and heating them up. That was what was happening as Harry, Bill Laurie and Varley were sitting drinking their rum-laced coffee, discussing how and when they'd get a pop at sinking the engineer's ship.

It was what they were still doing when *Shosei's* engineer reported to the bridge that they'd be ready to get underway in two hours. When everything was warmed up and running, he'd send superheated steam from the fire room to the engines to begin turning the screws; and once they'd steadied the load on them, he said, the captain could recover her anchors and *Shosei* could proceed to sea.

*

Out beyond the entrance to the straits, *Saraband* was well into her long wait, pacing her patrol box with barely way on her, all the power from her diesels going to cram charge into her batteries. Harry, flat out in his hammock at the back of the bridge, was gazing up, amazed at the amount of starshine there was under the vast vaulting arc of the Milky Way. He was also thinking about de la Pole on *Sittang*, back out at the IP; he would know by now it had all gone wrong; that the *XEs* were all overdue, and so was *Saraband*. Harry wondered what was going though his head, feeling impotent there was no way to let him know.

Saraband's crew knew what was going on, however. Harry had made sure of that before he'd come up. A brief word through the boat's tannoy speakers; Bill Laurie detailed to go back and relay the message by yelling in the engine spaces with the diesels going flat out.

About how the *XE* craft attack on *Shosei* had failed, but all that meant was *Saraband* was now going to get a shot at the bastard instead. They already knew how big she was, the punch she packed, the threat she posed to any Allied invasion of Malaya; he'd told them that when they were towing *XE10* to sink her.

'… so it is my belief the enemy will now try to put to sea,' he had said. 'And we shall be waiting for her.'

His mind had been in a tumult before he'd stepped to the mic; about how his crew of citizen sailors would react. They weren't going to be just shooting up junks here, or trying to torpedo some wheezing tramp steamer; they were about to engage an enemy battleship in the enemy's own backyard. Suddenly he was back, in his mind, on other submarines he'd served aboard; in *Pelorus'* control room when *Von Zeithen* had come over the horizon, and on *Umbrage* waiting for the Italian cruisers to show up, his captain lost overboard and Number One lying concussed, with a broken shoulder, so there was only him left to fight the boat; and on *Scourge* that night in the Tyrrhenian Sea with the Italian battlefleet in his periscope, watching as it had zigged away from *Scourge's* full salvo. How had he been, back then? The half daft undergraduate who had once, 'done a bit of sailing'.

He just needed them to do their job; and to help them do that, it was going go better if he could let them know they weren't alone; that men just like them had been here before, and prevailed; and that they could do it too. No fluffing; no jitters. Which was why he'd had word with Cantor, and who had come into the control room while he talked, and started fiddling with a line on the control room ladders.

What happened next had probably never happened before aboard a British man-o-war going into action; it was not the way Royal Navy officers were expected to exercise command over their crews. But this lot weren't your regular Jack tars; they were citizen sailors, civvies in blue suits.

'Now most of you can't see this,' he'd gone on. 'But the Yeoman is now rigging the Lieutenant Commander Gilmour Patent Underwater Signalling Halyard and is about to hoist, "am engaging the enemy more closely" …'

Cantor, had given the end of the line a round turn with a flourish, and let the two flags hang free. Harry's voice was commanding, grave, '... it was Nelson's final signal to the fleet at Trafalgar before the battle, hoist before a single British cannon had been fired at the enemy. It remained up until shot away ...'

He could even see as well as feel the utter deflation in the control room; he could practically put words to it, *oh God, the skipper's lost it* ... the heavy dread that he was going to come away with some atrocity like, *so it'll be as if Nelson's watching you* ... Or worse. Some infantile platitude ... after everything they'd all been through ...

'Now I know what you're all thinking,' he continued, and he'd been right, ' ... about what I'm going to say next ...'

But instead, he hadn't said what they'd been thinking, he'd said what they'd felt.

'... somebody pass me a basin so I can be sick in it ...'

And suddenly there'd been laughter; the laughter of relief. Which was good. It was what he'd wanted. And just as suddenly he'd gone all chatty, 'No, listen, imagine what it's going to be like when they make the movie.' Heads turned, expressions, half worried, half smiling. 'It's going to look great. Seriously. I'm telling you. Up there on the screen. You lot. So no spoiling the ending by making a bollocks of it and missing, right?'

He'd felt the electricity in the control room; throughout the boat. Chuckles and grins everywhere he'd looked. He'd got his message across, and rammed it home with laughter. *Saraband* was a happy boat, and only happy boats were proper fighting boats. In the radar cubby, McTeer, sitting next to Meek, grinning ear to ear, had said, 'See him, he's one gallus bastard.' And Meek, grinning too, had asked, 'Gallus? What's ...'

'Gallus. Ye know, wide ... full of it, and a mile wide,' then going all posh-sounding, '...derived from the word gallows,' then back again, '... cos that's where he's heided.'

And then Harry had topped the whole skit off with, '... and bagsy Errol Flynn to play me.'

Laughter out loud had followed, McTeer calling from the cubby, 'Who's gonnae play me, sur?'

'Silence in the radar cubby!' Harry, suddenly all formal again. There had been shocked inhalations all round, until Harry had come back, 'George Formby to play McTeer … in a kilt.'

And then everybody had dissolved. If you'd asked the *Sarabands* before, singly or in mobs, they'd have said they probably quite liked having a wild one for a skipper. Now they knew it. Meek had especially liked McTeer's description, 'gallus'. He thought that would stick.

Lying in his hammock, back up on the bridge now, Harry thought if he was going to lead them into the jaws of death, because that was sure as hell where they were headed, it was better they went laughing. 'Citizen sailors,' he said to himself. 'You'll do.'

He'd told them to expect a long wait. But he'd been wrong.

He heard the voice coming up through the voicepipe from his hammock, and was there before Caudrey, on watch, could turn to call him. It was Meek on the other end, reporting multiple high speed HE coming down the strait. Harry immediately hit the general alarm, and *Saraband* closed up for action. Caudrey, now standing at the TBT, began dialling in the range and bearings.

Harry wished he could light up his radar, but he couldn't. Especially here, the Japs must have kit for detecting radar emissions; so just one turn of the array, and they'd know.

Harry had already explained to his officers and the control room crew what he intended; had already passed the order for 25 foot depth settings on all torpedoes in the forward tubes. *Shosei* drew 32 feet of water, and no destroyer in the Jap navy more than 13 feet; he didn't want any escort taking a torpedo meant for their battleship. He also ordered that the tubes be flooded the instant the general alarm sounded.

Bill Laurie was on the dive board, ready to trim them down before beginning their attack.

Harry called down the pipe with an order to break the charge and put both diesels on line, and he rang for slow ahead together. He then ordered *Saraband's* head round so as she was creeping north west out of her box, across the approach to the strait, moving away from the course *Shosei* must steer if she was heading for the open sea; all the time closing the Changi shore of Singapore Island. No blackout there, the island too far for Allied bombers to reach; the ones they had in SEAC anyway. So a glittering frosting of lights telling him, and Gowers, exactly where they were.

'If she comes tonight, I want to hit her close in,' he'd told Number One. 'Right up against the minefields. If she's coming, she'll be coming with escorts, line astern, down the strait. I want to get her before her destroyers fan out, form a screen … before they're looking for me, or anyone like me. Then I want you to get us under fast.'

Harry looked around the bridge, at the lookouts, binoculars scanning the night, and at Caudrey. He couldn't remember whether he was 21 yet. And Gowers, with his folded chart and chinagraph pencil propped on the binnacle, taking bearings on the lights and the buildings, marking up his erstwhile plot as they crept along. *At least he'll tell me before we hit the minefield*, Harry thought to himself by way of reassurance.

Meek's commentary was becoming more detailed; he was calling a daisy-chain of HE running fast between the Changi shore and Tekong Island – the entrance to the strait. The big ship was there, with three smaller ships, running ahead of her. More behind them, but he couldn't count them yet. And then, at last, he was interrupted by the starboard lookout.

'Bow waves!' he called, and the bearing, coming at them, almost directly on their beam. 'Shapes! Multiple dark shapes, sir … Enemy in sight!'

Caudrey was turning the TBT onto Meek's bearing, confirming it. He worked the machine, calculating the range.

Harry lifted the bridge mic. 'Torpedo room, bridge. Open all bow caps.'

Even he could see the shapes now, running fast from the north, and as he did, he saw the leading bow waves appear to open out. From the voicepipe he heard Meek call, 'First three targets are under helm, sir.' The Jap destroyers were fanning out to form their screen. He risked his night glasses; he could see enough of their silhouettes to name them as *Kagero* class, sleek 2,000 ton state of the art fighting ships, almost 400 feet long, armed to the teeth and capable of over 35 knots. He noticed from their bow waves that the phosphorescence was not so heavy tonight; which was good, if any Jap lookout was going to be watching for torpedo tracks.

And behind them, there was the towering stack of *Shosei's* pagoda mast, running out of the shadows like the rain-swept monochrome photo he'd once seen of the Old Man of Hoy, except this stack was moving at a ridiculous speed. Good grief but they really weren't that far away.

'Target's range is six thousand yards, sir,' said Caudrey from the TBT. 'We are three thousand yards off the target's track. I estimate his speed to be twenty five knots, course one five five degrees, sir.'

'Very good, Mr Caudrey,' then into the pipe he said, 'Helm, steer zero six five. Engine room, give me revolutions for three knots.'

When you looked at the stark facts, it didn't look too good for *Saraband*. Her element, the sea, was very shallow hereabouts, with often less than 100 feet beneath her keel, and the waters enclosed; even out here in the Singapore Straits, they were surrounded by scores of islets and shoals. And to port was Japan's main base in the region, Singapore itself. Opposing her in this tight corner were probably more than half a dozen frontline units of the Imperial Japanese Navy, known for its skill in night actions, if not anti-submarine work. Not that the anti-submarine stuff mattered much, since there was hardly enough water for a hundred miles for a submarine to dive in. So it would have been okay to be frightened; sensible even. But Harry sniffed not a pheromone of fear on his bridge; he doubted there was one in the whole boat. What was it about battle that made even ordinary men shrug off perfectly rational terror? And instead made them feel more alive, more real? It was all a matter of losing yourself, he supposed. *Saraband* right now was living testimony to the fact it happened; right now she was no longer just a steel tube full of an ad hoc collection of Tom, Dick and Harry. The immanence of battle had forged them into one. It was how you could tell whether you had a crew instead of just a rabble. And right now *Saraband* had become a single weapon; he could feel it in his hand as she slipped through the dark, warm water towards her quarry.

Looking at *Shosei's* advancing pagoda, he wondered absently if that would be the last image he would ever see. All that rot about surviving the war; gone in a puff of the hot, humid air. He was going to sink this bastard, and the future would have to look after itself. He no longer bothered about wondering how he'd become this new beast anymore. He knew the light of battle was in his eyes.

He looked across at Caudrey. When he'd first clapped eyes on him he'd been about as much use as ... what had been McTeer's expression? As a one legged man at an arse kicking party, that had been it. And now look at him, hunched to his work; no longer a boy; a proper fighting sailor now, about to set about the King's enemies. It was going to be his job to order their torpedoes fired; his eye on the TBT's graticule when *Shosei's* bow crossed it; and not even a flutter or a twitch. His mother wouldn't recognise him.

'We're going for as ninety five degree track angle, Mr Caudrey,' Harry said, his eyes back on that towering pagoda. 'What's your range now?'

'Three thousand six hundred yards, sir,' the he read off the bearing.

'Bow waves emerging from astern of the main target, sir!' It was the port lookout. Harry swung his night glasses. It was the afterguard; the destroyers following *Shosei* out of the Johore. The lead one had a huge bone in its teeth; going flat out, almost running to cut off *Saraband* from her prey.

Time.

Meek reported the destroyer closing, high revs, another behind her. Then that *Shosei* was under helm.

'She's turning towards, sir,' said Caudrey. 'Ten degree change, sir. Course is now ...'

But Harry wasn't listening. Turning towards? Not along the strait and out to sea? Of course not! She was heading for another, safer anchorage, in the tangle of the islands to the south, where any other midget subs would never find her. And those bloody afterguards were fanning out to clear the way, coming right at *Saraband*.

'Number One,' he said, all polite. 'Trim us down now, please.'

He looked at his watch; two minutes had passed since Caudrey's last call. He didn't have to ask however.

'Range to target, two thousand three hundred,' called Caudrey. 'DA for ninety five degree track angle is red two nine.'

'Call it, Mr Caudrey, when you're ready.'

There was a mic clipped to the front of the TBT; Caudrey opened the channel and fixed his eyes on the graticule. Harry spoke into his own mic. 'Torpedo room, bridge. Stand by to fire. On the stopwatch, seven seconds.'

'Bridge, torpedo room. Aye, aye, sir.'

In the torpedo room, the six huge steel torpedo doors in front of him, sealed, covering *Saraband's* main weapons, Jowett, the Torpedo Gunner's Mate delicately pulled the pins from all the small activating levers on the firing board. The torpedo room crew, bodies glistening in the leeching humidity and garish light, in their gaudy sarongs and their skivvies, all eyes on him, and on the rating with the stop watch.

Saraband was lined up to fire the first shot at *Shosei's* bows, and every seven seconds after the first one away, another would follow; no extended ship length gaps to allow that the target might be running faster or slower than the speed dialled into the TBT. Harry was betting on them all to hit, to be sure.

'Fire One!' called Caudrey. Jowett pulled down the first lever and *Saraband* bumped as the first shot was ejected from the tube by a blast of compressed air. And as it went, Jowett fixed his stare on the rating beside him, the one with the stopwatch; not even bothering to wipe the sweat drips from his nose, so that every seven seconds, when the rating said, 'fire,' Jowett pulled the next lever.

In the control room, Bill Laurie, and Priestly adjusted the trim every time they felt her bump, to adjust for the sudden loss of one and a half tons of torpedo, and also the instant flooding of the displaced space in the tubes. The bubble barely wavered.

On the bridge, Harry was watching as the torpedoes' wakes sped away into the night; very little green froth bubbling from them. They were nearly done when the port look out called again, and he looked up to see that *Kagero* class destroyer charging across his vision, into the 2,000 yard gap between *Saraband* and her target. The lookout had called it, and he hadn't paid attention. Too busy concentrating on his torpedoes; their tracks now running right under the destroyer's track. No matter; the torpedoes were set for 25 feet and a *Kagero* only drew 13 … then suddenly the *Kagero* was slewing towards them, and out of the night air came the scream of her siren; rocket trails zoomed into the sky; signal rockets; a Jap code for submarine attack? And then the crack of a gun. It was a starshell going up; Harry watched the trail, knowing any second he would be dazzled by its igniting. *Saraband's* last two torpedoes were still to fire; time would be frozen for 14 seconds.

The next torpedo went; one more to go. The *Kagero* was coming right at them now, and suddenly, from nowhere, everyone, everything, was bathed in chemical light.

'Clear the bridge!' he shouted. And to Caudrey, reaching to release the TBT from its mount, 'Leave it, Mr Caudrey, down you go!'

Except Harry couldn't go. Not yet. Nor could *Saraband* dive. There was the last torpedo. Seven seconds and counting. And then the bump as number six cleared the tube, and Harry hit the klaxon twice and was sliding down the conning tower ladder, pulling the hatch stirrup behind him, shouting, 'one clip on, two clips on!'

He landed in the red light of the control room, breathing hard, '… keep eighty feet, Number One. Helm, port thirty, please, right away, thank you. Group up, ring for full ahead starboard.' The boat was already heeling, LS Poulter on the helm expecting the order. Before anyone could say another word there was a sudden, terrible thrashing roar racing over their heads, as if some machine was about peel off their deckhead and open them to the ocean; the *Kagero* running over them. Harry didn't even want to think by how little the charging destroyer must be clearing them. All he felt was his gut clench, waiting for the depth charges. But they never came. No time, he supposed. It must've all happened too fast for their quarterdeck crews to arm and roll them.

'Full ahead together,' he said. Just as Meek reported, 'New high speed HE closing fast from starboard … the other one's under helm, sir … he's coming back.'

Harry now leaning over Gower's plot, said, all matter of fact, 'Let's see if they're as keen to follow us into the minefield.'

Saraband's track on the plot showed her heading directly into the field, that the chart showed garlanding the Changi shore. Harry had no idea where the Admiralty had got the intelligence to plot it, or how accurate it was; or if the field extended further, or was even still there. But he didn't have anything else to go on, so it was just full ahead together and I love Jesus.

He noticed Gowers had his stopwatch out. For a second he was puzzled, and then laughing out loud; he'd forgotten the bloody torpedoes! The range had been nineteen hundred yards, and they'd had less than two minutes to run. But Gowers hadn't forgotten; he was counting down. He said, '… eight seconds … four … three …' Then the sickening gut-punch *BUUMMM!* of their first torpedo hitting home.

On hearing the *Kagero's* siren and seeing the signal rockets, *Shosei* had opened her throttles; even for such a big ship, the power in her steam turbines saw her take off like a greyhound; so *Saraband's* number one shot, instead of hitting her in her bunker tanks for'ard, struck just abaft her 'A' turret where the belt armour was eight inches thick; a lot of noise, and a stumble in her forward momentum, but the only damage was distorted steel.

Seven seconds, and the next torpedo also hit the belt armour with the same effect.

Another seven seconds … and nothing. Harry and Gowers looked at each other; had the torpedo gone rogue? There was far too much roar in the water now for Meek to tell them anything. And then the next seven seconds were about to elapse … *BUUMMM!* reverberating through the boat. Harry looked around, Garbutt was making a fist, and muttering, *yes!* under his breath. Harry assumed it'd be much the same through every compartment.

It was the fourth torpedo however, that was to wreak all hell aboard the speeding *Shosei*.

It penetrated her hull just for'ard of where her starboard outer propeller shaft entered the hull. The shaft turning at maximum revolutions, catastrophically distorted, bursting all the packing out the glands that sealed the shaft tunnel from the sea. Over 3,000 tons of water immediately flooded the tunnel and poured into the Number One engine room, sending *Shosei's* engineers scrambling up ladders for their lives and drowning dozens of others.

The thrashing shaft also split the tunnel top, jetting seawater into starboard dynamo room, which generated half of the ship's electrical power. Number two starboard boiler room also began to flood, and the main starboard auxiliary machinery room.

The fifth torpedo blew one of her rudders off, and the sixth sped off into the night, astern, to sink un-detonated, into the shallows.

The two *Kageros* were still hunting, although with all the noise in the water, Meek's set was still deaf. Then, '… both targets have started pinging,

301

sir,' reported Meek. 'I can hear it above the racket … trying to find us with some kind of Asdic of their own.'

'Thank you Meek,' said Harry, thinking to himself, *now is not the time to go quiet and try and hide … where do you hide in ninety three feet of water anyway?*

He picked up the sound powered telephone, 'Torpedo room, it's the Captain here. Mr Jowett, reload the forward tubes, please.' They might as well; give the lads something to do while they were running for their lives.

'We've crossed the minefield boundry, sir,' said Gowers, before adding, 'Coming up on zero feet beneath our keel according to the chart, sir.'

'What? Oh, thank you Mr Gowers,' said Harry, too busy thinking about the *Kageros.*

'Number One, keep sixty feet. Group down, ring for slow ahead together, starboard twenty. Everybody listen for wires scraping the hull.'

Wires. Mine wires, securing them to the seabed. Even in a minefield it wasn't that easy to hit one head on and blow yourself up, given there was a lot of water for you to swim in, and mines weren't that big. Much more likely some sticky out part of you would snag a cable and pull it on to you.

And all this while the sea had become a very noisy place, the blasts of their torpedoes still echoing off the shallow seabed, and the indistinct tearing sounds of tortured steel that must be *Shosei* … crippled? Dying? Nobody'd had a moment to spare to cheer their hits on her.

On *Shosei,* nobody was cheering either. With half her electrics out, there was no power to the starboard pumps and the rising water in the starboard boiler rooms was now causing a series of firebox explosions that could be dimly heard on *Saraband.* In minutes, all power to the battleship's starboard screws died, and her speed dropped to less than 12 knots. She was also now listing 15 degrees to starboard. Then the water reached her electric steering gear, rendering her helm unresponsive.

'Sir, the destroyers' HE bearing is opening,' it was Meek. 'They're moving from aft down our starboard side … running back towards the original track … HE from the main target, sir … low revs, sir, lots of mechanical sounds … her screws are barely turning, sir.'

Harry looked at the plot; were the destroyers running back to mamma? Was she so crippled?

He said, 'Hmmn.' Which was the right thing to say. Nobody was in the mood for commentary; the air was fraught in the control room, everybody concentrating. What the hell was happening?

Then into the febrile atmosphere came Meek again.

'Sir … ? Sir! I heard an explosion in the water, sir! A long way off, sir … to starboard … green seven zero … it sounded like a torpedo hit, sir.'

'*Sittang*,' said Harry out loud, without even thinking.

His new chum, that daft, posh bastard de la Pole, coming back for them in *Sittang*; that lovely daft, posh bastard. A torpedo hit far away to starboard; it must have been him, bagging one of the Jap destroyer's from the screen ranging ahead.

'… depth charges now, sir.' It was Meek again. 'I'm hearing multiple depth charges, a long way off.'

There had been no HE from the two destroyers or the battleship for at least 20 minutes when Harry decided to take a look. He had crept *Saraband* out of the minefield and to within 2,500 yards of *Shosei's* last position, marked on Gowers' plot.

The distant depth charging had continued for some time, but was now silent. Harry didn't want to think about that. He ordered the main search periscope up and swivelled it onto the bearing as it rose. And there, dim in the starlight, was what appeared to him to be a great confused heap of metal floating on the water that he couldn't quite make out; only the huge pagoda mask was identifiable, and then only after he'd realised it was lying at an impossible angle.

'Number One, take a look. What can you see?'

Harry handed the periscope over, and Laurie studied the heap for several long seconds before ordering it down.

'Both destroyers are alongside the battleship, sir,' he said. 'One's for'ard and it looks like they are trying to get a tow onto her. The other … it looks like they're trying to lash her to the battleship's starboard side. '

'So we've crippled her, you reckon?'

'She does look pretty bloody embuggered, sir.'

'Well bloody good show, *Saraband*,' said Harry trying to hide his disappointment.

'Multiple high speed HE closing from red four zero, sir,' said Meek. 'Light stuff, sounds like escorts …'

Harry looked at Bill Laurie. 'You know I've always hated taking torpedoes home,' he said, with that glint in his eye Bill was getting too used to.

'Give me heading to put me on a ninety degree track to *Shosei*, Mr Gowers,' said Harry.

*

Saraband went hard and fast for the Sunda Straits.

After firing her final full salvo at the confusion of ships, she had turned and dashed south, submerged, grouped up and flat out for 20 minutes, before Harry took her up and they ran for the rest of the night on the surface, on diesels, between Batam and Bintan islands and out into the South China Sea. The escorts Meek had picked up coming out of the straits for some reason hadn't chased them, even though *Saraband's* salvo had caused one of the destroyers in the tangle of ships round *Shosei* to blow up; so they'd known she was still around.

Then Meek, still listening for the pursuit that hadn't materialised, had started picking up the tell-tale sounds of rending steel from the water; bulkheads collapsing, boilers blowing, engines tearing loose from their securing bolts; big engines, big boilers; battleship-sized machinery, all sounding their death throes. *Shosei* sinking now.

But they weren't home yet. So no cheering. And on they'd rushed through the night and the following day.

The atmosphere in the boat stayed grim, tense, business like, until they raised the bottleneck of the straits. They'd got so far without encountering a single Jap patrol, at sea or in the air. But if the Japs were going to pinch them off from their base; from Flying Fish Cove; here would be the place to do it. However, there'd only been fishing boats in the way when they'd shot through on the surface on the second night, diesel throttles opened wide and racing along on the powerful tide and current.

It was only after they'd cleared the southern end that Harry decided he was prepared to risk turning their radio on, and ordering Yeoman Cantor to transmit a short coded signal to Captain Fell on HMS *Bonaventure*, announcing *Shosei* sunk and *Saraband's* ETA.

When they motored into the cove to trot up alongside *Bonaventure*, the depot ship's decks had been lined with sailors to cheer them home. I was a beautiful day, the pure, azure, vaulting sky showing the scrubby outcrop that was Christmas Island in her best light.

The casing crew stood at ease, caps on, socks pulled up, chests out, Harry even put on his best watch cap with the white top, and *Saraband's* jolly roger sported her new needlework; a double-sized red bar with a pagoda mast for *Shosei* and a single bar for the destroyer.

Captain Fell met Harry at the brow as he stepped aboard.

'A happy return indeed, Lieutenant Commander Gilmour,' said Fell, no stuff about saluting, just stepping forward and pumping his hand. 'It didn't quite go as planned, eh? But you sunk her anyway. Bloody good show, sir. Congratulations. Now Captain S's cabin, quick time for large gins, and you can tell me all about it.'

There had been a flatness aboard *Saraband*, all the way as she escaped the Japs, and all the way alongside *Bonaventure*, despite all the cheering. It hadn't been because nobody had appreciated the scale of their victory; it was because everybody on board had liked Percival and his crew. And they weren't here. Somehow it wasn't feeling quite right to be basking in glory that their friends might have paid for with their lives.

And sitting in Fell's cabin, Harry felt more or less the same way.

'I noticed your jolly roger's up to date,' said Fell, handing Harry his tumbler. 'Now clap your laughing tackle round that Mr Gilmour.' Harry took a sip while the angostura bitters were still roiling; the Captain knew how to pour in the finest traditions of the Trade. Harry felt his eyes water. 'Yes,' he said, 'the cox'n's very punctilious about matters like that. Any news of *XE10*, sir?'

'Yes as a matter of fact,' said Fell. 'Good news. Well, good-ish. Japanese radio's been crowing for the past two days about capturing three terror submariners …'

'Just three, sir? asked Harry.

'I'm afraid so. And God knows what state the poor buggers are in if the Japs have them.'

'And *Sittang*? Anything … ?'

'No. But's it's early yet to be worrying. Now young fellow, I want you to tell me, blow by blow, everything.'

They had a party that night in the wardroom, and another on the mess decks. The *Sarabands* were the returning heroes and their victory was well 'wetted'. The crew began to feel better about themselves, and then quickly started to revel in it. Weren't they the lads! A bloody Jap battleship! The skimmers had already bagged theirs in this war, and the wafus! And now the Trade could boast one too; all thanks to them. There should have been a defaulters' list the next day, but the Captain S said not to bother. The next day the signal traffic started to arrive. 'I'm to take lots of photos of you and the crew with your jolly roger,' said Captain Fell. 'And there's a mountain of signals addressed to you in the radio room. You appear to have incurred their Lordships' *pleasure* for a change, and lot of other people's.'

There were operational signals too. *Saraband* was not to return to Trinco, she was to sail directly to Fremantle. She was to be re-assigned to Eighth Flotilla; HMS *Maidstone* was already on her way to deploy there.

When *Saraband* got to Fremantle a gaggle of launches met them off Rottnest Island, and on the harbour quay there was a band waiting, and lots of press; flashbulbs going off like flares, and a bank of newsreel cameras. Harry just clenched his jaws and gritted his teeth, and let it all pass in blur; a blur that lasted three days. In the end, it turned out a lot of the crew loved the attention, especially his two younger officers, Caudrey and Verrell. Harry and Bill Laurie, and the likes of Eddie Garbutt and Bert Kershaw just did what was expected of them for the press, and then just slipped off to the pub. This was leave in Fremantle after all, a town that loved the navy.

After all the frenzy Harry knew he had letters to write. The news must've reached home by now, so there was his mother to write, and old Lexie would expect a letter. Then there was Shirley. And he'd have to write to Victoria too.

Shirley. He sat himself down on the veranda of one of the beachfront hotels, put a chilled schooner of VB in front of him, and put pen to paper.

At first he couldn't think what to write, then after the third VB, he did. He wrote everything he thought Shirley probably wanted to hear – mainly because he knew now that he wanted her to hear it.

Victoria was another matter.

He and the *Sarabands* also got to meet for the first time their comrades in arms in the US Navy's submarine service. Although Harry's first impression was not at first hand; it was bumping into Warrant Engineer Kershaw and his wrecker, Priestly, just after they'd come ashore from a visit to the Yank submarine tender, USS *Anthedon*. Both men had been treated to a tour of her workshops and stores, and when he saw them, they looked like they'd just had a religious experience. Kershaw kept repeating, '… the machine tools … the machine tools …', and Priestly looked into the distance as he told him, 'they've got a periscope shop that was fitted out in heaven, sir.'

Then there were the shore parties and the ship visits; or rather the US submariners' visits to *Saraband*, US ships being "dry", and Royal Navy ones definitely not. The *Sarabands* even learned to live with the endlessly repeated sharp intakes of breath every time a Yank sailor encountered the relative squalor of their boat; and its tiny size compared to the seemingly cruise liner dimensions of their own big USN Fleet Boats. But most surprising, there was next to no fighting between the two navies; which was not to say there was no joshing. While walking behind a group of *Sarabands* on their way to help re-store the boat for a patrol they'd never make, Harry had heard a good one; that he would often, in years to come, dine out on. They had just passed a big Yank *Balao* class boat, moored alongside, a huge bloody thing the size of a Royal Navy destroyer, when a group of hands on the Yank's deck called up to Jack strolling along the dock, 'Hi guys! How's life these days … in the world's *second* biggest navy?'

Everybody knew the US Navy had, some time ago now, overtaken the Andrew in terms of numbers of men and ships.

'Awright Yank,' one of the matelots had called back, all cheerful and friendly. 'How's life in the world's second best?'

It was not long after that he heard *Sittang* had been posted overdue, presumed lost.

Harry eventually did sit down to write that letter to Victoria. He had always told himself their brief interlude spent in the Galle Face Hotel had been one long idyll. But there had been one moment; one thing, looking back on it from the distance of Fremantle, that seemed to put a perspective on everything. After dinner one night, sitting out on the verandah, he had begun a train of conversation with her.

'The war's probably going to be over soon.' Not something he usually talked about.

'Indeed,' she had replied.

'D'you think, when it's over, you would like us to go on seeing each other?'

Victoria had given him a long, appraising look, then said, all airy, 'You'll be going back to university, I assume? To finish your degree?'

'Yes, I suppose so.'

'Which means you'll be back to being an undergraduate again. A student.' She'd paused to give him another long appraising look. 'Can you really see me introducing people to my boyfriend, the student? I mean, submarine captain, yes. But a student? Me? With an undergraduate student for a boyfriend? Honestly?'

She had been smiling by then, a warm smile. But her words spoke a truth that Harry thought he now understood.

He didn't, of course; mainly because she never said what lay behind those words; about how she too had thought about a future for them. A future where the war finished, but Victoria and Harry went on and on. Oh, how she'd wrestled that one. Long and hard, working through every possible permutation of how it all could come to pass; until the essential preposterousness of it all had finally defeated the yearning of her heart.

In his letter, Harry explained his posting, without giving enough away to annoy the censor, wrote that he could always be found, wherever he ended up, through his mother's address in Dunoon – it no longer felt like his home any more – and said that if she ever felt like meeting up, he would love to see her. There were no flowery phrases, no declarations of undying love, no lies.

He did get a note back from her; but that was much, much later. All it said was, 'I regret nothing. In fact, my time with you remains one of the happiest memories of my life – so far.' It made Harry smile when he read it.

After *Saraband's* next planned patrol had been scrubbed, he'd had an interview with the S8 and the Fremantle navy yard's principal marine surveyor. 'What can I say, mate,' said the big, bluff Aussie. 'I don't know whether it was you or the Japs that done it to your boat, but she ain't up to it any more. The war has not been kind to her. Too many shrewd dunts. The effect's been cumulative. What I'm saying is, we reckon your boat's not fit to go back out again, and your boss here agrees. We're giving you a sick note for her, for a one-way trip back to Blighty.'

Saraband sailed the day after the New Year's day, 1945. Her passage took her back through the Suez Canal, and along the Med, with calls at familiar ports, including Malta and a memorable night with Louis, sitting outside the long since rebuilt café on the Sliema seafront that had once been a favourite haunt. All the lights were on in Malta; it looked so very pretty.

Their passage continued, the days ticking by, no need to dive, every mile on the surface now; the boat performing her daily routines with the smoothness of a Swiss watch. *The Bugle* continued to publish every week, and with a British general election now looming, the content became more political. Harry didn't care as long as no-one advocated mutiny. After all, they were going home. And now there was plenty of time to think about what that meant.

He often found himself contemplating this new half ring on his jacket sleeve, wondering how it got there. Imagine? Him, a Lieutenant Commander?

The war might not be over, but it really did look as if he was going to survive it now.

Going home was another matter. For it felt that, for every mile travelled, the further away his old self seemed. The rank and the medals were merely the truth of that writ large. Home couldn't know the man he had become; whoever that was going to end up being; especially after he had unpacked all those boxes he'd been carrying around with him for so long.

Once through the Straits of Gibraltar Harry gave the crew a stern lecture. The Jerries might well be on their knees, but there were still U-boats operating in the Atlantic and he was buggered if he was going to die this close to home because some slack arse couldn't be bothered keeping his eyes open on watch. *Saraband* would steer a zig-zag pattern from now on, and daily trim dives were back. Bridge and radar watches must also pay special attention to aircraft. Even though at this stage in the war, every aircraft would be an Allied one, he reminded them again of the standard aircrew assumption that *all* submarines were U-boats, which was why, on sighting any aircraft, the officer of the watch must immediately dive the boat.

It was on one of those Bay of Biscay days Harry found himself alone at the wardroom table with Gowers, both of them lunching on ham and cheese sandwiches.

'Have you thought about when you want to sit for your Perisher, Mr Gowers?' Harry asked, not out of politeness; but because he was genuinely curious how his shy, enigmatic yet supremely competent regular RN Vasco saw his career progressing post-war.

'Can I stop you right there, Sir,' said Gowers; not words Harry ever expected to hear from him.

'Of course. Why?'

'I don't want to do this anymore, Sir. I intend to resign my commission at the cessation of hostilities, Sir.'

'Oh,' said Harry, dumb-struck. 'To do what?'

'I want to be a teacher, sir. Maths. I'm going to teach maths.'

Later, on the bridge that night, Harry gazed up at the vaulting sky and the rippling, sparkling band of the Milky Way, and then out over the vast boundlessness of the ocean stretching to the curve of earth, and he thought, *so that was what Gowers' wanted. What did Harry want?* Standing on *Saraband's* bridge right then; the boat he commanded, alive beneath his feet, her bows rising and cleaving the Atlantic swell; he couldn't imagine wanting to be anywhere else in the whole, wide world.

After they had rounded Ushant, everybody got 'the channels', as everybody told them they would; that electric charge that passes through every ship when she's on the home straight. *Saraband* sailed into Haslar Creek on a drizzly, blustery day, her paying-off pennant fluttering and her crowded jolly roger flying proud from the periscope stands for all to see – except there was hardly anyone around to notice. No bands or flashbulbs or cameras. *Saraband's* victory was old news by then. There was only a clutch of Wrens who stood dutifully on the wet quay, waving and sending up a cheer that was instantly whipped away in the wind. *Saraband* had returned to a country still at war, even though the war might seem far away, with Germany in her death throes, and the fighting against Japan back halfway round the world.

Harry and Bill stood on the bridge watching all the lines fly aboard to secure her to the quay, and the gangplank come aboard.

'You do it, Bill,' Harry said. 'Ring for finish with main engines and motors.' And Bill, grinning a lop-sided grin, rang the engine room telegraph for the last time.

Ashore, they drew up the leave bills, and started wrapping up the boat's paperwork. Until Harry was interrupted by a rating messenger presenting him with a signal relieving him of command with immediate effect, and sending him on leave, pending his next posting. Rail warrants were offered, but HMS *Dolphin*'s SOO told him *Sirdar* was heading up to Holy Loch the next day. He lived up that way, didn't he? The SOO was sure her skipper would give Harry a lift. Save the nightmare of a train journey.

Harry telephoned home, and when his mother heard his voice telling her where he was and that he was coming home, he feared she would faint dead away. He told her when *Sirdar* was expected and hung up, smiling to himself, feeling slightly silly at the emotions he knew were lurking there in his chest, that he was trying to ignore, like annoying children you know are never going to leave you alone if you give them an inch.

Mrs Gilmour of course told Shirley everything, and she alerted Mrs Wilson, the postmistress at Sandbank, to be on the lookout. Two days later Mrs Wilson telephoned Shirley to let her know that the submarine she said was coming was just rounding Lazaretto Point just when she'd said it would. Shirley had jumped on her bike and was standing at the top of Ardnadam pier when Harry's crew tender from the depot ship touched, just like she had first done all those years ago.

Even though it was spring, she was wearing her old duffel from back then too. Her tumble of chestnut hair had grown again and was tucked carelessly into her hood.

Harry did not see Shirley when he stepped off the crew tender; he was gazing around, looking up at the wooded hillsides of Glen Eck, none of it much different today, from that day six years ago when he had wished it all goodbye; laughing at the boy he had been then, telling himself, *Harry, the boy who left here in 1939, he isn't coming back, you know.* Thinking maybe that wasn't such a bad thing after all, and laughing at *this* Harry; still alive, with a big new world coming.

But Shirley saw him. Suddenly, there he was, the face in the crowd, standing back to let the ordinary sailors off first; his hair too long, tucked into a disgraceful battered watch cap, the shapeless white pullover under a faded reefer, with a ratings' kit bag on his shoulder, and carrying the Bergen with Lexie Scrimgeour's sextant in it; ambling along, grinning to himself, like he hadn't a care in the world.

She smiled. She'd soon knock that out of him. Although that wasn't her immediate priority. No. All that mattered now was that her sailor was home.

Glossary

In the course of all six Harry Gilmour novels, a great number of ships, aircraft and other weapons of war are mentioned. For those readers curious enough to wish to know what they actually looked like and how they performed, I have compiled a detailed, illustrated glossary that can be found on my website: www.theblackscibe.co.uk

Historical Note

31 July 1945, Royal Navy midget submarine XE.3 attacked the Japanese heavy cruiser Takao in Singapore harbour. The craft was commanded by Sub Lieutenant Ian Fraser and his crew were Sub-Lieutenant William Smith, Engine Room Artificer Charles Reed and the frogman diver Leading Seaman James Magennis.

Having been towed to a point some 40 miles from the target by HM Submarine Stygian, Fraser navigated his tiny craft on a dangerous passage across shoals and through minefields and an anti-submarine boom into the Johore Straits to where Takao lay between Singapore Island and the Malay mainland.

The plan was to drop two huge explosive charges under Takao's 15,500 ton hull, as well as attach six limpet mines. However, there was so little water between the cruiser's keel and the seabed, Fraser took several attempts to get XE.3 under the enemy. Even then, when diver Magennis tried to exit the craft, he found the proximity of the cruiser's hull wouldn't allow the hatch to open properly. He had to strip off his equipment and squeeze out.

Once outside the sub he found the hull was too dirty for his limpet mines to stick, so he had to spend 30 nerve-wracking minutes carefully scraping clean a series of patches with his knife. Magennis eventually returned to XE.3 and Fraser then released the two large explosive charges. However, one failed to detach. Although exhausted from his first dive, Magennis insisted on going back out to free the stuck charge using a heavy spanner.

XE.3's ordeal was not over. When Fraser then sought to manoeuvre astern to get out from under Takao, he discovered their craft was jammed between the cruiser and the floor of the strait; and on a falling tide. By repeatedly going full ahead, and then astern on the tiny 30-ton craft's puny electric motor, he finally freed XE.3 and she was able to make good her escape.

Fraser and Magennis were both awarded the Victoria Cross for their part in the attack. Sub Lt. Smith, who was at the dive controls of XE3, received the Distinguished Service Order and ERA Reed, who was at the wheel, received the Conspicuous Gallantry Medal.

Takao had a hole 60 feet long blown in her keel and finished the war sitting on the bottom of the Johore Strait, where the crew of XE.3 left her.

My technical adviser was Captain Iain Arthur RN, OBE, a former Captain S of the Royal Navy submarine service's Devonport Flotilla.

Lightning Source UK Ltd.
Milton Keynes UK
UKHW040044040720
365937UK00004BA/1243

9 781912 982035